A girl's best friend

Lindsey Kelk is an author, journalist and prolific tweeter. Born and brought up in the UK, she worked as a children's editor before moving to New York and becoming a full-time writer. She now lives in LA.

Lindsey has written ten novels: *I Heart New York*, *I Heart Hollywood*, *I Heart Paris*, *I Heart Vegas*, *I Heart London*, *I Heart Christmas*, *The Single Girl's To-Do List*, *About a Girl*, *What a Girl Wants* and *Always the Bridesmaid*. You can find out lots more about her here: http://lindseykelk.com and by following her on Twitter.

@lindseykelk
www.facebook.com/LindseyKelk

By the same author

I Heart series
I Heart New York
I Heart Hollywood
I Heart Paris
I Heart Vegas
I Heart London
I Heart Christmas

Girl series
About a Girl
What a Girl Wants

Standalones
The Single Girl's To-Do List
Always the Bridesmaid

Ebook-only short stories
Jenny Lopez Has a Bad Week
Jenny Lopez Saves Christmas

A girl's best friend

LINDSEY KELK

HARPER

Harper
An imprint of HarperCollins*Publishers*
1 London Bridge Street
London SE1 9GF

www.harpercollins.co.uk

A Paperback Original 2015
1

ISBN: 978-0-00-758239-6

Set in Melior by Palimpsest Book Production Limited,
Falkirk, Stirlingshire

Printed and bound in Great Britain by Clays Ltd, St Ives plc

MIX
Paper from
responsible sources
FSC™ C007454

#TeamJeff

Prologue

New Year's Eve

Doesn't everyone wish they could go back in time and change the past?

First, I'd do the world a favour and kill whoever invented the front-facing camera on the iPhone; second, I'd try to convince the parents of some of humanity's worst offenders to use more advanced family planning methods; and third, I would never, ever have kissed that man.

Or possibly any men. Just to be safe.

It had been the most ridiculous six months on record, not only of my life but quite possibly ever. I wasn't sure if there was a way to check against everyone else's cockups but my list was pretty impressive as far as I was concerned. Yes, there had been a lot of fun parts. Hawaii, Milan, New York, Nick . . . but dear God, the mistakes I had made. And, as Amy always said, there was no 'clear history' button for your heart. Actually, Amy always said there was no clear history button for your vagina but still, the sentiment was the same.

But there I was, against all the odds, standing in a dressing room, wearing a dress I never thought I'd wear, minutes away from changing my life for good.

No pressure, then.

'Is it too late to elope?'

The door to the dressing room cracked open and Kekipi slipped inside, smiling.

'It might be,' I replied, looking at myself in the enormous, three-paned mirror that almost took over the room. 'I've got the frock on, you're in a suit, all the guests are here. Probably going to have to go through with it.'

He took both of my hands in his and kissed me on the cheek. 'Well, it's so easy to get a divorce these days, I'm not too worried. Let's be honest, I'm not actually sure it will be entirely legal in the first place.'

I managed a half-smile and nodded. 'You, sir, make a very good point.'

'You look beautiful, by the way, white is your colour.' Kekipi reached out to brush one of my semi-tamed curls back behind my ear. 'You get a pass.'

The curl he had tried to tether sprang back in front of my face and Kekipi rolled his eyes. The rest of my hair had been bullied into something like a bun, although there were so many curls involved it looked more like a Danish pastry gone wrong. I had to stop believing I could do something just because I'd seen it on YouTube. The hairdresser had given up after an hour and I really, really should have taken her advice and left it well alone.

'I think you look very handsome,' I said with a mini curtsey, ignoring my mullet. It was true, he did. His bronze skin shone and his hair, usually slightly wavy and a little bit wild, had been brushed into a very dapper side parting.

'You should wear a suit more often. Especially one with so many sparkles.'

'Love the sparkles, hate the suit,' he confided, tugging at his stiff collar. 'I still think this whole thing would have been much easier if we'd gone with my suggestion of a beach wedding.'

'Well, bear with me.' I held a finger up in front of my false eyelashes. 'We could ditch these outfits, jump out the bathroom window and run away to Hawaii together?'

'Tempting,' Kekipi replied. 'Very tempting.'

'No one is running away anywhere without me,' a sharp voice called out from behind the toilet door. 'Do you know how long it took me to get her in that dress?'

'How long?' Kekipi whispered.

'Too long,' I replied, breathing in. 'I should never have let her loose with corseting.'

Amy, my dresser, and my best friend, emerged from the toilet with a very serious pout on her face and a very silly unicorn T-shirt on her back. 'I mean it,' she said, a pair of jeans in her hand. The girl was so afraid of missing out on something she had run out of the bathroom, half-naked. 'You're going nowhere.'

'And may I ask why you aren't dressed yet, dearest Amy?' Kekipi leaned in with a kiss for each of her pink cheeks, eyes averted from her pants. 'I do believe the ceremony starts in fifteen minutes.'

'I'm putting it on now,' she muttered, eyeing me with defiance.

'Ever since the hot Ribena and holy communion incident of 2001, Amy isn't allowed to wear nice dresses for very long before an event,' I explained as Kekipi watched a look pass between us. 'Amy spills things.'

Kekipi blinked. 'Say that again?'

'AMY SPILLS THINGS,' she repeated loudly. 'I'm putting it on now. I can't fuck it up in the next fifteen minutes, can I?'

I fought the urge to raise an eyebrow. As she had proved to everyone a million times in the last three months, Amy was not a child. Not that she was doing a much better job of passing as a grown-up than I was. I watched as she hunted around the bodice of the bridesmaid dress hanging on the back of the door with her tongue sticking out the side of her mouth, looking for the tiny covered zip. Eventually she found it, pulled it down – and leapt back as the entire dress fell to the floor in a silky puddle.

'Tess?'

The door to the dressing room opened again and a tall, beautiful blonde, wearing the same dress Amy was attempting to gather up off the floor, peeked inside.

'Are you in here?'

I held my breath.

'We're all in here,' Kekipi replied before I could grab anything appropriately stabby. Could you bludgeon someone to death with a can of hairspray? Probably, if you were motivated enough. 'Paige, you ravishing beast,' he went on, 'let me get a look at you.'

'I was looking for you too!' A shining smile lit up her anxious face for a moment as she became the latest recipient of Kekipi's kisses. 'I couldn't find you out front – oh, you look fabulous.'

'Oh, hello,' Amy said across the room. Her stern tone might have carried more weight if she hadn't been stood with her hands on her hips, wearing nothing but mismatched underwear and a frown. 'What a *lovely* dress you've got on there – are you going somewhere nice?'

'Amy,' I said quietly, 'don't.'

Paige pressed her lips into a thin line and shuffled her shoulders. I kept my eyes on the floor.

'Oh, the tension!' Kekipi said, settling into an over-stuffed armchair by the window to watch the show. 'If you two were gay men, I'd send you into the bathroom to bone and get it over with.'

'I don't know what else to say, other than I'm sorry.' She fussed with the full skirt of her dress. 'I didn't want to miss today.'

'You're such a twatfink,' Amy said with a low growl. 'Bros before hos, Sullivan.'

'Are they Mr Men knickers?' Paige asked, squinting over at Amy.

'Yes, they are – what of it?' Amy braced herself for a fight. 'I swear, Sullivan, just give me a reason.'

'Look, can we not?' I jumped in between my friends, hoping the ridiculous whiteness of my dress might blind them both momentarily. 'Paige, I don't really know what to say. I was a bit worried you might not show up and I would have felt horrible.'

'And *I* would have been furious at you messing up my Charlie's Angels bridesmaid theme,' Kekipi interjected.

'I've been feeling horrible.' Paige grabbed my hand and wrenched me across the floor into a hug I wasn't ready for. 'I should have talked to you, this really wasn't how I wanted you to find out.' I felt her arms tighten around me.

'You're both ridiculous.' Amy threw herself into the group hug, burning rage beaten out by overwhelming FOMO. 'Daft cows.'

Even though being the meat in a silk- and shiny-hair sandwich was wonderful, I still felt weird. So much had happened, so much had been said, and there was still so much to sort out.

Suddenly, the dressing room door slammed open, hitting the wall behind it and making everyone and everything in the room jump.

'You shouldn't be in here!' Amy said, charging directly at the door and attempting to close it on Charlie's bewildered face. But his six-foot-something versus her five-foot-nothing held its own quite nicely.

'Charlie!'

My arms instinctively wrapped themselves around my body, I felt so vulnerable in my dress.

'Charlie?' Paige said, her perfect hair whipping back and forth between the door and me.

'Charlie!' Kekipi cheered, tucking into another chocolate chip cookie as we all turned to look at him. 'Sorry, nothing to add, just didn't want to be left out.'

'I came to talk to you,' Charlie started, eyes darting around the room while Amy recommitted to her Mighty Mouse efforts to knock him out of the room by charging directly at his midriff. He didn't even flinch.

'Me?' I asked.

'Tess?' Paige asked.

Charlie nodded. He looked rumpled and rushed, his tie not quite straight, his hair all a mess.

'Can I have five minutes?' he said, stuffing his shirt down his trousers. Typical Charlie, never tucked in properly. 'Just, want to explain everything. I've been a real tit.'

'At last, I agree with somebody in this room,' Amy said. She stood up and took a deep breath before renewing her efforts to shift Charlie out of her sight.

'Thanks, Aims.' He picked her up, one giant hand under each arm, and placed her gently outside the door and closed it firmly. 'I want to explain before it all kicks off.'

'You've got to do it now?' I asked, my hands tucked underneath my armpits. The dress was so much more revealing that you'd have thought. 'Really?'

'It's not brilliant timing, Charles,' Kekipi agreed. 'I'm fairly certain you're not supposed to be in here right now.'

'Let me in!' Amy's voice yelled from the hallway while she pounded on the door. Suddenly she stopped the pounding. 'What are *you* doing here?'

The door began to open again and Charlie slammed it shut, or tried to, hitting something hard as he did so. But it wasn't Amy trying to get back in – it was someone bigger and considerably stronger. It flew open again, this time with such force that it knocked Charlie off his already shaky balance, sending him across the room to crash onto the floor at my feet, cracking his head on a chair leg as he fell, a spray of blood slashing across the white silk skirt of my frock.

'That'll do, pig,' Kekipi said, picking him up under the arms and dragging him away from my ruined dress. 'That'll do.'

'Who slammed the fucking door in my face?' Nick asked furiously, pressing the arm of his shirt to a bloody nose. 'And why is Amy out there in her knickers?'

I felt sick and hot. I felt my heart race and my pants hurl themselves on the floor, right before my pride raced down to pull them back up and weld them to my lady parts. I felt everything and I felt completely numb.

'Nick?' I whispered.

'Tess . . .' he replied, his eyes travelling up and down my dress.

'Charlie!' Paige yelped.

'Help me,' Charlie whimpered, lying on the floor, staring at the stars only he could see on the ceiling.

So there I was, standing in the middle of an elegantly appointed dressing room in an exquisite Milanese palazzo, wearing a beautiful white dress that was now accented with a charming slash of blood, while one former lover lay concussed at my feet and another stared at me, bleeding, in the middle of the room, and one best friend choked back a surprised sob while the other was silently jumping up and down in her inside-out underwear, fists pressed to her mouth and eyes so wide I thought they might pop out of her head.

'Oh my.'

I turned to see Al, resplendent in a gorgeous grey suit, surveying the scene from the hallway.

'This looks to be a fantastic start to a wedding,' he announced, walking in as a string quartet began to play somewhere in the distance. 'Now, remind me, who's walking who down the aisle again?'

CHAPTER ONE

Two and a half weeks earlier

'OK, that's it, you look amazing,' I yelled as my friend Paige perched uncomfortably on a bench. 'Don't move, you're a statue, you're frozen.'

'Frozen is right,' Paige shouted back. 'I am not comfortable, Tess.'

'Are *you* trying to take photos while wearing ice skates?' I shouted back, wobbling on the spot in the middle of the rink. 'No, you're not, so shut up.'

She raised a perfectly pencilled-in eyebrow in silent protest.

'That still counts as moving,' I replied. 'So stop it.'

'You know I hate having my photograph taken,' she muttered as the Zamboni ice-resurfacing machine whirred quietly around the rink behind me. 'How much longer is this going to take?'

Paige Sullivan was not only the art director at *Belle,* a super swanky fashion magazine, she was also one of the best human beings I had ever met. Knowing I was desperate to get more experience with my camera, she had called in favours and pulled so many strings that we had the entire Somerset House ice rink all to ourselves for a whole hour after her work Christmas party. She couldn't get me into the actual party itself, but then she was only human. And not being allowed into the party didn't mean I couldn't show up early and steal snacks from the kitchen anyway.

'And you know you're my favourite model,' I replied, pulling a mini mince pie out of my pocket and shoving it into my mouth when she looked away. 'It'll be over much faster if you stop moving.'

'Stop moving, look softer, point your toe, tilt your chin,' Paige grumbled. Even when she was sulking, she was still beautiful. 'Are you all packed for the wedding of the century?'

'Bags packed, ticket booked,' I nodded. 'Kekipi is so excited and I can't believe he's getting married.'

'There's someone for everyone,' she said sagely. 'Except for me and you, obviously.'

'Obviously,' I agreed. 'I think it's going to be incredible. Maybe we can pretend we're getting married instead of playing bridesmaids. Though Kekipi and Domenico's wedding is bound to be more impressive than anything I could pull together.'

'I do feel a bit weird about it, though,' Paige said, tilting her head upwards and catching the light perfectly. Whether she liked having her photo taken or not, she was a natural. 'I barely even know Kekipi but he said he needed a blonde bridesmaid or he couldn't fulfil his *Charlie's Angels* fantasy.'

'The bride wants what the bride wants.' I snapped and my flash filled the rink with bright, white light. 'And a custom-designed Bertie Bennett bridesmaid dress has got to be something of a sweetener for you?'

'It doesn't hurt,' she said with a shrug. 'And it'll be fun. New Year is always such a let-down, attending the wedding of the year in Milan doesn't sound like a bad way to spend it.'

Inching left with staccato steps, I tried another angle. Good God, she was pretty. The cow.

'In all honesty, I thought it was a bit odd for him to ask us to be bridesmaids but, you know, I don't think he knows that many people,' I said, my ankles beginning to ache inside my slightly too tight skates. How long had we been out here? It only felt like a moment.

'Obviously, he *knows* a lot of people but I don't think he has that many friends. He and Al were holed up in that house in Hawaii for so many years he was practically bouncing off the walls every day in Milan. I can't imagine what Amy's putting up with in New York.'

'*I* can't imagine the two of them living together, I'd be hard pushed to say which one is more mental. Poor Al,' Paige said with a shudder. 'Are we nearly done? I'm freezing my jacksy off.'

'And a fine jacksy it is too,' I said, gazing at her through my viewfinder and forgetting how cold I was, how much my ankles hurt, and everything else that wasn't the perfect picture. 'Almost done. Two more minutes.'

London had decided to play nicely for the *Belle* Christmas party and the miserable, rainy weather that had been bothering the city all day had been replaced with a beautiful crisp, clear night sky. Paige, wrapped up in long scarves and fluffy mittens, looked like a winter fantasy dream girl and with the beautiful backdrop of Somerset House behind her and bright white ice shining below, it was like a Christmas card come to life.

'Apart from bullying your friends into playing model, what else have you been up to since you got back?' she asked, reaching up to pull her perfectly imperfect blonde fishtail plait over her shoulder. 'I've hardly seen you.'

'That's because you keep cancelling on me to play with your fancy new fashion magazine friends,' I pointed out. Paige had moved from *Gloss* to *Belle* while I was working in Milan and now it seemed like she never had time for anything but work. Her new job sounded just like *The Devil Wears Prada* only without so much eye candy or free Chanel accessories. 'I've been working for this photographer, Ess? He's doing a shoot for *No-No* mag and he needed a second assistant. Do you know him?'

Paige screwed up her face and gagged.

'You have had the pleasure then.'

'Repulsive little turd,' she nodded. 'But his photos are amazing. I've got him booked in for a celeb shoot in a couple of weeks.'

'Really?' I wobbled on my skates. 'You're using him at *Belle*?'

'The editor loves him and all the celebs want to work with him,' she nodded. 'Otherwise, you know, I absolutely would have asked you if you were available.'

Personally, I thought his photos were cheap, overexposed and tacky but who was I to judge? It wasn't as though I could do a better job. Oh wait, yes I could.

'Oh, that's not what I was getting at,' I said, waving away her embarrassment. 'I mean, I'd love to shoot for *Belle*, but really, I'm not loving assisting. Today I had to pretend to be a giraffe to give his model "inspiration".

Do you know what noise giraffes make? I didn't. I had to google it.'

She frowned, flexing her cold fingers and blowing on them, just in case I hadn't realized how cold she was.

'Do giraffes even make a noise?' she asked.

'It sounds like an angry cow that's being strangled,' I said, wincing at the memory. 'I think that's the reason we don't hear their dulcet tones all that often.'

'I can't even begin to imagine it.' Paige wrinkled her tiny nose. 'That sounds horrible.'

I let my camera hang around my neck and cleared my throat. 'Yeah, it's like, ngggghhhh—'

'Tess!' She cut me off loudly. 'Dear God, woman, pull yourself together. This is why I can't take you to nice places.'

'Oh my God!' I stared at her. 'I've turned into Amy.'

'Yeah, that's a thing that's happened,' Paige said with sympathy in her voice, but not on her face. 'Are you wearing her clothes?'

I looked down at the cropped black T-shirt emblazoned with a neon unicorn that was peeking out from underneath my skimpy black cardigan and accessorized with a strip of very white stomach, covered in goose bumps. I'd had to take my bulky coat off to shoot and I could barely feel my fingers any more. And Paige thought *she* was cold?

'The T-shirt is hers,' I agreed, making a mental note to do a load of washing as soon as I got in. 'And the cardigan. When did this happen?'

'Oh, doll,' she sighed. 'So long ago.'

There was a time when I would never have gone out on a Friday night looking like such a tramp. Admittedly, not much of a time since I had spent almost every Friday working late since I graduated six years ago, but still. I would have been in my casual Friday best and neon unicorns were definitely not covered by the office dress code.

'How's she getting on with Al?' Paige asked. 'Everyone is talking about the AJB presentation. It's crazy.'

'She seems OK,' I said. 'It's hard to tell with Amy; she doesn't really take things very seriously.'

'A lot of fashion people were annoyed he's launching at Christmas instead of at fashion week,' she said, reapplying her lip gloss as she spoke. 'The powers that be don't like it when you don't play by the rules.'

'I don't think he cares about the powers that be,' I admitted. 'When I last spoke to him, he said he was dead set on Christmas because it was his wife's favourite time of year. Amy tried to convince him to show in Milan or Paris but he wasn't having it.'

'Must be nice to be so sure of yourself,' Paige replied and I nodded in agreement. 'So, other than working for a tosspot and swapping lives with your sartorially challenged best friend, what else has been going on with you? I've been so busy with work and Christmas parties and everything, I feel as though I haven't seen anyone.'

'Oh yeah, all those parties must be a nightmare,' I said, trying to capture the white light of the fairy lights that decorated the giant Christmas tree as they bounced off her pointy chin. 'You sound gutted.'

'You know work parties are never that much fun,' she argued. I zoomed in on her face and clicked as her pale cheeks flushed. 'There are always a lot of events at this time of year and none of them entertaining. And the weather's been awful. And there's nothing on TV. And, you know, stuff.'

I hadn't known Paige nearly as long as I'd known Amy but it didn't matter. She was a terrible liar.

'Paige Sullivan.' I narrowed my brown eyes and zeroed in on her green ones. 'Why are you babbling? What aren't you telling me?'

'Nothing, there's nothing,' she scoffed, her face glowing more brightly than Rudolph's red nose. And since there was a twenty-five-foot illuminated version of everyone's favourite reindeer right behind her, it wasn't a difficult comparison to make. 'Like, what are you even talking about?'

'Oh, no way!'

Delighted, I clapped and immediately lost my balance, the skates sliding underneath me. I threw my arms to steady myself as she tried to cover up a quiet laugh.

'There *is* something! Spill, immediately. You have to tell me, I'm brilliant at keeping secrets.'

'You can't even keep your own secrets,' Paige pointed out. 'Why on earth would I tell *you* anything?'

'Fine, I'll guess.' I stared until I had her locked in uncomfortable eye contact. 'New job?'

'No, no and there's nothing. I'm not keeping any secrets,' she protested, looking anywhere but at me. 'You know, you didn't have to wear skates to go on the ice. You could have worn your trainers.'

'Where's the fun in that?' I asked. 'Oh my God, are you pregnant?'

'Christ no!' she yelped. 'At least, I hope not.'

And then it was obvious. She was calmer than usual. She had only complained about her terrible luck with men once all night *and* she was wearing flats. Paige Sullivan. Art Director at *Belle* magazine. Out on a Friday night. In London. In flat shoes.

'Oh!' I threw my hands in the air, knocking myself off

balance and landing on my arse with a hard bump. 'You've got a boyfriend!'

At first she didn't say anything, she just sat there, concentrating on her mittens and shaking her head, while smiling. 'I haven't,' she said eventually. 'I haven't, Tess, honestly.'

'You're a filthy liar,' I replied in a strangled voice, waiting for my breath to come back. *Ow ow ow*. Broken coccyx for Christmas, brilliant. Maybe, if I was really lucky, I could spend Kekipi's wedding sitting on an inflatable doughnut. 'And lies make Baby Jesus cry. Do you want to make Baby Jesus cry this close to his birthday?'

'I don't have a boyfriend,' she insisted, pulling out the hair tie in the end of her plait and looking up to meet my eyes. I took this to mean the photoshoot was over. 'God's honest truth. I don't want to talk about it.'

'Fine,' I said, crawling over to the edge of the ice and taking her hand as she helped me up, my camera swinging wildly around my neck. 'I won't ask any more questions. I'll just assume you're secretly boning some wonderful man's brains out on the sly and when you're ready to talk to me about it, you will.'

I stared at her for a moment, holding her eyes before she looked away. She looked sad. Which made me sad. Which I did not care for.

'Or I could have him killed?' I offered. 'The mood I'm in, I'd be very happy to do it.'

She considered it for a moment then shook her head. 'We can let him live for now. I'm all right, Tess, I promise.'

'Well, of course you are,' I said as we flopped down on the bench next to the ice. I sucked up a sharp breath as my bruised bum bones hit the cold, hard stone. 'That goes without saying; you're amazing. Whatever's going on, you know you can talk to me about it though, don't you? Absolutely no judgement.'

'I know,' she nodded. 'You're a good friend. It's all right though, there's nothing to talk about.'

It couldn't have been clearer that that was not the case. I wondered what it could be. Did they work together? Was he famous? Was he married?

'What about you?' Paige fingered a delicate gold chain around her neck and gave me a nudge. 'You still haven't—'

'No.' I cut her off before she could ask. If she didn't want to answer my question, I certainly didn't want to answer hers. 'I haven't.'

'And he hasn't?'

'No.' I shook my head firmly and turned on the screen on the back of my camera, flicking through the fruits of our photoshoot.

'Tess,' Paige said, pushing my camera down onto my lap. 'Don't you think it might be worth giving him a call? It's been months.'

'Nope,' I replied swiftly. 'For now, I think it's best I pretend it never happened.'

'If only it were that easy,' she agreed. 'Why hasn't someone invented a pill for that yet?'

'Because there aren't enough women scientists yet,' I replied. 'The ones we do have are busy trying to cure terrible diseases while all the men scientists work on inventing vibrating razors with five blades. We'll get there eventually.'

'I hope it's sooner rather than later,' she said. 'It's only two months until fashion week in New York and I've got outfits to think about. All this man drama is taking up altogether too much brain space.'

'Priorities,' I agreed, resting my head on her shoulder

and watching the Zamboni buzz quietly around the ice in a graceful figure of eight. 'And that's another reason why I haven't called him. I can only deal with one massive brain drain at a time. At least it's nearly Christmas.'

'I'm thinking about getting really fat and then juicing for all of January,' Paige said.

'I'm definitely in for the first bit,' I said, pulling Amy's T-shirt down over my belly. 'Might give the second bit a miss.'

'Me too,' she admitted. 'Kale makes me retch. Maybe I shouldn't plan on porking out this close to fashion week.'

'Or you could always quit your job,' I suggested, patting her knee while she shrugged, considering her options. 'Let's go and get a proper drink before my fingers fall off.'

'Now you're talking,' said my model as she hopped off the bench and helped me untie my ice skates. 'First round's on me.'

Seriously, one of the best human beings I had ever met.

CHAPTER TWO

'Jess, can you lift that reflector up, please?'

'It's Tess,' I said, stretching my arms higher above my head, wobbling as I went. My arse was still killing me from the coccyx incident the night before and I did not feel steady on my feet in the slightest. 'My name is Tess, actually. Sorry.'

Celebrated celebrity photographer extraordinaire Ess – no last name – took a moment to throw me a filthy look, then went back to staring at nothing through his viewfinder. I couldn't really complain, it was the first time he'd looked me in the eye all day, having been far more interested in my tits ever since I'd arrived on set at 6 a.m.

I had been so excited when my agent got me the job with Ess. It was a real opportunity, she said. I'd learn so much, she said. So far, I'd made four cups of tea that hadn't been drunk, been out on two coffee runs in the pouring rain and contorted myself into more uncomfortable positions than the average yoga instructor, all while holding an arm-breakingly huge reflector. And that was just today. The closest I had been to a camera all week was when Ess accidentally hit me in the arse with his while I was underneath a desk, plugging in the MacBook. This was not the hands-on training I'd been hoping for.

'Jess, I need it higher. For Christ's sake, woman!'

I closed my eyes, prayed to whoever would listen that I wouldn't be spending Christmas with a broken leg to go with my bruised bum and pressed up onto my tiptoes, swaying back and forth.

'Sorry,' I said through gritted teeth. 'Is this better?'

'Not really. Doesn't help that you're waving it around like a fucking flag,' he replied, snatching the camera away from his face and throwing it at his first assistant, a small, scared-looking bleached blond boy called 7. Not the word seven, the number seven. He had been quite clear about that. Never the word, always the number, he'd said defensively. 'It's supposed to be still. You're supposed to reflect light. Do you even *know* how to stand still, Jess?'

'Nope,' I whispered before pasting on my brightest smile and holding my breath. 'Any good?'

'No. Get down and we'll find something for you to do that isn't as taxing as standing still,' Ess said. He scratched his muttonchops and leered at my backside as I clambered off the stool he had balanced on the chair that stood on top of a suitcase. He did not offer to help. 'Veronica said you were going to be good at this.'

It was delivered as a statement, no obvious question, no definitive inflection.

'That's nice,' I said, tiptoeing across the all-white studio set-up. 'And not at all like her.'

'You doing her?' he asked.

'Sorry?' I blinked.

'Shagging her?' he said.

'No,' I replied, shaking my head. 'I don't think so. Is she gay?'

'She's never tried it on with me,' he said, shrugging as though that was an answer. 'If you were good, you'd be able to hold up a reflector properly.'

He signalled for me to stand on the T-shaped mark 7 had created on the floor with duct tape. 'Veronica isn't usually wrong about people. You sure you're not shagging her?'

'I'm definitely not,' I said, pulling the elastic from around my ponytail and securing as much of my curly copper hair as I could. 'And I'm sorry if I'm not getting everything right straight away. I've never actually assisted before. I'll get it, though, I promise. I'm sorry.'

It was as though I had apologetic Tourette's. I couldn't stop saying I was sorry even though an apology was not owed and unlikely to ever be deserved.

'Oh, so you're one of them,' Ess said, eyes narrowing as a tight smile took over his bristly face. 'You think you're a real photographer so you're too good to dirty your hands assisting me.'

'Not at all,' I replied quickly. 'I mean, I *am* a real photographer but I don't think I'm too good to assist you.'

I did though. I thought I was far too good but since no one had hired me to be a 'real' photographer for nearly three months, I didn't have a lot of choice. It turned out that lucking into two jobs, no matter how brilliant they might have been, did not a career in photography make.

'Yeah? You got lots of nice pictures of your dinner on Instagram, have you?' he asked while 7 tittered in the background. 'Maybe the odd cat? Few nice duckface selfies?'

'No,' I replied, tossing my head like an indignant pony. 'I mean, yes, obviously, but not just that. I shot Bertie Bennett for *Gloss* magazine and I worked with him on the book he's writing.'

'Never heard of him.' Ess dismissed my job of a lifetime without a second thought. '*Gloss*'ll be closed inside six months, mark my words. All those gash mags are going under.'

Apparently the look of horror on my face didn't faze him one little bit.

'Gash mags?'

'Mags,' he nodded, making a chopping motion with each word. 'For gash.'

'I'm not following,' I replied. 'Sorry.'

'You,' he pointed at me with a thick, unappealing finger, 'are gash. Mags for you. Gash mags.'

Agent Veronica had warned me not to mess up this job. Those weren't her exact words because Agent Veronica loved to swear like most people loved to breathe, so the whole exchange had been a lot more colourful than that but when she told me not to mess up, I just thought she was warning me not to be late or break anything. Dropping a camera seemed as though it would be considerably less damaging to my career than sprinting across the room and stabbing Ess through the heart with a biro.

'Jess, are you with us?' Ess snapped his fingers in front of my face and pointed at the mark on the floor. 'I need to check lighting on this shot. You're tall, well done. Get down on your hands and knees so I can see where to position the daft model tart when she finally shows up.'

Taking a short, sharp breath in, I reminded myself of how important this job was, of how much I wanted to get somewhere in my career. How this was all vital experience for my very light CV. Besides, what else was I going to do with my Saturday? I only had three episodes of *Game of Thrones* to watch and then I was completely caught up. After that, I was going to have to put myself into a medically induced coma until the new season started if I didn't find something else to do.

'Shall I just stay here?' I asked, kneeling down and holding a hand over my eyes as 7 turned on the blinding studio lights, all aimed directly at my face. 'Is this good?'

'Look up at me,' Ess directed, looking through his camera and edging closer to me. 'Look right into the camera.'

'I can't really see it for the lights,' I replied, blinking. 'Am I looking at you? Can you see me?'

'I can see you just fine, Jess,' he said. 'Now bend your elbows down a bit and look up. And stick your arse in the air.'

When Agent Veronica told me I was going to have to start at the bottom, I didn't realize that meant I would have to start with my actual backside. Reluctantly, I did as I was told. Making my arse centre of attention went against everything that I was, I was worried that if I kept it up there any longer, planets would be drawn into its orbit.

'God, it's not easy, is it?' I said. My arms were already shaking with the effort of holding the pose and the air conditioning whipped around the exposed strip of skin between my shirt and my jeans. Hello builder's bum, farewell dignity.

'Now open your mouth,' Ess said, coming ever closer. 'And stop blinking, look right at the camera like you want to suck it.'

I jolted backwards, backside crashing to the ground. 'Excuse me?'

'Oh, for Christ's sake, can't you be professional for one

minute?' He turned on his heel and threw the camera at a waiting 7. 'I asked you to hold a pose for one minute and you're giving me bleeding Naomi Campbell.'

'No, I'm sorry, I'm sorry,' I said, the words tumbling out of my mouth before I could think better of them. 'I misunderstood. Where do you want me?'

'On your knees, with your mouth open, waiting for me to come all over your face,' he replied.

'OK, yeah, sorry, no.' I leapt to my feet, standing up and hitching my jeans back up over my backside, my face bright red. 'That is totally not cool.'

Now I was standing up, and less than three feet away from him, it was clear that I was a good six inches taller than Ess, even in my Nikes. And with the righteous indignation jacking me up another foot, it felt as though I was towering over him.

'You can't say things like that to people,' I said. My face was hot and my mouth was dry. 'It's not OK.'

'It's art, Jess,' he said, hammering a fist into his hand as he spoke, his face even redder than mine. 'It's editorial. It's a method. Didn't you just say you were a real photographer?'

'I *am* a real photographer,' I stated as clear and loud as I could manage, while 7 skittered over to the computer, visibly shaking in his overpriced silver boots. 'But I'm not going to sit there and let you talk to me like that. It's horrible.'

'It's art,' Ess repeated, not quite as sure of himself. 'It's my style. It's why the magazine hired me and not you. It's not like I'm really going to jizz all over your chops, is it? I'm just trying to make you look sexy – although clearly I'm fighting a losing battle on that front.'

'It doesn't feel sexy,' I replied, flushed and upset. 'It

feels horrible. Why can't 7 stand in for the lights? He's exactly the same height as me and he's probably skinnier. He looks more like a model than I do.'

Ess and 7 turned to look at each other and burst out laughing. True, hysterical, body-shaking guffaws.

'Oh, Jess, he does, you're right,' Ess wiped away an actual tear. 'That is priceless. I didn't realize you were funny, I just thought you were shit.'

'Do you think I might be able to set up some of the shots this afternoon?' I asked. It had to be worth a try. 'Or shadow you? Rather than, you know, just make the tea?'

The smile on his face evaporated in an instant.

'Until you're capable of making a drinkable brew, you're on tea duty,' he sniffed. 'You don't come within ten feet of my camera until I've decided you're ready. Now go and get the kettle on before the model gets here.'

I wanted to argue. I wanted to tell him he was a complete arsehole who didn't deserve his job, his assistant or the air that he breathed. But I didn't. I was broke, I was bunking down with my best mate and I needed the job. So I did what millions of women had done before me: shut my mouth and went to put the kettle on.

Tea soothed all ills. And failing all else, I could always piss in the teapot. That would probably make me feel a bit better.

'And then he said he was going to jizz . . .' I paused for effect while Agent Veronica stared at her laptop. 'On my face.'

She looked up for a moment, fag hanging out of the corner of her heavily lipsticked mouth, her glasses hiccupping across her nose as she sniffed before turning her attention back to her computer.

'And?'

'Well, he can't say things like that to me!' I exclaimed before squeezing my eyebrows together with concern. 'Can he?'

'He can say whatever he wants as long as people keep hiring him,' she replied. 'Can I ask you a question?'

'Yes,' I said, dropping my bag on the floor and my arse into a chair. I'd been too incensed to sit until now but her non-reaction had taken the rage right out of me.

'What the fucking fuck is wrong with you?'

My arms froze in mid-air as I tightened my ponytail.

'What's wrong with *me*? Seriously?'

'It's got to be something,' Agent Veronica said, stubbing out her cigarette and immediately lighting another. 'Because I can't think of a single reason why you'd be in here, complaining to me about working with one of the best fucking photographers in London.'

'Because he said he wanted me to look at him as though he was going to jizz—' I started.

'Yeah, we covered that,' Agent Veronica cut me off before I could finish. 'It doesn't get funnier the more you say it. Actually, it does, but I digress. What are you complaining about?'

I was stunned. In my old job, people were sent to HR for as much as showing an ankle to a chimney sweep and we worked in advertising, an industry that saw itself portrayed as a misogynistic, glass-ceilinged nightmare on *Mad Men* and thought, nope, that's not sexist enough.

'I felt uncomfortable,' I said, trying not to choke on her cigarette smoke. 'I didn't like it.'

'Oh, I *am* sorry,' she replied, pressing her hands to

her heart, a look of faux concern on her face. 'My precious little baby angel! Did that bad man upset you? Did he hurt your feelings?'

I pouted. 'Yes.'

'There there.' She reached across the table and patted me on the head. 'Now calm down. Did he actually come on your actual face? No, he didn't.'

'That doesn't matter,' I muttered, beginning to feel stupid. And hungry. Terrible combo. 'It shouldn't matter. He shouldn't be able to say things like that.'

'No, he shouldn't but welcome to the world.' Veronica sat back in her chair, blinking through the fug of smoke around her, and shook her head. 'Do you want to be a fucking photographer, Tess?'

Six weeks ago, when I left Milan and arrived home, bright and shiny, full of ambition and pasta, I had been fairly certain that I was one. Apparently I had been mistaken.

'Yes,' I said hesitantly.

'Do you want to book actual fucking jobs that pay actual fucking money?'

'Yes,' I said quickly. That one I was sure about.

'Then, I hate to be the one to tell you but there's worse coming your way than Simon fucking Derrick telling you to get on your knees and make kissy faces at his tiny knob,' she sighed. 'You should have told him to whip it out and then pissed yourself laughing.'

'Simon?' I asked, the first smile I'd managed all day creeping onto my face. 'His name is Simon?'

'What? Did you really fucking well think his Mancunian mother took him down the swimming baths and shouted "What a fucking brilliant backstroke, Ess!"?' She took a drag and blew it out hard. 'I've had him on the books since he was taking pictures for the Argos catalogue. And they were shite.'

I would have killed to shoot the Argos catalogue.

'And 7?' I asked.

'You mean Colin?' Agent Veronica grabbed her mouse and began clicking manically. 'Little shagweed. Went to Eton, daddy owns half the internet. I hate that child.'

'It's harder than I thought it was going to be, that's all,' I admitted, scratching at a blob of white paint on the knee of my jeans.

'There's nothing easy about breaking through as a photographer, Brookes,' she replied. 'It takes some people years. Early starts, late finishes, working weekends, hours spent photoshopping some wanker's sausage fingers so he doesn't look like the smackhead that he is on the cover of a magazine. And that's when you get good enough to pick up that sort of job. Have you considered that maybe it's not for you?'

I felt my mouth fall open and immediately choked on Agent Veronica's cigarette smoke.

'It is for me!' I said, my eyes stinging from the same smoke. The air in her office was so dense with thick white fug, it could have passed for the set of a Bananarama video. 'It definitely is. I'll put in the hours, I don't care about hard work, I'll do whatever it takes.'

'And that's a fandabidozi attitude, Pollyanna, but it doesn't mean it's going to happen for you.' She stubbed out her cigarette and immediately lit another. 'It might be time to admit that I was a bit bloody ambitious in taking you on. I don't really work with assistants, Brookes. I'm an agent, not a charity. Do you think I'm at work on a Saturday afternoon for fun?'

'But I won't be assisting for long,' I protested, swiping at my watering eyes, desperate to convince her to let me stay. 'I'm going to be booking shoots really soon, I promise.'

'That's not your decision to make though, is it?' she grimaced, eyes flickering back and forth over emails I couldn't see. 'I've had you on the books near enough six months and you've booked two jobs for the same person. I can't babysit you for another six. There are only so many bleeding hours in a bleeding day and, no offence, but I need to concentrate on clients who are bringing in money.'

'But I will,' I said again. 'I just need time.'

'News-fucking-flash.' Veronica spoke in between intense inhalations. 'No one knows who you are, no one's worked with you, no one gives two shits. I know it's nearly Christmas but it'd be a bigger miracle than the virgin sodding birth for me to get you another job like the one you blagged at *Gloss*.'

I opened my mouth to speak but she cut me off with a stab of her cigarette.

'And you've got a dubious reputation at best, depending on who you ask.'

A dubious reputation? I was clean as a whistle. I'd won the attendance prize in school every single year, apart from that one time when Amy made us bunk off to meet Justin Timberlake but that was hardly my fault. If I hadn't gone, she would have been arrested. Instead of just being cautioned.

'Word gets around in this industry,' Agent Veronica said, seeing the confusion on my face. 'And your cuntychops former flatmate has made it her business to make sure everyone has heard her side of the story.'

Oh, bollocks. Vanessa. Honestly, you steal someone's

job, their identity and let your best friend punch them in the tit *once* and you never hear the end of it.

'That said, I like you, Brookes.'

She had a funny way of showing it.

'I'd hate to see the way you talk to someone you didn't like,' I said behind a cough. 'But thank you.'

'You've got balls and I respect that,' she went on, ignoring me as usual. Agent Veronica only really listened when you were saying something she wanted to hear. 'But you've got to get used to throwing those fucking balls around a bit. Do you understand me?'

'You want me to throw my balls around?'

'You're not going to get anywhere mincing around and fucking well sulking in corners.' She pointed at me with her cigarette, causing a mini flurry of ash to fall into her keyboard. 'And you're not going to get anywhere crying to me about some arsehole asking you to polish his knob.'

'That's not going to be a regular occurrence, is it?' I asked, genuinely at a loss. I came from a world where you worked hard and you got ahead. Or at least, I thought I did. It turned out I'd been very naïve. 'I mean, tell me what to do and I'll do it.'

'That's more like it.' She sucked her second cigarette into nothing, grinding it out in her ashtray with what I supposed passed for a smile. 'I want you to go home, put your big boy trousers on and go back on set tomorrow and kick Simon Derrick's arse. That doesn't mean you have to take his shit: that means you stand up for yourself and be amazing. Yes?'

'What else can I do?' I asked, trying to change the subject before she knocked me out with a single punch. 'I'll do anything, really, I'm not afraid of hard work.'

'How about you take some fucking photos?' she

suggested. 'Cocking revolutionary idea, I know. I can't carry you much longer, Brookes, not when you're not booking jobs. I don't have the time to spend pulling assisting gigs that pay a pittance out of my wonderful arse.'

'I'll give that a try then,' I said, grabbing my bag from the floor. It didn't seem like the time to mention that she still took 15 per cent of that pittance. 'Thanks for the advice, I won't let you down.'

Before I could open the door, a tennis ball thwacked the wall, right next to my head. Bending down slowly, my heart in my mouth, I turned around to see Agent Veronica staring at me.

'You dropped this?' I picked up the ball and held it in the air, heart pounding.

She clapped for me to chuck it back. With a feeble underhand throw, I tossed it across the office, missing Veronica by a good two feet and knocking a massive stack of invoices off the desk.

'I'm not really a thrower,' I explained as they fluttered to the floor.

'Do your research.' She spoke to me without acknowledging the piles and piles of paper all over her floor. 'Never have that camera out of your hands, shoot everyone and everything and make the most of every opportunity that comes your way. If you want this, you're going to have to fight for it. It's not going to be handed to you on a plate.'

'I can fight,' I replied, clenching my hands into fists. 'I want this. I *really* want this.'

'If you don't book something in the next month, I'm going to have to drop you and then you'll see how hard this really is. I want to see those balls, Brookes,' she barked. 'Show everyone who you are. You're not Tess the shitty, sad office girl any more, you're Tess Brookes, photographer, and a photographer should have something to say, should have a message. Show me what that is, who you are. Got it?'

'Got it,' I confirmed as I closed the door behind me. 'Swing my balls around and show everyone who I am.'

It sounded easy. Only . . . I wasn't entirely sure who I was any more.

CHAPTER THREE

'And then Veronica said she was going to drop me if I didn't start booking jobs,' I said, shovelling salt and vinegar Pringles into my mouth by the handful. Damn Tesco and their seasonal three-for-two offers. Damn the woman on the checkout who asked if I was going to a party. There was absolutely nothing wrong with a twenty-seven-year-old woman eating two tubs of Pringles for dinner and saving one for dessert.

'No way!' Amy bellowed, the speakers on my laptop crackling with outrage during our daily Skype call. 'She did not? She can't do that, can she? She can't fire you?'

'She can,' I replied, exhausted, glancing down at all the pieces of paper and empty Pringle tubs around me. 'And she might. Looking at it from a business perspective, she probably should. She's investing a lot of time in me and I'm not bringing much money in. My ROI is terrible and—'

Amy clapped her hands together and I snapped back to the camera.

'Tess, please tell me you haven't worked out the return on investment on yourself.'

'No,' I replied, slowly pushing my pad and calculator out of view of the webcam. 'Of course not.'

'She can't drop you, you're just starting out,' she said, glancing away at her phone for a second. 'You're hardly going to be David Bailey overnight, are you? It's not fair.'

'It's not about fair,' I told her. 'It's about what's best for business. Also, there's a small chance I did think I would be David Bailey overnight. I suppose things don't work out like that though, do they? I just don't want her to give up on me.'

'I don't want *you* to give up on you,' Amy corrected. 'It's a minor setback, that's all. You're killing it. You're better than David Bailey. Fitter than him anyway . . . although I don't think I've actually ever seen one of his photos. Or a photo *of* him. Is he fit?'

'I appreciate that but it would be a massive setback,' I said. 'I haven't got a clue what I'm doing, I wouldn't even know where to start.'

But I was trying. The bed was covered in magazines and newspapers, every publication I could get my hands on lay open on top of the duvet, the name of every art director, picture desk and photo editor in London high-lighted with neon-yellow marker pen. I was down but I was not out. Not yet.

'You'll work it out,' Amy replied, her attention drifting. 'You always do.'

'Is everything all right? Do you need to go?' I asked as she frowned at her phone again. 'It's OK if you do.'

'Sorry.' She threw her phone backwards onto the bed behind her and I winced as it bounced twice and then hit the floor. 'I *am* listening, I've just got loads of emails coming in. This presentation is going to kill me.'

Amy was in New York to launch Al's brand-new fashion line, AJB, and, from what I could gather, it was going to be quite the event.

'If Kekipi doesn't first,' I replied. 'How are you going to grow your hair to waterfall-plait length in the next three weeks?'

Amy, Paige and I had received emails in the middle of the night, detailing our mandatory bridesmaid prep regime. I loved that man like a brother, but there was no way on God's green earth that I was booking myself in for a full body wax prior to my dress fitting. Yes, my legs needed shaving, but it wasn't like I was rocking a full tache, I thought, absently stroking my face.

'He's taking me to get fitted for extensions tomorrow,' she said, fingering her messy black pixie cut. 'Or at least he thinks he is. Anyway, less about Kekipi Kardashian and more about this job you're on. You didn't get a facial and the photographer is a sexist wankpaddle who isn't fit to wipe his arse with your negatives. What happened then?'

'Oh, don't worry about it, it doesn't matter, I should let you go.'

As much as I missed Amy, I was keen to get back to my project. I wouldn't be able to sleep until I'd found the contact details of every possible person who could hire me and worked out how to bribe them into hiring me. I had to show Agent Veronica I was a good bet. 'I haven't had dinner or anything yet, I'm starving to death.'

'There should be some spaghetti hoops in the kitchen cupboard,' she said with a nostalgic smile. 'God, I'd take your arm off for some hoops on toast right now. Bread here is shit. What's that all about?'

'Where are you going for dinner tonight?' I asked, hoping to distract her. I'd been living in her house for six weeks. The hoops were long gone. 'Somewhere amazing?'

'Everywhere here is amazing.' She puffed out her cheeks and slapped her belly. 'I've put on about a stone. Honestly, Tess, the food in New York – I want to eat everything. I *am* eating everything. You might as well burn all my clothes because they're going to have to roll me home when I'm done.'

'Sounds awful,' I said, forcing a smile. 'Speaking of home, any idea when you'll be back? Still looking at flying on Christmas Eve?'

Amy scrunched up her face and shook her head.

'Not sure,' she said. 'We're here until the presentation on the twenty-third obvs and then Al said something about going to Hawaii to work on some new concepts before we go to Milan. He wants to go through some of Jane's notebooks he's got back at the house. I'd probably have to go with him – the time difference between London and Hawaii is mental and we'd never get anything approved in time.'

Al, AKA Bertie Bennett, AKA fashion industry legend, Amy's new boss and one of my favourite people in the world, lived in Hawaii, which was where he and I had met. It was also where I had met another person who, for the time being, would remain nameless, lest I felt the urge to carve out my heart with a rusty spoon.

'Hawaii is amazing,' I mooned, eyes full of pineapples and palm trees. 'You'll love it, Aims.'

'I know, I really want to go,' Amy said, gurning like a

mad woman. 'And imagine Hawaii at Christmas. Wouldn't that be amazing? I wonder if they still have Christmas trees. Shit, what if they don't have Brussels sprouts? I hate them, obviously, but you've got to have them.'

Wuh?

'You're going for Christmas?' I squeaked far too quickly, finally understanding what she was saying. 'You're not coming home?'

The last few months had been hard work but every time I'd walked past a shop window full of brightly wrapped presents I couldn't afford or attempted to ignore drunk people wearing reindeer antlers on the Tube, I remembered that soon Amy would be home for Christmas and everything would be OK.

'I want to come home,' she replied, not quite quickly enough. 'I probably will. But I may not be able to, Tess, and I know you of all people understand how sometimes work has to come first, even if I can't quite believe *I'm* saying that.'

I hated it when my dedication to a cause came back to bite me in the arse.

'Of course I do,' I said, trying not to pout. Amy hadn't held down a job for more than weeks at a time in years and working for Al was an incredible opportunity. I was so happy for her. And only the tiniest possible bit envious. 'I miss you, that's all. I can't believe you're in New York and I'm stuck here. I'm so jealous. But don't worry about it, it's fine.'

I couldn't imagine getting through Christmas Day without my best friend. We'd spent it together every year for as long as I could remember, from being tiny tots skipping down to church with our families, right through to sneaking out while everyone was in a post-turkey coma and necking Baileys out of the bottle by the village pond. That tradition had lasted much longer than going to church ever did.

'Christmas is still ages away,' Amy added when I didn't paste on my fake smile fast enough. 'We'll work something out.'

There wasn't a woman alive who didn't know that 'fine' never really meant 'fine'. A man, maybe, but a woman? No way.

'It's only nine days away,' I said, checking my half-eaten chocolate advent calendar as the terrifying prospect of having to spend the day alone with my family reared its ugly head. Nope, not worth thinking about.

'Loads can happen in nine days, Tess,' she replied, messing with her hair again. It had got so much longer since I'd left Milan that her shaggy fringe hung low over her big blue eyes. She looked gorgeous. 'Don't stress about it.'

'I won't stress about it,' I echoed, stressing. 'So, you're busy even today then?'

'I am. I'm busy *every* day. It's mental,' she said, eyes flicking up towards the top of my screen. 'Cockmonkeys, is that really the time? Tess, I've got to go, I'm late.'

'You're always late,' I reminded her. 'It's one of those wonderful annoying things I've come to love about you.'

'I'm only late, like, half the time now,' she said proudly. 'I am the all-new and improved Amy Smith. Well, 50 per cent improved. Call you tomorrow?'

'Of course,' I said, giving her a swift salute. 'Now, go on, before you're any later.'

'Yeah, yeah.' Amy brushed at her hair one last time and blew a kiss into the camera. 'Love you, skankface.'

'Love you too,' I said, waving before my best friend disappeared and the screen went blue.

My cheery smile faded. The suggestion that Amy wouldn't be home for Christmas was worse news than the prospect of getting dropped by Agent Veronica. It was worse than my black-and-blue backside and Paige not telling me what was going on with her love life and never talking to Charlie any more, and it was almost worse than the fact I hadn't heard from Nick Miller in nearly five months.

'I'm pleased for her, I am,' I said, stepping into the not-really-hot-enough bathwater fifteen minutes later. 'It's amazing, she deserves it.'

The rubber duck sat on the edge of the bath and eyed me with suspicion.

'Don't look at me like that.' I shuffled around until I was somewhere near comfortable and tried not to knock a crusty looking bottle of Head & Shoulders off the side of the bath with my massive copper-coloured topknot. 'She *does* deserve it.'

He still didn't say anything.

'I mean, yeah, I suppose if I really tried, I could be a bit annoyed that she's never kept a job for more than three months and now she's running all over the world with Al.' I shrugged. 'And she's having this amazing adventure while I'm making tea and holding lights and letting a man pretend to ejaculate on my face but, you know, whatever.'

The duck wrinkled his rubber bill and I knocked him into the bath.

'I hate you,' I said, holding my breath and sinking underneath the bubbles, but there he was, all judgemental painted-on eyes, when I re-emerged.

'I'm not jealous,' I told him/myself. 'She's had so many shit jobs, this is amazing for her.'

'Remember that time she got fired from the dog walking service for bringing the wrong dog back from the park?' he asked.

'I do,' I admitted.

'She took a Great Dane out and brought a Labrador home.'

'She did,' I admitted. 'The owners weren't that happy.'

And now she was more or less running the show at Bertie Bennett's new label. My friend, Amy, working for my friend, Al. He was fashion royalty and she was a woman who couldn't get a second interview at Topshop because she laughed when they told her she'd have to work Saturdays and every other Sunday.

The duck still looked sceptical.

'She likes to have her weekends free,' I mumbled. 'But I think it's nice that she's finally found something she loves.'

Silence.

'Maybe we could brainstorm some ideas that would help me, that might be more productive?' I suggested, poking my toes up out of the water.

'One, you could assume your flatmate's identity and run away to Hawaii to shoot a feature for a fashion magazine,' he suggested.

I gave him a level stare and said nothing.

'Oh right,' he said. 'You've done that already. Two, go to Milan and shoot a retrospective of Bertie Bennett's fashion archives and document the creation of his first designer collection.'

'Come to think of it, that sounds familiar as well,' I said. 'What do you want me to say? Stop sulking, accept the photography isn't working out, be a grown-up and get a proper job?'

The duck gave me the beady eye.

'Or four,' I finished. 'Drop a little rubber duck into the toilet and wait for one of Amy's flatmates to flush him?'

Before he could reply, the handle on the bathroom door began to jerk up and down.

'There's someone in here!' I yelled, sloshing around in the bath water. The door was only held shut with one rusty old bolt and I wasn't convinced it would hold.

'What?' a male voice shouted on the other side.

'I said there's someone in here!' I shouted back.

Why would you keep trying the door when someone was clearly inside? Amy lived with idiots. Correction, Amy lived with Al and Kekipi in amazing houses and hotels all over the world. *I* lived with idiots.

'Are you going to be long?' the voice called.

'As long as it takes for the hot water to come back on,' I called back, trying the tap with my toe. Still freezing. 'I need to wash my hair.'

And washing my ridiculous mop required enough water to cause a hosepipe ban in the Home Counties.

A loud sigh rattled through the wooden door. 'I'll have to have a shit downstairs then.'

I made a sour face at the duck and waited for the disgruntled footsteps to fade away.

'I'm so glad I decided to take Amy up on her offer of a place to stay,' I said to the duck. 'I'm having such a wonderful time here.'

The duck sailed past my kneecap with a quirk of his little plastic eyebrows that suggested I could have come up with other options.

41

'Maybe we could pack up and go and stay with Charlie?' I suggested.

The duck gave me a death stare. He and Amy both had Charlie Wilder at the top of their shitlists.

'Oh, wait. We can't, he hates me.' I paused. 'So you can stop looking at me like that or we're off up north to live with my mother.'

As much as I missed Amy, I knew she had to come home sooner or later. It was nothing compared to how much of a gaping hole Charlie had left in my life. He was the third member of our squad but even I had to admit I could understand why he wasn't busting my door down to be best friends forever.

I'd been nursing a crush on Charlie Wilder since the first day of university and when it seemed as though we had finally found a way to be together, we managed to cock it all up. Him by sleeping with my former flatmate behind my back and me by falling in love with the worst man alive. And the more I thought about it, the less sense it made.

The duck gave a reassuring quack and floated back down towards the taps.

The hardest part was having absolutely no idea what was going on in his life. We used to talk or see each other almost every day, but after an ill-fated trip to Italy earlier this year, when Amy and I were out there with Al, he had blocked the pair of us from all forms of social media. No status updates, no tweets, no Instagrams, Snapchats, Vibers, WhatsApps or even so much as a Periscope update to give me a clue as to what was going on in his life. When someone declares their undying love and then you declare *your* undying love to someone else, a freeze out is to be expected. I'd stopped trying to talk to him after thirty-six unanswered text messages.

I missed Charlie. I missed Amy. I missed the certainties and straightforwardness of my old life.

The handle jerked into life again, the bathroom door rattling on its hinges.

'I'm still in here!' I yelled. 'I'm in the bath!'

I missed being able to have a bloody bath in peace.

'There's no bog roll downstairs,' the man's voice bellowed through the door. 'Can you chuck us some out?'

I looked over to see one sad piece of toilet paper fluttering from the draft that blew in around the warped wooden bathroom window frame.

'There's none in here, either,' I shouted back. 'Sorry.'

'F'king hell,' the voice grumbled outside the door. 'What am I supposed to do, wipe my arse with my hand?'

I gave the duck a desperate look.

'First things first,' I muttered. 'Let's get out of here ASAP.'

The duck's buoyant bob seemed to suggest he agreed. As soon as possible. If not sooner.

An hour later, I was safely wrapped up in Amy's giant bed, in Amy's tiny bedroom, holding a letter in my wrinkled fingers. It was one hundred and thirty-six days since I had been given this note. One hundred and thirty-six days since I had opened the envelope and seen his handwriting for the first time. It was something I'd never thought about before, his handwriting. Between emails and texts, I hardly ever saw anything written down these days, but as soon as I saw this, I knew it was from him.

My handwriting had always been flagged as an area for improvement in school, and now that I hardly ever so much as picked up a pen, it was a disgrace. Nick's handwriting was perfect, of course. Elegant, joined up, and entirely sure of itself. His beautiful, heartbreaking words, etched into a page he had torn from the expensive leatherbound notebook he carried around with him and then hidden away in my passport for one hundred and thirty-six days.

Dear Tess,

I told you I didn't know if I could do this and it turns out that I can't.

I've been thinking about it all week and I just can't see another way. Even if you hadn't left, I still would have been on a plane to New York in the morning – you gave me a coward's way out. Don't think this is your fault.

I'd been fooling myself into thinking this was fun and easy and that I could do it but there's nothing fun and easy about the way I feel. Everything you said last night was incredible. I love you so much, my bones ache. You, Tess, are spectacular and everyone should be so lucky to have you in their corner but I'm not ready for you and it's not fair.

I could stay and we could keep playing this game but eventually, I'd hurt you one too many times and you would put up with so much before that happened, so I'm saving us both the heartache by leaving now, before I turn you into me.

You deserve better. I want to be better.

All my love,

Nick

Given how fast and how fiercely I had fallen in love with him, I only realized after he left that I really didn't know all that much about Nick Miller.

The fact I'd never seen his handwriting until he wrote this letter should have been the least of my worries but, looking at it now, it was all I could think of. Before the tears could start, I folded the note along its one crease, once sharp, now so soft I worried it would tear in two from being opened and closed so very many times, and tucked it back inside my passport, back underneath my pillow.

Maybe I didn't know that much about him but what I did know was how much I missed him. I missed the sound of his voice when he laughed and when he said my name. I missed the little growling noise he made before he ate. I missed the way he would kiss the top of my head before I fell asleep and how he let me put my cold feet on his warm legs in bed and how he always laughed at his own terrible jokes and how he made me feel brave and proud and utterly myself. Ever since he'd called things off, it was as though someone had taken all of that away and no matter how hard I looked, how determined I was to work these things out for myself, I could not find the answers. I didn't want to need him like this but I did want *him* to need *me*. It was all so confusing.

It turned out I could lie to myself about a lot of things if I thought they were for the greater good. I could tell myself that Charlie would forgive me and that we would be friends again. I was happy to pretend I wasn't at all jealous of Amy's sudden success and I almost believed it when I told people I didn't regret walking away from a career in advertising to make cups of tea and sweep up studios but I couldn't keep telling myself stories about Nick any more.

We had spent two weeks together and one hundred and thirty-six days apart. He hadn't called, he hadn't written, but then neither had I. Every time I opened my inbox, I looked for his name; every time my phone rang, the split second before I saw who was calling, I hoped it would be him. The fact he hadn't even tried to speak to me since he left me in Milan was the reason I found it so hard to fall asleep every night but the thought of calling him and having him tell me he didn't want me and never really loved me? That was the thing that woke me up in a cold sweat. I wasn't lying when I told Paige I hadn't contacted Nick because I wanted to concentrate on work but I wasn't telling the whole truth either. I'd lost Charlie's trust and friendship, my career was in shambles, Amy was thousands of miles away and only moving further from me, but with Nick's letter safely under my pillow, and the tiniest spark of hope that we could still be together one day, that I could get back the things I had lost, I got to keep something.

When anxiety woke me in the middle of the night, it was the memories that lulled me back to sleep. I let myself remember the time we walked through Milan, hand in hand. The time we kissed in the square in front of the opera house. The look on his face when I told him that I loved him. I indulged in our days in Hawaii, swimming in the waterfall, sitting on the beach at sunset. The memories I kept locked away, day in and day out because, in the middle of the night, they felt like a warm blanket pulled right up to my chin on the coldest of nights but in the daytime, they were blinding. A constant reminder of what I no longer had.

It was easy to believe in dreams at night but the tiny spark of hope that I carried around all day was starting to burn my fingers. Something was going to have to change.

CHAPTER FOUR

'You sound a lot happier today,' Amy said. 'Way less like you're going to kill someone.'

'I do feel a bit less homicidal,' I replied, running to the underground station to avoid the sudden shower that had started the second I left the studio. 'Today is definitely an improvement.'

'I can't believe you're working on a Sunday,' she clucked, disgusted. 'You know how I feel about that.'

'I do but lots of people work weekends and the world doesn't end. Actually, it would be more likely to end if they didn't. Anyway, I've only got today and Monday left with the lovely Ess, I think I can manage that.'

I *thought* I could, I wasn't absolutely certain.

'Then I ought to get this out the way while you're in what passes for a good mood,' Amy said. 'I'm definitely not going to be home for Christmas.'

'Oh.'

'Obviously it would have been better if Kekipi wasn't dead set on this bloody New Year's Eve wedding but he's been such a bridezilla about the whole thing and

Domenico was insistent that they had to get married in Italy and we could only get the Park Avenue Armory on the twenty-third so we were kind of stuck with all the dates.'

'Oh.'

'Between the presentation on the twenty-third and flying to Milan for the New Year's wedding, going anywhere else in between is just impossible – I'll have so much to clear up on Christmas Eve and Boxing Day. You know they only take Christmas Day as holiday here?'

'Makes sense.'

I wondered whether or not I still had the receipt for her Christmas present so I could take it back and swap it for a sackful of coal.

'I completely understand.'

'But here's what I was thinking . . .' Amy was still talking, the strain in her voice breaking into a familiar giddiness. 'You should come here!'

'To New York?'

'To New York!' Amy confirmed. 'It would be amazing. I miss you so much and Al and Kekipi would love for you to be here at Christmas. God knows how I've managed this long without you, so please come? I need you!'

'No you don't,' I replied. 'You've done everything by yourself so far. You're going to be fine.'

I looked up at a snowman hanging from the telephone pole above me. His big white bum shone yellow in the smog but the bulbs had gone in his top half and nobody had bothered to replace them. His cheery grin and corncob pipe were lost in the drizzle and the whole effect was really rather sad.

'All right, I might not need you but that doesn't mean you shouldn't come,' she replied. 'I want you there. I want you to see the presentation – we're using your photos and I know you got an invitation – and take me for drinks when I'm crowing on about how amazing I am to anyone who will listen. Tess, Christmas in New York – you know you want to.'

I did. Amy knew I'd always wanted to go to New York but I'd never had the time, Amy could never afford it and Charlie hated to fly, so year after year, it had passed me by. But New York for Christmas . . . I had a sudden vision of myself, wrapped up in a cosy coat, mitten in mitten with Amy, buzzed on good cocktails, laughing with Kekipi and getting a grandfatherly hug from Al.

God, it was tempting. It would definitely be better than curling up on the settee with my family, drinking five cups of tea and putting away an entire box of half-price Christmas chocolates. Well, the chocolate part didn't sound that bad but the rest of it sounded incredibly depressing. And all too familiar.

'Well?' Amy was as impatient as ever. 'Unless you've been stunned into silence by my genius, this is the part where you're supposed to make agreeing noises. Wow, Amy! What a good idea, Amy! I'm on my way, Amy!'

'I want to come,' I said, having already talked myself out of it. It was way too expensive, it was way too far, I didn't even have any mittens – and what if Veronica got me more work? 'But I'm saving for somewhere to live. And you're supposed to be working, aren't you? I know it's going to come as a shock to you but you're expected to do it nearly every day.'

'You can put it on your credit card and I *will* be working,' she protested. 'I have had this job for over four months now, titface, surely that calls for a celebration?'

'New record,' I said with a heap of approval. 'I'm proud.'

'I'm good at it,' she replied simply. 'Come on, Tess, it would be awesome. I hate being here without you, it feels weird. I had my knickers on inside out all day yesterday and I didn't have anyone to tell. I need you.'

I smiled in spite of myself.

'And what would I do with myself while you're swanning around New York being the world's most amazing . . . you?' I asked, all my features pinching together as I tried to remember what her job title was supposed to be.

Amy cackled triumphantly.

'I'm the Vice President of Special Projects,' she said. 'Can you even effing believe it? Kekipi came up with it, he's amazing. It was that or Head Bitch in Charge and he said I couldn't have that title because that was him.'

It was impressive. The most special project Amy had worked on before now was the time she tried to work out if you could make toast with an iron.

Amy made a huffing sound down the line. 'And if I'm not enough to tempt you, there's at least one other really good reason for you to come over here.'

My ears prickled and I felt my entire body tense up. She didn't even need to say his name, I only had to think it.

'Unless you're about to say "hot dogs" I don't want to hear it, Amy,' I warned her.

'OK, don't be mad at me,' she began, knowing I would immediately get mad. 'But I did a bit of internet stalking and, you know, as luck would have it, someone else is in New York as well.'

'Is it Michael Fassbender?' I asked, refusing to play along.

'I know you're going to say you don't care but we both

know you do and what harm could it do to say hello if you're in the same city coincidentally and don't tell me you're over it because you're not and it's horrible and I hate it.' She barely broke for breath, afraid I would cut her off. 'You should call him. What harm can come of saying hello?'

So much harm, I thought.

'Tess?'

'I've got to go,' I lied. 'I'm just about to get on the Tube, I'm late for something.'

'For what? Get on a plane and come to New York.'

'I've got to go,' I repeated. She didn't need to know the only place I had to be was in bed with a six-pack of Wotsits but I just didn't have an answer for her that wasn't hysterical sobbing and I didn't think anyone fancied sitting opposite a crazy person on the Tube. Well, not any more than usual.

'I think you should call him,' she said. 'I think you should pick up the phone and say, "enough of this radio silence, you wankpaddle, we need to talk."'

'OK, really going now,' I told her, blocking out all her arguments. 'I'll talk to you later. Love you.'

I dropped my phone back in my bag, wincing at a regrettable thunk as it hit my camera.

The camera Charlie had given me.

It was funny to think about it now, but if he hadn't given me this camera, I might never have gone to Milan. And if I'd never gone to Milan, he and I might be together. Amy would still be in London and none of this would be happening.

It was Amyisms like 'get on a plane and come to New York' that made me miss him the most. Before, I would have gone over to his flat and told him all about my day, he would have made fun of Ess, we would both have laughed and then one of us would have made a cup of tea and put the telly on and everything would have been fine. With Amy all the way in New York and Paige so wrapped up in her work and her love life, I'd been feeling so alone. Which was silly, really, when one of my best friends in the whole world only lived half an hour down the road.

I stood in front of the turnstiles of the Central Line, trying not to get in everyone's way while I thought hard and fast. Everyone was so keen for me to take charge, swing my balls around, show everyone who I was and take what I wanted in life. Maybe they were right. Maybe it was about time I did something I'd been thinking about but too afraid to act on for months. Amy was right.

What harm could come from saying hello?

The rain had stopped by the time I got to Charlie's flat.

All the way over on the Tube, I'd run over every single scenario of how my first attempt at ball swinging might turn out and each one was worse than the last. What if Charlie was still so angry with me he didn't even open the door? What if he did open the door but he shouted at me? What if he had a girlfriend and she was there and he had told her what a terrible person I was and she was a Brazilian jujitsu fighter and she killed me with her bare hands? All entirely possible.

I was scared. I hadn't been this nervous to talk to Charlie since our media studies seminar in the first semester of university. I filled my mind with happy memories, laughing, smiling, cheerful Charlie. Not the face of the miserable, angry man I'd watched ride the train out of

Milan. The first man that evening who told me he didn't want to see me again. Unfortunately, not the last. Really, even by my standards, that was an incredibly poor twenty-four hours for me.

It was almost seven by the time I had forced myself down his street and even if Arsenal had played, he would be home by now. It was the best time to catch him. Unless Arsenal had lost. Oh God, I thought, grabbing hold of the railing beside me, what if they had lost? That was the only possible thing more dangerous to my health than a Brazilian jujitsu-fighting girlfriend. I scrambled in my bag for my phone, pulled up the app that still had a place on my home screen and madly flicked through the fixtures. They didn't play every Sunday, did they? I hoped against hope that this was one of their weeks off.

'Tess?'

I looked up and there he was in front of me. Red shirt, striped scarf, copper curly hair that looked just like mine, only considerably shorter, soaked from being out in the rain all afternoon.

'Did you win?' I asked, frozen to the spot, phone still in my hand.

'We drew,' he said, not moving. 'One-one.'

I slipped my phone carefully back inside my bag, painfully aware of the four feet of space between us.

'That's better than losing,' I said.

Charlie pulled out his house keys and I stepped aside so he could open the door. He turned to look at me again, blinking as if to make sure I really was there.

'Yeah,' he said, holding the door open and nodding me inside. 'You coming in or are you just going to stand there like a lemon?'

'I'll come in,' I said, skittling through the door and letting a little smile grow on my face.

So far, no violence, so good.

CHAPTER FIVE

'Look at you,' Charlie said, throwing the soggy scarf onto his blue sofa, his keys into the bowl on the bookcase and marching straight into the kitchen to put the kettle on. I immediately picked up the wet scarf and laid it on the radiator. Nothing had changed. His flat was exactly the same as the last time I'd been here.

'Look at *you*,' I echoed, not sure what else to say. The whole way there I'd run over what I would say to him in my head but I couldn't find the right words. I figured I'd know when I saw him but I was absolutely none the wiser. If anything, now I was inside his flat, all warm and cosy and familiar, I was more confused than ever.

'No, really.' He ducked out of the kitchen, all six feet three of him, and smiled. I felt my stomach fall to the floor and smiled back. 'Look at the *state* of you.'

My smile didn't last very long.

'Are you wearing denim dungarees?' he asked, trying not to laugh. 'And what has happened to your hair? It's massive.'

'It's raining,' I said defensively, pulling my hair back

into a cack-handed ponytail and wrapping a hair tie around the split ends. 'I got caught in it. And yes, I'm wearing dungarees, only we call them overalls now and they're very trendy.'

'You look like a giant toddler who's come round to fix my toilet,' he replied. 'Why are you covered in paint?'

'It's make-up,' I muttered, scratching at the multi-coloured smears on my clothes and wondering if he had noticed the extra pounds I'd picked up in Italy. Amy said you couldn't tell, but I could. Why had I come over without sorting myself out first? What a bloody rookie mistake. 'I was working.'

Charlie cocked an eyebrow. 'As what?'

'Photographer's assistant,' I replied. 'We were doing a shoot for a magazine.'

He nodded slowly. 'Better than a magician's assistant, I suppose,' he said. 'Milk and sugar?'

'The usual.' I sat down on the edge of his settee and tried not to read too much into the fact he was asking how I wanted my tea when he'd been making me tea almost every day for the last ten years.

'Two cows of milk and three sugars it is then,' he replied, disappearing into the kitchen. Phew. He hadn't forgotten, he was just being weird. Brilliant. 'I haven't got any biscuits so if that's all you've come for, you might as well go now.'

'How can you not have any biscuits?' I shouted, still searching his flat for evidence of what he had been up to for the last one hundred and thirty-seven days and coming up with nothing but a well-thumbed copy of *GQ*. Even for a slow reader like Charlie, that hadn't taken almost five months. 'What's wrong with you?'

How could nothing have changed in five months? The

same books sat on his coffee table, the same pair of trainers lay at the side of the door and the same dusty red Netflix envelope was wedged between his Blu-ray player and the PlayStation. My entire life had been turned upside down and he hadn't even sent his DVDs back. How was that possible?

'Health kick,' he said, emerging from the kitchen with two mugs in his hands. The same mugs. His mug and my mug. 'No biscuits, no sweets, no chocolate.'

'Are you dying?' I asked, only half joking.

'Just trying to take better care of myself.' He held my mug out to me and went to sit down on the sofa. Just before his bum made contact he shot back up and perched himself decidedly on the armchair he never used instead. 'Can't live on biscuits forever.'

'That's a lie and you know it,' I said, wrapping my hands around my mug, even though it was far too hot. 'Biscuits are the staff of life.'

'Isn't that bread?' He pinched his shoulders together and fell silent, the awkwardness of the moment finally winning out over our terribly English desire to drink tea and pretend nothing was wrong.

I stared into my mug and tried to remember the last time I'd been so tongue-tied around Charlie. It hadn't been this bad since the first week of university when I'd watched him playing a Smiths' song on his guitar outside our halls of residence. A verse and a chorus of Morrissey's finest and, just like that, I lost the power of speech.

'So . . .' He broke the silence, pulling off his Converse and kicking them underneath his uncomfortable chair. 'What's going on?'

'Not much,' I said in a voice much squeakier than I had intended. 'I've been running my toddler plumbing company and Amy's in New York. She's working for Al Bennett – you know, the man I was taking photos of in Hawaii? She's his Vice President of Special Projects, isn't that amazing?'

'What kind of projects?' he asked, puzzled. 'Is he building a house out of Dairylea Triangles?'

'No, he's opening these clothes stores, these boutiques.' I held my tea in one hand and waved the other around as I tried to explain. 'And starting a clothing line and, you know, she's got loads of experience in—'

'I don't really care, if I'm honest,' he said, interrupting. 'I meant, what's going on with *you*?'

I opened my mouth to answer but nothing came out. Instead, I held on to my scorching hot up of tea and sat in silence.

'Why are you here?' he went on. 'It's been months since, er, since I saw you. Why did you come today?'

Pulling on the end of my ponytail, I sipped my tea and focused on the Netflix DVD, wondering if he even knew it was still there.

'Why not?' I asked quietly.

Now it was Charlie's turn not to have an answer.

He was sat right on the edge of his chair, his white-socked toes curled underneath each other, clenching and unclenching every other second. I waited another minute, watching him watch me, not saying a word, before I gave up.

'Do you want me to go?' I asked, then stood up to leave. At least if I offered, he wouldn't feel like he was kicking me out. 'I'll just go. I shouldn't—'

'No.' He jumped to his feet. 'Sit down, stay. I'm sorry.'

'It's fine.' I grabbed my bag and swung it onto my shoulder, my camera smacking me in the shoulder blade to remind me what an imbecile I was. 'I'll go. I should have called or not come or got run over on the way or something. My mistake.'

'Tess, stop.' As I made for the door Charlie grabbed hold of my dungarees by the shoulder strap and my mug flew out of my hand. It bounced off the blue cushions and clattered onto the floor, breaking into three large chunks as it landed. 'Just stop.'

'Oh balls, I'm sorry,' I whispered, as I bent down to pick up the pieces. 'I'm so sorry, Charlie.'

'I know,' he said, yanking me by my shoulder strap until I stood up to face him. 'So am I, *I'm* sorry.'

Chewing my bottom lip so hard I thought I might break the skin, I turned towards my friend.

'Come here, you daft cow.' He wrapped his arms around my shoulders, pressed his lips against the top of my head and sighed. I felt one hundred and thirty-seven days fall away from the calendar as I buried my face in his armpit, greedily breathing in his teenage boy deodorant, smiling and ignoring the tickling in my ears and lump in my throat.

'Your hair smells like a wet dog,' he said, squeezing me tightly.

'I know.' My voice was muffled by his damp football shirt and smiles. 'It's a new thing I'm trying. All the rage in Milan.'

'I'm glad you're here.' He squeezed my shoulders once more and then let me go. Without the weight of his arms around me, I felt so light I worried I might float away. 'I've been feeling like shit for months.'

I'd never been so happy to hear that someone I loved had been miserable because of me.

'I wanted to say something but the longer I left it, the

more I felt like a dickhead,' he said, avoiding the broken mug and throwing himself onto the settee, arms and legs all over the place. I sat down next to him, our denim-clad knees just touching, just barely. 'And then you went quiet and I thought it was too late.'

'You didn't answer any of my texts,' I said, working very hard to resist the urge to clean up the broken mug. Now was not the time. 'I didn't think you would want to be friends again.'

'I didn't.' He leaned back against the settee and closed his eyes. 'I was so angry with you, Tess. I don't think I've ever been so angry about anything. But, you know, feelings go away eventually.'

I pursed my lips and cocked my head thoughtfully. Did they? Just like that?

'I should have been honest with you,' I said slowly. The peace between us felt fragile and every word out of my mouth seemed heavy and dangerous. 'About you know, about the other situation.'

Nick. Nick Nick Nick Nick Nick.

Charlie took a deep breath and let it out, hard and heavy.

'Yeah, maybe,' he said. 'But I understand.'

'You do?' I really hoped he had more to say on the subject because I definitely didn't.

'Yeah, I understand.' Charlie wiped the palms of his hands over his face and I realized what he meant. Just because he said he could understand it didn't mean he had to like it. 'You were confused and you were going through some stuff and I didn't exactly help, did I? Then you go off on an adventure and you meet this . . .'

He paused to take another deep breath while I held mine.

'You meet this bloke . . .' He kicked the 'k' out hard. 'And it's exciting and fun and it is what it is. We've all done it.'

And by 'done it' what he actually meant was that what *he'd* done was 'shag your awful flatmate without telling you', but in this instance I was prepared to give him a pass.

'It doesn't matter now,' he said with a shrug. 'We've been friends a long time, Tess. I should have called you and I didn't, more because of hurt pride than anything else. It was stupid. I was stupid and I'm sorry.'

I chewed the inside of my cheeks, admittedly a little confused. In my heart of hearts I had to admit it stung that he wasn't crying himself to sleep over me, just a little bit. I'd nursed my agonizing, unrequited crush on Charlie for the best part of a decade. He got over me in less than six months.

'I just want to be mates again,' he said. 'And Paige told me that, well, she told me you and this bloke were the real thing.'

'Paige?' I turned to look at him so fast my ponytail whipped around and whacked me in the chops. '*My* Paige?'

'Yeah, when we were working on the Peritos pitch,' he explained. 'And I suppose, while I'm being the bigger man, I'm glad you've met someone. Not to be a girl about it but, you know, maybe me and you weren't meant to be.'

'Maybe.'

Even now, when I knew he was right, it was hard to say.

Charlie rolled his eyes and smiled, looking just like my Charlie, the one I'd been in love with for so long, and my heart began to beat just a little bit faster. The last time

I had been in his flat, I thought, running a hand over the settee, the last time we'd been sat here together . . .

'So can we call a truce?' he said, holding out his hand. 'Go back to how things were before: Tess and Charlie versus the world?'

Ten years I'd waited for Charlie to tell me that he loved me, and as soon as he did, I went and fell in love with someone else. Brilliant bloody timing, Brookes.

'I suppose so,' I said, taking his hand in mine and shaking it hard, sad for what could have been, happy for what was – and still confused, but more than anything else, relieved. 'I need someone to watch the last five episodes of *Breaking Bad* with me, I've been too scared to watch it on my own.'

'Your bloke not into television or something?' he asked, his face looking like he had tasted something bitter. 'Because you know how I feel about people who don't like telly.'

'He actually hasn't got one,' I admitted. 'But that doesn't really matter, given that we're not together.'

Now it was Charlie's turn to look confused.

'I told you,' I reminded him. 'Remember when you told me to piss off and I said I wanted to make things right and you asked if it was because he'd dumped me?'

Ah, happy memories.

'Bit of a blur to be honest,' he said. 'I thought you were all loved up. I thought that's why you stopped texting me?'

I shook my head. 'We were never really together, if I'm honest.'

I hopped up off the settee, gathered up the pieces of broken mug and carried them into the kitchen so he wouldn't see the tears in my eyes. Dumping them in the bin, I turned on the cold tap to rinse off my hands, holding my wrists under the cold stream for a moment with eyes closed. I took a deep breath in and blew it out slowly through pursed lips.

'I can't really remember exactly what I said the last time I saw you.' Charlie's voice made me jump. I turned around to see him in the doorway, arms raised above his head, fingers clinging to the kitchen door frame and his pale, perfect arms peeking out of his shirt, his head ducked low.

'It wasn't pleasant,' I said. 'But probably not entirely undeserved.'

'I was so angry,' he said. 'But I didn't mean it, whatever it was. You know what I mean, don't you?'

I nodded automatically, wishing I could forget so easily. I remembered every word. Every cruel, carefully selected insult. I'd replayed it so many times, each time running it through a guilt filter, I'd probably made it worse than it really was. What I wouldn't give to trade that searing accuracy for a comfortable blur.

'I thought you were still seeing him,' Charlie said. 'I didn't know it didn't work out.'

I wrapped my fingers around the stainless steel of the sink, the cold tap dripping in time to my heartbeat as I stood there, waiting. 'Well, it didn't,' I said in a tight voice. 'Sometimes it doesn't, does it?'

'I know that shouldn't have made any difference,' he went on, scuffing his toes along his floor tiles. 'Because you have been my best friend for so long and even if I can't remember what I said, I know it wasn't very nice. I wanted to hurt you because I was hurt. My ego was hurt; I thought that you loved me. You said you did.'

'I do,' I said without thinking.

He looked up suddenly.

'You do?'

'I did,' I corrected softly, crossing one arm in front of myself, cradling my elbow in my other hand.

With a sad smile, he choked out a half-laugh in the back of his throat.

'And how do you feel now?' he asked.

Drip drip drip. Thud thud thud.

'I don't know,' I said. 'I missed you.'

Charlie looked around the kitchen, his head gently nodding up and down as he considered my response.

'There have been a million times in the last few months when I've thought, "I wish Charlie was here."' I carried on talking, scared of what would happen if I stopped. 'Or, "Charlie would think that was so funny." But you weren't there and it was my fault that you weren't there. I really want us to be friends again.'

'Friends then?' He turned his golden eyes on me and there was nowhere to go.

Friends. It was all I wanted. Or was it?

I'd worked so hard for the last few months, trying to get on with my life and over my feelings for Nick, thinking Charlie and me had been a mistake. But here, now, I wasn't so sure. Nick was gone but Charlie was here. Would it be incredibly stupid to even think about giving us a chance?

Suddenly, Charlie burst out laughing.

Apparently it would.

'I'm so happy I've got my mate back,' he said, crossing the kitchen in a single stride and wrapping me up in the least sexual embrace in human history. 'You know, I've had no one to watch *Vampire Diaries* with, it's been a disaster.'

'Your secret shame,' I winced as he rubbed his knuckles across the top of my head and pawed at my hair to smooth out the frizz. 'Good to know I'm good for something.'

Charlie looked down at me and our eyes met as he reached out a hand, his knuckles brushing my cheek.

'Watch out,' he said, opening the cupboard behind my head. 'I've got an emergency pack of Hobnobs in here somewhere. I say we crack them open, make another cup of tea and get the telly on. You in?'

'I am,' I agreed, trying to shake off the tension that apparently only I felt. 'But only if you've got the Hobnobs. Otherwise you're going back out to Tesco in the rain.'

He rifled around behind the dinner plates for a moment before producing a bright blue package. 'Milk chocolate Hobnobs at that,' he said, tapping me on the head with the packet. 'Best Sunday night ever.'

'Best Sunday ever,' I replied, happy, sad, and with a Hobnob craving like you wouldn't believe.

CHAPTER SIX

'Morning.'

'Nnueeughh,' I groaned, my face buried deep into a pillow that I immediately knew was not my own.

'You've always been such a delight first thing in the morning,' Charlie said as he opened the living room curtains. I rubbed my eyes with tight, tired fists. 'Nice pants.'

'Thanks,' I said, rolling myself up in his quilt and promptly falling off the settee. 'God, I feel rubbish, I should have gone home.'

'I'm not sure sleeping on my settee is why you feel rubbish,' he said, tapping an empty bottle of white wine with his foot. 'But you were in no fit state to go home, madam.'

'And apparently you were in no fit state to give up your bed for a lady,' I replied, clambering back up onto the settee, curling my legs up underneath myself and pressing my head back into the pillow. 'What a gent.'

'You refused,' he reminded me. 'You said you didn't need to be patronized, you were perfectly fine on the settee and you wanted to be closer to the toilet in case you threw up.'

'Oh yeah.' I looked across into the bathroom and saw the toilet seat up. 'It's coming back to me now.'

'And you said I'd have to carry you and, honestly, I couldn't be arsed,' he said, stretching upwards and tapping his fingertips on the ceiling. His T-shirt pulled up around his flat belly, showing off a trail of brown hair that disappeared under the waistband of his shorts as well as some abs I definitely didn't remember seeing before. His no-biscuit regime was clearly paying off.

'I should get to work,' I said, sitting up and trying not to cry. Charlie's settee was not the place to get a good night's sleep. 'If you're late, Ess makes you wear the Hat of Shame.'

'Hat of shame?' Charlie asked, flicking at his phone, a look of concern on his face.

'It's a bright pink baseball cap with the word "cock" embroidered on the front.' I tried to run my fingers through my curls but last night's rain, sleeping in a plait and a night on the settee had worked together to create one giant dreadlock. Wearing the hat might actually be preferable.

'I can't believe you're working as an assistant to an arsehole.' He leaned over the back of the armchair to give me a sad look. 'I know you're a complete martyr when it comes to work but at least at Donovan & Dunning you were getting somewhere.'

'I worked eighty hours a week and I was the first person they made redundant when the shit hit the fan,' I replied. 'Yes, totally getting somewhere.'

'But this is better?' he asked. 'Fetching and carrying for a wanker?'

'This is how it is,' I told him. 'You know how people

say, "you've made your bed, now lie in it?" This is my bed. This is me lying in it. You have to start at the bottom, Charlie.'

He made a humming noise and tucked his phone away in his back pocket. 'You say it like you don't have any options, but you do. You could get another job in advertising tomorrow.'

'Firstly, who would want me with a six-month gap in my CV? And secondly, I don't want to go back into advertising,' I said, almost surprising myself with my certainty. 'I love photography. I'm a photographer.'

'You're also a brilliant creative director,' he replied simply. 'And I'd have you.'

I pressed my lips into a tight, silent line.

'I mean, I'd hire you,' he clarified. 'I'm serious, I was thinking about it when I woke up. I interviewed someone for creative director last week but it's not too late. You could still take photos on the side and you wouldn't have to do all this assisting shit. You're better than this, Tess.'

I methodically worked my fingers through my hair and pretended he hadn't just made me the most spectacular offer.

'That sounds really amazing,' I said, overwhelmed by the sudden vision of myself striding into a meeting with nice clean hair and a lovely pair of shoes on my feet instead of balancing on a chair, covered in sweat, wearing a pair of dirty trainers. 'But like I said, I'm a photographer now.'

'I'm serious, Tess,' he repeated, squatting down on his uncomfortable armchair, elbows on his knees. 'I'm not saying you don't love photography and I'm not saying you're not good at it but I'm offering you something else.

You've had six months out and maybe you needed a break. There's no shame in saying the photography thing didn't work out as a career and keeping it as a hobby. You could be a director. If you wanted, you could be a partner, we'd be a team. The business is really starting to take off.'

It was something I'd wanted for so long. I'd worn my corporate blinkers for years with partnership the only goal in sight and here it was, being dangled in front of my face. And it was tempting. Going back to the beginning, a month before I turned twenty-eight, starting back at the bottom? Less appealing.

'Think about it,' Charlie said. 'I told the bloke I interviewed I'd let him know after Christmas so he can sort everything out with his old job in the new year. That gives you time.'

'I will,' I promised. 'I'll think about it.'

'Yeah, well,' he said, clearly a little bit offended. 'Don't think you've got to stick this out because you don't want to admit you made a mistake. Tea?'

I nodded and waited until he had disappeared into the kitchen before I gave him the finger. Did he really think I'd made a mistake? Did everyone?

I knew that going back to advertising would be easy and working with Charlie would be fun, but what I didn't know was whether or not it would make me happy. Nick always said I was too worried about the things I thought I *should* do, rather than the things I *wanted* to do. This definitely felt like a 'should'. But since when was I taking Nick Miller's advice?

Pulling the blankets up around my chin, I grabbed my phone to check my messages. There was a late night text from Paige, asking if I wanted to get a drink. A message from Kekipi attached to a photo of him and Domenico singing karaoke in some dimly lit dive bar and seventeen texts from Amy, half written exclusively in Emojis, the other half more or less unintelligible swearing but the general gist of them was that I should get my arse on a plane to New York ASAP.

'Maybe I should be Amy's assistant,' I called through a yawn. 'She'll be queen of the world in six months at this rate.'

'Maybe this Al dude is her Mr Miyagi,' Charlie shouted back. 'She's going to be the fashion equivalent of *The Karate Kid*.'

'Karaoke kid, more like,' I muttered, flicking through her Facebook posts. Kekipi and Domenico were not alone in that bar. 'I don't really see Al as the wax on, wax off type.'

'I don't know.' Charlie stuck his head out of the kitchen. 'He made a big impression on you.'

'He did,' I admitted. 'He's a really great man, you'd like him.'

Growing up, it hadn't really occurred to me to miss my dad. My mum remarried a couple of years after they got divorced and he was never more than an occasional visitor after that. Brian, my stepdad, was a total champ, but the fact of the matter was always there: he wasn't my real dad. Whether I knew it or not, I'd missed out on something. Al, or Bertie Bennett as most of the world knew him, was the kind of granddad everyone wished for. A kind, generous, gentle man armed with all the wisdom of old age combined with the same curiosity and preference for neon T-shirts as your average six-year-old. Al was the kind of person you needed in your corner, only you didn't know it until you met him.

'Hasn't he got a job for you somewhere in his empire?' Charlie asked. 'Personal photographer to the Bennett estate?'

'It's not like I haven't thought about it,' I admitted. 'But I don't want to take the piss. He helped me out loads by getting me in to work on his book. I can't expect him to hand me a job every time I'm on my arse.'

'Don't be afraid to ask people for help,' he said after a moment's consideration. 'It's nothing to be ashamed of.'

'I do need help,' I told him as the kettle whistled for attention in the kitchen. 'I need help getting to work in an hour and I need help explaining to Amy why I'm not going to New York for Christmas.'

'First one's easy, I'll get you an Uber,' Charlie said, setting a cup of coffee down in front of me. 'And don't understand the second one. Why aren't you going to New York for Christmas?'

It was a fair question.

'I do want to go,' I said, scooting up the settee so he could sit down beside me. 'But I can't go. I've got work and I don't really have the money and, you know, I should spend Christmas with my family. Or something.'

Charlie did not look convinced.

'Christmas Day at your mum's house makes *Eastenders* look like a sitcom,' he reminded me, needlessly. 'And as for work, most people take time off at Christmas, although I know that's going to come as a shock to you.'

'It's less shocking than the thought of going to New York to visit the Vice President of Special Projects at Bennett Enterprises,' I said while searching for my overalls. Ah, there they were, rolled in a ball in the bath. Of course, where else would they be?

'Do you know what I do whenever I'm not sure what to do?' Charlie asked.

'Lie down on the floor and eat Maltesers?' I suggested. 'No, wait, that's me.'

'I sit down and I ask myself, what would Tess do?' he said with a knowing smile and a smug nod. 'Works like a charm.'

Amy was right: he really was a cockwomble.

'And there was me thinking you were going to say something helpful,' I said with a filthy look on my face. 'Thanks, Charlie.'

'Good to have you back, Brookes,' he replied, slapping a heavy hand hard on my arse as he strode back into the kitchen. 'Now get your arse to work, your Uber'll be outside in two minutes.'

'Jess, I've got a mouth like a badger that just went down on a camel and liked it,' Ess declared later that morning. 'Go and get us a coffee, I am parched.'

Across the studio, I gave him a startled look from the make-up artist's chair. 'Right now?' I asked.

'No, next Tuesday,' he replied. His flat cap and mutton-chops clashed with his flashy silver tracksuit, making him look like a disgruntled sheep farmer who had come to work in fancy dress as a twat. 'I wouldn't ask for it now if I didn't want it now, would I?'

'It's just, I'm not really in any shape to pop to Starbucks right now.' I bit my lip and got a mouthful of something rancid.

Ess dropped his camera, 7 diving across the room to grab it before it could hit the hardwood floor. 'What's the problem? The model is going to be here any minute.'

I looked at Rachel the make-up artist with wild eyes.

Well, I assumed I did; it was very hard to tell under all the face paint and false eyelashes and cock cap.

I had been three and a half minutes late.

'I'll go,' she offered, turning to Ess. 'I can be there and back before Tess washes all that off her face. What does everyone want?'

'Why would she need to wash her face?' he asked, trying not to laugh. 'I need you here, Rach, the model will arrive in a minute and we'll have to get started.'

'I can't go out like this,' I said. 'You're not serious.'

'You look grand to me,' he said, staring right at me. 'Doesn't she look grand to you, 7?'

'Grand,' he squeaked, hands pressed over his mouth. Wanker.

'You said you'd look at my portfolio today before the model came in,' I reminded him, stalling for time. 'When are we going to do that?'

'When you've got my coffee,' he replied. 'I'm dying on my arse over here, Jess. If I don't get a coffee in me in the next two minutes, I'm going to turn into a right old – Kelly, you're here!'

A six-foot-something goddess with glowing black skin and a weave that would make Beyoncé weep strolled into the studio, only to be swept up in Ess's arms and lavished with kisses.

'Jess is going out to get coffee,' Ess said in between gratuitous snarfs of her neck. 'What do you want?'

'Oh, I'm fine,' she said, taking off her sunglasses, giving me a double take and then putting them straight back on so she could stare more freely. 'Thank you.'

'You need a juice, she'll get you a juice,' he reassured her before turning back to me. 'If you're back in less than ten minutes, I'll look at your portfolio.'

'Can I wash my face first?' I asked, bouncing my weight from foot to foot.

He sneered. '7, start a timer for ten minutes,' he called across the studio. 'I don't know, can you wash your face and get coffee in less than ten minutes?'

'Bollocks,' I muttered, grabbing hold of my bag and running for the door. 'I'll be back in nine.'

'She's not going out like that, is she?' I heard the model ask in a low voice as I left. 'Does she know what's on her face?'

'Yeah,' Ess said gleefully. 'Yeah, she does.'

Starbucks was exactly two minutes away from the studio and the juice bar was next door but one. I'd spent all week bouncing between the two and had my coffee run down to six minutes exactly, I could absolutely do this.

'No one will be in Starbucks,' I told myself, shaking out my ponytail and trying to cover my face with my hair. 'It's East London, no one will be in Starbucks. It won't be busy.'

No, the voice in my head reminded me, they'll all be in the organic juice bar, you fool.

Whatever, I argued, as if I would be the strangest thing on the streets of London today. What were the chances of bumping into someone I knew, anyway?

'Tess? Is that you?'

The chances were high.

'Raquel?' I squinted through my hair to see a small, squat blonde woman staring at me, slack-jawed, in the middle of the street. 'Hi!'

Because there was no better time to bump into the woman who had fired you from your last proper job than when you were wearing dirty denim overalls with unspecified muck all over the knees and an entire make-up artist's palette of unblended contouring slap all over your face.

'Are you . . .' She peered up at me, half confused and half delighted. 'What's going on with your face?'

'I'm working,' I told her, trying very hard not to touch my face. 'I'm doing a thing.'

'What kind of thing?' She kept staring, her eyes flickering from red triangles underneath my eyes and lavender circles on my chin to the brown shading all around my cheeks and nose. 'Are you a clown?'

I gave her as ferocious a look as I could, given the circumstances.

'Do I look like I'm laughing?' I asked.

'Sort of,' she replied tartly. 'That's an interesting hat.'

'Thank you,' I said graciously, touching the peak of the Hat of Shame. 'Anyway—'

'I'm glad you found work,' Raquel said, interrupting me to be even more condescending. If that was possible. 'You disappeared off the face of the earth and I was wondering where you'd got to. What agency are you with?'

'I'm not in advertising any more,' I said, aware of every single person on the street turning to stare as they passed. 'I'm a photographer.'

Raquel looked at me with her dead shark eyes. 'You're a what?'

'A photographer,' I replied. It was hard to sound confident when you looked like a Picasso painting of a clown. Brown blocks on my cheeks, silver triangles around my chin, bright red circles under my eyes. It was a grand look.

'I see.'

'I've been in Hawaii,' I said, folding my arms around me. 'Shooting for *Gloss* magazine.'

'Is that right?'

'And Milan,' I said, nodding. 'I was working with Bertie Bennett. You probably won't know who he is but he's basically a fashion legend. He's huge. Just an incredible man. An inspiration really.'

'And this . . .' She gestured towards my face, reminding me of my current situation in case I'd somehow forgotten for a split second. 'Is something to do with that?'

'It's a make-up test,' I said, hoping she didn't have any follow-up questions. 'I'm testing make-up.'

Playing make-up guinea pig was another in a long line of Ess's super-fun challenges. Like how he'd had me wear a necklace of sausages for two hours last Wednesday morning and then source fourteen gerbils and six guinea pigs for a 'concept', only to discover that the model was allergic to rodents, meaning I had to return them before she would even walk into the studio.

'And what about Charlie?' Raquel asked. 'How's lovely Charlie?'

'He's fine,' I told her. 'I saw him last night.'

'So exciting to see him go out on his own,' she said, her over-tweezed eyebrows arching high into her hairline. 'And picking up Peritos as his first client? Impressive.'

'He's very talented.' I shoved my hands in my pockets and wished I'd brought my gloves. It was windy and cold and I very much wanted to be inside. 'He's going to do very well.'

'I was surprised to hear you weren't working together, you two were always so buddy-buddy.'

'You know, I'm actually late,' I said, looking past her to see a queue forming out the door of Starbucks. 'I'm shooting a feature for *No-No* magazine – have you heard of it?'

'I can't say I'm familiar with it, but I'm sure it's very

good,' she said, flipping her bleached blonde head around, stretching up to her full five-foot-nothing.

I stood in the street, looking down at the woman who had taken away my job with a smile, and suddenly realized she didn't matter. None of it mattered. She could stand in the middle of the street and try to make me feel shit every single day for the rest of the year and it wouldn't mean a thing. She couldn't fire me again; I was the only one who could fuck up now. So why waste another second worrying about what she thought of me?

'You know, you actually did me a massive favour,' I said, giving her a big, bright smile. 'And I never said thank you.'

'I did?' she asked, her smile fading as mine grew. 'How's that?'

'Sacking me,' I explained. 'Best thing that ever happened to me.'

'Oh.' Her thick foundation formed deep orange creases on her forehead as she frowned. 'Well, I'm glad you've been able to find a positive in such a difficult situation.'

'Absolutely! And not just because I never have to see you again!' I replied, quickly looking at my watch. 'Ooh, is that the time? It's been so great to see you—'

'I'm at Eskum now,' she said, interrupting before I could make my escape. 'Director of people—'

'Wow, yeah? I actually really don't care,' I said, taking my turn to interrupt. I flashed her one more smile as she visibly shrivelled in front of me. 'But gosh, those poor, poor people.'

Raquel looked as though I'd slapped her in the face and I wished I had.

'I wish I could count all of the fucks I don't give but I've only got eight fingers and two thumbs and that's not nearly enough,' I said, giving her a brief hug and ever such a tiny shove. 'Have a lovely day, Raquel. Or don't. Doesn't really matter.'

I turned on my heel and marched off down the road, ridiculous painted head held high in my cock cap.

'Ess!' I shouted as I pushed the door open against the wind.

'Thank God, my stomach thinks my throat's been cut,' he said, holding his hand out for his coffee with one hand and scratching his crotch with the other. 'You were gone more than ten minutes though.'

'I haven't got your coffee,' I replied, marching across the studio and throwing the Cock cap at 7. 'I want to go over my portfolio.'

'We haven't got time,' Ess replied, pointing across the studio to the styling area. 'Now sod off and bring me a coffee.'

'We won't be done for at least an hour,' Rachel the make-up artist called over to us with a thumbs up. 'Take your time.'

Hands on my hips and feeling only slightly less confident than I had been thirty seconds earlier, I stared Ess down until he gave a sigh and shook his head in defeat.

'Fine, pass it here,' he said, holding out his hands. 'But if they're shit, I'll tell you they're shit.'

'Good.' I pulled my portfolio out of my bag, bouncing across the room. 'Whatever advice you can give me, I'd appreciate it.'

'Most of the time my advice is stop trying to take photos,' he grunted, flicking through the pages, skipping over my shoot for *Gloss*, my pictures of Milan, without even stopping to take a proper look. 'It's quicker.'

Biting my thumbnail, I crossed my fingers.

'Shit,' he said, flipping through the pages without really looking. 'Shit, shit, shit. Ready to give up yet?'

'No,' I said, barely breathing. 'You can keep going.'

He paused on a shot of Al, sat on the beach in Hawaii and staring out at the ocean.

'I don't hate this one,' he announced, slamming the book shut. 'Now go and get my coffee.'

'That's it?' I asked, crushed. 'You don't hate that one so we're done?'

'I don't hate that one so I'll look at the rest later,' he clarified. 'Now you go and get my coffee and we'll go through the rest of them after the shoot if I don't decide it's a complete waste of my time before then.'

'Oh my God,' 7 whispered, pulling me away after Ess shoved my portfolio into my chest and walked away, muttering to himself. 'That's the nicest thing I've ever heard him say about anyone's photos.'

'Really?' I asked, a tiny spark of hope lighting up inside me. 'That was nice?'

'Have you met him before?' he asked. 'Don't push it. That was a big compliment.'

'Why are you still here?' Ess barked, looking over his shoulder at me. 'Why isn't there a cup of coffee in my hand?'

Nodding, I threw my portfolio back in my bag and ran out the door. Two weeks I'd been there and I'd finally got him to look at my photos. If I could get Ess to give me some genuine feedback, I felt as though I could do anything. This must have been that ball-swinging feeling Agent Veronica had been talking about and I didn't hate it.

As I jogged down the street I made another big ball swinging decision. Pulling out my phone, I opened up the internet browser and tapped in 'New York flights'. There was nothing stopping me taking photos while I was in New York, was there? Maybe there would even be a course I could take. Donovan & Dunning's American office barely closed for the holidays so I was far more likely to find something useful in New York than I was hanging around my mum's house getting squiffy on Baileys and ignoring my sisters.

As soon as I'd picked up four flat whites, two Frappuccinos and a green juice, I told myself, I was going to book my flight to New York and work the rest of it out from there. Well, after I'd done that and finished the day at work, washed my face, gone home and had some tea. And packed. And called my mum. And done the online paperwork.

But once all that was out of the way, New York City, and the rest of the world, had better get ready for me.

CHAPTER SEVEN

'TESS!'

Resplendent in a red velvet Santa hat, gold-glitter leggings, neon-blue fur coat and clutching roughly enough balloons to float a house, Amy Smith was impossible to miss as I walked through the arrivals gate at JFK. She fought her way through with the helium-filled herd, the biggest balloons practically lifting her off the ground as she hurried across the airport, bashing people in the head as she went.

'You're here!' She threw herself at me, wrapping her arms around my neck and her legs around my waist while Kekipi clapped and cheered behind her and half the balloons floated off up to the ceiling.

'I'm so happy to see you,' I said, dragging my case behind me with Amy still clinging around my middle like a glittery little spider monkey. 'It feels like forever.'

'It's been forty-nine days and fifteen hours,' Amy confirmed as she hopped to the ground. 'God, Tess, you look knackered.'

'That's because I *am* knackered,' I replied, trading air

kisses with Kekipi. 'I had to change planes twice to get any kind of cheap flight. Turns out it's expensive to fly at Christmas. What time is it?'

'It's 1 a.m.,' Kekipi said, taking custody of my suitcase as Amy grabbed hold of my hand. 'What time did you leave London?'

'Yesterday?' I said, shaking my head. 'But Amsterdam was today I think. And I got to see Chicago! Or at least I got to see the airport. But I'm here now, that's all that matters.'

'At least you can fly directly from here to Milan,' he said. 'Amy told you I've booked your flights? I want no arguing from either of you.'

'You won't get any,' I said wearily. 'Usually I would fight you on it but this one bankrupted me, so thank you.'

'You're welcome. I couldn't have my bridesmaid missing the wedding, could I?' he asked. 'And you look wonderful. Look at those charming overalls, you're so Madonna circa 1986.'

'No, she's right, I look like a tramp,' I replied, stifling a yawn. 'I can't remember a time when I wasn't wearing these. If it's 1 a.m. here, what time does that make it at home?'

'Party time,' Amy said confidently. 'Maybe a little bit past.'

'That's funny, it feels more like bedtime to me,' I said, trotting through the airport, hand in hand with my best friend. I was tired, I ached from cramping my stupid long legs up in an economy seat, but I was so, so happy. Of all the spur-of-the-moment, credit-card-destroying flying decisions I'd made in the last year, this felt like the best one. 'Can party time be tomorrow?'

'I suppose,' she replied. 'I've got a few meetings in

the morning but then we're going to have the best time ever! I'm so excited. We're going to do everything – carriage ride round the park, boat ride round Manhattan, sunset walk over Brooklyn Bridge – everything.'

'Sounds like the most romantic holiday ever,' I said as I craned my neck to peer out the windows, trying to catch a glimpse of the city. 'Maybe Kekipi can keep me entertained while you're busy.'

'I will be drowning in wedmin,' Kekipi said, miming himself hanging from an imaginary rope. 'I can't believe it's so soon.'

'Don't listen to him.' Amy slapped his hand back down by his side. 'He's been a total bridezilla. Domenico is a saint to put up with him.'

'I'm actually going to Tiffany to look at china patterns,' he confided. 'I don't know why I didn't get married years ago, it's wonderful. All you have to do is throw a party and people buy you obscenely expensive presents.'

'Don't worry, you don't have to babysit me,' I told them, a wave of exhaustion rolling over me. 'I made a list of things I want to see on the plane and I can get started on my own.'

'Of course you made a list!' Amy clamped her arm through mine. 'Just when I thought you'd really changed.'

'Shut up,' I told her sweetly. 'I was researching courses and exhibitions and stuff, to see if there was anything I could do while I was here, and there's a thing I want to enter. It's a photography exhibition in a Manhattan gallery but they have a new-photographer type thing that's open to anyone and the winner gets an apprenticeship with a working photographer. I'm going to enter.'

'And *win*,' Amy replied. 'Are you going to enter a photo of me?'

I looked at her, smiling sweetly up at me, framed by red velvet, blue fur and a shimmering background of sequins.

'We'll see,' I said, glancing over at Kekipi and his impeccably groomed and impressively raised eyebrow.

The double doors of the airport slid open and a blast of cold air slammed into me, turning every inch of exposed skin to fire and then to ice. My fingertips burned as I tried to hide my hands inside the sleeves of my jumper and my eyes began to water immediately.

'Oh my God,' I gasped, the wind catching in my throat. 'Oh my God, it's *cold*.'

'Winter is coming,' Amy said in an ominous voice. 'Sorry, I should have told you to bring a proper coat.'

'You should have told me not to come,' I corrected her through chattering teeth. 'It's freezing! Amy, it's so cold.'

'Tess hates the cold,' she told Kekipi as she breezed along towards a line of yellow taxis as though it was the middle of a sunny Tuesday in June. 'She's such a baby about it.'

'I'm not being a baby!' I protested, excited about the taxis but still wondering whether or not my nose had fallen off. 'It's about a million degrees below freezing!'

'Not yet,' Kekipi said, hustling me across the road. 'But it will be tomorrow.'

I paused and looked up at a plane screeching above us.

'Is it too late to go back?' I asked.

'Get in the taxi, you twatknacker,' Amy instructed. 'We'll get you a proper coat tomorrow.'

'A coat, a cocktail and a big handsome man to keep you warm at night,' Kekipi added. 'Something in a blond, maybe? With a beard for added warmth?'

'Don't get her excited,' Amy told him as a taxi driver hopped out of his cab and popped the boot for my suitcase. 'We've got to share a bed.'

'I'm very glad you're here,' Kekipi said, wrapping me in a bear hug while the taxi driver screamed at Amy as she tried to force the remaining balloons into the back of the taxi. 'We've missed your civilizing influence.'

'And the scary part is,' I said, watching as the driver began popping the balloons with a lit cigarette faster than Amy could get them in the car, 'I've really missed her.'

For the third time in three days, I woke up without a clue as to where I was. Rubbing my eyes, I looked around the room. It wasn't Charlie's living room and it definitely wasn't the departures lounge in Amsterdam. Thick cream carpets and heavy matching drapes made it look like the inside of a very swanky igloo, although it was considerably warmer than that, thank God. Turning over on my white pillow, underneath the white duvet, I saw Amy, flat on her back and snoring with her mouth wide open.

'Amy,' I whispered. 'Are you awake?'

'No,' she replied, snorting twice and then rolling across the bed. 'Go back to sleep.'

'I can't,' I said. A quick glance at the clock showed it was 6 a.m. I'd only been in bed for five hours and I was wide awake. The wonders of jetlag. 'Wake up!'

'I am awake,' she said, pulling the thick, fluffy duvet over her head. 'I might not reply but I'm definitely awake and I'm definitely listening.'

I shuffled upright for a better look at the bedroom. I'd always imagined homes in New York to be either poky little shoe boxes or huge industrial loft spaces but I really should have known better than to expect any of that from one of Al's homes. Amy's room was huge, the bed taking up more space than her entire bedroom in London. The furniture was simple, with clean modern lines that made it look as though it had been brought in from the set of some sixties TV show, and huge, long swathes of heavy fabric hung all the way from the ceiling down to the carpets. Pin-thin lines of a brightening dawn ran all the way around them, promising a world outside these four walls.

'Amy?'

My best friend snored in response.

Wired and tired and generally suffering from my impromptu long distance flight, I rolled out of bed and headed for what I assumed was the bathroom. The mattress didn't even dip and Amy's delicate snorts kept on coming.

'Definitely awake, my arse,' I mumbled, tiptoeing into the bathroom and shutting the door as quietly as I could.

The sun had only just begun to rise when I stumbled out onto Fifth Avenue, big sunglasses and an even bigger smile on my face. Bumbling towards a zebra crossing in the dawn light, snow seeping in through my Converse, my knees bound together by a floor-length sleeping bag of a coat I had borrowed from a wardrobe by the front door, I was cold, uncomfortable and ridiculously happy.

'I'm in New York,' I whispered to myself, not caring whether or not anyone could hear me. It felt so improbable. I was finally here, walking around a city I had dreamed of visiting for so long, just as though it was a perfectly normal thing to do. It was all I could do not to grab hold of passers-by, just to explain to them how excited I was.

Even though it was still early, not even seven, there were already so many people on the street. I sensed a certain solidarity in our matching coats and gave a small, smug nod to everyone I passed, feeling like such an insider. No touristy, inappropriate-but-visually-appealing jacket for me. Less than twelve hours in and I was practically a born-again New Yorker as I stopped at the edge of the pavement, waiting for the little white man to tell me it was safe to walk.

'Hey! Watch it, lady!'

A tall man in a black version of my blue coat bashed into me, phone in one hand, coffee in the other, a frustrated look on his face.

'Sorry,' I spluttered, starting left then right as he tried to get around me. 'I was waiting for the light to change.'

'There's no cars,' he replied, waving his phone hand down the street before he stepped right into the street. 'You need me to hold your hand? Watch where you're walking.'

'I'm walking here,' I whispered, delighted as he walked off, giving me a surly look as he went. '*Fugeddaboutit.*'

I couldn't think of another time when I'd felt this excited just to be in a place. Hawaii was paradise, Milan was beautiful but New York was electric. The green street signs, the slightly off spellings, the threat of parking tickets and towing fines in dollar signs all made my heart beat slightly faster. I held my camera in my freezing cold fingers and clicked away at everything I saw.

Without any idea where I was going, I started walking south along the park, following the flow of people and letting my mind begin to wander. How many times had Amy walked down this street since she got here? And Al? I knew Jane had chosen their house in Milan because it faced the park – had she picked this place for the same reason? I wondered how things had changed since they'd moved to New York in the sixties and how much was the same. Everything in my life seemed temporary at the moment; twenty-seven years of the same followed by six months of madness. It was so hard to know what I was supposed to do now. Carry on down this road of not knowing or go back to my old life with my tail between my legs? A partnership in an advertising agency with one of my best friends shouldn't have felt like second prize but I couldn't shake the feeling that accepting that would be settling.

And try as I might, I couldn't stop my eyes from searching the crowds for his face. I stopped for a moment, reaching into my handbag to rest my hand on my passport, to find his note. It was strange sometimes, the thought of Nick was always there in the back of my mind but every now and then it popped up to say hello, punch me in the stomach and stop me dead in my tracks.

Nick lived here. I was in Nick's city.

But New York was a big place, wasn't it? I wasn't about to bump into him on the street, even if I wanted to. I didn't know which area he lived in, but I couldn't see him rubbing elbows with Upper Eastsiders. That said, I could absolutely imagine him running up here. Every few minutes, a Lycra-clad jogger whizzed by me and disappeared into the park, like a lululemon-sponsored ninja. And in that moment, he was real again. He wasn't a fading holiday hangover memory, he wasn't the super human I'd built him up to be. He was just Nick, a man who might go running around the park of a morning. A man who walked and talked and breathed and ate and did everything the same as everyone else, here in this city. And all the arguments I'd had with myself, all the reasons I'd come up with not to call, suddenly seemed silly.

'I could call him,' I whispered, my fingertips finding my phone in my pocket. 'I could send him a text to let him know I'm here.'

Before I could act, my Nick-induced trance was broken by a loud snuffling and heavy breathing around my shins. I looked down to see a huge, smiling golden retriever wearing a purple puffa jacket and slobbering on my jeans.

'Hello,' I said, bending over as far as my coat would allow to pat his happy head. 'What's your name?'

'Don't touch my dog!' His owner, wearing his very matching purple puffa jacket, yanked on the dog's lead and pulled him away down the street.

'So friendly,' I muttered as the dog made eyes at me over his shoulder.

I stared at the phone in my hand but the moment was gone. I wasn't ready. What if he didn't want to see me, or speak to me? I didn't want to ruin my first day in New York. I'd call him later.

With my phone safely zipped away, I carried on my march along Central Park, washing away thoughts of Nick Miller by filling my brain with a million new memories. Across the street I saw tall men in grey coats and top hats, hurrying in and out of buildings with snow-covered green awnings, opening the doors of long black cars for women wearing floor-length furs and sunglasses, and on my side, men in jeans and two pairs of gloves were setting up shiny steel food carts as far as the eye could see.

The carts looked so out of place, all bright colours and unappetizing photos of greasy doner kebabs hanging from them, right in the middle of the elegant, icy neighbourhood. It would make a great picture, I thought, as I watched one of the men blow into his hands while he watched out for a customer.

'Excuse me . . .' I sidled up to one of the carts and gave the sullen-looking owner my brightest, non-teeth-chattering smile. 'Hello.'

'Hot dog?' he replied. 'Two dollar.'

'Oh, yes, I do want a hot dog,' I said, pulling my camera out from inside my coat where it was safely nestled in my armpit. 'And a coffee—'

'Three dollar,' he said before grabbing the handle on a silver lid to reveal a bucket of hot dog sausages, resting in an inch of unpleasant-smelling hot dog juice. 'Onion?'

'Oh, no!' I waved my hands madly as he started fishing for a limp sausage with a bun in the other hand. 'If it's all right, I want to take your photo first?'

He didn't say anything.

'Me, take photo?' I pointed at my camera and held it up to my face, making clicky noises. 'Photo of you?'

'You wanna take my picture?' he asked, dropping the hot dog back in the grey water with a splash. 'Sorry, it's early, I didn't get ya' right away. No worries, hun, snap away. This is my best side.'

Shamefaced, I kept the camera in front of my burning cheeks and nodded. I hadn't only turned into Amy; I was also morphing into my mother. The man straightened his baseball cap, put on his biggest smile and puffed out his chest.

'I was actually thinking something a bit more natural?' I said as his cheeks began to vibrate with the effort of his smile. 'Like, as if you were just going about your day.'

Crestfallen, he pulled his thumbs out of his lapels and went about his business.

'Oh, gotcha,' he said. 'All natural, like.'

Taking a step backwards, directly into a cold, filthy

puddle, I crouched down, looking for the perfect angle. The early morning light streamed through the trees above, bouncing off the hot dog cart, making it shine like solid silver. Ice-white puffs of air came out of the man's mouth as he worked, frying up onions and fishing for hot dogs. Sensing he was losing patience, I took as many pictures as my stiff, frozen fingers would allow.

'You still want the hot dog and the coffee?' he asked, ending the session with an impatient glare directly into my lens.

'Absolutely,' I replied, fishing around in my pocket for the small bills I'd stashed in there. Anything over a twenty was strapped around my body, underneath my coat. You could take the girl out of Yorkshire . . . 'Three dollars, you said?'

'Twenty,' he replied, holding out a limp wiener. 'For the photos. And the hot dog's on the house.'

Grudgingly, I handed over a twenty and took the hot dog in one hand and the blessed paper cup filled with scorching hot coffee in the other.

'Nice doing business with you,' he said as I pumped bright red ketchup and bright yellow mustard all over the hot dog. 'Have a nice day.'

'I will, thanks,' I said, walking quickly down the narrowly ploughed pavement and chomping through the world's most expensive hot dog. Fifteen minutes on the streets of the city and I'd already been grifted by a hot dog vendor.

Giant coat or no, I was clearly not a New Yorker just quite yet.

'Ms Brookes?'

Two hours later I was creeping back into the townhouse

and stashing my borrowed coat back in the closet when a tall woman in a stylish grey dress appeared out of nowhere. Al's homes were always staffed by domestic ninjas, invisible housekeepers who kept your room cleaner than your average five star hotel and telepathic cooks who knew exactly what you wanted to eat before you did. Clearly his New York pad was no exception.

'Yes, hi, hello.' I raised a hand awkwardly, not sure if I was expecting her to shake it or I was just giving a pleasant wave.

There would never be a time I didn't feel weird meeting someone's 'staff'. Having people work for you was something I just couldn't get my head around. The one and only time I'd hired a cleaner for my old flat, I ended up spending two hours bottoming the place before she arrived so she wouldn't judge me for being a scruffy cow. It was pointless: she totally did anyway.

'I'm Genevieve, the housekeeper,' the woman said, ignoring my proffered hand and gesturing for me to follow her. 'Mr Bennett will be pleased to see you. He's dining in the breakfast room.'

'He is?' I couldn't hide my excitement and did a little skip as I followed her down through the seemingly never-ending hallways. 'Have you worked here long?'

'Just eight years,' she said, as though it was nothing. I'd been in my job for seven and it felt like a lifetime. 'Before that I worked with the Spencers and moved here with Miss Spencer when she returned from school.'

'Miss Spencer?' I repeated. 'This isn't Al's house?'

'Delia Spencer,' Genevieve replied. 'Mr Bennett's god-daughter. She lives here, yes.'

'Oh, I see.' I didn't really. 'So, Delia lives here while Al is in Hawaii?'

'Mr Bennett hasn't been in residence for the past eight years,' she said. 'But Miss Spencer is very happy to have him home for the time being.'

'Tess! There you are.'

Al jumped to his feet as I walked in, always the gentleman. His Grateful Dead T-shirt and lime-green board shorts were at complete odds with the gentle greys and pale blues of the breakfast room and his white hair and wiry beard rubbed against my cheek when he hugged me. It made me think of Brillo pads and Father Christmas and home.

'How marvellous that you're here,' he said, pulling out a chair and waiting for me to sit. 'I must say, Amy was over the moon when you called to say you would be joining us. I felt terrible taking her away from her family at Christmas.'

'It's usually best to take Amy away from her family whenever possible,' I reassured him while he poured me a steaming cup of tea. 'But I'm glad I came.'

And right then and there, I really was. Knowing Al was in the world was a wonderful thing. Sitting across the table from him with a fresh mug of Earl Grey in your paws was another entirely.

'And what can we get you for breakfast, Ms Brookes?' Genevieve asked. 'Anything particular you'd like the chef to prepare?'

'She'll have the works,' Al answered before I could underorder out of politeness. My tongue had been locked in a battle between my English reserve and my howling stomach: my early morning walk around Central Park had burned off my hot dog snack. 'She's a good eater, this one.'

'So you have noticed that I've gained some weight?' I

said, patting my stomach. It was really misdirection; actually it was my arse that had ballooned since I'd last seen him. 'Thanks, Al.'

'Not a single pound where it shouldn't be,' he protested. 'You know I don't stand for this skinny-minnie nonsense. I'm always starving after I fly and I can't have you staying at my house without a proper breakfast in your belly.'

I'd really only put on three or four pounds but I felt like a heifer. It didn't matter how many compliments your surrogate grandfather threw at you, if you couldn't fasten your jeans without breathing in, sometimes it was hard to feel good about yourself.

'Now, tell me everything you've been up to since you left us,' he insisted. 'Where should I be looking for your fabulous photographs?'

'I've been mostly making tea for a man called Ess and wearing a hat with the word "cock" embroidered on the front,' I said. 'Oh, and I was watching the first three seasons of *Scandal*.'

'I've heard that's very good,' he said as he chewed thoughtfully. 'You haven't been taking photos?'

'I've been taking them,' I said as Genevieve brought out a stark white plate full of food, 'but they haven't gone any further than Instagram. It's a bit harder than I thought it would be.'

'Anything I can do to help?' Al asked.

I smiled and shook my head. 'My friend has offered me a job,' I said, pushing the words out fast. 'In advertising.'

'And you're considering it?' He pushed a jug of warm syrup towards me as I tackled a fresh, fluffy pancake.

'I'd be stupid not to,' I said. 'It's a pretty good offer.'

It was true. I couldn't simply write off Charlie's offer, I wasn't a child. I had bills to pay; I needed somewhere to live. If I couldn't pay my way by taking pictures, could I really call myself a photographer? 'It's a really great offer.'

'Then you should certainly consider it,' Al said. 'I'm sure you're not the kind of person who would run away from a situation when the going gets tough.'

'I might be,' I admitted. 'Don't most people?'

'Are those people happy?' he countered.

'I don't actually know,' I replied through a mouthful of pancake. God, it was good. Why didn't we have pancakes for breakfast in England? It wasn't like we didn't know about them. 'They seem pretty chipper.'

'You'll do what's right at the end of the day,' he said. 'I have faith in you.'

'I'm going to enter a competition while I'm here,' I told him, while he jammed a huge forkful of hash brown into his mouth. 'It's an exhibition, really, but they have a competition for new photographers and the prize is a paid apprenticeship with one of the photographers in their programme. I sent in some of my other work and they accepted me, so that's a good sign, isn't it?'

'I would think so,' he agreed, a broad smile on his face. 'A very good sign.'

'Well, that and I paid $500 to enter.' I frowned. 'I'll probably get there and find a million entrants and one bloke sat in the corner counting piles and piles of money. You don't think it's a scam, do you?'

'Let's assume it isn't,' he said, supportive to the end. 'Tell me, which of your photographs do you think you might enter? You're free to include anything we've done for the book, of course.'

'It has to be of New York,' I told him, my eyebrows knitting together as I flipped through my portfolio in my head. 'Not like a landscape, necessarily, but it has to be about the city. I don't even know where to start.'

'New York is a glorious place for clearing your head and finding inspiration,' Al said. 'Every time you step outside, you live a dozen lives. My Janey always said that.'

'I went for a walk when I woke up,' I said, smiling softly at the mention of his late wife. I really wished that I had known her. 'It was weird, I expected it to be impressive but I didn't think it would be actually, straight-up beautiful. The snow and the trees are so pretty and the light was amazing. I took loads of pictures but I wasn't really awake so I have no idea what they'll look like.'

'Spectacular, I'm sure,' Al assured me. 'Now, when and where is this competition? So I can make sure it's in the diary.'

'Oh, you don't have to come,' I said, shaking my head quickly. 'It's on the twenty-eighth at the Spencer Gallery? Do you know it?'

'Actually I do and I'm sure you'll submit something you can be very proud of,' he said with a chuckle. 'What I'm not sure about is this "cock hat" nonsense. Although there is a chance I'm out of touch with the fashion world. I suppose we'll see shortly, won't we?'

'Is everything all ready for the presentation?' I asked as Genevieve returned with a plate so full of food, I didn't know where to start. I couldn't even name everything in front of me and, what's more, I didn't care.

Al waved his fork in the air, a so-so gesture. 'It'll have to be,' he said, covering his mouth with his hand as he spoke. 'Seeing as it's the day after tomorrow. I hear the blogs are alive with chatter. Whatever that means.'

'I imagine Jane would be incredibly proud of you,' I said. 'I think it's amazing that you're doing this.'

I'd never met Al's late wife but he talked of her so often, with so much love, I couldn't imagine she could feel any other way.

'Let's hope you're right,' he said, his eyes twinkling. 'They're really her dresses, after all. If everyone loves them, she'll get the credit, but if they hate them, it'll be on me.'

'The world is going to go crazy for them,' I promised. 'I can't wait to see everyone's faces when they see the whole collection.'

When we'd been working on his book in Milan, I'd seen all of Jane's original sketches and they were incredible. Al had taken the designs she had worked on decades ago and created the most beautiful collection of gowns I'd ever seen. Each and every one was timeless; any woman from any era would have swooned. We'd revealed a few at his launch party in Milan but the rest were being saved for the presentation, the details of which Amy and Paige had filled me in on. Everyone from the fashion world would be there, editors, buyers, bloggers – even if Al didn't really know who they were. Putting on an event like this outside of fashion week was a big risk but even in his seventies, Al was a rebel. And if you can't work outside the system in your seventies, when can you?

'I couldn't have done it without Amy,' he said. I dove into my breakfast, swallowing down the pangs of jealousy and smothering them with perfectly cooked eggs. 'She's been quite the revelation.'

'She's amazing,' I choked, taking a big swig of tea then realizing my friend was missing from the breakfast table. 'And not here. Amy never misses food – I should go and check on her.'

'Oh, no, she didn't miss a feed, *you* missed *her*,' Al said. 'She left for a breakfast meeting a little while ago.'

I almost dropped my fork.

'Amy had a breakfast meeting?'

Al nodded. 'With the caterers. And then she was headed to the venue to meet with the lighting design people.'

'That all sounds very . . .' I searched for the right word, struggling to pair anything that seemed to fit the situation with my best friend '. . . professional?'

'As I said,' Al quirked an eyebrow and sipped his coffee. 'Quite the revelation.'

'Amazing,' I mumbled, wondering how I had missed the memo on Amy and me switching lives.

'She is,' he agreed as a very tall, very slim and far too pretty blonde slipped in from the hall and came over to the table to kiss Al on the cheek. 'As is this young lady.'

'Good morning!'

She held out a hand with perfectly manicured pink nails and I realized I was supposed to shake it, not just stare at it. I had never seen anything so glossy and well put together and I knew Paige Sullivan. This girl looked airbrushed. There was literally not a single pale blonde hair out of place. She had to be wearing a wig, I decided, no one's hair was that good. Especially not when it was snowing outside.

'You must be Tess,' she said, confirming that everyone in the house had received the memo about my arrival. 'I'm Delia Spencer.'

I shook her hand and returned her friendly smile, reaching up to smooth down my own damp bird's nest of a mullet with my other hand. She was wearing a beautiful navy-blue sheath dress, the kind of thing that would make me look like I was on my way to court to argue a parking ticket, but on Delia it gave an air of polished professionalism. Combined with her impossibly shiny bun and simple, black-framed glasses, I couldn't help but wonder as to whether or not she was really a Hollywood actress playing a plain-but-not-really professional type, shortly before her grand makeover. It was all I could do not to grab her glasses, pull out her bun and scream, 'But Miss Spencer, you're beautiful!'

Genevieve practically ran across the room with a cafetière of freshly brewed coffee as Delia took her seat, the housekeeper fussing around her charge like an overprotective mother bird.

'I'm so glad you could join us for Christmas!' Delia said, leaning back while Genevieve poured her coffee. 'Amy was so excited when you said you were coming.'

A penny suddenly dropped. 'Spencer?' I looked at Al and he nodded. 'Like the gallery?'

'Like Spencer Media,' he replied. 'The gallery belongs to Delia's grandfather.'

'What gallery?' she asked, adding the tiniest splash of cream to her coffee. 'Amy and Uncle Al have told me so much about you.'

'Al's your uncle?' I asked, trying to work out how much make-up she was wearing, because it looked like none and I refused to believe it. '

'I'm Delia's godfather,' Al answered on Delia's behalf. 'Her grandfather, Bob, is an old, old friend of mine, hence, Uncle Al. Old habits die hard.'

'I can't just call you Al,' she said, laughing lightly as an egg-white omelette was set down in front of her. 'It would be too strange, you're family.'

I inwardly sighed with relief as I watched her transform from Upper East Side perfect princess to standard issue

Al worshipper before my eyes. And I liked her all the more for it.

'So, I hear you're a photographer?' she asked, digging into her breakfast. 'And you were working for UK *Gloss*?'

'Delia never forgets a thing,' Al said, beaming with pride. 'She's my baby elephant.'

'Hey, I've lost a lot of weight since I was a kid,' she replied, drawing her spine up straight with a grin. 'But he's kind of right, I do remember everything. It's a curse. Even after one too many cocktails. Not that I ever have one too many cocktails, Uncle Al.'

'A likely story,' he replied, a smile hidden underneath his beard.

'So, do you know anyone over at US *Gloss*?' Delia asked. 'That's sort of where I work.'

'I don't,' I admitted, still inhaling my stack of pancakes. 'Are you in the fashion team? Did you know Paige Sullivan in the UK? She's now at *Belle*.'

'Ah, the name isn't familiar,' she said, flushing slightly. 'What is it that she used to do?'

'What Delia doesn't want to say is, she doesn't work at *Gloss* exactly,' Al said, interrupting smoothly. 'She's the VP of business development at Spencer Media.'

'And acquisitions,' Delia added, her cheeks bright red now. 'Humblebrag.'

'That's amazing.' I was trying not to stare but I couldn't help it. I had dreamed of being my company's youngest creative director at twenty-seven. She was a baby and she was running a multimedia empire. 'You're so young.'

'Not that young,' she said, shaking pepper over her omelette. 'I'm thirty-three.'

'I'm sorry, that was really rude,' I said, biting my lip

in disgrace. 'But just so you know, that's still really bloody young.'

'Yeah, I guess it is,' she laughed. 'But I've been in the business basically my whole life. Like, actually my entire life. My sister and I were almost born in the Spencer Media building – my mom's water's broke in a shareholders' meeting.'

Now that would have been a photo.

'You're a twin?' There were two of her? Dear God, how was that fair on the rest of us?

'Uh-huh,' she confirmed. 'Identical. But Cecelia is way cooler than me. She moved downtown a while back, though she still has a room upstairs. She'll be here for Christmas – I'm sure you'll get to meet her then.'

'That would be great,' I said, keen to add to my gaggle of Al fans. 'I'm sure she's awesome.'

'She's . . . something,' Delia said reluctantly. 'Actually, she *does* work on a fashion team at Spencer, at *Gloss*.'

'The US edition?' I asked. Ooh. US *Gloss*. Fancy. 'Not to be incredibly rude but, do you think she would meet with me? Just for ten minutes? I'll bribe her with coffee and everything but I'm trying to get to know as many editors as possible, just to get feedback on my portfolio.' I held my breath a bit. It had been a while since I'd pushed for work.

'I can ask,' Delia offered. 'But Cici can be a little prickly sometimes.'

'That's a very polite way of putting it,' Al muttered. 'She's a strictly take-no-prisoners sort, Tess. Even I'm a bit scared of her.'

'Well, maybe my friend Angela would be a better bet,' suggested Delia. 'She's the editor-in-chief so I can't promise anything, she's always super busy.'

'Anything with anyone would be amazing,' I said, celebrating with one final bite of one final pancake. 'And really, I can take harsh criticism.'

'Let me email them,' she said, pulling a shiny iPhone out of an unseen pocket. 'I can't imagine they'll be super busy this week. I mean, who works that hard over the holidays, right?'

'Right,' I replied weakly. Last year, I had been the only person in the office for the last three days in the run-up to Christmas and, as such, had finished off six different peoples' advent calendars. Hashtag no regrets.

'OK, I have to run, I have a meeting. I just wanted to stop in and say hi to you both,' she said, pushing away two-thirds of her omelette. So that's how she stayed so skinny, I thought, looking at my almost empty plate. 'But I'll let you know what they say. What's your number?'

'Oh, um, here.' I handed her a tattered-looking business card and tried not to look ashamed. Amy had them made for me when I finally agreed to consign my Donovan & Dunning cards to the wheelie bin and they'd been floating around in the bottom of my handbag ever since. Proof of how far I had fallen – there was a time when I would have been able to locate my business-card holder with my eyes closed. 'That's my mobile and my email.'

'Thanks,' Delia said, slipping it into a pocket on her phone case. 'Have a great day, you guys. Lots of fun stuff on the agenda?'

'Sadly I have a lot of dull meetings with journalists almost as scary as Cici,' Al said, smoothing his unruly hair closer to his head. 'But I'm sure Tess is up for an adventure all on her own.'

'Absolutely,' I agreed. 'Do you think it will warm up at all?'

'You'll forget about the weather in five seconds flat,' Delia promised, a polite way of saying no. 'There's nothing like your first day in New York. You're going to have a ball.'

'I'm going to have pneumonia,' I said, checking what 35 degrees Fahrenheit was in Celsius on my phone. 'But still, where better to have it than New York?'

'We have excellent doctors,' Delia said. 'Just the best.'

'Quite,' Al replied, shaking his head and finishing up his tea. 'That's the spirit.'

CHAPTER EIGHT

'Der de, der-der-da, der der der-der-da . . .' Charlie answered his phone singing. 'Tess! You're in New York!'

'I am! And in a coffee shop! With coffee!' I said, shuffling as close to the radiator as it was possible to be without setting my coat on fire. 'Well spotted.'

'I can't believe you went,' he said, his voice clear as day all the way across the Atlantic Ocean. 'I really thought you'd find a reason not to.'

'It wouldn't have been hard,' I admitted, peeling off my top layer. I didn't have pneumonia yet but it was definitely on its way. 'And if I'd known how bloody cold it was going to be, I would have used any of these excuses. Honestly, I'm not sure I'm going to live through the day.'

Running off to tropical climes was much more my style. It was hard to feel like a powerful, accomplished woman who could achieve anything when you were walking around a city with a steaming paper cup held against your nose, just so you could breathe.

'But it's amazing, yeah?' he asked, ignoring my moaning. He had a gift for that. 'How's Amy?'

'It is and she's good.' I pressed the tips of my fingers against the radiator and waited for them to defrost. 'She had to work today but we're having dinner together tonight. I passed out as soon as I got here last night, so I'm in trouble.'

'Amy working while you swan around all fancy free,' he said, laughing. 'Unbelievable.'

'I know,' I replied, considering our switcharoo once more. 'Although there hasn't been so much swanning as cautious tiptoeing. It's like an ice rink out here – I've fallen over twice already.'

And I had the bruises to prove it, I thought, poking myself in the thigh.

'What have you been up to so far?' Charlie asked, the sound of the clicking of a keyboard and random radio chatter in the background. It was 1 p.m. in New York, 6 p.m. back in London, and he was still beavering away. I wondered what he was working on, if it was an existing client or a new pitch. 'What have you seen?'

'So, I was reading this photography magazine the other day and it mentioned a competition out here – I'm entering that. No big reason, just it's something to do.'

I wanted to play down just how strongly I felt until I'd made my absolute final decision on taking his job.

'I've mostly been sightseeing and taking photos for that this morning.'

So far since I left Al's townhouse for the second time, I'd taken more than three hundred photos. I'd seen the Empire State Building, the Chrysler and the Freedom Tower. I'd watched yellow taxis run up and down Park Avenue and hung out with a man with a cat on his head. I'd taken photos of big brown shopping bags, little blue coffee cups and a rat the size of a dog. And not a small dog, at that. But none of them seemed quite right.

'What's next on the agenda?' Charlie asked. 'Have you bought me a Christmas present yet?'

'Oh, I meant to put it in the post before I left!' I said, stifling a yawn. The jetlag combined with more physical activity than I'd seen in weeks had left me wiped out. 'I'm so sorry. I can't believe I won't see you at Christmas this year.'

'I know, mental,' he replied, yawning right back at me. 'First year in how long? You can make it up to me at New Year though, OK?'

'Except I'm going to a wedding in Milan.' I frowned at the mishmash of sugar packets in the little white bowl in the middle of the table. 'Unless you want to come to that? I'm sure there's room for one more.'

'I can't even keep up with you these days,' he said, a light laugh in his voice. 'No wonder you don't want to work with me. Who wants to slog away in an office with all this jet-setting you've got going on?'

'I didn't say I didn't want to,' I said quickly. Too quickly. 'I need a bit more time to think about it. I'm not being difficult, it's just a big decision.'

'It wouldn't have been a year ago,' he said, sounding somewhat resigned. 'But I want you to know I'm not just trying to help you out, Tess; this is entirely selfish on my part. You're the best and I want the best working for me. This isn't a pity offer.'

'I know,' I replied, taking out the sugar packets and stacking them back in the bowl in order: pink, blue, yellow, brown, pink, blue, yellow, brown. 'Like I said, I just need a bit more time to decide.'

'Not a problem, but like I said, I already interviewed that bloke so I need to let him know after Christmas,' he said. 'I've got to go. Call me when you've had a hot dog.'

'I've already had two,' I told him. 'And they were delicious.'

'Class act, as always,' he laughed. 'Miss you.'

Hanging up the phone, I stared at the sugar packets. There were three pink ones left over. Knitting my eyebrows together, I pushed the neatly organized bowl back against the wall before switching on my camera and taking another look at my day's work.

I was a good photographer. I knew I was. Paige and Al both said I had natural talent and Agent Veronica wouldn't have taken me on if I wasn't. Even Ess had grudgingly admitted he didn't hate all my photos after I strong-armed him into looking at my portfolio. But at the same time, Charlie was right. I might be a good photographer with lots of potential, but I was already a brilliant creative director. And that wasn't arrogance speaking, it was seven years' experience, hundreds of campaigns and dozens of awards. If it took me another seven years to get anywhere as a photographer, I'd be thirty-four before I was anywhere while Charlie ran his own advertising agency and Amy took over the world. Why was it so much harder to make these decisions as we got older? I thought, tearing open one of the extra pink packets. Shouldn't it be easier? The more I did, the less I knew and the older I got, the more afraid I was. It felt as though it should go the other way, to me.

Weird.

Before I could delve any deeper into my existential crises, my phone flashed into life with a text message. It was Delia Spencer.

Hi Tess! Angela and Cici can see you at 2 p.m. They're in the Spencer Media building, 1757 Seventh Avenue. Ask for Angela's assistant Candace at reception.

'Spencer Media Building?' I muttered

The woman sat beside me with three pieces of pizza piled up on a paper plate looked up as I spoke this last bit aloud.

'That's not far from here,' my neighbour announced. 'Three blocks. You're good, honey.'

'Thank you,' I said, immediately cheered by the kindness of strangers.

'No worries,' she replied, stacking all three slices on top of each other, covering them in chilli flakes and folding them down the middle into one giant pizza sandwich before wedging the entire thing in her mouth. 'Always happy to help.'

Even if it was disgusting, it was impressive.

I looked at the time on my phone and realized I had less than half an hour until my meeting. At a fashion magazine. In Manhattan. My shoes were stained from the gritty grey slush I'd been walking through all morning, almost every single one of my nails was bitten to bits and my hair was a mess after having been shoved inside my coat all morning. And that was before I even considered the state of my face.

Trying not to panic, I closed my eyes and shut out the sounds of the noisy café. If I was preparing for a meeting in my old job, what would I do? Research the company, reach out to any contacts who had dealt with them before and make sure I had as much information as possible. I wanted to make a good impression on these people. I couldn't turn up to a fashion mag dressed as a nail-biting, sleeping-bag wearer with dirty feet.

'Please answer,' I muttered into my phone, picking it up and dialling the only person I could think of who would consider this as much of an emergency as I did.

'Tess?' Paige answered on the second ring. 'You're in New York!'

'Um, yes?' I replied, slightly surprised. 'Are you psychic?'

'Oh, I, no,' she said, her laugh fluttering down the line. 'Amy posted. On Facebook.'

'Of course she did,' I replied, shaking my head. I started boycotting social media when my sisters began posting photos of their assorted children in various seasonally themed ensembles. 'But yes, I am and I need your help.'

'Of course you do,' she replied simply. 'What's going on? Did you pretend to be Vanessa again? Do I need to bail you out of somewhere? Tess! Am I your phone call?'

'No,' I sniffed. 'I haven't been arrested yet. I came to see Amy for Christmas, all a bit last minute. But the problem right now is that Al's goddaughter got me a meeting at *Gloss* magazine.'

'That's fantastic,' she cheered. 'They're doing really well. Who are you meeting?'

'The editor-in-chief and the fashion editor?' I said. 'Do you know them?'

I heard Paige suck the air in through her teeth, sharp and slow.

I blanched.

'That bad?'

'The editor is supposed to be lovely,' she said. 'But I haven't met her. The fashion editor, not so lovely. I met her at New York fashion week in September. What. A. Bitch. It's not the same as the UK, they're far more intense over there. Even more than they are on *Belle*. I hear it's all very Miranda Priestly.'

More intense than Paige's job? Christ on a bike.

'Reassuring,' I said, beginning to wish I hadn't bothered

calling in the first place. As if mucky shoes weren't enough to worry about. 'I met her twin sister this morning, she was lovely.'

'Then she must be the nice twin,' Paige replied. 'Cecelia is definitely the evil twin. What are you wearing?'

'Black jeans and a black polo neck,' I said, peeking inside my unattractive coat. 'I accidentally dressed as a mime this morning.'

'No, that's OK,' she sounded relieved. 'Everyone wears black in New York. But you're going to want to touch up your make-up.'

'How do you know?' I asked, peering at my reflection in the screen of my phone. 'Maybe my make-up is fantastic.'

'Tess,' she said. 'Get real.'

'You're always so charming,' I told her, steeling myself to venture back outside. 'That's why I love you.'

'Thank your lucky stars you aren't wearing that bloody unicorn T-shirt,' she warned. 'Or I'd have called a bomb threat into the office to stop you from going at all. I'm only thinking of you, I want them to love you.'

'Me too.' I said, waving at my pizza-eating table neighbour and heading outside. I pushed the coffee shop door open and felt my breath catch in my throat as the wind slapped me in the face. 'I'll let you know how it goes.'

'I'll keep my fingers crossed for you,' she said. 'And my legs. And my eyes.'

'It's nice to know you have so much confidence in me,' I told her as I strode out onto the snow-covered street. 'And really, she can't be any worse than you.'

'Oh, Tess,' Paige laughed. 'You just wait.'

'So.' I blinked, struggling to pull my heavily mascara'd eyes apart. 'Any questions?'

Cecelia Spencer stared at me across her huge glass desk.

'What's wrong with your face?' she asked, squinting.

'My face?' I replied. 'What's wrong with it?'

'What. Is. Wrong,' Cici repeated, slower this time. 'With. Your. Face.'

'Nothing,' I replied, pulling out my iPad and opening my portfolio. 'Why don't I show you some of my work?'

'You're wearing so much make-up,' she said in a low, confused voice. 'Like, *all* of it.'

It was possible that asking Paige for advice hadn't been my best idea. I'd been pretty pleased with my make-up after a quick go at myself in the café toilets with a kohl pencil and the mascara I found in the bottom of my handbag. With a little smudging and a touch of translucent powder, I'd even convinced myself I looked quite good.

But somewhere between Forty-Second Street and the Spencer Media building, I was caught in an unexpected slushy shower and my smoky eyes and nude lips had bled into what might happen if Alice Cooper, all the members of *Kiss* and a couple of giant pandas decided to hang out together at a goth night. Of course, I hadn't seen my reflection until I walked through the mirrored doors of *Gloss* and by then it was too late. No wonder the lady on reception had looked at me so strangely.

'It must be the light,' I replied, skipping through to my photos of Al's archive dresses while trying to wipe around my eyes with my little finger. 'Let me show you some of the work I did with Bertie Bennett.'

'You look like one of those dolls little kids have to practise make-up on,' she whispered, never taking her cornflower blue eyes off my face. 'Only with worse hair.'

'This was actually his wife's wedding dress,' I said,

clenching every muscle in my body and powering through. The sooner I got to the end of the portfolio, the sooner I could leave, wash my face and kill myself. 'I shot it at his house in Hawaii and no one had seen it since their wedding back in the sixties. Would you like to see the shoot I did for *Gloss* UK?'

'I'm so sorry I'm late.'

The glass door to the office bustled open as a pretty woman with an English accent and an anxious look on her face rushed in, her blonde-brown hair in a messy ponytail and her arms full of papers, printouts and cardboard coffee cups.

'The exec meeting ran over and I had to grab the pages from the features desk and entertainment are having a crisis and – anyway, that doesn't matter, does it?' She dumped everything on the circular table behind me, dusted off her bright blue patterned dress and held out her hand. 'I'm Angela Clark. You've met Cici?'

'Angela, what's wrong with her face?' Cici asked, resting her pointed chin in her hands and resting her elbows on the desk. 'It's not just me, right? You can see it, right?'

'You've met Cici.' Angela nodded, dropping her hands on her hips. She turned to the fashion editor with wide, fierce eyes. 'Could you do me a massive favour? Candace is out picking up some props for the shoot tomorrow and I'm dying for a coffee.'

'You can go.' Ceci pointed at me with a silver nail file. 'I got this.'

'I was actually thinking you could go and get coffees for me, you and Tess.' Angela's chin lifted as she spoke. 'If that wouldn't be too much trouble.'

Cecelia pushed her chair back with something that

couldn't quite be considered a sigh but certainly wasn't a happy noise. Standing, she smoothed out her jumper and strutted towards the door, in heels so high just looking at them made my ankles hurt.

'What do you want?' she asked, her eyes focusing somewhere to the left of my head.

I glanced at Angela who was busy taking Cici's seat and straightening various papers. I looked around at all the cute, funny things pinned on the walls. Images of Alexander Skarsgård in various states of undress, an empty bag of Monster Munch, a Union Jack and a Christmas card showing Rudolph and his red nose in a very compromising position. Of course this was *her* office. Cecelia Spencer did not eat Monster Munch.

Cici cleared her throat loudly.

'Just a coffee. Milk and sugar, thank you,' I said. 'Two sugars.'

'Sugar is terrible for your skin,' she informed me in a conspiratorial whisper. 'And, you know, your ass.'

Sucking my stomach in, I slouched down in my chair as she walked out the room.

So far, so astonishingly awful.

'Sorry again,' Angela said, pulling out her ponytail and running a hand through her long, straight bob. 'I know Cici can be a bit prickly.'

'Not at all, she reminds me of someone I used to live with,' I replied, the tension in the room fading out as Cici walked away. 'I've never seen identical twins that are so, well, identical.'

'Thankfully Delia focuses all her cut-throat energy into her career,' she assured me, swiping on a pink chapstick. 'Cici's *Mean Girls* stage lasted a bit longer but she's mostly over it now.'

I raised a blackened eyebrow.

'Oh man, you should have met her before,' Angela replied. 'Believe me, this is a million times better than she was a few years ago. Anyway, what can I do for you? Delia said you're a friend of her godfather or you work for him or something? Sorry, my brain isn't quite with it today and I'm a bit rushed for time – we were hoping to close the magazine early to get more time off over the holidays so everything's gone to shit, obviously.'

'I really appreciate you seeing me,' I said, happy to pull the meeting back on track. If there was one thing I was good at, it was a PowerPoint presentation. The sooner I could wow her with my portfolio, the better. 'I shot a feature spread with Bertie Bennett for *Gloss* UK and then we worked on a book together, a retrospective of his work.'

'That's cool.' She looked impressed and I felt proud. Two emotions I had missed over the last few weeks. 'How long have you been working as a photographer?'

'Not that long, if I'm honest,' I said, hesitant. 'I'm only just starting out, really.'

Angela smiled, tucking her hair behind her ears.

'Still struggling to say it?' she asked.

'Yes,' I admitted. 'It feels weird. I'm a photographer . . . I'm not entirely sure I believe it.'

'What were you doing before this?' She grabbed a handful of red and green M&Ms from a bowl on her desk before pushing them towards me. I took them gladly, popping a couple in my mouth before I could worry what the sugar was going to do to my skin. Or my arse.

'I was in advertising,' I told her, noticing the beautiful emerald ring on her wedding finger. Fancy. 'I was a creative director at an agency in London.'

Angela began twisting the emerald around her finger.

'Bit of a drastic change there. What made you swap careers?'

'I was made redundant,' I said, not sure whether or not I should be telling her everything. 'And I always enjoyed taking photos so I thought I might as well give it a shot. No pun intended.'

I handed her my iPad and watched her eyes flick back and forth over my photos. I noticed that she smiled a lot more than Ess had when he was looking at them but she was still very quiet.

I looked around her office while she looked at my photos, my eyes automatically drawn to a bunch of silver-framed photos of Angela and various people on top of her bright red filing cabinet. In one, she was posing with a blonde woman and a baby outside a church; in another she was laughing hard and clinging to an improbably beautiful woman, who had the hair my hair dreamed about. The same woman cropped up in two or three others; some of the backgrounds I recognized, lots I didn't. Angela looked so happy in every picture.

'Was that really it? You got made redundant?' Angela asked, looking up from my photos. 'And that was enough to make you change your entire life?'

'I did get made redundant,' I admitted, weaving my fingers in and out the ends of my hair. I couldn't see any good in not telling her the truth. 'But then I sort of shagged my friend, found out he'd been shagging my god-awful flatmate and I went a bit mental.'

'Fair,' she said with an accepting shrug. 'Happens to the best of us.'

'Not finished,' I said, wincing. '*Then* I stole her identity, her camera and her job, went to Hawaii to shoot Al – I mean, Bertie Bennett – for *Gloss*, met another bloke

– and that ended horribly – then went to Milan to shoot the book with Al and well, now I'm here. So, basically I was completely sorted with what I was doing with my life and now I haven't got a clue. Except I really, really want to make it work as a photographer.'

'Classic,' Angela said. 'I knew there was more to it. Sorry, it's the journo in me, I can't resist a good story.'

'How did you end up here?' I asked, staring at the New York skyline that stretched out behind her, wondering how she ever got anything done. 'What made you move to New York?'

'My boyfriend was shagging another woman in the car at my best friend's wedding and I accidentally broke the groom's hand,' she said in the most disarmingly offhand manner. 'I came over here to get away for a bit. That was, what, six years ago?'

'You're my hero,' I said.

'I don't know about that,' she said, taking another look at my iPad and handing it back to me. 'I am so glad Delia sent you over.'

'Me too,' I said with an unexpected bubble of laughter. I felt my entire body relax as Angela retied her ponytail and sat back in her spinny chair. 'It's ridiculous.'

'I'm the worst person on earth to give someone life advice,' Angela said, running a finger underneath her eyes to wipe away mascara smudges that didn't exist. I did the same and came away with hands that looked like I'd been down a coal mine. 'But I have dealt with more than one curveball, I know how hard it can be when things start going off track.'

'Really?' I replied, looking at a gorgeous black-and-white wedding photo over her left shoulder. If the man in the picture had given her that ring on her finger, she officially had no grounds for complaint, ever, about anything.

'Things are good now.' She waved her hands around her office. 'But trust me, that was not always the case. I turned up here with nothing but a very unflattering bridesmaid dress, a pair of Louboutins and a credit card I've literally just finished paying off. As in last week.'

'What happened to the Louboutins?' I knew Paige would ask me later so it only made good sense to find out now.

'They were blown up in a controlled explosion at Charles de Gaulle airport,' she replied. 'Honestly, don't ask, it's not worth it. My point is: if I can get it sort of kind of almost together, anyone can. Really.'

'I'm going to have to trust you on that,' I said, nodding towards the window. 'But it's amazing that you've done all this in six years.'

'A lot of people will tell you it's not what you know, but who you know,' she said. 'But I'm a big believer in right place, right time and making the most of opportunities when they're given to you. I could have turned down the blog I was offered and gone back to England but I didn't. I knew staying would be harder than leaving and I had to put a lot of trust in people I didn't know that well, not to mention myself. I didn't know if I could do it but I did. Or rather, I am. It's a work in progress.'

I smiled before a massive chunk of mascara fell into my eye, causing tears to start pouring down my cheek.

'Do you want a tissue or something?' Angela asked as I scrubbed at my face with the cuff of my jumper. 'Or a wipe? Or a sandblaster?'

'I don't normally wear a lot of a make-up,' I explained, happily accepting the packet of make-up remover wipes she produced from her desk drawer. 'I just thought, you know, *Gloss* is a fashion magazine and I'm supposed to be a fashion photographer so I ought to make an effort. This is what happens when I try.'

'Or when you stop trying to be yourself,' Angela corrected. 'I hate to be rude, but I've got a bitch of an afternoon in front of me and I think I'm going to have to kick you out.'

'Oh, of course,' I said, jumping to my feet. 'Is there any chance I could grab five minutes with your art director or whoever books the photographers? I don't want to be a pain, I just really need some advice.'

'Honestly,' she sucked the air in through her teeth as she stood, 'this is the worst day. That would be the art director and she's already in LA to run a shoot that I just had to kill because the actress she was supposed to be working with has checked into rehab. I'm sure you'll be able to read all about it on the internet.'

'Ooh.' I felt terrible for her but, more importantly, I really wanted to know who the actress was.

'So yeah, today isn't the best. I've got until tomorrow morning to come up with a brand-new story that we can pull off on practically zero budget to fill six pages of our New Year's Eve issue that we have to close in two days unless we all want to be working on the weekend, which just so happens to be Christmas, and between you and me, I'm more than a bit hungover. I thought we were all but done with this issue and everyone out there hates me right now.'

'Well, if you need a photographer, I'm available,' I quipped, carefully sheathing my iPad. 'And will work for wine.'

'Be careful what you wish for,' she warned. 'If I can't

119

get hold of anyone else in the next hour, I might well take you up on it.'

'No, really?' I dropped my bag back on my chair. 'I would love to do it. If you really don't have anyone, I have my camera and my laptop and I've shot for *Gloss* UK before. I know I'm just starting out but I wouldn't let you down.'

Angela looked up at me and gnawed on her thumbnail.

'I don't know if it's that easy,' she replied. 'We're pulling something together with really experienced models and I wouldn't want you to feel like you were out of your depth. It wouldn't be fair on you and I won't have time to reshoot.'

'All the better that they have experience,' I argued. How could I convince her? This was my chance; I knew it. 'That makes everything easier for me. I've worked with models and I've worked with non-models. Angela, I'm really good. Please give me a chance to prove it.'

'I just don't know,' she said reluctantly. 'It's not that I don't believe you . . .'

'I'll do it for free,' I blurted out. 'That'll help costs, won't it?'

'It would,' she admitted. 'But we would pay you, it wouldn't be right otherwise.'

'But you could pay me a lot less than anyone else available at such short notice, couldn't you?' I added. 'Tell me about the shoot.'

'It's a "New Year's Eve in New York" article,' she said, sitting down slowly and looking at her computer as I swiped my iPad back into life. 'I've called in a couple of favours with a couple of friends so it'll be Sadie Nixon and James Jacobs, celebrating on the town and then telling us their New Year's resolutions.'

'Brilliant, I love both of them.' No, I didn't have a clue who either of those people were. 'And that sounds like so much fun. Look, here's one of the shots I did for *Gloss* that was a party scene. And we pulled all this together so quickly, adverse weather conditions in Hawaii, if you can believe it. Angela, I promise I can do this. I won't let you down.'

I felt such a fire in my eyes, I was worried I might turn into Superman and burn the place to the ground. Angela looked back at me, not nearly as certain as I felt.

'I am a really great photographer,' I said, my voice so certain I barely recognized it, even though I was shaking from head to toe. 'And I will not let you down if you give me this chance.'

'It's a huge job,' she said, giving me a level stare. I realized she hadn't made it to editor-in-chief of a magazine in New York by being all charming and English. 'You're putting a lot on yourself and you're asking a lot from me.'

'Right place, right time,' I reminded her, my spine turning to steel as I kept my chin up high. 'I can do it.'

She didn't say anything, just stared at her computer and up at my iPad and then down at her desk. After a huge sigh, she turned her eyes back towards me.

'If this turns out to be a complete disaster, we're both buggered,' she said, sighing as she began to type. 'But you're on.'

'What?' I felt my knees wobble as she spoke and everything inside me melted. 'You really want me to do it?'

'You're not bottling out on me now, are you?' She looked up, her eyes flashing with concern. 'Because this is a now-or-never situation.'

'No, I'm in,' I said quickly, throwing up my arms and jumping back into my seat. 'I'm definitely in. I definitely want to do it.'

'It's a pretty straightforward concept,' Angela said, her forehead still creased with a lack of conviction. 'And James and Sadie are total pros so they shouldn't give you too much trouble.'

'It'll be perfect,' I promised as Cici reappeared, hurling herself at Angela's office door with three paper coffee cups in her hands. 'Just give me the brief and I'll do the rest.'

'What's going on?' Cici asked, dumping the coffees on the desk with as much care and grace as a baby elephant. Streams of steamed milk trickled underneath the edge of the lids and pooled around the bottom of the cups, making a mess on the glass desk. I had to sit on my hands to stop myself from reaching over to wipe it up with the sleeve of my jumper.

'Tess is going to shoot Sadie and James tomorrow,' Angela explained. 'She's a lifesaver.'

From the look on Cici's face, I had to assume she did not agree.

'Angela, I know it's Christmas,' she replied without taking her eyes off me. 'And it's a time for charity and all, but do you really think this is a good idea? Can we really not find a professional?'

If we hadn't been on the millionth floor of a skyscraper in the middle of Manhattan, I would have dug a hole in the ground, crawled into it and tried my very hardest to die. All the fight and fire I'd felt while convincing Angela to take a chance on me melted away in front of this very mean girl.

'Cici.' Angela spoke with a warning in her voice and her fashion editor rolled her eyes in response. 'Don't.'

Taking my cue to leave, I stood up, pleased to see I was at least more or less the same height as Cici Spencer, even if I was not the same size. The woman was a twig. How could legs that skinny support hair that big?

'Oh, look,' Angela pointed at the two of us. 'You're wearing the same outfit. How cute is that?'

I looked down at my skinny black jeans and Topshop polo neck then over at Cici's black leather leggings and cashmere sweater.

'We're really not,' we said at the exact same time.

At least we agreed on one thing.

After an intense fifteen minutes spent washing off the rest of my eyeliner situation in the very fancy Spencer Media bathrooms, I jumped in the lift back down to the lobby, feeling considerably happier than I had on my way up. Cici Spencer aside, that had to rank as one of the best hours of my life. Right next to arriving in Hawaii, eating in Hawaii, and the time Amy and I met Justin Timberlake. Right before the police took Amy away. I had a job! I didn't know exactly what it was but I had an actual job, taking actual photos.

Maybe I'd be able to take something for the competition, I pondered, fishing around in my pocket for my phone so I could let Charlie and Amy know right away. Or maybe my pictures would be so good, *Gloss* US would want to hire me again and I could stay in New York forever. I could spend some proper time with Amy and then my Charlie decision would be made for me. I could only imagine the looks on the faces of the girls we'd gone to school with. Amy Smith and Tess Brookes, living in New York, working in fashion and definitely not being lesbians. Everything they'd been saying about us since year ten proved entirely wrong. We weren't gay and we were cool, so there.

Bouncing out of the lift, I tapped out a text to Amy before gleefully wrapping the ten-dollar scarf I'd bought from a charming man on the street all the way around my head until only my eyes were visible. It had taken me almost an entire day but I finally had this New York winter ensemble down. Hood up, scarf on, sunglasses at the ready and not an inch of bare skin showing. I looked like an absurdly cheerful Ray-Ban-wearing mummy and all I wanted to do was get back to Al's townhouse and prep for the shoot. Because I had a shoot to prep for. I was in New York and I had a shoot to prep for and I was deliriously happy.

Until I saw him.

Nick Miller was standing in the lobby of Spencer Media.

I didn't believe it at first. I'd been dreaming about his face for so long, I'd almost forgotten what it looked like in real life; part of me had even worried that I wouldn't recognize him but there was no such luck. There he was, wearing no more protection from the bitter cold than a pair of jeans, leather jacket, and a tired expression, and it was all too much. In one heartbeat I went from freezing cold and full of joy to a burning bundle of shredded nerves. Biting off my gloves, I tore at my scarf, at my sunglasses, all the noise of New York getting louder and louder inside my head, my heart thudding and drowning out everything else. In the middle of the city, surrounded by constant car horns, shouting, banging, screaming and laughing, skyscrapers and snow and millions and millions of people, there was only me and only him and he hadn't even seen me.

With one hand still caught up in my scarf and my sunglasses in my mouth, I felt every part of me just stop. I couldn't breathe, couldn't move, my arms were stuck at odd angles and every muscle in my body contracted. It was one hundred and forty days since I had seen him. His hair was one hundred and forty days longer; there was one hundred and forty days' more grey mixed into the blond. One hundred and forty days since I had kissed his chapped lips and held the hand that was pulling a travel card out of his back pocket and replacing it with his phone. One hundred and forty days since I had told him that I loved him and he had run away.

Without breaking stride, Nick sighed, turned the collar of his jacket up against the wind, walked out of the building and into the snow, as though I wasn't even there. But now that I'd seen him, even with the thrill of my new job echoing in my ears, even here in the middle of Times Square, in the overwhelming heart of the city, there was nothing and no-one else for me in the whole world.

If I was certain of only one thing in this world, it was that private detective was not amongst my future career plans. I had chased Nick out into the street without a second thought. As soon as I laid eyes on him, it all came flooding back, all the reasons why I loved him, all the reasons why I hadn't been able to let him go and I followed blindly as though there were an invisible string pulling me along. Tailing him through the crowds, I had no idea what I was going to say to him when I finally caught up with him and so, I didn't catch up with him. I stayed a few feet behind, my eyes trained on the back of his head, dodging people as he strode confidently through streets he knew like the back of his hand. He hopped on and off the edge of the pavement, turned tightly around corners and spun himself this way and that, avoiding the tourists with their ever-present mobile phones and the Christmas shoppers, wielding their weaponized shopping bags. I bumped against everyone I passed, scraping my legs on Big Brown Bags, tripping over toddlers and skidding on patches of black ice in my attempt to catch up.

Eventually, he stopped and I paused, ten feet away, trying to catch my breath. I really had to start working out. Perhaps I should join a gym in January then stop going in March, like everyone else. Sweating underneath my scarf and hood, I peeled off my sunglasses as they began to steam up. Freezing cold air and hot, sweaty face was not a good incognito combo. Nick was almost lost in the crowd when I saw the back of his head dart across the street, ignoring the Don't Walk sign, and sprinting into a restaurant with half a pig hanging in the window.

Trying not to gip, I waited for the walk signal and crossed the street in an orderly fashion, hovering outside the door of the restaurant. I was pleased with my amateur sleuthing prowess but now what was I supposed to do? I peered inside the window, fingertips touching the glass, and watched Nick clap a tall man on the back in the most manly of hugs before shuffling himself into a booth and slipping off his jacket. The place was pretty big and pretty busy. I felt as though I might go mad, to be this close to him but not be with him. I wanted to hear him, I wanted to smell him, I wanted to grab a handful of his hair and dig my fingers into his arms until they left a mark and never let go, ever again.

Or, I could pop in, order a drink and listen in on his conversation for five minutes instead. It wasn't like I was being a complete stalker, I was really thirsty, after all, and I hadn't eaten anything in over an hour. That was a new New York record for me. Maybe this place had cronuts? I'd heard nothing but wonderful things about cronuts. Nick would never need to know. I could nip in, get a pastry fix and my Miller fix at the same time, then decide what I wanted to do. It was a completely rational plan. Mentally swinging those balls, I pushed open the door and lowered my scarf to smile at the hostess inside, never taking my eyes off Nick Miller.

'Hi, welcome to McCall's,' she said. 'Table for one?'

'Yes please,' I croaked, pointing at my throat. 'Sorry, I have no voice today.'

'Oh no,' she said, a look of concern on her face as she grabbed a little laminated menu and walked me towards the bar. 'I hope you're not getting sick for the holidays?'

'I'm sure I'll be fine,' I whispered in an indeterminate accent. 'Just have to keep warm.'

She placed the menu down on the bar, so far away from Nick and his friend, I couldn't possibly hear a single thing.

'Would it be all right if I sat at a table?' I asked, looking pointedly over at an empty booth that backed up on my ex.

'We usually seat people at the bar when they're on their own,' the waitress said with a furrowed brow. 'But I guess the lunch rush is dying down. There's a spot in the back over there?'

'Just here will be fine,' I replied, throwing myself onto the brown leather banquette, back to back with Nick. 'Thanks.'

I was a superspy mastermind.

'All right then.' The hostess rediscovered her fake smile and nodded. 'I'll send over your waitress.'

Settling in, I shuffled around under my hood, pulling my scarf over my telltale copper hair, and then unzipped my coat, audibly sighing with relief as I felt the AC of the restaurant hit the disgusting sweatiness of my clammy skin. Nothing said 'I love you' like stalking-induced sweat patches.

'What's up, man?' Nick's friend asked as I placed my phone next to my folded napkin, the official 'I'm OK' accessory of the lone diner. 'I thought maybe you'd already be headed home. The airport is brutal at this time of year.'

'I'm headed out Sunday,' he replied. 'Flights back to the UK are always cheaper on Christmas Eve – no one wants to land on Christmas morning.'

That's because Christmas morning is when you're supposed to be with the people you love, I explained in my head, silently stabbing the menu with my finger. Ooh, chicken noodle soup.

'Yeah, man, good call,' his friend agreed. 'Glad I caught you.'

'I know, it's been ages. This year has been too much.' Nick broke off while his friend ordered a beer and a sandwich, then ordered a bourbon and a burger for himself. Of course he was drinking whisky in the middle of the afternoon, of *course* he was. 'I can't wait for it to be over. It's been nothing but one kick in the arse after another.'

Well, that was nice to hear.

'I hear you, man,' his friend said. 'Has anyone had a good year?'

I had, I thought. Sure, I started it with an amazing job and a nice flat and a lovely, manageable crush on my friend and was ending it homeless, sort of jobless and double dumped but, well, I still thought it had gone all right. I'd had an all-expenses paid trip to Hawaii and so had he – that was nothing to be sniffed at where I came from.

'Next year needs to try harder, that's all I know,' he replied. 'How are the kids?'

'Hi!' A cheerful-looking woman with a nose ring and a smile placed a huge glass of ice water down in front of me. 'I'm Debbie and I'll be your server today. Do you have any questions about the menu? Is there anything I can get you?'

'Chicken noodle soup?' I whispered, hoarse with pretence. 'And a tea?'

'Hot or iced?' she asked, scribbling on her pad.

Iced tea? In this weather?

Demon.

'Hot, please,' I replied, desperate for her to get out of my way before I missed any more of their conversation. 'With milk. And sugar. Thank you.'

She nodded politely and hopped away to the kitchen while I tried to tune back in to Nick's friend telling delightful tales about his children, who sounded horribly spoiled and like they needed a good talking-to.

'I don't know,' he said as I watched Debbie sail by with a bottle of Bud in one hand and a small glass of whisky in the other. 'I can't see what she has to complain about. They're at school all day and then all she's gotta do is pick them up and take them to their activities. It's not like I've got her chained to the sink, dude.'

I would have liked to chain him to something, but it definitely wouldn't have been a sink. Possibly the stocks? Did villages still have stocks? Perhaps I could bring them back.

'Maybe she means some time without the kids,' Nick suggested. 'I can't imagine it's very easy to get anything done when you've got to go back out to pick two toddlers up from coding class as soon as you've got started.'

My heart swelled as he defended his friend's poor wife – that, or I was having a stroke from all my layers.

'Are they really taking coding?' he added. 'When I was four, I couldn't even organize my Meccano.'

'August is really into his iPhone,' the friend replied. 'So we figured we might as well start him early. Allanah wanted to go too but she's got to finish out her yoga series before she can switch.'

Coding class and yoga series? What happened to Brownies or gymnastics? I felt a sudden flash of pity for my sisters and wondered if I should have got my nieces and nephews iPads for Christmas instead of Lego. I was a terrible, out-of-touch aunt.

'I don't think wanting a bit of time to herself is asking too much,' Nick argued. 'It must have been hard for her, giving up work when you had Allanah, that's all I'm thinking. She's probably missing the real world.'

'I wish I could quit my job and knock out babies,' the friend moaned in response. 'I can't see nothing fun about dragging my ass on the subway every day when I could be at home watching *Doc McStuffins* and spending time with my kids.'

As Debbie placed my tea down in front of me, I fought the urge to knock the Doc McStuffins out of him.

'It does sound like fun,' Nick said with a half-laugh I recognized. I could tell he didn't agree with his friend but he didn't want to get into an argument. I knew that tone well – I'd been humoured by Nick Miller more than once in this terrible year he had been forced to endure. 'But I imagine it's not as entertaining as all that.'

'Relationships, man.' His friend echoed Nick's laugh

and I heard two glasses clink together. 'You're so smart. Stay out of the deep end altogether. How is life in the shallow end of the pool?'

'Shallow,' Nick replied instantly. 'Easier to wade around and considerably simpler when you want to get out.'

'Right, right,' the friend agreed, laughing again. 'Sometimes I wish I'd never bothered to dive in. Why didn't you say anything at my wedding, dude?'

I heard Nick huff out a deep breath and concentrated on pouring the little metal jug of milk into my lukewarm tea.

'You'd spent a lot of money,' he replied. 'I didn't want to be rude.'

'Fair,' the other said. 'But you're still strictly one and done? What happened to that chick you met over the summer?'

I must have poured fifteen spoonfuls of sugar into my tea before I realized what I was doing. Summer chick? Was I the summer chick? I had better be the bloody summer chick or I was going to jam this spoon into his jugular.

'Here's the soup.' Debbie reappeared with an enormous bowl of soup and three packets of cream crackers. 'Can I get you anything else?'

'No,' I shook my head manically, trying to hear what Nick was saying over the radio and the other customers and Debbie's fantastic customer service. 'Thank you.'

What was with the cream crackers?

'No chance of working it out?' his friend asked.

What had I missed? What had I missed?

'Can I get you more hot water for your tea?'

More hot water? I looked at Debbie as though she had just asked if she could consume the soul of my firstborn.

Partly because she was making me miss a very important part of a very important conversation and partly because adding hot water to an already made cup of tea was clearly a crime against nature.

'I don't think so,' Nick replied as I tried not to vomit on the table. 'There was this whole big thing and I left and now she's not talking to me. I don't even know where she is now.'

If this had been a movie, that would have been the moment that Debbie the waitress dropped my chicken noodle soup in my lap and I would have torn off my coat, jumped to my feet and Nick would have realized I was there, pulled me into his arms and kissed me while his friend burst into song and some bluebirds flew in through the front door to serenade us with the dead pig in the window. Instead, I knocked my phone off the table and watched it skitter across the tiled floor and come to a stop right in front of Nick's feet. I sucked in my breath and fumbled for my woolly hat, pulling it down over my telltale hair and poking myself in the eye as I went.

'Like you said, relationships are confusing,' he told his friend, absently bending down to pick up the phone and hand it to Debbie the Waitress. 'I thought this was it, you know? It was the first time in so long I'd felt anything at all.'

'Here you go, darl.' Debbie placed my phone back on the table, eyeing me with concern as unwelcome tears streamed down my cheeks from all the accidental eye poking. 'You doing OK?'

I nodded, wiping my cheeks and biting my lips, and willed her away.

'Poked my eye,' I explained as she backed away. 'I'm an idiot.'

She didn't argue.

This was it. This was my moment. I took a deep breath and opened my mouth. To say what, I wasn't quite sure.

'But she turned out to be just like the rest of them,' Nick concluded. 'Not worth it. I'm better off on my own.'

What?

I mean, what?

My mouth hung open for so long, I began to choke on the air conditioning and had to soothe my coughing fit with my manky cup of tea, all too aware that Nick and his friend were looking my way. I shrank back against the booth, forcing more of my hair inside my hat. How could he think that? I'd explained everything! I'd told him that I loved him! He was the one who left the bloody note!

'Chicks, man,' the friend said, clearly Manhattan's greatest philosopher. 'Thank the sweet Lord for Tinder. If that shit had existed five years ago, I would never have gotten married.'

'Ha,' Nick said, no laughter in his voice. 'I can't say I blame you. I'm going for a slash before the food comes.'

He stood up and I dropped my head towards my bowl, pulling the scarf further over my face as he stalked by to the back, shaking his head and flexing his knuckles. The restrooms were right on the back wall of the restaurant and I saw a dimly lit, white-tiled bathroom as he pushed the door open and turned the corner.

'Oh shit,' I muttered. If I was still sitting here when he came out, he would see me and I couldn't talk to him now, not after that. I needed time to work out what I wanted to say. Pulling a twenty-dollar bill out of my wallet, I threw it down on the table, grabbed my bag and shuffled out of the booth to my feet. I had to get out of there. As I stood up, I paused at Nick's table to get a look at his friend, the inaugural winner of my Worst Husband of the Year award.

'You,' I said, pulling up my hood, 'are a terrible, terrible human being.'

He looked up at me for a moment before shaking his head and turning his attention back to his phone. 'This city is full of crazy bitches,' he muttered as I walk-ran towards the door.

Better a crazy bitch than a total wanker, I thought to myself, bursting out onto the street and walking fast, no idea of what direction I was headed in. Fingers crossed Allanah and August took after their mother and not their selfish shithead father, otherwise the world truly was doomed.

CHAPTER NINE

'And then I had a meeting with the movement choreographer,' Amy said, stuffing a meatball in her mouth as she spoke. 'Because that's a thing. Can you believe that's a thing? We're paying someone to tell the models how to move and they aren't even moving. They're coming in, standing on platforms and that's it. We're paying someone to choreograph standing still.'

I nodded, pushing a sliver of garlic around my empty plate.

'Then me and Al went over the guest list and then we had a conference call with the factory and *then* I went to the venue to make sure everything was ready for the run-through tomorrow.'

'Is it?' I asked.

'Yeah,' she said with an easy shrug, her pink cropped jumper riding up to show her bare belly. Amy never felt the cold the way I did. 'More or less. It will be.'

'I can't believe how relaxed you are about everything.' I took a long drink of my cocktail and shivered at the vodka in the bottom. 'I'd be freaking out by now.'

She eyed my empty glass with suspicion. 'I can't believe how quickly you put that away. Are you feeling all right?'

'Yes,' I lied. I was not a good drinker and Amy knew that all too well. 'Long day, jetlag, I'm just tired.'

'Yeah, work has got me literally knackered all the time, I don't know how you coped doing this for all those years,' she said, grabbing a chip from the bowl between us and inhaling it. 'I'm so glad you're here though. I can't wait for you to see the presentation; it's going to be incredible. Al says it's the most amazing thing he's ever seen.'

Amy's dad took off about the same time my parents got divorced, only her mother never remarried. Or had a nice word to say to anyone, ever again. If anyone else was deserving of some positive reinforcement from my surrogate granddad, it was Amy.

'I can't wait,' I said, snaffling a chip before she ate them all. 'I've never seen you work so hard on something.'

'I worked very hard that time I was handing out yoghurts at Wimbledon,' she reminded me. 'They were delicious.'

'No you didn't,' I corrected her. 'You turned up late, spilled a pint all down your tennis whites at lunch and then you nicked off early with two hundred yoghurts. I was eating those things for a month.'

'Oh yeah,' she sighed. 'Didn't they give you the shits?'

'I should have checked the sell-by date,' I said stiffly. 'That was my fault. But still, I'm impressed.'

'And you didn't think I could do it,' she said, shimmying her shoulders. 'Oh ye of little faith.'

'I never said that,' I replied, only slightly awkward. 'I've always believed in you.'

Amy stared hard at me across the table.

'I have!' I protested with slightly less conviction. 'I'm so proud of you.'

Possibly, I was a little bit surprised. And maybe a tiny bit jealous. And perhaps I was expecting things to go a tiny bit wrong while really hoping that they wouldn't. But she didn't need to know that, it really wasn't constructive feedback.

'I'm glad you're going to be here,' she said, raising her own half-full glass. 'I really, really want you to see it. Now tell me everything about your shoot tomorrow. Are you nervous? Is that what's wrong?'

'Yes?' I pulled out my phone to reread Cici's email. 'A little bit. The brief looks good, it's a New Year's resolutions thing. Sounds simple enough but you never know. I'm more excited, I think. It'll be good to be the one taking the photos again instead of doing everything but. Kekipi is going to play assistant – Domenico has given him a day off wedmin to help me out.'

'Oh, good,' Amy said, clinking her glass to mine. 'I *was* going to take some time off so we could hang out but it's cool. I know how important work is to you.'

'You have a massive event in two days,' I reminded her. 'That's important too. We can hang out after.'

'Not as important as my best mate flying all the way out to New York to see me,' she countered. 'I had kind of cleared the morning but it doesn't matter.'

'Well, you could come with me,' I offered, trying to change the disappointed expression on her face. 'You could be my assistant again? If you really want to hang out?'

'That's not really hanging out,' she said. 'And you're right, I should be working.'

I nodded, chewing on a piece of delicious bread while Amy gave a small sigh that I couldn't quite translate.

'Who are you shooting?' she asked, changing the subject and spearing one of my uneaten meatballs, popping it into her mouth without asking. One of the benefits of being best friends since before you could speak was unspoken permission to steal each other's food without retribution.

'Call time, location, phone number, phone number, phone number,' I muttered, scrolling down the email on my phone. 'Oh, James Jacobs and Sadie Nixon.'

Amy's fork clattered loudly against her plate.

'James Jacobs?' she asked through a mouthful of meatball. '*The* James Jacobs? You don't know who he is, do you?'

I shrugged.

'Excuse me . . .' Amy prodded a checked-shirt-wearing man at the next table. 'Do you know who James Jacobs is?'

'The actor?' he asked, pushing his black glasses frames up his nose. 'The British guy?'

'See?' Amy turned back to me without replying to our table neighbour. 'He's so famous hipsters can't even pretend not to know who he is. And this man is wearing plaid. I bet those glasses aren't even prescription, are they?'

The man shook his head at her through his non-prescription glasses.

'See' she said, triumphant.

'Whatever,' I said while the man at the next table continued to stare at Amy as though she was insane. It wasn't a rare occurrence at dinner with her. 'It's fine. That probably makes this easier anyway, doesn't it? He'll have had his photo taken loads of times.'

'Yeah,' she said, raising her eyebrows. 'By *everyone*. Like, loads of proper, famous photographers.'

'Thanks, Amy.' I picked up my glass, rattled the ice cubes around and emptied what dregs were left in the bottom before looking for the waitress to order another. 'You're really helping build my confidence.'

'I mean, he should be thanking his stars that he gets Tess Brookes to take his photo right at the beginning of her career,' she squeaked, quickly correcting herself. 'How bloody lucky is he? And if he gives you any shit, I'll ban him from Al's party – pretty sure he's on the guest list. Seriously, he even looks at you the wrong way and I'll rip off his balls and give them to you for Christmas.'

'Just what I wanted,' I said. 'I still need to fill your stocking. Anyone's balls you're after?'

'Other than that twatknacker, Wilder?' she answered with a grimace. 'Seriously, I can't believe you're being all buddy-buddy with him again. I can't stand it, Tess. He's a cock. He's a cocking cock who should be sent to The Island of Lost Men, abandoned until he goes completely batshit mental and then blown up by a drone.'

'Do you even know what a drone is?' I asked, giving her a look she understood.

'That's not the point,' she said. 'The point is, he's a cock.'

'And it was very well made,' I said. 'But we've been friends for a long time and I missed him. Can't you just pretend none of it ever happened?'

'Uh, have you met me?' she asked.

'Fair point,' I replied.

'And you've not been friends with him as long as with me,' she pointed out. 'So I should get some say in this.'

'He wants to add you on Facebook,' I said. 'He said he's missed you.'

Her face lit up for half a second.

'He did?'

I nodded.

'That's so sad. Oh wait, no it isn't. Let him miss me, he's a cock.'

'I feel better knowing things are OK with me and him,' I said, attempting to draw a line under the cock banter. 'So can we just leave it at that?'

'Only if you promise not to bone him ever again,' Amy agreed. 'Seriously, I'll rip—'

'Off his balls and wrap them up for Christmas, I know,' I finished for her, ignoring the looks from our plaid-wearing table neighbour. 'I'm not planning on boning him, I promise. He did offer me a job though.'

She stopped what she was doing, her fork halfway to her lips.

'You're not going to take it though,' she replied with a statement, not a question. 'You're not going back into advertising?'

'I don't know.' I pushed my food around my plate, concentrating on my hands. 'We'll see.'

'But you don't want to?' she asked. 'Do you?'

'No, not right now,' I said again, putting down my cutlery and pulling my sleeves over my hands. 'But what if something goes wrong at the shoot?'

'Nothing is going to go wrong at the shoot,' Amy assured me. 'The worst that could happen is Kekipi and James Jacobs fall in love and we have to cancel next week's wedding and Domenico comes after us all with a machete. Which, now I think about it . . .'

'James is gay?' I asked and she nodded, gulping wine. 'Well, at least now I understand why Kekipi was so keen to volunteer.'

'Also because he loves you,' she said. 'But yeah, I think the allure of James Jacobs was probably a little stronger than the thought of spending the day holding up lights.'

'Amy, I need to talk to you about something,' I said abruptly, incapable of holding it in any longer. 'I saw Nick today.'

'WHAT?'

Amy's knife and fork clattered to her plate before falling to the floor.

'I know,' I said, reaching down to pick them up and smiling broadly at our table neighbours. 'He was at Spencer Media when I was there. But he didn't see me.'

'What was he doing there?' she demanded. 'Is he stalking you? Oh my God, he's stalking you. This is so romantic.'

Typical response from the girl who thought *Fifty Shades* was the most romantic film she had ever seen. I decided to leave out the part where I was actually the stalker for now.

'He was probably just there for work,' I reasoned. 'He is a journalist, they do have magazines there.'

'No, he's definitely stalking you,' she said. 'I've decided. I can't believe you didn't tell me until now. What happened next?'

'I didn't know what to say,' I looked at my friend, hoping I'd know what I wanted to do after spending all afternoon obsessing over our encounter. But I hadn't got a clue. 'To him or you. He was gone before I could say anything.'

'God, if only there was some way to contact him,' Amy said, blowing her hair up out of her eyes. 'I mean, if only someone would invent some sort of telecommunications device you could use to send him a message. Damn this dark age of communication we live in.'

She took her phone out of her handbag and hurled it at me across the table.

'Call him!' she shouted.

'Very funny,' I said, fumbling to catch her phone before it could assault anyone at the neighbouring tables. 'I know, I could email him.'

'Or text him,' she added. 'Or Facebook, tweet, WhatsApp, Snapchat, Viber or Instagram him.'

'I bet he isn't even on half of those,' I sniffed as she held her hand out for her phone.

'Oh, you bet?' Amy said. 'As if you haven't internet stalked the shit out of him. Even I've found him on Twitter and, dear God, have you read his blog? What a pretentious tit.'

'I know he has a Twitter,' I said quickly. She was right, his blog was terrible and even though he hadn't updated it all summer, I had read every single entry. 'But he doesn't tweet.'

Amy grinned. 'Now who's the stalker?'

'Yeah, I know,' I said with a sigh. 'I just check in sometimes. I like to know he's OK.'

And by sometimes, I meant almost every day.

'And maybe I followed him a bit.'

'Of course you did,' she replied, all matter of factly. 'Why wouldn't you?'

'Because that would make me a mental?' I suggested. 'It did feel like I was losing the plot, a bit.'

'It would make you human.' She reached across the table, dipping her sleeve in butter, and took my hand in hers. 'And you haven't lost the plot, you've fallen in love. That's what happens, Tess. What happened next?'

'He was having lunch with his friend.' I cringed at the memory and tapped around my eye lightly. It was still quite sore. 'And they were talking about me. He said he thought we were going to be something but that we're not because I'm no different to the others and we're all the same.'

'That cockwombling weasel.' Amy's eyes burned. 'I'll kill him. I'll do worse than kill him. I'll skin him alive. I'll sign him up for the Justin Bieber mailing list. I'll—'

'Amy, it's fine,' I said. 'It threw me a bit though.'

'Well, yeah,' she replied. 'But he clearly didn't mean it. He was having lunch with his friend, you said?'

I nodded.

'Then that totally explains it,' she scoffed. 'Trying to save face in front of the dudes. He's hardly going to tell his mate that he got all over-emo and left a drama queen note about his poor broken heart, is he?'

She had a point. 'I suppose,' I agreed half-heartedly.

'The fact that he's still talking about you says enough really,' she went on. 'If he didn't give a shit, why would you even cross his mind? Why would he bring you up? Men don't work that way.'

It wasn't like I had a lot of experience in the ways men worked but it was certainly true that Charlie stopped bringing up his exes in conversation as soon as they were out of the picture, especially when he felt as though he was the wronged party.

'He was acting the big man, Tess,' she reasoned. 'But enough about him, are *you* OK?'

'No,' I replied, pushing my hair behind my ears. I'd washed and dried it properly since my afternoon adventures and my big, bouncy curls were completely at odds with how I felt inside. 'It was so surreal. He was right there in front of me.'

'I get it. The first time I saw Dave after we broke things

off was strange.' She looked down at her empty plate, pinching her delicate features together. 'They really should have the decency to stop existing when they skedaddle, shouldn't they? But no, there he was, walking around town, wearing a T-shirt I'd never seen before. That was the main thing that weirded me out. That he had this new T-shirt on. Even though I'd been the one to end things, I felt totally offended that he was going on with his life.'

'Is it still hard?' I asked, watching as she wrinkled up her nose and her eyes glassed over for a moment. 'Do you still miss him?'

'No . . .' She didn't sound sure. 'Maybe. If I think about it, I suppose it is. He's in London, having a baby, I'm in New York, working. It's all changed anyway.'

She shook herself off, blinking away the tears in her eyes, and took a quick swig of her cocktail.

'Anyway, enough about Boring Dave and his shit T-shirts,' she said. 'Let's go back to what we were really talking about. How did you feel when you saw Nick?'

More shrugs from Team Tess. It was no wonder I'd turned to photography to express myself, I am useless with words.

'You miss him though,' Amy stated, not a question. 'I know you do.'

'Yes,' I admitted. Now that I'd seen him in the flesh, there was no hesitation. 'But it's complicated.'

'Then *call* him,' she said, her eyes wide and kind. 'You'll never know how he really feels unless you ask him. He'd probably be mortified if he knew you'd heard all that shit at lunch.'

'But what if he—' I started, only for Amy to reach across the table and clamp a hand over my mouth.

'I'm going to stop you there,' she said, hitting me lightly on the top of the head with a pepper grinder. 'My Tess doesn't live with "what ifs".'

It was news to me.

'She doesn't?'

'Not any more,' Amy confirmed. 'You've got to call him. Please? It can be my Christmas present.'

'Then what will I do with those Topshop boots I bought you a month ago?' I asked as her face lit up. 'Remember the ones you had to have and "accidentally" ordered on my credit card?'

'Oh yeah,' she said, eyes on the ceiling. 'I forgot about those. And no, I'm having them. *And* you're calling him.'

'What if I text him?' I bargained as the waitress carefully set our drinks on the table. I'd been mentally composing messages all afternoon. Now I'd seen him, now I knew how he felt – or how he claimed to feel – I couldn't imagine actually talking to him. But texting could be OK. How did anyone get together before texts were a thing? 'And you don't leave my side until he replies?'

'Done.' She picked up her glass and clinked it against mine. 'And if he in anyway disappoints, hurts or fails you, you can keep the Topshop boots *and* I'll chop his balls off, box them up and put them under the tree for you.'

'I have been very good this year.' I gave Amy a half-laugh, half-sob, relieved that I'd made a decision, excited that I was going to text him and already terrified of what his response might be. 'And balls are so versatile.'

'I've heard they're all the rage for spring–summer,' Amy replied, pulling down the hem of her neon-pink sweater to reveal half an inch of her bright yellow bra. 'I think they showed them at Chanel.'

'And who can argue with Chanel?' I asked, looking down at my not-in-any-way-revealing blue stripy top.

'No one,' she answered. 'Did you see where that waitress went? I physically need dessert before we write this text message.'

I sipped my drink and thanked my lucky stars. Pudding and Amy Smith. The only two things on earth that were 100 per cent guaranteed to make everything better.

'I can't believe I'm going to meet James Jacobs,' Kekipi said, sitting in the back of a black Lincoln town car with his hands pressed against his mouth. His brown eyes were alive with excitement and I wasn't sure I'd ever seen him this excited, not even when we stayed up until 3 a.m. so he could make sure he got Taylor Swift tickets.

'You've met a million famous people,' I reminded him. 'What's so special about this one?'

The look on his face suggested I'd just made a truly terrible joke about his mother's sexual proclivities. Which I would never do – because he would have done it first.

'James Jacobs is an icon,' he replied. 'And James Jacobs was on *Downton Abbey*. I've never met anyone who was on *Downton Abbey*, this is a life goal realized.'

'Well, I appreciate you coming to help out,' I said, bouncing my camera bag on my knees and tapping my toes up and down. 'I know how busy you must be with the wedding.'

'Oh please,' he said, straightening his hair. 'I can have a *hundred* weddings. Who knows when I'll get another chance to oil up James Jacobs?'

'We're not oiling up anyone,' I pointed out. 'He's going to be fully dressed for the whole thing.'

'Spoilsport,' he muttered.

He had let his hair grow out since I'd last seen him and the extra length suited him. All these months away from Hawaii had taken an edge off his golden skin but the gently curling waves gave him a certain softness, and then I realized what it was. He looked happy. Falling in love suited him. In love with his fiancé Domenico, that was, not James Jacobs.

'Maybe you can help the stylist,' I relented. 'I'm sure we can engineer some semi-nudity as a thank you for helping me out. I really appreciate you helping me, I know it's a boring job.'

'Don't worry, I'm not really going to be much help, am I?' he said, pushing his glossy black waves into place. 'What is it I've volunteered for anyway? Other than to make sweet, sweet love to my celebrity crush?'

Really, I should have known better.

'How is your fiancé?' I turned to look him straight in the eye. 'So nice of him to leave everything behind in Milan and follow you to New York. Monogamy working out well, is it?'

'Oh, splendid,' he said, smiling in the face of my sarcasm. 'He's the love of my life.'

'Apart from James Jacobs?' I asked.

'Oh, Tess.' Kekipi gave me a pat on the shoulder. 'I would sell my grandmother for a go on James Jacobs and I fully expect Domenico would do the same. As long as he filmed it and let me watch, I would completely understand. I'm very excited to marry him and that's one of the reasons why.'

'Relationships are confusing,' I sighed, watching the townhouses trail away and a grey, frozen river take their place as our car sped down the west side of Manhattan.

'Speaking of which . . .' He never missed a good segue.

'Miss Amy tells me you and Mr Wilder are on speaking terms again.'

I nodded. 'Yep. We're friends again.'

'I see,' he purred. '*Friends.*'

Turning my attention out of the window, I concentrated on the sights that sped by, beginning to regret my decision to bring Kekipi along on the shoot.

'And I also heard you happened upon a certain Mr Miller.'

'When did she tell you all this?' I asked. 'We were together all night.'

'She texted me when you were in the toilet,' he replied, taking a bite out of a bagel. I had declined Genevieve's offer of breakfast to go when the nerves Amy had asked after had showed up and brought all their friends with them. 'And she said you sent him a text message?'

'Then I'm assuming she also told you he didn't reply,' I said, looking at my watch. 'And still hasn't, twelve hours later.'

And every minute that went by was killing me.

The rush of anticipation, every time my phone buzzed, followed by the crushing realization that it wasn't from him. Every minute that passed by I felt less and less like he was going to respond. The only obvious explanation was that he had got so cold the day before his hands had fallen off and he was in hospital, waiting for replacements so he could text me.

'How long has it been exactly since you last spoke?' Kekipi asked.

'A while,' I replied. If by a while, he meant one hundred and forty-one days.

'Then I think we can give him a bit longer than twelve hours,' he said, patting my knee. 'Have a little faith. It is Christmas, after all, goodwill to all men and all that jazz.'

'I suppose I'll have to wait until Easter if I want to crucify him then,' I muttered. 'When is that exactly?'

'What did your text say?' he asked, ignoring me. 'Amy wasn't specific, the swine.'

'Just, you know, hi.' I tried to give the impression that I couldn't remember word for word what I had written but given that Amy and I had spent nearly forty minutes crafting the perfect breezy, noncommittal but totally genuine and heartfelt message, clearly that was a lie. 'I think I said I was in New York and that it would be great to see him if he's in town. That kind of thing.'

'That kind of thing, right,' Kekipi echoed. 'And what exactly are you hoping he'll say?'

That he's sorry and he loves me and he wants to try again, I answered in my head.

'I don't know,' I answered out loud. 'There's no point thinking about it because he's not going to say exactly what I want him to say, is he?'

'Probably not,' he agreed. 'Have you thought about what you'll do if he doesn't reply at all?'

'Murderous Godzilla-esque rampage in downtown Manhattan?' I suggested. 'But you know, wearing a Santa hat so it's nice and seasonal.'

'Can it be after the wedding?' Kekipi asked. 'We've spent a freaking fortune.'

'Go on then,' I promised, as we slowed down and turned onto a narrow cobbled street, still sparkly and white. New York was like a Christmas snowglobe come to life. 'I have to tell you, I'm pretty bloody excited about this wedding. My expectations are high.'

'Your expectations have nothing on what we have

planned,' he assured me. 'Wedding of the century – of the millennium, even. It's going to be a great big gay Hawaiian-Italian Christmas spectacular. Did Domenico tell you he wanted Kylie to play the reception?'

I shook my head.

'I nixed it of course, too much of a cliché,' he said. 'We're going much classier.'

'Who did you get?' I asked, a little bit sad not to be able to live out Tiny Tess's Locomotion fantasies.

'Amy lobbied pretty hard for Justin Timberlake but there was something about a restraining order?' he asked, plucking my phone out of my hand as I checked it one more time. 'Anyway, it'll be a surprise. I'm taking your phone away. You need to concentrate and you can't do that when you're waiting for a man to send you a message that will no doubt be infuriatingly vague even if it does come.'

'You're right,' I admitted, Business Tess taking over. 'I need to concentrate on the job and the more I think about Nick, the harder that's going to be.'

'Good girl.' Kekipi grinned, straightening his hair. 'You concentrate on the job and I'll concentrate on James Jacobs's wang.'

I flashed him a stern look as the driver opened the car door onto the snowy street.

'And look after your phone and be a fabulous assistant,' he added. 'Professional to the end, of course.'

'Of course,' I replied, staring up at the big black building where we were supposed to meet Cici, excitement for the shoot bubbling up inside me. 'I didn't doubt it for a second.'

'I wonder what he's wearing,' Kekipi pondered, jumping out behind me and striding straight into the studio. 'Do you think he'll sign my butt? As a surprise for Domenico?'

Professional to the end.

'Oh look, you showed up.'

Cici was already in the studio, a cup of coffee the size of her head in one hand and an iPad in the other. Angela had sent me an email explaining that because her art director was stuck in LA, Cici had graciously offered to step in. Lucky old me.

'Are we late?' I asked.

'Yes,' she replied.

I looked at my watch: we were twenty minutes early.

'But I'm kind of surprised that you showed up at all. So thanks for that.'

'This is Cici?' Kekipi whispered over my shoulder. I nodded, gripping my camera bag tightly. 'She's a delight,' he said. 'Permission to spend the day insulting her with very clever asides that go right over her head?'

'Permission granted,' I whispered back.

'Cici!' Kekipi opened his arms for a hug and was greeted with a look so filthy, it made me want to pop home for a shower. 'I'm Kekipi,' he said, lowering his arms to his side. 'I work for your godfather. We haven't met but I know your sister somewhat.'

'Then why are you here?' she asked, not even slightly impressed. 'Aren't you his butler or something?'

'Or something,' he replied coolly. 'I'm assisting Tess today.'

'Fantastic, another amateur,' she said with a dramatic sigh, beckoning the two of us through the reception and into a large empty space. 'If we could all pretend to be professionals, that would be awesome.'

'What a proper, good old-fashioned bitch,' Kekipi said, giving her outfit the once over. 'Under any other circumstances, I'd like her.'

'Under any other circumstances, I'd kill her,' I replied. 'But I really want this job to go well. These shots need to be amazing.'

'James Jacobs is going to be in them,' he reminded me. 'They're going to be the best photographs ever taken.'

'The idea is New Year's resolutions, so we have two set-ups,' Cici explained, ignoring our whispered conversation as we followed her through to the studio. 'The first is black-tie wardrobe and we're shooting against a green screen. We'll drop something behind them later—'

'Something?' I asked.

Cici turned her blue eyes on me.

'Something,' she repeated. 'You don't need to ask questions, you just need to take the picture.'

'But shouldn't I know?' I asked, flashing back to the photoshoot debacle in Hawaii. I had learned my lesson about not thoroughly discussing the brief *before* the shoot got started. 'I mean, I'm the photographer.'

'I mean, you're not really,' Cici sniped back. I heard Kekipi take a deep breath behind me as he gripped my elbow tightly. 'And if I knew what we were putting behind them, I'd tell you. But I don't know, we're still working on it. Just tell them it's a party or something. It's a New Year's party.'

'Do you want me to find an image?' I asked. I'd worked on some greenscreen stuff with Ess so I knew what I was doing. 'I think I'd rather, if it's OK with you.'

'I want you to take a photograph,' she said, speaking very slowly. 'The art team are on it.'

'Fine,' I muttered. Some people didn't want you to be helpful. 'Then what?'

'Second set-up is individual portraits to run with their New Year's resolutions, James first, then Sadie. We want them to look like normal people – only not. At home in their pyjamas, putting on a face mask, eating ice cream, watching TV.'

So the concept was dressing a supermodel up as me. As if I didn't feel bad enough seeing a supermodel in a bikini, now I had to feel inadequate when I was watching Netflix in my PJs.

I shunted my camera bag up my shoulder. 'Do we have the resolutions, do you know what they are?'

'No,' she replied, still messing about with her iPad. 'So don't ask me for them. Angela is writing the piece today.'

'Got it,' I said. 'I'll just stop talking altogether.'

'And the world will be a better place,' Cici said with a big smile. 'Like I said, we don't have a lot of time. I can't believe that bitch dropped out at the last minute yesterday. I hope her film flops so hard she ends up in reality TV.'

I really, really wanted to know who it was. The internet gave away nothing.

'That's it. Do you think you can manage?' she asked, a look of faux concern forcing her Botoxed eyebrows as high as they could go. Which wasn't very high. 'You're representing my magazine today and I know Angela wants to throw you a bone or whatever but this is still important.'

'Tess is an amazing photographer,' Kekipi answered before I could punch her perfectly aligned teeth out. 'You're going to be blown away.'

'I'll settle for mildly disappointed as long as I have

153

usable photographs at the end of the day,' she said with a saccharine smile. 'So don't let me down, yeah?'

'Christ, she's better at guilt trips than my mum,' I said as she marched away to the make-up area where two girls stood quaking in their extremely stylish boots. 'They should send her out to schools to tell kids not to do drugs.'

'Please, do you know how many of her I've come across over the years?' he huffed. 'She's ten to a penny, all hair extensions and attitude. And she'll stay that way until her husband has an affair with the nanny.'

'Have I mentioned that I love you?' I asked him, setting my equipment on a table and giving him a hug. 'I owe you one.'

'Anything for my bridesmaid,' he said, squeezing me back. 'Although I will hold you to that. I do hope you won't end up regretting it.'

'Me too,' I agreed, tossing my ponytail over my shoulder, Cici-style. 'Now, can we at least pretend to be professional?'

'We can try,' he said. 'But I make no promises.'

'Good enough for me,' I told him, unzipping my camera bag and smiling for real. 'Let's do this.'

'I don't want to do this!'

Two hours later and Sadie Nixon, my gorgeous model, was standing in front of me in a gorgeous midnight-blue gown that fell all the way to the floor, intermittently slashed with sheer panels that showed off her perfect body. Combined with her gorgeous hair and gorgeous make-up, she pretty much looked gorgeous.

'I look awful,' she pouted as I tried to line up the shot. 'I am hideous.'

'You look beautiful,' I told her, glancing over at Kekipi

for support. But Kekipi was too busy watching James Jacobs getting an epic make-up job on the huge bags underneath his eyes. Shockingly, I really did feel like the most professional person on set. 'That dress is incredible.'

'I look like a fat cow,' she replied, grabbing at a tiny ripple of fabric and somehow mistaking it for a slab of human flesh. 'Look at this. I'm enormous. I can't wear this.'

'Uh, I think you look amazing,' I searched the room for Cici. Nowhere to be found, of course. 'Incredibly beautiful. Unreal, even.'

'Fine, just take the shot.' Sadie stopped sulking for one second, stared directly into the camera and became the most beautiful creature on the planet. I clicked off ten fast frames before she started pouting again and the moment was over. 'Have we met before? You look familiar.'

'I don't think so,' I said, reviewing the images on my camera. It was amazing how she had transformed. Models really were a different species to the rest of us. 'I haven't been to New York before.'

'Did you shoot me in Paris?' she asked, picking up the skirt of the dress and letting it fall, another second of perfect beauty. 'Maybe it was London?'

'No, I'm pretty new,' I replied, trying to capture the shot before her mood changed again. 'We definitely haven't met.'

'I'm really only doing this as a favour to Angela,' Sadie said, turning away from me and glancing back over her shoulder. She was so beautiful I could barely stand to look at her. 'I'm kind of a big deal.'

'Must be nice for you,' I said. 'That's amazing, what you're doing now. So beautiful.'

'I broke up with my boyfriend last night,' she said in a stage whisper. 'I feel awful.'

'Clearly he's an idiot,' I said, checking in on Kekipi to see him holding a glass of water and a straw up to James Jacobs's lips. 'You're a goddess and he's not worth it and, um, forget that guy. Could you stand on that mark right there?'

'Yeah,' she said, her eyes brightening a shade. 'Forget that guy.'

'I know . . .' I held up my camera triumphantly, hoping to get her on side. 'Let's take the most incredibly beautiful, sexy photos and make sure he sees them. That'll teach him. And could you please stand on the mark?'

'Uh, yeah, there's a photo of me in my underwear in Times Square,' she pointed out. 'And like a million on the internet. I'm a model?'

Model break-ups were presumably very different to civilian break-ups.

'Oh yeah.' I walked over to the green screen and physically moved her onto the taped-out mark on the floor. 'Well, let's think of something else.'

'Guys always break up with me over the holidays,' she whined. 'Or around my birthday. Or Valentine's Day. It's like any time there's a thing, you know?'

I nodded, although clearly I did not know. Personally, I would have broken up with her any day that had a 'y' in it, but, thankfully, I did not have a penis and it would never be a problem I had to deal with.

'It's like, every time I meet a guy, he only wants to date me for five minutes.'

Without a second's warning, she sank to the floor and rested her chin in her hands.

'I don't know what I'm doing wrong. It's super-confusing.'

'I'm sure you're not doing anything wrong,' I told her, running over to pull the hem of the dress off her spike heel before twelve hundred dollars' worth of shoes tore through five thousand dollars' worth of dress and I was fired immediately.

These were the situations where an assistant was useful, I told myself, looking back at the Kekipi/James Jacobs love-in. If only I'd thought to bring one with me . . .

'Yeah, I totally am,' she sighed and rubbed the heel of her hand against her eye, destroying the make-up that had taken fifty minutes to apply. 'I mean, it's got to be me, right? It's like my roommate says, I'm the only common nomination.'

I frowned and sat down beside her.

'Nomination?' It took me a minute to work out what she meant. 'Well, I think all it means is you haven't met the right man. You shouldn't have to change yourself to make a man happy, should you?'

Sadie pursed her lipstick commercial lips into a perfect pout for a moment while she thought about it.

'I guess,' she said finally. I was very glad she'd taken so long to come up with such a considered response. 'I'm, like, so nice to the guys I date.'

'There you go then.' I began to stand up but she grabbed by elbows and dragged me back down.

'You're right,' she said, the pout replaced with determination. 'I'm gonna be me and when the right guy comes along, he'll appreciate that.'

'Hell yeah,' I said, holding out my hand for a high five. And holding it. And holding it. Eventually, I put it back down by my side. Apparently we weren't there yet. 'You be you.'

'Yeah.' She sounded more and more convinced by the second. 'I mean, it's their problem if they can't deal with my job, right?'

'Right,' I agreed.

'And it's not weird to want to do nice things for your boyfriend, is it?'

'No,' I said, frowning slightly 'What kind of nice things?'

'And what kind of dude doesn't want to give his girl-friend a key to his apartment?' She held up her hands in despair. 'I mean, clearly he is the one with intimacy issues there.'

'Well, I don't know if a man would want to give you a key right away,' I said. 'But you know—'

'And he should *want* to buy me gifts.' Oh dear God, she wasn't finished. 'And I don't see why he would be mad at me having his cat re-homed when I am so allergic. Who chooses a cat over the love of their life?'

I placed a hand on her wrist as two bright pink spots developed in her cheeks.

'How long were you going out with this man?' I asked. 'Just out of interest?'

'Forever,' she said, whacking down the billowing edges of her gown. 'Like, two months.'

My breath caught in my throat and I choked down a gasp, coughing like a dying seal instead.

'Forever, right?' she blew a strand of hair out of her mouth. 'What an A-hole.'

'A-hole of the highest order,' I nodded. 'You're better off without him.'

And lucky he didn't take out a restraining order, I added silently.

'Your boyfriend would never behave like that,' she

said, patting my hand absently. 'I can tell. You wouldn't take that shit.'

'I don't actually have a boyfriend,' I said.

'Girlfriend?' she asked, raising an eyebrow.

'No, not gay, just single,' I replied. 'Did you think I was gay?'

'Not so much,' she said with a shrug. 'Just maybe your shoes. And your pants. And—'

'Well, I'm not,' I interrupted, folding my gay feet underneath my gay jeans. 'Just single.'

'But there must be someone you like,' she said, a conspiratorial smile on her face. 'There's always someone.'

'It's complicated,' I said, returning her smile. 'When is it not?'

'You just gotta go for it,' Sadie said, shrugging her delicate shoulders as though it was that simple. 'You gotta know what you want and you gotta go get it.'

'Good advice,' I admitted. 'But what if what you want isn't a good idea?'

'Oh, it never is,' she laughed. 'But since when did that stop anyone?'

I wriggled my toes, shaking off pins and needles in my left foot. She had a point. But was I really going to take romantic advice from a woman who gave her boyfriend's cat away because it made her eyes water?

'I hate being single,' she went on with a moan in her voice. 'All my friends are coupled up. I'm the last old hag who can't keep a man.'

'If you're a hag, I'd hate to think what I am!' I laughed as Sadie opened her mouth to respond. 'That was a rhetorical question,' I explained. 'You don't have to answer.'

'I wasn't going to call you a hag,' she said, laughing as she spoke. 'Silly. You're not a hag. You're just normal.'

Normal. Was that what I was?

'And normal's OK,' she whispered, as though it wasn't something everyone needed to know. 'I'm sure you'll find a normal dude to date eventually.'

'Shall we take some photos?' I asked brightly. 'Before we run out of time?'

She gave a nod and shrug before rising from the floor, her dress floating out all around her, her face soft and delicate.

'You look incredible,' I said, speaking without thinking. I'd worked with what felt like a lot of models over the last few months but Sadie was something else. Maybe it wasn't so irrational of her to expect a man to lose a cat on her behalf.

'Thank you.' She shook out her loose blonde curls and leapt on her mark, all drama over, all concern forgotten, suddenly the consummate professional. 'Is this good?'

'Perfect,' I told her, snapping ecstatically. It was impossible to put a camera on this woman and take a bad photo and I was almost guaranteed to get something for the competition. Relaxing into the shoot, I felt a wave of certainty wash over me. I'd got this. I knew exactly what I was doing and I couldn't imagine doing anything else.

'I'm not sure about this,' I said, watching a group of deliverymen wheel two giant black boxes onto the set. 'Cici, they seem awfully big for the space.'

'They're perfect,' she snapped, signing the clipboard of a large, greasy man who seemed far too sweaty for the temperature outside. 'And you should be grateful I managed to get hold of them at all. Maybe now we'll be able to get a photo we can actually use.'

'I thought the photos looked good,' Sadie whispered,

checking the monitor over my shoulder. 'Don't they look good?'

'They look great,' Kekipi said. 'She's actually lost her mind.'

'We're going to do the picture of the two of you one more time.' The edges of Cici's voice frayed as she spoke to James and Sadie, ignoring me. 'But with a snow machine. For the drama.'

'I don't know if we need to do this,' James said, flapping his hands at Kekipi as he fussed with his bow tie. 'I really do think we've got the shot. We've been at it all day, darling.'

'We'll have it in five minutes,' Cici said. She gave the clipboard back to the large man and wiped her hands on her skintight jeans. 'Trust me.'

Sadie stared her down for a moment, then turned to me.

'Tess, what do you think?' she asked.

'What do I think?'

I blinked as James, Kekipi and the make-up artists all turned to look at me. I'd been contemplating checking my phone if Kekipi would let me. Surely Nick must have replied by now? Across the studio, I saw Cici with her hands on her hips and a foul expression on her face.

What I thought was that we already had the shots we needed.

Everyone was tired and bored and wanted to go home; it had been a long day in the studio and there wasn't a person there who wasn't ready to swing for Cici Spencer, but Cici Spencer was technically the client. And wasn't it my job to keep the client happy? Could I even say no? We were taught never to say no to a client in my old job. If this were an ad campaign, I'd put together a couple of other options to humour her and eventually talk them round to the original idea. Surely this was the same?

'The longer you all argue with me, the longer it will take,' Cici said before switching her attention to the men who were setting up, while James and Sadie reluctantly hovered around the make-up chairs. 'It's all set up and ready to go?'

'Uh-huh.' One of the men nodded, talking directly to her cleavage. 'Press the green button to start it up. The red button turns it off.'

'Can we stop wasting time?' Cici said, waving the deliveryman away. 'This is going to make the shot and you'll all be thanking me once it's done. Start now and we'll all be home inside an hour.'

Was it possible we really did just want the same thing? I looked outside at the pitch-black sky and then back at the set, trying to imagine the image with the snow. Maybe it could work. Maybe she was right.

'Let's try it,' I relented as everyone around me deflated with a mass of sighs. 'It won't take long.'

'Thank you,' Cici crowed. 'You wait and see, this is going to be epic.'

Taking a deep breath, I climbed my little stepladder and set the camera as Sadie and James found their marks. 'OK, Cici, turn it on.'

The second after she flipped the switch, I asked myself a thousand questions. Why didn't we test the snow machine before we put Sadie and James in the shot? Why did I think it was a good idea to climb a ladder in front of a wind machine? And why had Kekipi crawled underneath the food service table?

But there was no time to answer any of them.

As soon as Cici switched on the wind machine, I was

blown right off the ladder into a blizzard of wet snow. I came crashing down into James, who tried to throw out his arms to catch me. Unfortunately, even though he was a tall man, the laws of physics were against us. Tall man plus tall woman holding heavy camera and blown off a stepladder by twenty-mile-an-hour winds was only going to end one way.

'My camera!' I yelped, trying not to hit the movie star in the face as hundreds of pounds of photographic equipment clattered onto the floor. 'Are you OK?'

'Never better,' James grunted, flat on his back on the ground as I curled around my camera, protecting it from the mounds of watery snow blowing towards me, just in time to see my laptop go flying on the other side of the snowstorm. 'Thanks for asking.'

'Hey you guys, how's it going? Is everything—?'

Blinking through the driving snow pinning us all to the ground, I saw a tall, curly haired woman I vaguely recognized from Angela Clark's office wall walking into the studio.

'Holy shit!' she yelled, stopping dead in her tracks. 'What the hell is going on?'

It was a fair question from where I was standing. Or rather, lying.

'Stop screaming!' Cici yelled over the roar of the powerful snow machine. 'Everyone stop screaming.'

There was actually only one person screaming but Sadie was doing such a good job of it no one could have been blamed for thinking we'd brought a bus full of toddlers into the room and introduced them to a knife-wielding circus clown.

'Turn it off!' I shouted as loud as I could, cradling my blinking camera as James tried to scramble to his feet, grabbing a handful of boob as he went. 'Please just turn it off!'

'I'm trying!' Cici wailed back. 'The button is stuck.'

'Help! Sadie screeched. She was pinned to the green wall behind us, the wind machine hurling relentless gobs of semi-frozen snow at her beautiful face. 'I can't move.'

Dropping her handbag by the door, the woman pulled off her suede high-heeled boots in the doorway and ran across the studio.

'Get out of my damn way!' She gave Cici a shove as she took over the controls of the snow machine, bashing every button with the flat of her hand.

'Make it stop!' Sadie wailed, ineffectually flapping her hands at the oncoming blizzard. 'I can't see!'

'Cici, get her out of there!' the woman shouted. Whoever she was, Cici knew not to mess with her. Without so much as an eye roll, she nodded and crawled into her homemade snowstorm on her hands and knees, spitting out snow as she went. I was impressed. I couldn't even get her to stand up to pass me a pencil earlier in the day.

'Oof,' I grunted as a boot hit me in the back of the head as I tried to wriggle towards dry land.

'Sorry,' James called as he scurried out of the danger zone and joined Kekipi underneath the table. 'Didn't mean to.'

'No problem, gents,' I shouted back, spitting out a mouthful of snow and shoving my camera down the front of my jumper. 'I'm fine.'

'She's fine,' Kekipi insisted, grabbing hold of James's hand. 'She's a feminist.'

'I have a T-shirt with that on,' James replied cheerfully, brushing the snow out of his hair. 'Good for her.'

'I can't turn it off,' my curly-haired hero yelled, hitting

the snow machine with the heel of her boot before turning her attention to the power cable. I watched as she followed it to the wall and gave the plug a short, sharp tug. 'But there's always a way.'

I opened my eyes as the swirling snowstorm petered out into a delicate dusting of soft flakes and took a deep breath.

'Are you OK?' a loud American voice asked. Looking up, I saw a hand reach out towards me and pull me up to my feet. 'I'm Jenny.'

Glancing across the studio, I watched while Sadie kicked off her insanely expensive and utterly destroyed shoes and turned them into weapons, bashing Cici in the head as she attempted to slither away from the scene of her disgrace.

'Tess,' I said, snapping my wet jumper away from the cold skin on my belly. 'Should we stop them?'

'Eh?' Jenny slipped her boots back on, holding onto my arm for support. 'If we help Cici now, she'll never learn, and between you and me, I think there are a few lessons she could stand to learn the hard way. Is your camera OK?'

'I don't know,' I said, taking it out and pressing the on and off button. Nothing happened. 'Is the laptop all right?'

Kekipi reluctantly emerged from his James Jacobs occupied den and picked it up from the floor.

'I'm sure we can fix it,' he said, holding the screen in one hand and the keyboard, mostly parted from it, in the other. My stomach dropped to my feet and I felt the sudden urge to sit down and never get back up.

'Come on.' Jenny pulled me out of my trance and back into the safety zone behind the snow machine. 'You need a drink.'

I nodded and watched a supermodel chase a Park Avenue princess around our accidental winter wonderland, cracking her across the arse with a shoe.

Now, *there* was a photo. If only I had a bloody camera so I could take it.

CHAPTER TEN

'I've got to tell you, it was the most amazing thing I've ever seen.' Jenny Lopez, snow-machine maestro, and my new personal hero, shoved her phone under Angela's nose and swiped back and forth through this afternoon's chaos. 'You know I love Sadie, but man, I wish I'd thought of getting a snow machine for the apartment when she first moved in.'

Angela took the phone and zoomed in on the catfight.

'Dear God,' she whispered. 'I wish I had been there to see this.'

'I am so sorry,' I said, wishing Jenny would put the phone away. 'We definitely got the shot, though. And nothing was damaged, well, nothing much was damaged.'

Apart from my camera and my laptop, I added silently. They were both drying out inside bags of rice, stashed in the boot of the town car Al had loaned us for the day, a dark secret between me and Tony the driver; as far as everyone else was concerned, I had salvaged my equipment with nothing more than a little scratch. Even Kekipi seemed to believe that a laptop that had been virtually severed in two could be clipped back together.

According to the internet, there was nothing I could do for at least the next twelve hours while they dried out and I didn't want to worry Angela unnecessarily. She had given me this amazing chance and I couldn't even process the idea that it might be completely ballsed up. I was fairly certain the pictures already on the memory card would be OK, but I couldn't be certain about anything on the laptop.

'I got an email from Cici telling me she was very concerned about her shirt,' Angela said, still swiping through the photos as though it were Tinder. 'It was dry clean only.'

She skipped back to the picture of Cici, spreadeagled in the snow, with Sadie holding a stiletto above her head.

'I wish I'd had this before we sent out the company Christmas cards,' she said, enlarging and enlarging until she could properly see the look of terror in Cici's eyes. 'This is priceless.'

I had emailed Agent Veronica to tell her about the job but all I'd received in response was a curse-littered note about working below her set rate and bleeping me and her up our bleeps, so it was safe to say she was annoyed with me. The last thing I needed was bad feedback from the one job I'd managed to book. If I lost my agent *and* gained a reputation for almost killing people on set, I'd be utterly buggered. Two steps forward, three steps back was no use to anyone.

'I don't think it was as bad as it looks in those pictures,' I lied. 'Really, it was all over in a matter of seconds.'

Which was just long enough to destroy all my equipment.

'It was carnage,' Kekipi qualified. Always so helpful. He leaned across me to take a better look at Jenny's photo of him and James, clutching each other underneath the folding food table. 'Could someone forward me that?' he asked.

'You're not helping,' I hissed, kicking him in the shin as Jenny and Angela went over the pictures one more time.

'Tess, love . . .' Kekipi pierced a fat-looking olive with a cocktail stick and patted me on the back, 'it was a disaster. We're lucky no one died. But you got the photos you needed, so why worry about it?'

Why worry indeed? I thought, swilling my wine around in the glass. I still felt sick to my stomach and it really wasn't going down well.

'Yeah, Tess, no one is blaming you for this,' Jenny said, still unable to take her eyes off her phone. 'Shit like this happens to everyone.'

'Really?' I said, peering down at a photo of Cici crawling in front of the camera while Sadie lay on the floor, locked forever in an open-mouthed scream in the background.

'Well, OK, no, it doesn't,' she replied. 'But shit like this happens to us. Don't sweat it. You've been shooting all day, you coped with Cici all day, you took a bad spill from the top of a stepladder – if anyone deserves to unwind with a drink, it's you.'

I looked hopefully at Angela who had already turned her attention to the dinner menu.

'Oh, yeah,' she agreed. 'Remind me to tell you about the time we fell in the fountains in Las Vegas. Classic Clark. As long as you got the shots and no one died, I'd chalk this one up as a win.'

'And there was the time I was living with a hooker in

LA,' Jenny added. 'And remember when James wanted you to be his beard? And when Cici had your luggage blown up in Paris?'

'I already told her about that,' Angela nodded. 'Good times, happy memories, everyone's a winner.'

'I feel so bad,' I said. Of course they thought everything would be OK; they didn't know we might have lost 90 per cent of the photos I'd taken. 'I should have told her we didn't need the snow machine. I knew we'd already got the shots we needed but I didn't know how to explain it to her without pissing her off.'

'Firstly, you can't tell Cici Spencer shit without pissing her off,' Jenny said, topping up her glass. 'Secondly, you need to learn how to use your voice and thirdly, drink up. I want to order another bottle. How long are you going to nurse that glass?'

'Jenny is very wise,' Angela said, grabbing an olive before Kekipi ate them all, proving Jenny wasn't the only wise one. 'She's read more self-help books than anyone else I've ever met. Also, I would like more wine, please.'

Jenny nodded. 'I'm basically Oprah only not a sellout.'

'Translation, "without the billions of dollars",' Angela added, giving her a sly look.

'I don't whore out my powers,' she countered, nipping the olive right out of Angela's fingers. Best friend food thievery, I noted; it was familiar. 'I can't be bought.'

Angela almost choked on her sauvignon blanc. 'That's a lie and we both know it.'

'Whatever,' Jenny said, smiling as she swatted her with a menu. 'But seriously, if you knew you were done, why didn't you tell her? You're the photographer, you're in charge.'

'But she was the client! Wasn't I supposed to do what

she asked?' I said, looking to Kekipi for help and not getting it.

'You were in charge,' she said, pointing a perfectly painted gold nail in my face. 'You should have told her you had the shot.'

'You'll pick it up with experience,' Angela offered, playing good cop to Jenny's downright terrifying one. 'Next time you'll know.'

'If there is a next time.' I raked my hands through my hair and fought back my frustration.

'We can sit here all night and kiss your ass,' Jenny added, taking hold of my ponytail and flicking through the ends. 'But if you just want to wallow, there's nothing anyone can do to help you.'

I sniffed and sipped my wine. 'I guess . . .'

'I *know*,' she countered. 'Also, you need to drop by the office tomorrow, I have some conditioner you need.'

'Oh, I have conditioner,' I said, examining my own dry ends. 'Thanks, though.'

'It wasn't a suggestion,' she told me, a severe clip to her words as she dug a business card out of her handbag. 'Here's the address, come by any time. I'll be there all day.'

'She's right, though,' Angela said. 'Not about the hair stuff, although she's usually right about that too. So much of getting ahead nowadays is believing in yourself and you seemed pretty bloody convinced of yourself in my office yesterday or I wouldn't have given you the job. You can't let someone like Cici bring you down. There are an awful lot of those in this world.'

'Agreed,' Jenny said. 'And for the record, I'm always right about hair stuff.'

'There are going to be a lot of people telling you you're shit,' Angela carried on. 'Either because they're jealous of you or because they really think it. You have to be able to go out there with your photos and say, "oi you, look at my photos, they're amazing," no matter what anyone else says, not only when people are nice to you.'

Jenny turned to look at her friend. 'Were you drinking before you got here?' she asked.

Angela pinched her shoulders together in a shrug. And then nodded.

'Yeah, I figured,' Jenny sighed. 'Your delivery is off but you're right. You've gotta believe in you or no one else will.'

'You think she's a mess at work, you should ask her about her love life,' Kekipi said, clucking his tongue. 'Now there's a story.'

Both of the other women picked up their glasses and downed the contents in tandem.

'Spill,' Jenny ordered.

'Please,' Angela added.

'I'd rather not,' I replied.

'I'll start,' Kekipi interrupted. 'So, we met in Hawaii and there was this man called Nick Miller there as well . . .'

Refreshing my texts one more time, I saw a sad face emoji from Amy. She couldn't make drinks because she was still working. Whatever topsy-turvy bizarro world I'd walked into, I didn't want anything more to do with it.

'And now we're waiting for him to text back,' Kekipi concluded, giving me a nudge as I tapped out a reply to Amy. 'We are still waiting, aren't we?'

'We are,' I confirmed. 'But it's been twenty-four hours, I think it's time to give up.'

'Doesn't sound like a bad idea,' Angela said, waving to the waitress for another bottle of wine as I got to work on my full glass. 'He loves you, he doesn't love you, he loves you, he doesn't love you. Trust me, I dated one of those wankers before I met my husband, Alex. The only person they love is themselves. All this "I'm so damaged and hurt" stuff is just an excuse to treat you like shit and then say "I told you so" with a smile on their face on their way out the door.'

'Fair,' Jenny agreed. 'He does also sound like something of an asshat. I want to hear more about this Charlie dude.' She turned to Kekipi with a very serious expression on her face. 'Which one is hotter?'

'Oh, please don't,' I muttered. 'Charlie is off the table. They're both off the table. There's nothing on the table but wine, really.'

He cocked his head to one side and considered the options. 'Charlie is taller,' he said, contemplating. 'But Nick is definitely sexier. That said, Charlie definitely has a "hot boy next door in a Reese Witherspoon movie" thing going on. I feel as though he is heavily involved in sports. Great thighs.'

'So, Charlie is cute and Nick is hot, am I right?' Jenny asked. 'And they're both assholes. This is a tough one.'

'It really doesn't matter which one is which,' I said, watching the waitress bringing our wine over from the bar. 'I'm not interested in Charlie and Nick isn't interested in me. End of story.'

No one at the table looked convinced.

'But, hypothetically, if they both came running through the door and begged you to forgive them,' Angela said, her face a picture of innocence. 'Which one would you go home with? Hypothetically.'

'If you had to,' Jenny added. 'If you had to or you'd *die*.'

Sloping back against the booth I fingered the ends of my hair. She was right, they were very dry.

'She'd choose Nick,' Kekipi said, picking up his glass and taking a long sip. 'Definitely.'

'I don't know,' Jenny said, regarding me carefully with dark eyes. 'She's taking her time. And everyone knows the Nicks of this world are not reliable. You can't reform an asshole. Once a douchecanoe, always a douchecanoe.'

'Didn't you say that about my husband once upon a time?' Angela asked. 'God knows he'd been round the block more than once before we met.'

'I don't remember calling him a douchecanoe,' Jenny frowned. 'But yeah, he and the block were super-familiar. Although I'm pretty certain Alex is the exception, not the rule. You caught him on a good day: with dudes it's all about timing.'

'And what if the timing is right with Nick?' Kekipi argued. 'What if he has spent the last couple of months thinking about how badly he screwed everything up and if only he had a chance to change things, he would?'

With newfound resolve, I finished my first glass of wine with two big gulps while the waitress waited and held it out for her to fill it to the brim.

'Have you eaten today?' Kekipi asked as I chugged my second glass.

I shook my head and the room shook with it. 'I'm fine,' I assured him. 'I'll be fine.'

'It was a long day and you deserve a drink,' he relented. 'But you can't vomit in a taxi, there's an extortionate cleaning fee here.'

Stopping mid-sip, I put my glass down on the table but kept my hand clenched around the stem. 'There is?'

'Ask your best friend,' he said, raising his eyebrows.

'I don't know. Life is short,' Jenny said, still debating my romantic situation, or lack thereof. 'What happens if she walks away from the Nick situation and spends the rest of her life asking herself what if?'

'I'm not going to,' I said, interrupting. 'I've texted him and he hasn't replied – that's a fairly clear indication of where his head is at, isn't it?'

'Perhaps we're overlooking something,' Angela said, turning to face me head on. 'Tess, do you love Nick?'

'Ahhdunno,' I replied with a shrug. 'Maybe, sort of?'

They all stared at me.

'Yes?' I said, miserable. 'I totally do.'

'Oh, you poor girl,' Jenny said, her big brown eyes full of pity. 'You're in so deep you don't even know it.'

'Oh God!' I covered my face with my hands. 'When does it stop? It doesn't make sense.'

'Hate to be the one to break it to you,' she replied as the rest of the table went silent. 'But love doesn't make sense. Can't rationalize this one, honey, you've got to go with your gut.'

'But my gut is scared.' I dropped my forehead onto the table, my hair spilling all around me in a lovely, tangled tent of isolation. It lasted approximately four seconds.

'Of course it is.' Jenny grabbed a handful of my curls and pulled my head back up, sulky face and all. 'If you're in love, you have something to lose. That's terrifying. Way easier to pretend it's not happening, am I right?'

I stared at her pretty face and perfect lipstick and wondered what she could possibly know about romantic problems. She was a goddess. I couldn't imagine she'd had so much as a dent in her heart, let alone a straight down the middle, keep-you-up-all-night-and-then-slap-you-in-the-face-every-morning-when-you-wake-up break.

'It's too hard,' I replied, grabbing my wine glass and drinking, my hair still wrapped up in Jenny's fist. 'I'm going to give up on men altogether. I'll just get a load of cats, lie down on the floor and wait for one of them to fall asleep on my face and smother me. It's a good way to go.'

'Very dignified,' Kekipi said, taking the wine glass out of my hand, sloshing sauvignon blanc across the table. 'Shall we order some food? Perhaps a lot of stodgy carbs to soak up your entire bottle of wine?'

'How many wines have I had?' I asked, rocking my glass back and forth and eyeing the bottle.

'Only two,' Kekipi replied. 'You're a disgrace.'

'Feels like more.' I pushed it around the table, making Spirograph patterns in the condensation. 'Can I have more?'

'I think Mr Miller is a very interesting man,' he said, taking away my wine and then taking my hand in his underneath the table. 'And they bring things out in each other that they're not used to. I think that makes them both uncomfortable but I don't know if he's as brave as Ms Brookes here. He may well have decided he doesn't want to risk it.'

Squinting in the semi-dark of the restaurant, I zeroed in on my friend.

'Really?' I asked. 'That's what you think?'

He nodded.

Everyone had been so busy discussing me and what choices I had to make, I'd forgotten that Nick had thoughts and feelings as well.

'You think I make him uncomfortable?'

'I love that the first thing you worry about is how you make him feel,' Angela said, shaking her head. 'You should be thinking about yourself first. Didn't you hear him say that you're brave?'

'I'm brave?' I repeated, the wine washing over my anxieties and stress, dropping my brain into an internal hot tub. What if they were right? 'I'm brave. Oh my God, I'm brave.'

'You seem pretty fearless to me,' she said. 'Stop over-thinking everything and you'll see it. If there's the slightest chance that this man does regret the way he left things and is too scared or too proud or too stupid to tell you, wouldn't you want to know?'

Well, when she put it like that.

'Hell yeah!' Jenny cheered. 'Guys are wimps, babe, they compartmentalize like mofos. It's one thing to run away from your feelings in a note, it's another when they're stood on your doorstep and staring you in the face.'

'I am not going to stand on Nick's doorstep and stare him in the face,' I replied. 'I can't think of anything worse. I cannot imagine anything I would rather not do in the entire world, thank you very much.'

'That's a shame,' Kekipi said, placing my wine glass back in front of me. 'Since I know where he lives.'

'No thank you,' I said again, draining the glass. 'Wild horses couldn't drag me to Nick Miller's apartment right now. Now, what's for dinner? I'm starving.'

CHAPTER ELEVEN

'Don't just stand there, ring the bell!'

Two hours and two more bottles of wine later, I was somewhere on the Lower East Side of Manhattan, surrounded by string lights and Christmas trees and dozens of drunk people wearing high-waisted jeans, staring directly at Nick Miller's front door.

'I'm just going to tell him off,' I shouted, wrapping my too small coat tightly around my too thin jumper. This wasn't the right outfit. My hair was all wrong and I needed to check my make-up. 'I'm going to ring the bell and tell him he's an asscat and then we'll do shots.'

'It's ass*hat*,' Jenny corrected. 'But you know what, asscat is great too. You do you.'

'Cockwombling asscat,' I said, swaying on the stoop. 'I'm not doing this with you all watching. Go away.'

This had seemed like such a good idea ten minutes earlier. Well, first it felt like a terrible idea but the more I drank, the more I came around to it. Now, if I could just focus for long enough to read the numbers on the buttons, I'd be golden.

'We're not watching,' Kekipi promised, clinging to the corner of the next building and peeking around with Jenny's head buried in his armpit. 'We're leaving.'

'We're gone,' she agreed, nodding madly. 'We already left. Just ring the damn buzzer already.'

There would never be a good time for this, I realized. My hair would always be wrong. Jenny was right, press the buzzer and take back my power. I was Tess Brookes; I was in control; I could do this.

Number one, Elizabeth Ziemacki. Number two, Peters and Alimena. Number three, N. Miller. This was his apartment. This unassuming block of concrete on this unassuming and only slightly terrifying street. The twinkling lights of the city sparkled with encouragement at my back and a rowdy drunk man unleashed a torrent of filth at a parked car.

'We'll be right here,' Angela called, hustling Jenny and Kekipi away from the curb and into the bar next to Nick's place. 'Text us from the toilet to let us know you're not dead.'

'Why would I be dead?' I muttered, taking a step forward and immediately skidding on a patch of black ice, just grabbing hold of the door before I could fall.

'OK,' I called back, clinging to the door handle. 'I will text you.'

Glancing over my shoulder, I saw them stumble through a glowing doorway, a blast of warm air and laughter and music swallowing them up. Maybe I should go with them, I thought. Maybe I should have one more drink.

'You're overthinking it,' I scolded myself. 'Just ring the damn bell and stop being a baby. A drunk baby.'

My fingertips were numb from the cold and my face

was warm from the wine but at least I was funny, I told myself.

'Ring the bell!'

I turned around to see Jenny hanging out the door of the bar.

'Sorry.' Angela ran out and shoved her back inside. 'She's a bloody nightmare when she's had a couple.'

As the door to the bar slammed shut, I closed my eyes and took a deep breath that was rudely cut short by the bitterly cold air catching in my throat. Of all the ways I'd imagined this scene playing out, half-cut on a downtown Manhattan doorstep, wearing a sleeping bag with sleeves and eyeliner I'd applied in the back of a town car that was carrying a broken camera inside a family-sized bag of brown rice in its boot had not featured in my top ten.

He was in there. Nick Miller was behind this door. And up some stairs. And behind at least one other door – but the point was, he was only moments away from me. I was buzzing with excitement and nerves and what might happen next. I wished Amy was there. Amy would know what to do.

'Amy would press the doorbell and bloody well run away,' I whispered to myself. 'So just do it and it's done.'

Closing my eyes, holding my breath, I jabbed the doorbell hard.

And nothing happened.

My anticipatory high fizzled into disappointment.

He wasn't home? How dare he not be home?

Staring at the buzzer, I jabbed it again. And again and again.

'Hello?'

A woman's voice answered. If the black ice hadn't

been so treacherous, I probably would have made a run for it. Unless Nick had undergone some extreme hormone treatment in the last twenty-four hours, that definitely wasn't him, but then nothing would really surprise me any more.

'You pressed the wrong button,' I said with a sigh. 'Because you're an idiot.'

And so I tried again. Deep breath, open eyes, press the buzzer.

'Who is this?'

So there was one thing that could still surprise me. The same woman's voice crackled over the intercom.

'Hello?' she asked again, all American and annoyed and inside my Nick's apartment. 'Elizabeth, I swear, if that's you and you've forgotten your key again, I'm going to rip you a new one.'

Who was Elizabeth? And why was she always forgetting her key?

'I'm not buzzing you in. You can stay down there and freeze to death.'

Whoever this was, she sounded like a real charmer.

'I . . . it's not Elizabeth,' I said, fumbling for the right words. Which was pointless because there were none. 'Sorry. I'm in the wrong place.'

'Hey, there's some weirdo downstairs,' I heard the woman call out to someone. 'Can you go check it out? He sounds wasted.'

He? Cheeky cow. Somewhere above me, I heard a shuffling noise and a flurry of frozen snow fell from a disturbed windowsill and hit me in the face as I looked up. I watched as a window on the fifth floor slid upwards and a face peered down at me.

'Hey you,' it called. 'Get the fuck off our stoop.'

Black ice be damned! I turned on my heel and ran as fast as I could along the street dark street. The fear of seeing Nick in his apartment with another woman was far greater than my fear of breaking my neck.

Once I staggered over to the street corner, I grabbed hold of a signpost and considered my options, heart racing. I could go back and talk to Nick like a grown-up, I could find Kekipi in the bar, laugh about what had just happened then drink until I destroyed an awful lot of brain cells or I could jump into the first taxi that drove past, hide under the covers and obsess over the fact that Nick had moved on, he didn't love me, he never had loved me, and cry myself to sleep.

Really, there was only one sensible decision as far as I could tell.

The taxi stopped outside Al's house but I didn't want to go inside, not just yet. Actually, that wasn't true. I only wanted to go inside because it was bloody freezing but Amy was still at work and the last thing I needed was one of Al's pep talks. I didn't want to be peppy; I wanted to wallow. Between the wine and the photoshoot and the wine and the doorbell incident and the wine, I was too worked up. My stomach was in knots and my dinner was in danger of making a second appearance in my day if I didn't calm down. I needed five minutes to myself to decompress.

Looking both ways, even though I knew by now the traffic only ran south, I crossed the road as quickly as I could and ran down to the gates of the park. Locked. I gazed between the iron bars, looking in on the lamplit pathways that sparkled silver in the night. I followed the footpath through the trees until it disappeared under a gently curving bridge. My fingers tingled as I reached for my camera until I remembered it wasn't there. It was in the back of a car downtown, hopefully drying out. But the light was too beautiful for me to walk away, I had to try to capture it, there had to be a way. I still had my phone, didn't I?

'This is too perfect,' I said, leaning against the wall, my feet slipping in the snow. 'Who locks up a public park?'

But since when did I let a padlock and no camera get in my way of taking photos of a gated park? Pushing up my sleeves, I hoisted myself up on top of the wall with steely determination. If Amy could climb over the security fence at Wembley arena to get five minutes face to face with Justin Timberlake, I could break into Central Park.

'OK, I'm OK,' I muttered, hoisting one leg across the wall and hurling myself over. I hadn't anticipated that the drop on the other side would be quite so far, but once I'd stood up, dusted myself down and made sure there were no broken bones, I was really quite pleased with myself. This could make a great story, I thought, envisioning myself at the Spencer Gallery, swanning around in a dress I didn't yet own and regaling the assembled crowds with my hilarious tale of breaking into Central Park to secure the snap.

'You climbed over the wall in the snow?' someone would ask, astonished and delighted. 'That's dedication.'

'And so worth the risk of a broken ankle,' someone else would add. 'This is the most astonishing work in the whole show.'

'Why, thank you.' I bowed my head graciously at the tree in front of me. 'I've always sought to find truth and beauty in my subjects but the truth of the matter is, the park was so beautiful, I couldn't not take its picture. Do you know, I actually took this with my iPhone! Ah ha-ha-ha-ha-ha.'

But once I was over the wall and inside the grounds, something had changed. I couldn't find the same shot now that I was on the ground and the light had shifted.

'I can't make adorable puns about *this* in front of complete strangers,' I said, looking through my viewfinder and seeing nothing but disappointment.

But I had not climbed over a wall and risked life and limb for nothing; I was not leaving without my photo. In the quiet park, the city seemed miles away. If only it could stay that way, I thought, marching through the undisturbed snowbanks, lost in my own little corner of New York City for as long as I could stand it. I stopped in front of a tall, thick-trunked tree with solid-looking branches jutting out like spokes on a wheel. If I could climb the tree and get high enough, I could get my picture. I could get a picture no one had ever taken before. It was too tempting. There had to be a million photos of Central Park in the world but the thought of capturing an image no one had ever managed to snag, ever before?

Rubbing my hands together and flexing my fingers, I grabbed hold of one of the middle branches, hoisting myself up and finding a foothold. Not too slippery, I thought, a white-hot rush of excitement pushing me on. All the tension I'd felt in the cab uptown shot through my arms and legs, helping me climb higher and higher, my lips pressed together with steely determination. I kept going until the branches began to feel slender and flexible in my hands. Wedging myself in safely, I grabbed my phone out of my pocket and searched for my shot.

'There,' I said, satisfied I hadn't risked my life for nothing. The picture really was special, a million shades of black and white, touched by silver as the park glittered for no one but me. Fifteen feet off the ground, wrapped around a tree in what felt like the last garden in Manhattan, I couldn't have felt further away from my old life. Charlie, the job offer, Amy's flat, my family, even Nick – it was all background noise. Up here I was just Tess, taking a photo. I felt calm and I felt safe.

At least I did until I heard footsteps in the park below me.

'Fuck a duck,' I whispered.

What on earth was I thinking? Who broke into a park at night? It was locked for a reason! It was almost as though I hadn't spent the last six weeks staying up too late just so I could watch New York crime procedurals on random digital channels. And this was a perfect holiday special, three days before Christmas: stupid tourist sneaks into the park to climb a bloody tree in the middle of the night. Well, at 10 p.m. but still, it was late and I was an idiot and now I was going to die.

My mother was going to be so annoyed.

Directly beneath me, I heard snow crunching and then silence.

Because the murderer is waiting for you to come down, I told myself. Even he's not stupid enough to actually climb a tree in Central Park in the snow.

I looked down to see a human shape loitering underneath my tree, turning in circles and shining a torch into the darkness.

'Miss?' a voice called out. 'This is Officer Hawkins of the NYPD. You do know it is an offence to be in the park after dark?'

I thought about arguing with him: I hadn't seen a sign and I was only a visitor, after all, but even the most stupid person would have to admit the locked gate was a bit of a giveaway. And so instead of calling politely to the officer and attempting to explain my predicament, I stayed up in the top of my tree, completely silent.

The policeman's radio fuzzed in the semi-dark but I couldn't make out the message.

'Copy that,' the officer said. 'I can't see anything. Maybe it was a big dog.'

A big dog? How big a dog were they used to seeing in this bloody park?

'Or a couple of raccoons.'

The sheer indignity.

'I'm heading back your way, over.'

Relieved that the policeman was leaving, I loosened my grip slightly and looked back down at the deserted ground. How big were raccoons, anyway? And they weren't violent, were they? Slowly, I stuck out a foot and attempted to find the next branch down. Enough of this stupid adventure, I told myself, it was time I was on my way home instead of on my way to hospital. I'd let my travel insurance policy expire and I'd heard no end of horror stories from my mother about what happened when Cheryl from Asda had to have her appendix out in Florida.

But I couldn't find the next branch. No matter where I stuck my foot, I couldn't find anything. I was stuck up a tree in Central Park with the temperature dropping every second and two police officers and a pack of rabid raccoons out to get me. With one arm wrapped around the trunk of the tree, I squeezed my thumb against the touch ID to unlock my phone and pressed the first number I had on speed dial.

'Amazing timing, I'm almost home,' Amy answered immediately. 'Are you still out? Should I come and meet you?'

'Sort of,' I said, my voice still low in case the police officer or the raccoons were within earshot. 'And yes please!'

'Where are you?' she asked. 'I'm getting really weird static on the line.'

'I'm in Central Park and I'm stuck up a tree,' I replied. 'I'm drunk and I'm scared raccoons are going to eat me and I can't get down.'

Amy sighed.

'I'll be there in five minutes or so,' she said. 'Don't fall out and break your neck.'

'I'll try,' I promised.

Five minutes seemed like an awfully long time.

'Are you going to explain to me why you're up there?' Amy asked from the foot of the tree, four minutes later.

'I was trying to take a photo,' I explained. Of course Amy hadn't asked how or why I'd broken into the park in the first place, just why I'd decided to climb a tree. 'And then a policeman came and I got stuck.'

Whatever frustrated energy had propelled me up the tree had disappeared and I couldn't move my foot even an inch.

'I can't move,' I said, closing my eyes and clinging tightly to the trunk of the tree. 'I'm stuck.'

'Was he hot?' she asked.

'I don't know,' I called down. 'But I do know we can get arrested for being in here if he finds us.'

'Hurry up and get down then,' she hissed. 'You know I'm usually the first one to suggest a fun sleepover in a jail cell but I've got the presentation tomorrow and if we have to ask Kekipi to bail us out again, we might get sacked from being his bridesmaids.'

'Getting up was easy,' I said. 'I can't see my way back down. I'm going to fall, it's too slippery.'

'It's fine,' she sighed. 'Don't think about it, just do it. One foot after the other, I won't let you fall. I'm here.'

With a deep breath, I loosened my grip on the top branch, eventually finding something solid a couple of feet below. Slowly, I picked up my left foot and lowered myself down.

'There you go,' Amy cheered. 'The first one was the hardest. You're almost down.'

'I am not almost down!' I replied, staring at the lights flickering on and off in the skyscrapers across the park. 'Don't patronize me.'

'All right,' she said. 'You're still a good twelve feet up a frozen tree. Try not to kill yourself and I'll see you back at the house.'

'I hate you,' I muttered under my breath, knowing full well she wouldn't leave me. 'Don't look at my arse.'

'It's basically blocking out the moon,' she assured me. 'I can't miss it.'

The sturdy branches I'd grabbed on the way up the tree all disappeared on the way down, replacing themselves with rubber chickens and icicles that threatened to bend and snap every time I put any weight on them at all. A couple of feet from the ground my foot slipped out from under me and I felt my whole body slam against the trunk of the tree, my knees taking the brunt of the hit and branches in my hands snapping clean off the tree, skinning my palms as I went.

'There you go!' Amy clapped as I collapsed onto my hands and knees at the bottom of the tree. 'You're down!'

'What happened to "I won't let you fall, I've got you"?' I asked, rising to my feet and brushing off my filthy hands.

'Oh yeah,' she replied, scratching her nose. 'I suppose that bottom bit did sort of count as a fall. It was a dead classy one though, well done you.'

'Whatever,' I said with a sigh as she wrapped her arm around my waist and helped me hobble back towards the path. 'Thank you. I really did think I was going to be stuck up there all night.'

'I don't know what possessed you to get up there in the first place,' she said. 'That's the sort of stupid thing I would do.'

'I went to Nick's apartment and a woman answered his intercom,' I said. 'And I'd had wine. All of the wine. Well, four glasses, that's a lot for me.'

'That's all the wine as far as you're concerned,' Amy replied. 'I thought maybe something had gone wrong at the shoot.'

'Oh, it did,' I nodded, picking bits of dirt and bark out of my palms. 'It really did. But climbing the tree was a stupid reaction to seeing another woman in Nick's place. Getting so smashed at dinner that I thought going to Nick's apartment in the first place would be a good idea was because the shoot went so badly.'

'So what you're telling me is, you've had a busy day,' she surmised. 'Cup of tea and a bag of Maltesers?'

'You wouldn't kid a girl, would you?' I asked, limping towards the streetlights.

'I've got a secret stash under the bed,' she said. 'I cleaned out Heathrow on the way over.'

'I love you,' I said. 'Take me to your chocolate.'

'What are best friends for?' Amy asked. 'Now, one more time, was the police officer hot or not?'

CHAPTER TWELVE

The next morning, I woke to find a cold cup of tea on the nightstand beside me, alongside a bottle of Advil and a bottle of water. Amy was nowhere to be seen.

It only seemed like moments since I'd fallen into bed and no part of me wanted to get up. But once my eyes were open, the last twenty-four hours came flooding back, whether I liked it or not. Grumbling quietly to myself, I opened the headache tablets and shook two into my hand, only whining the tiniest bit when I struggled to open the bottle of water. As much as I might have wanted to, there was no time for wallowing. I need to fix my camera, I needed to find a computer with Photoshop so I could edit the *Gloss* photos and I needed to figure out what the flip I was going to do about my picture for the Spencer Gallery exhibition. The man I had spoken to at the gallery had assured me I could hand-deliver it as late as the twenty-fourth but that only gave me twenty-four hours and almost every photo I had taken since I arrived was on my broken laptop.

Picking my jeans up from the floor, ignoring how crusty

they felt against my skin, I pulled them on, and grabbed a soft blue jumper from the armchair. I'd seen Amy wearing it as a dress, which meant it would likely be the perfect length for me. There were occasional upsides to having a friend who was almost a foot shorter than you, not many perhaps, but this was one of them.

Slicking lip balm on my dry, chapped lips and tying up my hair, I gave my reflection a determined look. It was time to go and see a man about a camera.

'Ah, Ms Brookes.'

Tony the Driver sat at the kitchen table, surrounded by sections of a newspaper and a mug of coffee so big I could have dunked my head in it. And it took all my restraint not to.

'I just dropped Ms Smith off at the Armory. It's nice having another early riser around, I'm going to miss her when you guys leave.'

It was very odd to hear someone refer to Amy as an early riser. My Amy preferred not to get out of bed until McDonald's had stopped serving their breakfast menu so she could start her day with a nice, healthy McChicken Sandwich. This new New York Amy was a different creature altogether.

'Your rice is over there,' Tony said, waggling his eyebrows up and down and nodding towards the kitchen counter. 'I got my fingers crossed for you.'

'Thank you,' I said, holding my breath and picking up my camera. 'I really appreciate this.'

'Not my first rodeo,' he assured me. 'Miss Cecelia went through a bunch of cellphones before I learned this trick. If only there had been a way to stop her puking in the back of my car when I went to pick her up . . .'

'Nice.' I picked up the camera and weighed it in my hands. It felt OK and it looked OK. Tony brought his mug of coffee to his lips and held it there, not drinking as he watched. Wincing, I pressed down on the power button and endured the longest half-second of my life.

'Yes!' Tony yelled, spilling his coffee as the camera whirred into life.

'Oh, thank God,' I breathed out as I began to scroll through the previous day's photos. 'I don't think I've ever been so happy.'

'What about the computer?' he asked.

I looked down at my sad MacBook and tried not to cry, but there had to be a chance, didn't there? Emboldened by my success with the camera, I jabbed at the power button and prayed for the irritating chime to tell me it was still alive.

But the chime didn't come. The screen stared up at me, blank and vacant, with no signs of life.

'I'm calling it,' Tony said. 'Time of death, eight twenty-three. Fifty-fifty ain't bad, kiddo.'

'I know,' I replied, choking down a sob. If the laptop was broken, the photos were useless. I knew there was a computer in Al's office but I doubted he had the programs I needed and I really, really needed them. What's more, I really, really needed a laptop full stop. 'Looks like I'm going shopping.'

'You need a ride?' he asked. 'Because I know a guy who has a car.'

'I might.' I tried a half-smile while calculating how much room was left on my credit card. I'd worked so hard to get out of debt, all my student loans paid off, all my credit cards cleared and now I was more in the red than I'd ever been. 'Thank you.'

'Gimme twenty minutes,' he said. 'And I'll run you to the Apple Store.'

'I might go and sort myself out then.' I looked down at my cobbled together outfit and scraped-back hair. 'The Apple Store is going to be busy, isn't it?'

'Pretty busy,' he nodded.

'And if I have to prostitute myself to get a new computer, I'm going to have to look half decent,' I said, cradling my sad electronics under my arm and heading back upstairs.

Without the will to try much harder than a hairbrush and some mascara, I was ready inside five minutes and didn't think Tony wanted to sit and watch me sob over a broken computer while he read his morning paper. Wrapped up in my borrowed coat, I shuffled upstairs to Al's roof terrace, blinking into the early morning sunshine without my sunglasses. We hadn't had any snow overnight and the air wasn't so cold, just sharp and electric. High up on the rooftop, I looked out over Central Park and felt a burst of something I couldn't quite put my finger on. Despite my frustration and underlying sense of doom, there was something else. I followed the pathways of the park with my eyes, looking for my tree, trying to spot where I had hopped over the wall, but I couldn't quite work it out.

Not that it mattered. There was plenty to see. The office buildings, apartments and hotels that lined the park jutted up and down, breaking up the bright blue of the sky with sharp grey lines, and on top of Al's townhouse, standing in silence above everyone else, at eye level with concrete giants, even in my current predicament I felt untouchable. It was as though last night was a million years ago, a sad scene from a bad movie. Something like that could never happen to someone who lived here.

The ordered cityscape gave way to a winter wonderland, all rolling hills and twisting trees dropped right in the middle of the structured streets. North and south, east and west – where else in the world could these two things exist so perfectly together? You would think walking out of your door to be swallowed up by this fantasy every single day would have been amazing, but as I watched the people below walking their dogs and rushing off to work, every single one of them had their heads down. I was the only one who could see how special it all was, as though Central Park had been made only for me, a magical world in the centre of a city and the real world seemed very, very far away. When I looked down on the park, it was like falling into a fairy tale.

I turned my camera on again, still relieved when it whirred into life, and tried to find the perfect shot but it was too much, too vast. I wanted to take hold of the whole city and wrap it up in a bow but my camera could only capture tiny parcels at a time and it wasn't enough.

My eyes stung from the early morning sun and the wind that whipped around the edge of the terrace burned my cheeks, chasing me away to a group of comfy-looking couches surrounded by outdoor heaters around the corner where a giant gas barbecue just waited to be fired up.

Settling myself on the sofa, I remembered one winter's day back when I was little, before my dad left and when my mum still smiled easily. For reasons that didn't need explaining to a six-year-old, Dad decided to cook Sunday dinner on the barbecue in the garage, with two feet of snow covering the garden. I remembered me and minia-ture Amy laughing like mad things, running back and forth from the garden to the kitchen, puffing out big clouds of frozen air and jumping from foot to foot while we waited for the next round of chicken drumsticks to be declared ready. I remembered thinking it was the most wonderful, ridiculous and spectacular thing that had ever happened.

I made a mental note to make sure we found time for a rooftop barbecue in the snow before we left for Milan and wondered what six-year-old Tess would make of all this. A little girl who couldn't even process the wonder of barbecuing out of season, sat on the roof of a town-house in New York, spending Christmas on the Upper East Side before flying to Milan for the wedding of her Hawaiian gay best friend. It didn't seem quite possible. Things like that didn't happen to people like me.

I opened my emails, hoping to find something inspiring, but instead I was faced with a message from my least favourite Spencer twin, demanding to know when she could expect my edited photos. My stomach rumbled, rolling in on itself and settling somewhere around my feet. Rather than dwell on things that made me want to lemming myself off the top of the townhouse, I opened a message from Paige, a forward of the daily *Belle* email blast with the subject header *Bertie Bennett Rides Again*. This had to be from the interviews he'd been doing the day before, I realized, happily clicking through, hoping to find something cheerful to brighten my morning.

> *Bertie Bennett, one of the fashion world's most*
> *colourful characters, returns to New York today with*
> *an off-season presentation of AJB, the first fashion*

collection designed by the retail magnate-turned-recluse.

Recluse was a bit harsh, I thought. He had lost his wife and he had been cursed with a shithead for a son. I imagined most people would choose to hang out in their beautiful Hawaiian holiday home for a bit if they had the option after all that.

Bennett was the mastermind behind Bennett's department store, beginning in Manhattan in the early seventies and expanding worldwide, bringing high fashion to people across the globe. Bennett's late wife, Jane, was known for working with young designers in each Bennett's territory, acting as mentor and patron and giving them space in their stores to sell their early collections. Many of today's leading designers owe their start in the industry to the Bennett family and there is no doubt that today's launch has been the most highly anticipated date in the fashion calendar ever since Bennett announced his debut collection at a special event in Milan this summer.

While few were surprised to see Bennett colouring outside the lines – the retailer-turned-designer will likely be remembered for his legendary parties as much as his revolutionary impact on the retail landscape – whispers inside the industry have cast doubt on whether or not Bennett should run the risk of tarnishing his legacy by branching out into design. It is understood the collection draws heavily on designs created by Jane Bennett, which some fear will appear dated, in spite of AJB design head (and long-time Bennett family friend) Edward Warren's influence. Added to this, the appointment of Amy Smith, a newcomer to the fashion industry, as VP of Special Projects has certainly caused raised eyebrows. For the past decade, the Bennett retail empire has been primarily run by Bennett's son, Archie, and even though age has no bearing on a designer's sensibilities (Bennett Senior still clocks in several years younger than a certain Mr Lagerfeld), his absence from the fashion world and the potential disconnect from his wife's dated designs has caused some to speculate as to how well equipped he might be to understand today's buyer.

Tonight, at New York's Park Avenue Armory, the fashion world will discover whether AJB will be Bennett's greatest success or his deepest regret.

Well, I thought. That wasn't very nice. And why was an entire industry raising its eyebrows at Amy? Sure, she had no fashion industry stuff on her CV and, OK, her retail experience was a little bit patchy and primarily consisted of a couple of Christmas shifts on the checkout in Woolworths but she wasn't the reason it had gone under. Probably. For all they knew she was an amazing VP of Special Projects. And actually, I realized, she was.

I went back to the original email from Paige and noticed the sad face above the link. I replied with a considered and succinct 'bollocks to this' and hoped against hope that Amy and Al were both too busy to have checked their inboxes that morning.

Looking at my watch, I realized it was almost time to hurl myself deeper in debt at the altar of Apple, but before I could heave myself up off the sofa I heard the lift ping as the doors opened and watched as Al trudged slowly over to the edge of the terrace. I opened my mouth to say hello but as he turned to stare out over the city, I saw an unfamiliar look on his face and my mouth snapped shut. His eyes were puffy and his nose was red.

'Oh, Janey,' he said, taking a deep breath and then leaning over the wall. The cityscape didn't seem to have the same effect on Al that it had on me. 'I cannot believe you're not here today.'

He shook his head.

'I could really use your advice now,' he said, wiping a calloused thumb against his cheek and stretching his long legs out behind him. Even in this weather, Al could not be parted from his beloved board shorts. 'I feel like such an old fool. What am I doing?'

Even though I knew he was in his seventies and his white beard and frothy head of hair were hard to miss, it had never occurred to me that Al was old. We'd met on a surfing beach in Hawaii, me stumbling along the sand and Al leaping out of the waves with more spring in his step than your average Slinky, but today, he looked fragile and, for the first time, I realized he could break. He looked like something that could be broken. Without thinking, I picked up my camera and snapped.

'Morning,' I called, the weight of my camera around my neck nothing but a relief. 'Have you been out here long? I was so busy with my camera, I didn't see you there.'

'Ahh, Tess.' A bright smile came over his face and whatever I had seen through the camera disappeared. Or he did a really good job of covering it up. 'I should have known you'd have found your way up here. It really is the only place to find some solitude in this city.'

'Not the only place,' I said, glancing down at the park.

'But definitely the most accessible. Are you excited about the presentation tonight?'

He nodded and looked down at his shorts and ratty fisherman's jumper. 'I imagine they're going to expect me to get changed.'

'Me too,' I replied. 'I can't wait to see the final collection. Amy won't tell me anything – she says I'm going to have to see it to believe it.'

'It's going to be quite the spectacular,' he confirmed. 'I'm very proud of her.'

I rested my elbows on the edge of the terrace beside him and stared straight ahead, wondering whether or not he had already seen the article.

'You must be missing Jane a lot today,' I said, slightly awkwardly. 'I bet it's weird doing all this without her.'

Al smiled and nodded slowly. 'It's all for her,' he said. 'And she's not here to see it. I have to admit, the nerves have been growing over the last couple of days. I'm starting to wonder if perhaps this was a slightly rash decision.'

'But you wanted to do it, didn't you?' I asked.

'I did,' he confirmed. 'I do. But it's a huge risk. I've tied quite a lot of money up in the venture and I'm not entirely sure why. I'm an old man, Tess. I could be back on the beach in Hawaii right now, not bothering myself with starting over.'

'That's true,' I agreed, curling my fingers to hide my grubby fingernails. 'But I think this is going to be worth it. Hawaii will still be there when you get home.'

'It will,' he said, patting my hand then stretching his arms high overhead. 'Where are you off to at such an early hour?'

'Oh, just some last-minute shopping,' I said, shaking

my head at the task at hand. 'I'll be all shiny and new for the presentation.'

'Sounds fun,' he said. If only he knew how wrong he was. 'Janey loved to shop.'

'Convenient, given that you owned a load of shops,' I commented. He smiled but his usual gruff chuckle was nowhere to be heard. 'Are you all right up here?' I asked. 'I could always go out later if you fancy a chat?'

I couldn't really, but I also couldn't bear to see him in so much pain. Al was my oracle, and not knowing how to defend him against these awful magazine mares, let alone his own demons, was the worst.

'No, no.' He shook his head and shooed me away. 'All I need is ten minutes to clear my head. And several cups of tea, I should think.'

'I'll ask Genevieve to get the kettle on,' I promised, resting my hand on his arm. 'Are you sure you're OK?'

'More than,' he promised. 'Now off with you. I'm sure you have a lot of fun adventures planned, so don't waste your day on a sulky old man.'

'Adventures,' I agreed weakly. 'I suppose you could call them that.'

Tony was right. The Apple Store on Fifth Avenue was busy. So busy, in fact, that I had to join a line of people queueing up around the bizarre glass cube that sat on Fifth Avenue, marking out the subterranean retail wonder below. Charlie would love this, I thought, as I inched towards the staircase. Not the queueing, per se, but the ridiculous design of the store and the overexcited tech heads would send him into gadget-geek overdrive. He always had the newest phone as soon as it came out, was always updating mine to the latest operating system.

He was on the list for an Apple watch before I even knew what an Apple watch was. In all honesty, I still wasn't entirely certain.

'You on Yosemite?'

I looked up to see a young woman with lilac hair looking at me as though she would rather be anywhere else on earth.

'Sorry?' I said politely. 'Did you mean me?'

'Yeah?' she replied. 'Are you on Yosemite?'

'I don't know what that means,' I said as we trudged another step forward en masse.

There was something very unsettling about standing in a crowd of people in the snow, all moving one step at a time and willingly walking into an underground bunker just because a man with a Madonna-esque earpiece told us too.

'The operating system?' Every sentence out of her mouth was phrased a question. 'For your computer?'

'Oh, I don't know,' I admitted. 'I'd had mine a while but my friend always updated it for me. It's broken, actually, that's why I'm here.'

'Yeah?' she replied, flicking her unlikely coloured hair over her shoulder and into the face of the man behind. 'I have to pick mine up? I ordered it online because I need, like, super specific specifications? This is way closer to the G?'

I understood about 50 per cent of what she had said to me but I was too scared to tell her.

'I just need a laptop that will run Photoshop.' I was determined to hold up my end of the conversation without coming off like a total loser. She could only be five years younger than me, tops. I was only twenty-seven; it wasn't like I had one foot in the grave just yet.

'Pro or Air?' Lilac Hair asked, her eyes lighting up. 'Or are you getting the new MacBook?'

'I don't know, I'm a photographer.' I said, my tongue still tripping over the word. 'I just need something to edit on.'

'You want a Pro,' she said with complete confidence. 'That's what I use for my photography.'

'You're a photographer too?' I was cheered to find some common ground that might help us converse like normal people, rather than leave me feeling like her nana.

'I have a blog?' she shrugged. 'I shoot for my blog but I don't like to label myself. I write also, but I mostly use my Air for that or my tablet, depending on how much travelling I'm doing?'

'Right,' I said as the group took another step forward. Did anyone really need that many computers? 'Do you work nearby?'

She looked at me, gone out. 'I, like, don't have a desk job?' she said with a sniff. 'I'm an artist.'

I pursed my lips together. An artist. Right.

'My mom is getting me an iMac for Christmas?' she explained. 'What camera do you have? I need to upgrade soon?'

I pulled my Canon out of my bag and held it up for inspection.

'Dude.' She tried to smother a splutter of laughter. 'That's so funny – I have one of those as my back-up shooter. You use that, like, for real?'

'Oh look,' I said, as we shuffled to the top of the stair-case. 'We're almost down. Well, enjoy your computer.'

Lilac Hair sniffed and looked away while I concentrated hard on the floor, more worried about this purchase than ever. How could a twenty-two-two-year-old artist with purple hair and no real job have three computers, an iPad and two cameras when I was twenty-seven and driving myself into debt just to own one laptop?

'Hi, welcome to the Apple Store!' a far-too-cheerful voice boomed as I hit the bottom of the stairs and watched Lilac Hair disappear into the crowd. 'How can I help you today?'

'I need a laptop,' I said, in my best, most polite English accent. 'Please.'

His face fell a little and I noticed the badge on his shirt read 'genius'. Thank God for that, I thought, it really would help if one of us had a clue what they were doing.

Several hours and a credit-card-cancelling amount of money later, I had managed to transfer the photos from my destroyed machine onto my brand, spanking-new laptop and pull together something resembling a passable selection of images from the *Gloss* shoot. It was already after three when I looked at the clock after transferring them over to the magazine's FTP site for Cici and Angela's approval, so I had less than four hours until the presentation and I was still wearing my dirty jeans and borrowed sweater dress; while that could pass for bohemian chic in the Apple Store, I had a feeling it wouldn't cut it at the AJB presentation. Amy had warned me she would be incommunicado all day, preparing for the presentation, and after seeing how upset Al had been that morning, I didn't think it would be a good time to ask if it was all right to rifle through his dead wife's closet for a frock to borrow. But who else did I know in America who had access to fancy dresses and wouldn't mind loaning one out for the evening? After getting Kekipi's voicemail three times in a row, I fished around in the bottom of my handbag for the next best thing Manhattan had to a fairy gayfather. My snow-shoot saviour fairy godmother and fashion PR maven . . .

'Jenny Lopez.'

A true professional, she answered on the second ring.

'It's Tess,' I said, fingers, legs and toes all crossed. 'Tess Brookes. I was wondering if I might be able to bother you for a favour?'

'Man, I am wasted in PR,' Jenny muttered, as a very skinny man with black skin and a pink Mohawk reached out with a lip brush to dab at my mouth one more time before setting it down on the desk and taking a small bow. 'You are a babe.'

'She's perfection,' he declared. 'Even I'm impressed.'

'Am I done?' I asked, struggling to hold my eyes open under the weight of my false eyelashes. 'Do I look OK?'

'Doll . . .' She flipped her caramel highlights over her shoulder and gave me everything but a finger snap. 'What a dumb thing to ask! Go look at yourself in the mirror. Razor is a master with a mascara wand.'

'I love my work,' he said modestly. 'But this is impressive, even for me.'

'Oh sweet Jesus,' I gasped, pressing my hands against my heart. 'Is that me?'

I'd walked into Jenny's office wearing my sleeping-bag coat, dirty Converse, and a smile. After sixty very committed minutes with a pair of very hot hair straighteners, my bushy curls had transformed into liquid copper that trickled over my shoulder in Veronica Lake waves that I couldn't quite believe while another thirty minutes in make-up had left my skin glowing and my eyes sparkling. I looked like an Instagram filter come to life. It was still me, only Photoshopped and soft filtered, and I barely dared move.

'I can't wear this,' I said, completely still. If I moved and the girl in the mirror moved at the same time, I was worried the world would end. It had to be a glitch in the matrix. 'It's too much. Isn't it too much?'

'Girl, you're going to a party with me – there is no such thing as too much,' Jenny replied, appearing in the mirror behind me and grabbing hold of my shoulders. 'Repeat after me: I am Tess Brookes.'

'I am Tess Brookes,' the girl in the mirror said.

'I look incredible.'

'I look incredible,' she echoed.

'I am a badass bitch,' Jenny said.

'Yeah – no! I can't say that out loud,' I cringed. 'But I'm thinking it.'

'Fine,' Jenny clucked. 'Let's finish with "when I need to use the bathroom, I will give Jenny ten minutes' notice because I am wearing two pairs of Spanx."'

'Only two?' I turned to the side and marvelled at the power of well-made clothes. 'This dress is incredible.'

And it was. As dazzled as I was by my hair and make-up, I'd seen my face a million times before. This dress was a one-off. The silk chiffon gown sparkled with rose gold sequins, or *pailettes* as Jenny insisted they were called, catching the light and ringing with sparkles every time I breathed. Through the wonder of amazing tailoring it clung to my curves but never accentuated my chub, nipping my waist to improbably tiny proportions and dipping low on the front to suggest tasteful cleavage rather than tons of boob. Soft straps slipped over my shoulders, forming a deep V in the back while matching strips of rose-gold chiffon floated out behind me, meeting somewhere around my perfectly lifted backside to create a romantic train.

'I feel like I want to propose,' Razor said, clasping his hands together under his chin. 'And I'm so gay I hit on my preschool teacher.'

'I'm not sure the camera goes with it,' Jenny said, shaking her head at my refusal to put my newly fixed camera down, even for the evening. 'But you look so good I don't even feel bad that I'm not wearing it.'

'This was yours?' I spun around, the train swishing behind me, eliciting a gasp and clap from Razor. 'Oh, Jenny, I can't take it. I'll wear something else. Seriously, you take it.'

'Your need is greater,' she said with great benevolence. 'It's what Oprah would want. Also, I'm pretty sure this is the only thing I have that will fit you, so shut up and wear it, OK?'

'OK,' I relented, swishing lightly from side to side, watching the light catch the sequins. Sorry, *pailettes*. 'It's soooo pretty! Who is it by?'

'It isn't pretty, it's a masterpiece,' she corrected, flipping out my train. 'And you don't know who it's by? It's AJB, you dumbass. It's Al's.'

I looked at myself again. Of course it was from Al's collection. The dress was exquisite. Defiantly feminine; flattering beyond belief, and timelessly vintage. It would have been just as at home in Janey's wardrobe in the sixties as it would on the red carpet at the Oscars. With a sad smile I thought back to the moment on the terrace and wished with all of my heart that I had said more. It was crazy to think that Al was in any way anxious, his work was stunning. Even if he *had* read that thing in *Belle*, surely someone as confident and sure of himself as Al wouldn't care. Tonight could only be a huge success.

'Hey, Miss Thing!' Jenny snapped her fingers to get my attention. 'When you've finished falling in love with yourself, you can sit your ass down. I still have to get ready and we're leaving in, like, thirty minutes. Can you be trusted not to eff up your dress before then?'

'If I sit very still,' I said, nodding solemnly as I backed onto an office chair. 'I can try.'

'You're already an easier project than Angie,' she said with a sigh. 'Do. Not. Move.'

Every year my company had gone to the annual advertising awards at this plush hotel in London. It was a fancy do; the men all wore what they believed was black tie and the women dressed up, either in actual ballgowns if it was their first year there or the sexiest dress their boss and their self-esteem would let them get away with every year after that. When Amy said they were organizing a presentation and a party for Al's collection, I anticipated something along the lines of the advertising awards, only with more flair. I'd been to one of Al's parties before so I knew we weren't talking hotel conference room and tired canapés but what I wasn't expecting was this. Really, I had to stop underestimating the pair of them.

'You ready?' Jenny asked as the car pulled up outside a building that made the V&A feel like it wasn't quite pulling its weight in the drama stakes. Red brick, tall windows – it even had turrets. Since when had Cinderella's castle been smack bang in the middle of Manhattan? Huge banners hung on either side of the gothic wooden doors, declaring the arrival of AJB, and it was only when our driver held open my door and the

December chill hit me in the face, I realized that the photographs on them were mine.

'As I'll ever be,' I finally nodded, ignoring all the popping flashes and screaming paparazzi while keeping my eyes on the banners and my feet moving forwards.

'What's it like to be on this side of the camera?' she whispered, slipping her arm through mine as we walked the red carpet. An actual red carpet, bleeding through the snow and up the stairs into the Armory.

'I think I prefer the other side,' I replied, watching people I recognized from TV and magazines posing for the paps in dresses I recognized from Al's sketchbook. It was surreal.

'So, what's the deal?' I asked as we made our way inside and followed the crowds through the echoing halls. Music throbbed all around us and the walls were lined with twinkling fairy lights, leading us ever onwards. 'When is the actual presentation?'

Jenny cast me a look I was getting far too used to seeing.

'What are you talking about?' she asked, her skintight, floor-length black crepe grown moving with her as she walked, a thigh-high split exposing acres of perfectly toned leg.

'The presentation,' I repeated, blushing. 'Isn't Al going to stand up and, you know, tell us all about the brand?'

'I take it back,' she said. 'You are worse than Angie. A fashion presentation isn't the same as a business presentation; there won't be any slides or handouts if that's what you mean.'

Part of me was slightly disappointed. I really did love a good PowerPoint.

'It means Al is presenting his collection to the industry,

209

like a runway show only not. Instead of having models walk the runway, they kind of stand still, like statues, while buyers and media look at them.'

'How long do they have to stand still?' I asked, eyes flitting all around me. Everyone looked like someone I should know and everyone I should know looked excited.

'At a regular presentation? Two hours, maybe three.'

'Christ on a bike!' I gave a low whistle. 'And they have to stay stood for all that time? No thank you. Imagine what a ballache that would be?'

'I don't have to,' Jenny reminded me. 'I live with a model, remember? She's plenty vocal about the hardships.'

'Are they usually done like this?' I waved my gold satin clutch around at the dozens of people, dazzling in their ensembles, wending their way down the hallway to whatever awaited us all. 'Are they usually such a production?'

'Nothing is done like this,' she said with an electric smile. 'Can't you tell how psyched everyone is?'

I looked around and noticed a smile on almost every face. I was so relieved, *Belle* magazine couldn't possibly consider this a mistake and neither could Al. 'Everyone looks like they're enjoying it.'

'That's how you know this is a big deal,' she laughed and pulled me along as the music swelled all around us. 'This is New York – no one smiles in public. What would people think?'

After what felt like a million miles in four-inch heels, we came to the end of the corridor and fell through the rabbit hole.

'Bloody hell!' I whispered, craning my neck to take it all in. 'Amy Smith, you are *incredible*.'

Once upon a time, the room we found ourselves in

might have been a big, empty hangar but somehow Amy had transformed it into something else. The lights that had led the way down the hall spread out along the walls, creeping across the ceiling like strings of stars. They came together in the centre of the room around the most extraordinary chandelier I had ever seen with strands and strands of lights casting a golden glow across the room, twirling and sparkling as though it was alive. Over in one corner, surrounded by towering fir trees, decorated with the same delicate lights, I saw a black-haired man in a cage of his own, playing an acoustic guitar and singing softly, seemingly oblivious to the commotion around him.

All across the room, women stood on raised platforms, inside giant brass birdcages, the fairy lights streaming along the floor, underneath our feet and climbing up the bars of each cage. Rather than standing frozen in place like Jenny had said, the models moved around inside, some sitting on delicate wooden chairs that were woven with springs of holly and blood-red poinsettias, others swaying to the music that filled the room, each one in a different AJB Collection gown. And every one was stunning, the gowns and the women. I knew right away that Al had been involved in the casting. As well as standard issue Sadie Nixon-type knockouts, I saw just as many normal-sized women, draped in AJB's finest. Tall, short, slender and curvy: every kind of woman was represented and they all looked incredible.

I stared all around the room, taking in one thing then the next, and I couldn't believe that Amy had created anything so incredible. I was so ridiculously proud of her, I could barely stand it. All I wanted was to knock the guitar player out of his cage, grab his mic and tell everyone, 'Listen, my best friend did this!' My best friend had made a dream – a dream I didn't even know I'd had – come true.

'This is amazeballs,' Jenny said, taking a glass of champagne from a passing waiter with a heavily burdened tray. 'Your friend is killing it.'

'She is,' I agreed. 'I can't believe she's never done anything like this before. She's amazing.'

'I'll say,' she agreed. 'This is the most impressive event I've seen. And I've been to a Halloween party at Gwyneth Paltrow's house.'

Ooh!

'You have?'

She nodded and screwed up her face. 'Not nearly as nice as you'd think. Also, I totally saw Sour Patch Kids in her kitchen even though she was only serving fruit snacks. Sugar free, my ass.'

As the room filled up with equally astonished guests, I searched for a face that was familiar because they actually were someone I really knew, instead of someone I'd seen in a movie or posted on someone's Facebook wall. But Al, Amy and Kekipi were nowhere to be seen.

'Hey, I have to go say hi to a few people,' Jenny said, her hand on my bare arm. 'You OK if I leave you for a few?'

'Yes, of course,' I said, waving her away but suddenly feeling very exposed. 'I'll be right here.'

'You don't have to be,' she said, smiling. 'Go mingle. Hell, you look incredible, Tess. Go find a millionaire and marry him. Just make sure you invite me to the wedding.'

'I'll do my best,' I replied, dying to take out my phone and check for messages. But this wasn't the time. Nick hadn't been in touch and I'd more or less given up hope that he ever would but that was something to worry about afterwards. Right now, the only thing to do was to find Amy and tell her how amazing she was.

Everywhere I looked there was something new to see and treasure: small, singing birds that couldn't possibly be real, hidden in the branches of the towering Christmas trees that lined the room but looking as though they would flutter down and sit on your shoulder at any second; tiny, golden pineapples glinting in the lights, reminding me of Al's beloved island home; and, as I got closer to the walls, I saw lines and lines of elegant hand-writing. Tracing out the words with my finger, I realized what I was reading. It was wallpaper made from Janey's notebooks, her original notes and sketches, yellowing and faded with time but brought to life for everyone to see. It was such a beautiful touch that I felt tears swelling in my eyes, threatening my false lashes. Before I could destroy my make-up, I raised my camera to my face and snapped at everything I could see.

'Miss Brookes, as I live and breathe! You are beautiful.'

I looked up to see Kekipi and Domenico in matching black tuxedos, Domenico tall and striking, Kekipi shorter and dashing, both with the same expression on their faces that I knew was on my own, utterly glowing with pride.

'This old thing?' I looked down at my dress and saw it sparkling in Amy's fairy lights. Almost as if she knew. 'Chucked it on at the last minute.'

'Then I insist that you really must stop taking so much care when getting dressed every day,' Kekipi said. 'Now, tell me everything that happened from the second I left you last night. I can't believe you've made me wait all day, it's downright cruel.'

'He's done nothing but bitch about it since he bothered to get up this morning,' Domenico added. 'Please put him out of his misery before I do it for you. My way will be much more permanent.'

'Dom, you're all talk.' Kekipi rolled his eyes at his partner before turning his attention back to me. 'Now, dish. What happened?'

'You haven't talked to Amy?' I asked in disbelief. 'I thought you might have had a summit about it or something.'

'As you can probably tell,' he said, waving his hand around in the air, 'Miss Amy was really quite busy today. And I was looking after our glorious leader while you were AWOL.'

'Of course she was,' I said, gazing around in awe. 'And I wasn't AWOL. I was working and then I was getting all pretty. This was not a short process.'

'I am guessing not.' He pressed a hand to Domenico's chest. 'How long do you think it took to tame her hair? I would not have had the patience.'

'Is Al all right?' I asked, thinking that neither would I. 'Where is he?'

'I don't know, he left before us. He did seem a little less chipper than his usual self,' he said, looking to his partner for confirmation. 'What did you think?'

Domenico nodded. 'But he was 100 per cent when we left him,' he said. 'This is a big day for him. It has to be hard without Mrs Bennett.'

'Did you see the *Belle* piece?' I asked in a low voice, fully aware that any one of the well-dressed women around us could have written said take-down.

'No,' he replied, holding out his hand for my phone. 'Gimme.'

Kekipi read quickly, Domenico scanning over his shoulder, scowling as they swiped down the page.

'That is ridiculous,' he announced, handing the phone to his fiancé to finish. 'Some airy-fairy asshole has their nose out of joint because Al doesn't want to play by the rules. It was the same when Alexander Wang showed in the Brooklyn naval yard and now they're all doing it. Forget this.'

'Trash,' Domenico nodded. 'I cannot believe this came from Spencer Media.'

'I imagine Delia doesn't see every email that goes out,' I reasoned. 'But it does feel a bit harsh. Maybe Al is hiding with Amy? I can't find her anywhere.'

'Amy isn't hiding,' Kekipi said, looking surprised, pointing off to the corner. 'She's right over there.'

And there she was.

While hundreds of people milled around in extravagant outfits, drinking champagne and marvelling at Al's designs, Amy was standing in a dark corner, head to toe in black, wearing a headset, with a look of concentration on her face the likes of which I hadn't seen since she vowed to beat the mechanical claw game on Blackpool seafront in 1998. She hadn't even seemed this fazed during her maths GCSE and that was routinely referred to as one of her life's greatest tests.

'She's been here the whole time?' I asked, my heart swelling with pride.

I couldn't stop staring. She pressed a hand against her ear, talking into her microphone and checking something on the phone in her hand. Even though she was practically invisible, as far as I was concerned, Amy was the most incredible thing in the room.

'AMY!' I bellowed at the top of my voice, barrelling into her with a hug. 'This is incredible. I can't believe you did all this.'

'Tess!' She almost yanked my head off with a hug. 'I'm so glad you're here. I'm freaking out.'

'I don't know why,' I said. It once took us three weeks to build an Ikea television unit and we still buggered it up. How had she done all this by herself? 'I'm *so* proud of you.'

'There's so much going on,' she said, shaking her head. 'Al isn't here yet, the media is totally out to get us, one of the ovens is on fire so we don't have all the edibles and one of the models kept throwing up before she went in her cage. She said she was OK but what if she pukes on her dress?'

'Which one?' I asked, glancing around the room. Amy looked at me with wide, terrified eyes. 'It doesn't matter,' I corrected myself. 'She won't be sick. Everything is going to be fine. Brilliant, even. Look how impressed everyone is.'

'I'm just glad you're here,' she said, squeezing my wrist before pressing the headset against her ear and looking off behind the tallest Christmas trees in the corner. 'What's that? What do you mean they won't let her in? She's the cocking editor of *Vogue*. Of course she isn't already inside! OK, I'm on my way.' She turned to give me another quick squeeze. 'I've got to go, there's a problem at the door. I'll be back, don't go anywhere.'

'I won't,' I promised. 'Don't worry about a thing, you've got this.'

She gave me a grateful smile and then disappeared through the trees.

'Full of surprises, that one,' Kekipi said, sidling up behind me with a drink. 'But you know how it is, you can do exactly what you believe you can do. If you spend all your time telling yourself you're no good at something, you start to believe it.'

'Suppose so,' I replied. 'Or listening to other people tell you you're shit.'

'Exactly,' he nodded. 'Lesson learned?'

'I've been ruining Amy's life by not encouraging her enough?' I asked, horrified.

'Actually, I meant more like *you* don't believe in *yourself* enough, but sure,' he said, 'if the shoes fits, go ahead and wear that bitch. Now, I do believe I'm still short of a few details from the last twenty-four hours, such as what happened after you abandoned me with those terrible women who led me astray and who is responsible for this vision of beauty that stands before me?'

'It was Jenny. One of those terrible women who led you astray.' I shimmied my shoulders and watched my entire dress come to life, scintillating from head to toe. 'They must have twisted your arm so far up your back, I'm amazed you can even hold on to that glass.'

'Champagne is a miracle cure,' he declared. 'I take it all back, we can keep her.'

'He did not get home until four in the morning,' Domenico said. 'And when he did finally roll into bed, he was singing Billy Joel at the top of his voice. I do not know how you did not hear him.'

'The soundproofing in Al's houses is always wonderful,' Kekipi explained. 'And you can't be mad at me: it's impossible to go to a karaoke bar in New York and not sing "Piano Man", but that isn't the point, what happened with Mr Miller?'

'Nothing,' I said, determined to retain a stiff upper lip. My nan always told me the reason we won the war was because there was no time for crying if it would ruin her eyeliner. 'He didn't answer the door.'

It wasn't a lie.

'He didn't answer the door?' Kekipi looked suitably unimpressed.

'That's what I said. The evening was Nickless.'

'And you're going to leave it at that, are you?' Kekipi asked.

'Hello Miss Photographer to the stars.' Angela appeared at my elbow, Jenny and Delia by her side, both of them showering Kekipi with kisses. 'Your photos were perfect.'

'I don't know about perfect,' I blushed, so thankful she didn't know about all the drama that had gone into their delivery. 'I'm glad they were OK.'

'How many times do we have to tell you about this false modesty shit?' Jenny said. 'I saw them, they were ah-mazing. Own it.'

'I'm owning it, I'm owning it,' I said, accepting a hug from Delia.

She and Angela both looked stunning, Angela in a navy knee-length shimmery cocktail dress with a flared skirt and adorable white collar while Delia had stuck to her classic style and was sheathed in a floor-length black shift dress that swooped dangerously low in the back, exposing her lack of bra in a way that made me very, very jealous. Bralessness was something I had always aspired to.

'What's going on?' Jenny asked, grabbing a yummy-looking canapé from a passing waiter and nibbling at the pastry.

'Tess was just telling me how Nick wasn't home last night so she's given up trying,' Kekipi told them. 'Which is nice.'

'I haven't given up,' I argued. 'I'm taking it as divine intervention. Maybe it was a bad idea.'

'I don't think so; I think it was a test to see how committed you are,' Jenny said, her long glossy hair cascading over one bare shoulder. 'Dude, you should call him.'

'I'm not calling him because he never answers,' I explained. 'It always goes to voicemail, always. Don't you think I would have tried that by now?'

'Then forget him,' Angela added quickly, much to Jenny's visible chagrin. 'If he doesn't call, he's not worth it. You shouldn't have to chase him.'

'Nick?' Delia asked, looking confused. 'I've missed something haven't I?'

'Superhot douchebag who's giving Tess the runaround,' Jenny summarized. 'She's totally into him though.'

'Right,' Delia nodded. 'Got you.'

'You know I'm all for the rules,' Jenny went on. 'But this is different. Don't be such a buzzkill, Angie, she looks incredible, we're basically at a ball, it's almost midnight—'

'It's seven forty-five,' Domenico corrected.

'It's almost midnight,' Jenny said again, as though she could change the clocks by sheer force of will. 'You should go to his place. Reverse Cinderella this shit.'

'I say let him turn into a pumpkin and stay and have a drink,' Angela said, grabbing two pink cocktails from a tray and waving them seductively in the air. 'I happen to know my husband has some friends here tonight who are very single and only 25 per cent knobhead. That's a really good percentage for New York.'

'Never let her set you up with one of Alex's friends,' Jenny insisted. 'If they're less than 75 per cent asshole, they're fug. Go get your man. Don't take no for an answer.'

'I agree with that one,' Kekipi said, taking the spare cocktail out of Angela's hand and pointing at Jenny. 'Let's go to his place.'

'You just want to go back to the karaoke bar,' I replied. 'You're not going anywhere. Can we just stay and have a nice time, please?'

'Only if you can put your hand on your heart and tell me you're not thinking about him right now,' he said.

I clamped my lips together and gave him a look.

'You're not curious? Not even the slightest, tiniest bit intrigued as to why he's behaving like a little girl?'

'Oi,' Angela interrupted. 'That is an insult to the good name of little girls. I was quite capable of using the phone when I was little.'

'Aren't you angry?' Jenny asked, changing tactics. 'Aren't you freakin' furious? Don't you want to pin him to the wall by his balls and make him explain himself?'

'Well, yes,' I admitted. 'A bit.'

'Then don't be so damn English,' she ordered. 'I've had six years to beat those bad habits out of this one and she still apologizes to people who walk into her on the street.'

Angela peered at us over the rim of her champagne flute with guilty eyes. 'They don't mean to,' she said. 'I'm sure.'

'If I were you, I would be exploding right about now,' Jenny said, fire lighting up her eyes. 'That guy would be wishing he had never been born. Messing you around like this. Are you kidding me?'

'I suppose if I was going to see him, I wouldn't hate to see him looking like this,' I said, flipping my skirts around my ankles.

'Do you really want to do this again for another six

months?' Kekipi asked. 'Or did you enjoy spending ten years not knowing where you stood with Charlie so much, you want to do it again?'

'Not really,' I admitted.

'I really thought he might show his face,' Kekipi said, pursing his lips and surveying the room. 'I mean, he RSVP'd no but you know what he's like.'

'He was invited?' I asked, flicking my eyes from one face to the next, slightly startled by the information. There was a chance he'd be here and no one told me?

'Of course,' he replied. 'He's a journalist, we've worked with him and Al likes him. Not to mention the fact we're all aware that the two of you need all the help you can get.'

'He's not here,' I murmured, quite certain now. 'He's flying back to London tomorrow.'

'Then why are you still here?' Kekipi asked gently.

I gulped and tapped my hand fast against my heart. 'How long would it take me to get down there, do you think?'

'Not long at all,' he said. 'You've plenty of time.'

'You're not missing anything here,' Jenny said. 'This is it. You've seen it all. Go!'

'I can go and come back.' I looked over my shoulder for Amy, to say goodbye, but I couldn't see her anywhere. 'You're right, I've got to go. Will you tell Amy and Al I'll be back?'

'Of course,' he said, taking a bow as I picked up my skirts. 'They'll understand, it's all in the name of true love. Don't do anything I wouldn't do.'

'That doesn't leave much,' I said, rubbing my fingers across my forehead before Jenny slapped them away.

'I'm going,' I said, taking a deep breath and nodding to

myself. 'There are things I need to say for me, forget what he wants. I'm going to go and see him, sort this all out.'

'Amazing!' Kekipi danced on the spot, spilling his champagne. 'Go get him, girl. Or something.'

'Good luck,' Angela said, giving me a quick hug as Jenny and Kekipi high fived each other. 'This is really brave.'

'So brave,' I said to myself. 'Don't be a chicken, Tess.'

Award-winning advertising slogan for chicken cook-in sauces *and* good life advice. Maybe I was wasted in photography.

CHAPTER THIRTEEN

'Where to?' the taxi driver asked as I struggled to stuff my dress's train into his car.

'It's downtown,' I said, trying to remember the street sign I'd clung to so hopelessly the night before. 'Um, Stanford Street? Is that a place?'

'You mean Stanton?' he barked, pulling into traffic to a chorus of honks and beeps.

'Probably,' I replied as I was hurled across the back seat. Clambering upright, I grabbed hold of the seatbelt and stared. Ruin the dress or break my neck? Tough choice.

'Stanton and what?' the driver asked, changing lanes with joyous abandon. 'What's the cross street?'

'Oh,' I replied, staring out the window and watching Manhattan blur by. 'I don't know. Is it a long street?'

'You don't know?' He turned to look at me, foot still firmly on the accelerator. 'Lady, are you fuckin' kiddin' me?'

The blank look on my face was all the answer he needed.

'What, you want me to drive up and down the Lower

East Side while you try to work out where you're going?' he asked, taking a drag on a cigarette.

Rather than ask whether or not smoking while driving a taxi was legal in New York, I simply shrugged. 'That would be lovely,' I said. 'It's an apartment building next to a bar.'

'The whole damn street is an apartment building next to a bar,' he said, hammering his horn at a pedestrian stepping into the street. Silly him, imagine you could cross the street safely when you had a walk signal. 'You gotta do better or I'm kicking you out when we hit Stanton.'

'But I don't have a coat,' I protested. 'And it's freezing!'

'That makes you the dumb one, not me,' he pointed out. 'If you don't know where you're goin', why you goin' there in the first place?'

'It's a long story,' I said, gazing into all the Christmassy shop windows and letting my eyes lose focus until it was all one pretty, illuminated blur. 'I'm sure I'll know it when I get there.'

'We got time,' he said. 'And if you want me to drag my ass around town looking for a needle in a shitstack, it better be good.'

Dropping my head back against the sticky plastic seat, I looked up at the stained ceiling of the taxi and wondered where to start.

'So,' I said, holding my hands up in defeat. 'I met this bloke . . .'

'You sure you don't want me to wait for ya?' Jerry the cabbie asked as I opened the passenger door. 'In case he ain't home again?'

'No, it's OK,' I said, fishing a fistful of bills out of my

clutch and shoving them through the window. 'Thank you so much.'

'Naw, man,' he said, a big cheerful smile on his beardy face. 'I'm a sucker for a love story. Y'all take care now, you hear me?'

'I will,' I promised. 'You have a lovely Christmas. I hope Karlena says yes.'

'Me too,' he said, gunning the engine. 'Maybe she won't be so mad about me working so many nights when she's walking around with a rock on her hand.'

'I'm sure,' I agreed, shivering in the street. 'Thanks again.'

'Happy holidays!' he yelled, pulling away from the curb and hitting his horn and holding it until everyone on the street was looking. 'Hey, Nick! Come get your girl, ya limey bastard!'

Admittedly, the bit at the end of *Pretty Woman*, where Richard Gear pulls up outside of Julia Robert's house in a white limo playing Verdi was a *touch* more romantic, but you couldn't fault his intention. With considerably more care than I had taken twenty-four drunken hours earlier, I tiptoed across the slippery sidewalk, keeping my pin-thin heels off the ice. A broken nose would not go with this ensemble and I would hate to see Jenny's face if I returned it covered in blood.

And there I was again. Right outside his door. But this time I was ready; this time I would get answers.

I pressed the doorbell, every inch of me buzzing with anticipation and a smile on my face I couldn't control.

No answer. I pressed it again and waited. And waited. And waited.

For the second time in twenty-four hours, Nick was not home. Maybe he went out of town for the holidays,

I thought. In which case you just look stupid. Or, the considerate voice in my head suggested, he is home, he knows it's you and he's not answering.

So much for taking control of the situation.

There were only two ways to shut up unhelpful inner monologues and those were with booze and online shopping and since I'd bankrupted myself at the Apple store and the roaming charges on my phone were already ridiculous, I decided to opt for the booze. I couldn't wait on Nick's doorstep until he decided to show himself unless I wanted him to find a ridiculously overdressed snowman outside his apartment, so I made my way to the bar next door.

'What can I get you?' the bartender asked, not even batting an eyelid at my haute couture as I manhandled myself onto a stool. These dresses were not designed for sitting down – no wonder all the actresses at the Oscars were so skinny.

'Do you have wine?' I asked.

'I do, but you don't want it,' he assured me. 'I'll make you something.'

I nodded and emptied my bag onto the bar, looking for my dollar bills. My phone, a pen, two lipsticks and a just-in-case hair tie clattered out and my phone lit up with seven new text messages, all from Amy.

I reluctantly opened the inbox to find four messages, saying 'WHERE R U?' two 'IM FREAKING OUT's and one last 'TESS?????'

Oh, fuckityfuckcockbollocks.

'Here you go.' The bartender set a tall glass down on in front of me, wet with condensation and chilled by one long spear of an ice cube that was almost as big as the glass itself.

I offered him a polite smile as I tapped out a reply to Amy but I didn't have a clue what to say. Why hadn't Kekipi told her I was coming back?

'It's a cinnamon and apple infused bourbon base,' he explained, leaning over towards me and pointing to the drink. 'Mixed with a little sweet and sour mix, a little sweet sugar syrup, ten fresh mint leaves and a paper-thin slice of a red delicious apple.'

I looked at him, picked up the drink and took a sip.

'Tasty,' I said, picking out the giant ice cube and dropping it on the bar.

'Thanks,' he said with an adorable lopsided grin. 'You muddle all of that together and then top it off with . . .'

The adorable lopsided grin faded as I pulled out the straw and chugged the entire thing in one go.

'Really, very nice,' I said, placing a twenty-dollar bill in his hand. 'Thank you. I have to go.'

Pulling my silky straight hair into a topknot, I threw the rest of my things back in my handbag and rubbed my bare arms as the cinnamon and apple infused bourbon warmed me up inside. It was only 8.30; I could be back at the Armory in twenty minutes if I left now. The presentation wasn't scheduled to end until 9.30. I had tons of time.

But leaving would have been a lot easier if Nick Miller hadn't been standing between me and the door.

'Of all the bars in all the cities,' he said, smiling at me, as easy as anything. 'Is it really you?'

I stared at him for a moment, my fingers clenching around my handbag.

'Tess Brookes.' His voice was just the same as I remembered. Heavy and dark and deep. 'You didn't have to dress up; this place is fairly casual.'

I've never been a violent person. When Verity Johnson challenged me to a fight after school in year nine, I showed up, I took one punch to the nose and I hit the deck. The last thing I remember from that day was watching as Amy leapt over my prone form with a battle cry that put Braveheart to shame and ever since, whenever confrontation became unavoidable, I found nodding and/or shaking my head while saying 'oh really?' over and over really helped take the sting out of most situations. Throwing hands was never really called for, in my opinion.

But right there, stood in the bar, full of fancy bourbon and five months of frustration, I saw red. I dropped my bag on the floor, pulled back my arm and slapped Nick Miller across the face, as hard as I possibly could.

'You absolute, total shitting wanker,' I yelled as Nick stood there, staring at me in a state of shock.

'Hey there, woah!' the bartender yelled. 'What the hell?'

Stunned by my own outburst, I stuck my throbbing hand under my armpit and stared back at Nick. He hadn't moved an inch but a bright red, hand-shaped slap was beginning to bloom on his left cheek. Blinking, he opened his mouth wide, moving his jaw slowly from side to side.

'Your hand all right?' he asked, bending down to pick up my bag.

'No,' I replied. 'It hurts.'

And it did. My palm stung like a bastard.

'Good,' he said before waving to the bartender. 'Sorry, Joe. It's all right.'

'If you say so, dude,' he said, shaking his hipster haircut. 'If you say so.'

Nick took a step towards me and I immediately took a step back.

'What?' he said, holding up his hands in surrender, sparkly clutch bag held aloft. 'I'm not the one who just decked you in the face. Can we go upstairs, please?' He held out his hand and looked me in the eye. Crossing my arms, I shook my head.

'You want to do this here?' he asked in a low, gruff voice.

'I don't think I want to do it at all,' I said, grabbing my bag and pushing straight past him, out the door and onto the street. 'I have somewhere to be.'

'Tess, wait!'

I was too angry to be cold this time, my arm flung out in the air as I tried to flag down a taxi with my camera bashing against my hip.

'Tess!'

'What?' I turned to look at him without lowering my arm. 'What do you want?'

'To talk.' He threw his hands up in the air. 'Come upstairs, please.'

'No,' I said, searching the street for a cab. 'I waited months to talk and now I don't have anything left to say.'

'You're the one who came here,' he protested. 'Don't pretend this is an odd coincidence, you being in the bar next to my house, because there's just no way.'

'No, I came to see you,' I admitted. 'But now I'm not sure why.'

'I think you are,' he said. 'I think you're just scared to admit it.'

It was almost as though he wanted me to slap him again.

'Will you do me a favour?' I asked.

'If I can,' he said, his fingers matching up with the mark I had left on his face, almost as though we were holding hands.

229

'Please tell me you're not interested,' I said. My voice broke as I spoke but I was determined to get the words out. 'Tell me we're not a thing and we never were, that it's over so I can put an end to it all, then let me leave.'

'Are you serious?' he asked, any trace of a smile gone from his eyes. 'You want me to tell you that?'

'It would be easier,' I said, knowing it wouldn't, not really.

'I'm not doing this out here,' he grunted, grabbing hold of my wrist so abruptly I almost lost my balance. 'Come upstairs.'

'No!' I tried to shake him off but the ice was too slippery and he was too strong.

'Five minutes,' he said, his eyes locked on mine. 'And then you can do whatever you want.'

'You've had five months,' I replied, not really fighting as he pulled me towards his door. Why was it so hard to walk away? 'What's different now?'

He turned towards me, the shoulders of his leather jacket dusted with snow. 'You came down here to see me, didn't you? Now I'm here, you're going to leave?'

A boxy yellow taxi rounded the corner and slowed down as he saw me waving manically in his direction.

'Tess.' Nick placed his hand on my arm and drew it gently down by my side. The cab drove on. Without me. 'I want five minutes.'

I studied him closely, almost afraid to look away, my bare skin tingling where he touched me. I was afraid he would vanish if I took my eyes off him.

'Five minutes,' I relented as his fingers slid down my arm and wove themselves around my own and a familiar feeling of excitement bubbled up in my stomach. 'And that's all.'

Nick nodded, a smile appearing on his face as he unlocked his front door and pulled me inside.

Seeing his home for the first time was like seeing his handwriting: if someone had shown me a photo without telling me it was his, I still would have known. Dim lighting glowed from industrial fixtures that hung low from the ceiling, a worn leather couch and mismatched armchair were placed carelessly around the low coffee table and I saw book after book after book lining the walls. There was barely a square foot of brick visible behind his home library.

With his hands on his hips, Nick closed the door behind me and inhaled slowly, deeply, before letting out a long sigh. With my arms folded, protecting myself, I lifted my chin in defiance and remained silent. I tried to live by the rule of if you don't have anything nice to say, don't say anything at all. And I had nothing.

'You look beautiful,' he said, observing me from a safe distance, the air between us crackling. Of what, I wasn't quite sure.

'Thanks,' I said, trying to step forward and immediately being yanked backwards. 'Oh, balls.'

Nick looked back at me with a raised eyebrow and tossed his leather jacket onto his sofa.

'My dress,' I explained, panic rising. 'It's stuck on something.'

'What?'

I tried to turn around to try to see where I was caught but every time I moved, I felt the delicate fabric of the dress shiver and froze.

'Can you see what it's hooked on?' I asked, terrified of destroying the dress. How many hundreds of hours had it taken to stitch on all these sequins? I mean, *pailettes*? It might have been incredibly heavy but I couldn't shake the notion that one pull and the whole thing would unravel.

Nick wiped a hand over his jaw, as if to cover an unwanted smile and bent down behind me as I looked up at the ceiling and held my breath.

'Don't move,' he said as he slid down onto his belly, his shirt riding up his back. I can't see . . . oh, there it is. Hang on.'

He reached behind me, one hand on my hip to steady himself and twisted his keys to open the front door. 'There,' he said. 'Your train was waiting for you outside. *Haute couture* with an in-built chaperone? Might catch on.'

I took a half-step forward and felt my dress sigh around my body, everything falling back into place. I looked down at Nick, still on the floor, still with his hand on my hip. It was just for a second, just as he got to his feet but a second was all it took. By the time I'd blinked, he was in front of me and the rest happened without a second thought. I grabbed the back of his head and kissed him, hard, and everything else was gone. I wasn't worried about work, Charlie, Amy, Al, what I should or shouldn't be doing because I was doing the only thing that mattered. Nick dropped his keys on the floor and backed me up against the door, his hands wrapped around my face, fingertips in my hair, his eyes closed. Nothing else mattered.

'I can't believe you're here,' he said, his words almost lost in his kisses. 'Why didn't you call me? You've been killing me.'

My head banged against the door and my breath caught

in my throat and I was completely lost. He pulled back, his breath caught in his throat, and ran his thumb over my lips. The way he smelled, the way he tasted, the way he knew exactly where to touch me, it was all too much in the best way and when he was kissed me again, I could taste blood. A Nick Miller signature.

Wait, why hadn't I called him? Is that what he just said?

As his hands travelled down my body, catching on each and every *pailette* as he went, I knew I had a choice. I could keep my eyes closed and let this happen or I could stop it and make him explain himself. His lips pulled away from mine, moving to my throat and following the low-cut neckline of my dress, down my collarbone.

'Nick,' I said, my voice little more than a ragged croak. 'Stop.'

'Why are you talking?' he asked, lowering himself to his knees and running his hands over my backside. 'Be quiet.'

'I mean it,' I pushed him away as hard as I could and watched as he sprawled backwards, a look of surprise on his face and an unmistakeable bulge in his trousers. 'Stop.'

The unreadable look on Nick's face disappeared and was replaced by an equally infuriating grin.

'Oh, Tess,' he said, rising to his knees. 'You are in so much trouble.'

'I know, Amy's going to kill me,' I replied, straightening my dress and moving quickly away from the door and over to the kitchen; I needed to be further away from him to keep a clear head. 'What do you mean, why didn't I call you? I don't understand, you're the one who ended things.'

There was something on his face as he stood slowly, adjusting the front of his trousers as he followed me into the kitchen. I understood the frustration – the annoyance perhaps not so much. I quickly sat down at a small wooden table – putting two pieces of furniture between us seemed like a good idea.

'Drink?' he asked, turning his back to me. 'I know I need one.'

'Water, please,' I chirped, placing my bag on the table. 'Why didn't you reply to my text two days ago?'

Nick was opening cupboards and running taps. He shrugged with his back to me.

'I was going to,' he replied. 'But I didn't know what you wanted me to say.'

He was the most frustrating man alive.

'Did you consider replying with what you wanted to say?' I asked.

He turned back to look at me with two glasses in his hands and smiled before turning back to the business of drinks. Why had I even imagined I would get an answer? When were things with him ever straightforward?

While he was busy I shamelessly stared around his apartment. So this was where he lived. This was where he had spent the last five months without me. The living room opened out into a tiny kitchenette, with a butcher's block in the middle, well-used stainless steel pots and pans hanging from a rig attached to the ceiling and a deep, white enamel sink full of dishes by a window.

The rest of the place was a study in careless perfection. Handwritten notes and recipes were stuck to the fridge with conspicuously tacky tourist magnets, and the kitchen walls were covered in unframed Polaroids. Other than the books, the living room walls were bare of decoration and the furniture was limited to the sofa, the armchair and a small coffee table that looked like it was made of concrete cinder blocks.

The heavy dining table where I had sat myself was pushed up against a big open window that let in the sounds of the city to soundtrack our evening. Even though the outside temperate was dropping fast, the apartment was sultry, a heat haze diffusing the air above an old metal radiator in the corner of the room. Predictably, there was no Christmas tree or fun decorations but he did have a few cards propped up on one of the bookshelves and I wondered who they were from. A small carry-on suitcase sat beside the door.

'Going somewhere nice?' I asked.

He shook his head and pulled a face. 'My mum's,' he replied. 'I'm flying back to London tomorrow.'

I nodded, knowing full well where he was going. I had just wanted to know whether or not he would tell me the truth.

He grabbed a bottle of whisky from the top of his huge fridge, gave himself a generous pour, and then sat down across the table, sliding my glass of water towards me before taking a long drink.

Propping his feet up on the empty third chair at the table and unbuttoning the cuffs of his white shirt, Nick methodically folded each sleeve three times and then pushed them up towards his elbows, revealing strong, tanned forearms. He clearly hadn't spent the last five months in New York – his arms were freckled and brown and the creases around his eyes revealed tiny white tiger stripes when he sipped his drink and stopped smiling. Disappointingly, the red glow of my slap was already fading away into nothing. I really did need to start working out.

'So,' he said, slowly. 'What *do* you want me to say?'

'I'd love an answer my question,' I said, my shoulders tensing as I spoke. I could still feel the imprint of his thumbs on my shoulder blades. I wondered if there would be marks. He was much stronger than me. 'Why didn't you call me?'

Nick picked up a box of matches from the table and rubbed his thumb against the striking edge.

'Why do you think I should I have called you?' he asked, pulling out a match, lighting it and immediately blowing it out. 'Why is it a "should" situation?'

'I don't think you *should* have,' I replied as he lit another match, wishing I had something flammable to keep my hands busy. 'But you were the one who ended this. With a note, Nick. You didn't even have the decency to say it to my face. Why on Earth should *I* have called *you*?'

'I thought you weren't into games,' he said, that same annoyed look on his face as his jaw tensed. I knew that look, he was almost angry. 'Why are you here?'

'No, really, why do you seem to think I should I have called you?' I asked again, determined to get my answers. 'Is your ego really that out of control that you were just expecting me to run after you and beg you to change your mind?'

'Isn't that what you're doing now?' Nick replied and I almost threw my water in his face. What a dick. He leaned back in his chair and raked a hand through his grey-blond hair. 'Anyway, that isn't how this game goes. You ask a question, then I ask a question.'

I was starting to wish I'd asked for a whisky.

'Fine,' I said, giving up and throwing myself back against my chair. 'You are the professional question asker, after all.'

For a second, I saw a smile on his face but it disappeared just as soon as I had seen it, like a shooting star or Michael Fassbender's penis in that sex addict movie.

'Why did you ring the doorbell and then leave last night?' he asked.

Right away, I felt my skin burn bright red. It was more than a little bit unfortunate that so much of it was on show.

'I didn't want to interrupt you and your guest,' I said. 'Why weren't you answering your own buzzer?'

'Had my hands full.' He swirled his whisky before taking a tiny sip, pleased with his answer. 'Me again. Who did your hair tonight? It looks nice.'

'No one you know,' I countered. 'Is the woman who answered your girlfriend?'

'No,' he replied, taking his tie off then holding it in the air and letting it fold over itself onto the table. He picked it up and did it again. 'She's not my girlfriend.'

Oh dear God, I thought, closing my eyes and trying not to vomit. They were married. They had three kids. He had written her name into that bit in the back of his passport.

'She's my neighbour. Now, about your hair?'

'Seriously?'

He nodded and raised his glass.

'My friend Jenny did it' I replied. 'My question: why are you being such an infuriating dickhead?'

'Pass,' he said. 'My turn. Why don't you have a coat? It's freezing outside.'

'Stop asking stupid questions,' I said, flustered. 'You didn't tell me we could pass.'

'You didn't ask,' Nick said. 'How was the presentation?'

'Pass.' I was trying very hard to retain my composure when all I wanted to do was slap him in his smug face.

'I didn't come here to talk about the presentation, Nick. You could have gone, you were invited.'

'I was,' he replied. 'And honestly, I really don't know why you're here but this is the kind of thing that made me write that note. I can't believe you're sat there with that look on your face, after everything.'

'I don't know why you're so angry at me,' I said, sinking my water and standing to leave. 'But I don't like this, Nick. You're being a complete arsehole. Maybe I dodged a bullet. Maybe you were right and this was a horrible idea in the first place.'

'Tell me why you came,' he insisted, rising to his feet to meet me, eye to eye.

'Tell me why you're so mad at me?' I replied.

I stared at him, my brown eyes locked with his stormy grey and he didn't say a word.

'Ok, I'm done,' I said, grabbing his whisky and taking a sip. Bleurgh. 'It always feels like a test with you, Nick, only I don't know how to pass. I told you I loved you and you walked away. Now I'm walking away. I'm done.'

He was on me before I could even stand to leave.

Yanking me to my feet, Nick grabbed the glass out of my hand and threw it down, not even pausing to look when I felt it shatter on the ground around our feet. His hands circled my waist and picked me up off the floor, dropping me on the table. I winced at my already bruised coccyx but nothing mattered. Frustrated, angry, and confused, I felt my breath coming hard and fast as I took hold of his collar and pulled him towards me, pressing my mouth against his as the whisky on his breath burned the cuts on my lips, closing my eyes and giving in as he pushed up the heavy skirts of my dress, hands running up and down my legs as I curled them around his waist and he lifted me clear off the table and carried me to the sofa. He was hot and hard and heavy and my hands found the familiar muscles in his back, moving under his skin as I tore at his shirt. I needed to feel his skin on me, just him and me and nothing else. All that was left were hands and lips and warm breath and whisky.

'Holy shit, my eyes!'

It took me a moment to remember where I was – my brain had turned itself off when my back felt leather – but it soon remembered itself as Nick scrambled upright, kneeing me in the crotch as he went.

'Susan!' He stood beside the sofa, one shoe on, one shoe off, while a petite, dark-haired woman about Nick's age stood with her hand on the front door handle, a key in the lock. The look on her face suggested she was annoyed but not in the slightest bit surprised.

'I left my glasses here last night,' she said, pulling out the key and kicking the door closed behind her before she disappeared down the hallway, out of sight. 'I'll go get them and then you can get back to whatever this is.'

I recognized her voice at once. It was the woman who had answered the intercom.

Nick looked down at me, speechless, as I pulled at my dress, making sure my boobs were securely tucked away.

'Tess, this is Susan, my neighbour,' he explained quickly. 'She lives downstairs.'

'This is Tess?' Susan called from the bathroom. 'The Tess? Man, have I heard a lot about you.'

She re-emerged with a patronizing smile and a bright purple glasses case.

'Susan, don't,' Nick pressed at the front of his jeans, high colour in his cheeks. 'Please.'

'You have?' I asked.

She had heard about me? Heard what about me?

'Wow, you are not what I imagined at all.' She crossed the room, holding out her hand. 'I'd say it's nice to meet you but, you know, it is kinda awkward.'

'Tess.' I stood up, shaky on my legs, and took her hand. 'Tess Brookes. And yes, completely understand.'

'I gotta say, I'm surprised to see you here,' she said, hands on her hips as she took in the scene. 'And Nick, she does not look like a psycho bitch at all.'

'That's nice to hear, thanks,' I said, straightening my hair.

'Oh yeah,' Susan said, walking back to the door. 'So, I'm gonna go. Leave you two kids alone.'

'Susan, don't be weird,' Nick said again, resignation in his voice. 'We're mates, Tess, that's all.'

I looked back and forth between the two of them, wanting to believe Nick but not sure that I could.

'It's true, I'm just his dumbass neighbour who should have realized that was all I would ever be a long time ago,' she said, holding her front door key in the air. I wasn't sure whether she was a bit pissed or just always this dramatic. Either way, I wanted to hear more about this psycho bitch business. 'So, you're gonna need to find someone else to water your plants and take in your mail and listen to you whine and drink with you till you pass out.'

There was an unreadable expression on Nick's face as he turned back to me.

'I'm just gonna give this to the homeless dudes who live in the park,' she said, pocketing his key. 'Maybe one of those guys can house-sit for you in future?'

'Christ,' Nick looked to the ceiling. 'Will you bloody well calm down?'

'Bye, guys. Happy holidays!' Susan called as she closed the door much too carefully and without a sound.

'She seems nice,' I said cheerfully. 'Why have you got to be such an arsehole to everyone?'

A shrill ringing sound came from my bag and I saw the screen of my phone light up inside the sequined fabric.

'It's hardly my fault if she's got a crush on me, is it?' he said, exasperated, reaching out as I picked my bag up from the floor. 'We aren't together. She's my neighbour, we're friends. She does stuff for me when I'm away; she must have got the wrong idea.'

'You can be such a knob,' I said, as mad at myself as I was with him. I grabbed my bag and saw Amy's name light up the screen just before it went dark. Bugger, I had to get back to her. I hadn't charged the bloody thing all day and now the battery was nearly dead. 'My five minutes were up a long time ago. I've got somewhere to be.'

'Wait.' Nick's voice was urgent and low but he didn't move. 'Please. I don't want you to go.'

'You've had such a long time to talk to me and now you're going to have to wait,' I said, flushed and confused, desperate to leave the apartment and dying to stay. There was too much to process and I knew if I stayed where I was, things would only get messier than they already were. 'Merry Christmas, Nick. I'm sorry, but someone else actually needs me right now. When you're ready to talk like a grown-up, let me know.'

Closing the door with a slam, I ambled down the stairs and out onto the street, unwelcome tears smearing my make-up. So much for Cinderella, I thought as I held my arm out for a taxi, half hoping Nick would fly through the front door and stop me before I could leave. But he didn't. Instead, a taxi pulled up across the street and honked for me to jump in. With a shake of my head, I skittered across in my heels, skirts held high in my hands, and opened the door. Pulling my phone out of my bag in the desperate hope it might have a nano-percentage of battery left to call Amy, I stared at Nick's front door and felt something sink inside me as we drove away.

CHAPTER FOURTEEN

I stared out of the window of the taxi at a sea of endless red brake lights.

I'd managed to squeeze precisely two texts out of my dying phone battery, saying respectively 'On way!!' and 'Shit traffic!!' before it died for good. I tapped my foot impatiently in the footwell while my driver honked his horn for the hundredth time. Strangely enough, it had absolutely zero effect on the traffic jam ahead of us. It really wasn't looking good for getting back by nine thirty.

Kekipi hadn't been in touch since I left on my crazy, ill-judged Nick mission, and I didn't need to re-read Amy's texts to know she was furious. I really did need to talk to Kekipi about how to deal with this. And then I needed to talk to everyone I'd ever met about whether I'd gone completely mad. But I couldn't. All I could do was sit in the back of that cab, banging my head on the roof every time we hit a pothole and regret the day I ever laid eyes on Nick Miller.

'I can't get you any closer to Park,' the driver announced

as I hung up. 'We're only a couple of blocks away but it's a long couple of blocks.'

'Don't worry,' I said with an inner sigh of resignation, scooting to the edge of the leatherette backseat. Goodbye presentation, hello Amy's wrath. 'Can you get me to Sixty-Sixth and Fifth?'

'Sure,' he replied, making a swift left turn that sent me flying across the back of the seat. 'No problem, sweetheart.'

On the back seat of the cab I'd found a plastic bag, emblazoned with an I Heart New York logo when I jumped in, and even though I felt terrible about it, I nicked the oversized Fire Department of New York hoodie I found inside and pulled it on over my dress. All the adrenaline that had kept me warm had worn away and all I felt was cold and tired and alone.

'Here you go,' the taxi driver said as he pulled up outside Al's house.

'Thank you,' I replied, throwing the last of my dollars at him as I clambered out. I needed to find a bank in the morning – New York was bleeding me dry. I never used cash in England, but here, I couldn't keep my money in my wallet. How was it possible to spend twenty dollars on coffee and a muffin?

I stood outside Al's house for a moment, my stomach in knots at the thought of Amy's texts. And growling because I hadn't eaten anything since lunch. Instead of going inside, I turned and walked quickly in the opposite direction, the train of my dress in hand, following the downtown lights as my breath turned into little puffs of grey-white smoke in front of me, like a really rubbish dragon.

A block away, I saw a little diner, spray snow decorating the windows and sprigs of plastic holly hanging over the door, and I didn't even look at the menu – whatever was inside smelled delicious. The lights were brighter than my messed-up make-up would have liked, but it looked warm and friendly and as though it was very likely to sell doughnuts, so I ducked in out of the freezing night.

Right at the back, sat a red leatherette booth with his elbows resting on a white formica table, was Al. He looked dashing in a three-piece tuxedo, a long wool coat hung up beside him, and a steaming cup of coffee in his hands.

'I would never have thought to style the dress that way,' Al said, holding up the coffee up in salutation as my eyes adjusted to the light. 'You youngsters and your high-low fashion. Very inspirational, I must say.'

'Hello,' I said and sat down opposite my friend, smiling at the waitress as she placed a clean cup in front of me. 'You are just about the last person I expected to see in here. Why aren't you at the presentation?'

'I could say quite the same to you,' Al replied, over the Christmas songs that crackled out of the radio behind the counter. 'There wasn't a problem, was there? Tell me the place hasn't burned to the ground?'

I looked down at the NY Fire Department hoodie and shook my head quickly. 'Oh no,' I said, leaning back as the waitress poured me a cup of coffee. 'Not as far as I know, anyway. I found this in a taxi.'

'I won't ask,' he pulled out the paper napkin that was stuck in his collar and wiped his hands, before brushing the crumbs of something from his beard. 'Yes. Well, I stopped in for a minute. It all looked as though it was going swimmingly.'

I stared at him in disbelief. 'You didn't stay??'

'She'll take one of the bacon doughnuts,' Al told the waitress, hovering at his elbow. 'Thank you, Marlene.'

'You're welcome, Al,' she replied, turning the edges of her lips upwards in a warm smile. Of course she knew him by name.

'They sound disgusting but you have to trust me,' he said, pouring an unquantifiable amount of sugar into his own freshened mug of coffee. 'If there's one modern New York habit I do agree with, it's putting bacon in everything. Really, who knew?'

'Al, why did you leave the presentation?' I asked. No wonder Amy was freaking out. 'Does Amy know you were there?'

'Amy had everything under control,' he replied, pushing the sugar towards me. 'People wanted to see the dresses, not me. Now, tell me the whole story of how you came by that fetching jumper? It's a little large but it does set off the *pailettes*.'

'They absolutely wanted to see you,' I argued. Poor Amy, she had worked so hard to create something so wonderful and we'd let her down, both of us. 'And you must have seen, it was incredible. I couldn't believe I was still in New York, everyone was saying how amazing it was, how they hadn't seen anything like it before.'

'Well, that's a relief,' he said, an uncertain look on his face I hadn't seen before. 'People were enjoying it?'

I sat back, confused. Clearly he had dressed for the occasion – he was wearing a tux instead of a Grateful Dead T-shirt – and someone had definitely brushed his hair but something was wrong. The easy certainty he had earned from seventy-something years of living was missing and, if I had to put a label on it, I'd say he seemed sad.

'Loving it,' I said. 'The collection was amazing, I really do think Jane would have been proud of you.'

We sat quietly while the waitress presented us with an enormous doughnut that took up almost the entire paper plate. I hadn't eaten anything since Jenny had squeezed me into two pairs of control pants and I was almost scared to even smell this in case I split all the seams on my borrowed frock.

'I thought working on the collection would help,' Al said eventually, a sad smile on his handsome old face. 'It felt like she was with me again for a while.'

I pushed the doughnut towards him but he shook his head. If a glazed bacon doughnut couldn't cheer him up, I worried nothing could.

'All that time I was in Hawaii, when everyone was calling me a recluse . . .' He pulled a napkin out of the holder between us and began to tear it up into little strips of identical size. 'All my friends and my family would ring me on the phone and tell me I couldn't hide out there forever, that no good would come of holing myself up and pretending nothing had happened. They all wanted me to get back out into the world and do something.'

He laid the strips down on the table, side by side, carefully matching them up together in perfect order like a feathery jigsaw.

'And eventually I agreed to do the interview when Delia asked.' He smoothed the shards of broken napkin until it almost looked like one piece again. 'And along came you and Paige and Mr Miller and, of course, dear Amy. Everyone was so happy and Kekipi was bouncing off the walls at having guests again. I thought, perhaps they're right. Perhaps spending the rest of my days walking up and down a beach, talking to a ghost, is a waste of whatever good years I have left. But I still didn't know what to do with myself. I didn't have any ambitions left, you see, all my dreams had come true, many years ago. And what are you meant to do with yourself when you don't have a dream to pursue?'

'Chase someone else's?' I guessed, pulling the sleeves of my sweatshirt over my fingertips.

'Quite right,' he said. 'I thought, if I could do this for her, bring her designs to life, it would be as though we were working together again. But now it's done she feels further away than ever. And everyone thinks I'm a laughing stock.'

'You read the *Belle* article,' I said.

He nodded and blew lightly on the napkin and all the little pieces floated away from each other.

'Industry nonsense, nothing changes on that front,' he replied. 'But if I'm honest, it all feels rather pointless.'

'My opinion might not be worth much,' I said, noticing how the fluorescent light above us made my dress glow a dark bronze, 'but I think what you've done is amazing. You've honoured your wife's memory, accomplished an ambition on her behalf, and you're going to make thousands of people happy. How is that pointless?'

Al didn't say anything, didn't look up, just drank his coffee. I frowned and shoved the doughnut out of my eye line. It was hard enough having to be the one who gave the life-affirming speeches without bacon-studded pastries messing with my concentration at the same time.

'You're not being fair to yourself.' I sat up straight and adopted a more authoritative tone but I'd never been terribly good at tough love. 'When I put this dress on, even with everything that's been going on and how difficult it's been, it made me happy. I felt special and beautiful and that was all because of this dress. Isn't that something worthwhile?'

'You *should* be happy,' Al admonished me lightly. 'And you are special and beautiful. A dress is just a dress, Tess, that's all.'

'And what would Jane say if you told her that?' I asked, tapping him on the back of the hand. 'She's waited how long for you to get off your arse and make these dresses for her and now you're going to turn your back on them?'

'They're just dresses,' he repeated, staring over my shoulder at something no one else could see.

'And I just take photos for a living.' In theory, I added silently. 'I'm not saving the world, I'm not curing cancer. Should I stop?'

Al stared at the table for so long, I didn't know whether to leave, shout at him or fuck it all and shove the doughnut into my face. Thankfully, Al cleared his throat before I had to make a decision.

'I have to say . . .' He picked up his knife and carefully chopped the doughnut in half. 'You're not bad at this motivational-speaking lark. If the photography doesn't work out, you could always give that a go.'

'One career change at a time,' I said, accepting my half of the doughnut with great pleasure. 'You should be happy. And if making the clothes doesn't do it for you, go home, go surfing – and forget it all.'

He picked up his half, took a bite and nodded.

'But I think you might have enjoyed it.' I picked off a bit of icing and popped it into my mouth. Oh dear God – it was incredible! 'Maybe just a little bit.'

'Perhaps a smidge,' he replied with a wink. 'Right up until this part. I really do miss my home an awful lot and dealing with all the buyers and the press, it's reminding me why I moved to Hawaii in the first place. New York isn't for old codgers like me, it's a city made for you young kids.'

'I don't feel that young right now,' I told him, moving from the icing to the cake. Sweet Baby Jesus in the manger, it was a good doughnut. 'Mostly, I just feel tired.'

'Unfortunately that's one of the side effects of youth,' Al clucked his tongue. 'You really don't appreciate it until you're at least forty-five. I thought I knew everything when I first moved to America, I thought I was going to take over the world and, you know, I think I probably could have. And then one day I woke up and I was married, I had a son and I was fifty years old and I realized I hadn't a clue about anything.'

'I don't think I could take over a sandwich shop,' I replied. 'But Amy could probably stage a pretty successful coup.'

'The only difference between you and Amy is that she knows exactly who she is,' he said. 'Does that make sense?'

'Yes,' I admitted. 'I thought I knew who I was before, but now it's all changing so fast. I wish someone would tell me, you know, describe Tess Brookes in three words, or something.'

'You should never let anyone else tell you who you are,' Al warned. 'Or you'll spend the rest of your life trying to be something you're not. The difference between you and Amy is simply that she has no fear. She doesn't compromise. You spend far too much time worrying about every possible outcome, whereas Amy acts first and worries later. Or sometimes never, as I'm sure you've noticed. She and I have that in common. Well, the younger me anyway.'

I laughed, and it felt almost as good as eating the doughnut. Almost.

'Is there a happy medium?' I asked.

'For some people,' he said, licking his fingers clean. 'But you can only change if you want to, not because someone else thinks you should.'

'The last few months have been so hard,' I told him. 'Everything I thought was certain in my life has changed, me included. I feel as though I don't really know who I am anymore.'

'That happens to the best of us,' Al said. 'And I'm quite certain you're going to be fine.'

'I wish I had your confidence,' I said. 'I'm getting really tired of making the wrong decisions.'

'You're going to have to let me know precisely what we're talking about before I can help on this one.' He dusted off his hands on another fresh napkin but left this one intact. 'Work or Mr Miller?'

'Mr Miller,' I said, shoving the remaining doughnut in my mouth. Maybe I'd give up on love altogether and concentrate on baked goods. 'I'm a glutton for punishment.'

'Things never seem to go smoothly with the two of you, do they?' Al mused. 'I wonder why that is?'

'Because he's the spawn of Satan?' I suggested, dropping my arms on the table and nursing my chin. 'And I'm an idiot?'

'You realize, one has to ask,' he said, leaning across the table to lower his voice. 'What is it that keeps drawing you back together?'

It was a fair question.

'Obviously, he's the only man left on earth and if I give up on him the human race will die out,' I replied. 'I can't think of anything else.'

'You're sure there isn't anything else?' Al asked.

'Nope.'

'Positive?'

'Yep.'

'You can't think of anything?'

I pouted, thinking back to the moment I got in the taxi outside his house and how badly I wanted him to see him at the door.

'If you're going to say it's because I love him, I'm afraid I'm going to need another doughnut and a machine gun.'

'Humour me,' Al said, stifling his laughter. 'Tell me what happened.'

With a bacony sigh, I gave him the PG version of events and then sipped my coffee while I waited for his verdict.

'I say sleep on it,' he said eventually. 'You've really done all you can do.'

'Oh.' I was actually surprised. I was sure he would tell me to pick up the phone and hear him out. 'I really thought you were going to tell me to give him another chance.'

'That's because really, that's what you want to do,' Al replied. 'You could call him.'

'But you just said not to!' I frowned, clicking my neatly filed but terribly short fingernails on the table. 'What should I do?'

'You should do whatever feels right,' he advised. 'No one else can make this decision for you, Tess, however much you'd like them to. You have to do what you can live with.'

'I can think of thousand reasons to call him,' I said. 'And a thousand more not to. I don't think I've ever been this confused.'

Al nodded. 'You're dealing with very confused young man.'

'He's not that young,' I pointed out. 'He's thirty-six. No, thirty-seven. I think he had a birthday.'

I knew full well he'd had a birthday. He was definitely thirty-seven.

'You're forgetting that troublesome Y chromosome,' Al said. 'Not predictable. And he's far too intelligent for his own good, another one who overthinks everything. If I'd been in his shoes, I never would have made a play for my Janey. Remember, she was engaged when we met but I couldn't ignore the way I felt.'

'I think that's exactly what *he's* doing,' I admitted and my sight sharpened as a fresh run of tears threatened to fall. 'But I can't force it, can I?'

'If it's meant to be, it's meant to be,' Al added unhelpfully. 'The path of true love never did run smooth.'

'If he's my true love, I might as well end it all now,' I said. 'Worst soulmate ever.'

'I think you're very lucky, Tess,' he replied. 'Very lucky indeed.'

'How's that?' I wasn't quite following.

'Not many people find their soulmate, most of them settle for someone they can live with.' Al rolled down his shirtsleeves and fastened the cufflinks. 'And you've gone and found two of them.'

I had?

'I have?'

'Imagine being so lucky as to have a Nick *and* an Amy,' he said, nodding. 'A surfeit of soulmates. Imagine that.'

'I don't think I've got either of them right now,' I said. 'Amy's going to be so pissed off when I get home.'

Al gave a big, granddad-sized sigh. 'She's every right

to be upset with me,' he said, pulling twenty dollars out of his wallet and placing it on the table. 'I let her down. Perhaps we both did.'

If he hadn't been paying for my coffee and doughnut, I could have really gone off him.

'I can't imagine what would have happened if I hadn't asked my Janey to take a walk with me that Saturday afternoon,' he said, pulling his long woollen coat from off his little metal chair and giving a whistle. 'Where would we all be now?'

I emptied my coffee mug and picked up my bag. 'Shall we?' I asked, nodding towards the door.

'You should,' he replied, wrapping a grey scarf around his neck. 'I'm going over to the Armory before they break down Amy's masterpiece. I do hope she can forgive me.'

'She'll understand,' I promised, certain she would forgive Al, not so sure I'd be let off so lightly.

'She is a remarkable young lady, that friend of yours,' he agreed. 'I consider myself very lucky to have met the pair of you.'

'I consider myself very lucky that you told me about that doughnut,' I said, looking longingly at the empty plate. 'Maybe I should take one for Amy?'

'Maybe you should take a dozen so we've got them for breakfast,' he suggested, tapping a finger to his temple. 'Full of good ideas up here.'

'One or two,' I said with a smile.

CHAPTER FIFTEEN

The plan was simple. I would go home. I would find Amy and, if she was a little bit mad at me, I would bribe her with doughnuts. If she was *very* mad at me, I would eat all the doughnuts myself and, if the fates allowed, spend Christmas in a diabetic coma. I was definitely due an extended nap, if nothing else.

But that plan was thrown out of the window before I arrived at the house – the plan and half the contents of Al's drawing room. At first I thought I'd walked too far but no, I was home. Apparently I'd missed the memo about an afterparty. The music was blaring out the house so loudly I could hear it a block away, all the lights blazing from every window. The shouting, screaming and smashing glass came later. As I tried the door handle, I realized the front door was unlocked and one of the carefully topiaried trees that sat inside the huge stone urns beside the front door had been draped in flashing fairy lights, while the other slumped sadly to one side, defeated.

Tiptoeing over two abandoned champagne bottles, I pushed the door and stepped inside, petrified. Was there such a thing as party robbers in New York? Because it definitely sounded like a thing. I could almost see my mum rolling her eyes and saying 'only in America' when they called her to tell her how I had died.

'Genevieve?' I called into the darkness. 'Are you there?'

She didn't strike me as the type to throw a rager while her boss was at a work do, but what did I know? We'd only just met.

'Hey.' A shirtless man with enormous pupils ran towards me, a red strip of silk tied around his head like a high-fashion Rambo. 'Great sweater. That's a hot look. That's totally slammin'. I'm Ivan. What's your name?'

'Tess,' I said, still trying to work out exactly what was going on. 'Have you seen an older lady? Grey hair, smart outfit, she probably looks really angry right about now?'

'Nuh-uh,' he replied, bouncing up and down on the spot, pupils so wide I thought I might fall in. 'I only know Amy. This is Amy's place. You should talk to Amy.'

'You know Amy?' I asked, all of this beginning to make a horrible sort of sense. He had to be confused. She wouldn't do this, not to Al.

'Hey, you're British!' Ivan said, grabbing hold of me around the waist and throwing me into the air. 'Amy's British too! She's the best, like, really, really, really the best. Do you want some Molly? Do you have any Molly? We should take some more Molly. If you have some.'

'I'm sorry, I don't,' I replied, holding the box of doughnuts high above my head as he carried me through the foyer and into the reception room. Someone was playing 'Do They Know it's Christmas?' so loud, I could feel the bass in my lungs. 'Although I think tonight might be a good time for me to start on the class As. Please could you put me down?'

'When we find Amy,' he promised, grinding his teeth. 'Amy will know who has the Molly. Maybe Amy has the Molly.'

'If Amy has the Molly, Amy's going to get a slap,' I said as I bounced around in midair. 'Ivan, please put me down before you hurt yourself; I'm bigger than you.'

With one swift kick to whatever body part was at foot level, Ivan went down like a sack of shit. With the doughnuts safely in one hand, I yanked off my shoes and slipped the straps over my other wrist. I'd made it to the presentation, to Nick's, to the diner and back again without an injury, I wasn't about to break my ankle now.

'Look who it is!'

Over the booming music, I heard a familiar voice. Standing on a side table in nothing but a lime green vest and a pair of stripy knickers was my best friend, a bottle of champagne in one hand and what I hoped was a cigarette in the other. She looked like a dark-haired Miley Cyrus on a particularly bad night.

'Snacks!' She leapt to the floor and took a swig from the champagne. She didn't offer it to me. 'You went out for snacks! So that's where you were.'

'What are you doing?' I asked, snatching the bottle out of her hand. 'Have you actually lost your mind?'

'What are you talking about?' She kept on dancing, arms high up over her head, her hips thrusting to the beat. 'Stop being a dick and give me whatever's in that box.'

'I'm not being a dick,' I shouted, my hands now full of shoes, booze and baked goods. 'Amy, what are you doing? Who are all these people?'

'Friends,' she said, looking around. 'Well-wishers. People from the presentation. That was the party, this is the afterparty. Next, it's the hotel lobby. At least, according to R. Kelly.'

Even by Amy's standards, this was bad.

When we were seventeen, her mum went to Cornwall for a week with a load of women from the village line-dancing club and we decided to throw a party. After three days of scrubbing puke out of the living room carpet and pooling our combined savings to replace the telly after Gareth Stevens fell on top of it halfway through his Taekwondo showcase, we swore to each other that we would never throw another house party as long as we lived. But here we were, one of us in a fancy dress and a shit sweatshirt and the other, smoking and drinking in her underwear. It was like being seventeen all over again, only this wasn't our house and I couldn't convince myself that 'there wouldn't be that much of a mess in the morning'.

'We've got to get all these people out of here!' I yelled, dodging a woman wearing a string of multicoloured fairy lights around her neck, a Santa hat and no clothes. 'Al will be home soon, he can't see this.'

'Why not?' she yelled back. 'He didn't come to the presentation! He doesn't give a shit. He's going to sack me anyway.'

'Of course he isn't.' My voice started to scratch from all the shouting. 'He did go, I saw him and he told me. He just didn't stay very long.'

'Why?' she asked, something that looked suspiciously like tears in her huge blue eyes. 'So, what? He saw it and he hated it? Or he's a selfish shit like you and he just didn't care enough to bother hanging around.'

Stunned, I stared at her, while the party raged on around me.

'Which do you think it is?' she asked, grabbing the bottle of champagne back out of my hand.

'I didn't leave because I didn't care,' I said, ashamed. 'I was on my way back and I didn't think I'd be gone that long.'

'Oh, no, I know,' she said. 'You left to go and see a man who keeps messing you around because that was more important than being there for me.'

I couldn't even think of a way to argue with her; it wasn't as though she wasn't wrong, I had just hoped she would understand.

'I didn't think it was more important,' I tried to explain without digging myself into a deeper hole because really, wasn't that exactly what I'd done? 'I didn't plan to go and see him at all but then I realized if I didn't go tonight he would be gone and Kekipi said I should go and—'

'That's right!' Amy shouted, two little red spots appearing on her cheeks. 'It's Kekipi's fault! He told you to go so you had to. I'm sorry, Tess, for a moment I thought you were a twenty-eight-year-old woman who made her own decisions.'

'I'm not twenty-eight until next month and you know it,' I said, my shame dissolving into frustration. 'And none of that explains why you decided to put on a rave in Al's living room.'

'Because I worked my backside off to make tonight a success and none of you cared,' she shouted over the top of the music. Mariah Carey was never meant to be played this loud. I pressed a finger to my ear to make sure it wasn't bleeding. 'So why not have a party.'

I hated myself so much. 'Amy, the presentation was incredible, everyone said so.'

'They did,' she agreed, furiously swiping at her eyes.

'Apart from my best friend and my brilliant boss, who both had better places to be.'

'I didn't have a better place to be and neither did Al,' I argued, fully aware that she could blow at any second. I kept a tight hold of the doughnuts. 'He had a bit of a meltdown; it happens to everyone, you know.'

'Right, right,' she said, her eyes burning fierce. 'He had a meltdown. And what about you?'

Clenching my jaw and pressing my lips together, I shook my head.

'I messed up,' I said, my words shaky. 'I let you down. And I'm sorry.'

Amy took another drink from the champagne bottle as Ivan ran past screaming with the naked girl on his shoulders. With a bitter laugh, Amy opened it, grabbed a doughnut from the big pink box in my arms, stuffed it in her mouth and then knocked the rest of them onto the floor.

I couldn't believe she would attack the doughnuts! I basically had nothing left to live for.

'The presentation was incredible, I couldn't believe it,' I told her, staring at the glazed mess at my feet. 'I mean, I do believe it, obviously. What I mean is, the whole thing was so beautiful, I was blown away. I took so many photos. And *you* did all that. It was the most amazing thing I've ever seen, Amy, I'm so, so proud of you.'

The fire in her eyes flickered for a moment. The power of that doughnut knew no bounds.

'And yes, I left to go after Nick and I shouldn't have. Definitely not without letting you know anyway, and the plan was always to come back before the end. I tried to but I got stuck in traffic.' I was going to ignore what might have happened if Susan hadn't interrupted us.

'You have to believe that I'm sorry and we have to get all these people out of here before Al gets home. Where are Delia and Genevieve? Where's Kekipi?'

Amy nodded across the room. 'Don't know about the others but Genevieve is over there.'

I followed her gaze across the room to see Al's housekeeper slumped in an armchair, the top four buttons on her blouse undone, her high and tight bun let loose and a bottle of vodka in her hand. She held a hand out in front of her face and laughed.

'There you are, you dumb hand,' she yelped, delighted. 'What are you doing there, hand?'

'I don't even want to know,' I said, turning back to Amy, stripy knickers, neon bra and all. 'We can fix this.'

'Why?' she asked, furious and heartbroken all at once. 'Why bother?'

'Because you love working with Al,' I said, beginning to lose my temper. 'Because you're good at it and because you're mad at me and disappointed in us both but you don't want to mess everything up.'

She stared at me for a moment and I really didn't know what she was going to do.

'Tess?' she said, looking around her as though she was seeing the party for the first time. 'I've dropped the biggest bollock ever, haven't I?'

'No,' I lied as two models jumped up on the coffee table in their stilettoes and started grinding on each other to the super sexy beats of 'Mistletoe and Wine'. 'We can sort this out. You turn off the music and I'll kick everyone out.'

'It's on Spotify,' she said, looking around the room. 'But I can't remember where I left my phone. Give me a minute.'

She grabbed a black polo neck from the back of the

settee and pulled it on, not bothering with the bottoms, and ran off into the kitchen in her knickers. Looking back at the packed living room, I gnawed on my bottom lip, not sure where to start, so I picked up the doughnuts instead and put the box on a side table. Then I turned round and faced the room.

'OK, everyone!' I bellowed at the top of my voice. 'You need to GO HOME.'

Strangely enough, no one budged.

The house was heaving with people, dancing on the sofas, kissing in corners and doing God knows what underneath the dining room table. I saw empty bottles of vintage champagne on every surface while someone had spilled tequila all over the polished wooden floors. The music was so loud I could barely think, and while that didn't seem to be a problem for all the gurning, grinding partiers, it was a problem for me. I needed Amy to shut it off. When the music stopped, the party stopped, I told myself. And lights, we needed lights.

'If I were a light switch,' I muttered. 'Where would I be?'

I grabbed the empty bottle Amy had abandoned and searched for switches. How hard could it be? I asked myself. But of course it was impossible. I vaguely remembered seeing Amy wielding some sort of Starship Enterprise-type handset when we got in from the airport on Monday night but I had no idea where it was hiding.

Picking my way through the party, I began to gather discarded bottles as I tapped individual party guests on the shoulder.

'You need to leave,' I shouted at a group of young-looking men, all over six-foot tall, all gorgeous. 'You have to go!'

'No, it's cool,' one of them replied, grabbing me around the waist and pulling me into the centre of their dance circle. 'You don't have to go anywhere.'

'Not me,' I replied, shaking off one pair of hands, only for them to be replaced by another. At any other time, being mauled by a gang of male models could only be considered a good thing but I was so, so frustrated. '*You. All. Have. To. Go.*'

But they were far too busy tearing off their clothes and grinding on each other to listen to me. With arms full of Cristal and Krug, I stepped over thousands of dollars of carelessly abandoned dresses, shirts and shoes, wending my way back towards the foyer. There had to be a fuse box somewhere, I decided. Since Amy didn't seem to be having any luck killing the music, shutting this thing down at the source seemed like the best option. Weighed down under half a dozen bottles and one pair of very expensive shoes, I heard a strangled sob escape from my mouth when the front door swung open again. Not more people, I couldn't take it.

'*Aîa!*'

Kekipi and Domenico, still in their dinner jackets but sans bowties, stood outside, shock written all over their faces.

'Help me,' I begged. 'Please, make it stop.'

'What is this song?' Kekipi replied, a smile breaking out on his face and his foot tapping along. 'I love it!'

'It's Cliff Richard and you're not helping!' I thundered. 'Please, Domenico, we have to get everyone out of here before Al gets home.'

Throwing off his jacket and rolling up his sleeves, he snapped into action. As he had managed Al's Italian home while taking care of his wayward son for decades, I had a feeling this wasn't the first time he had pulled the plug on an unplanned party. Kekipi, on the other hand, the patron saint of impromptu soirees, was no use to us whatsoever. By the time I had ditched my empties in the umbrella stand by the front door, he was already shirtless and swigging from a bottle of vodka with the male models.

A split second before I went completely deaf, the earsplitting EDM remix of 'Last Christmas' gave way to deafening silence before it was replaced by a loud chorus of disappointed grunts and yells.

And then the sirens started.

'Don't worry about the Po-Po,' Kekipi said, still dancing to nonexistent music only he could hear as everyone else began to rush towards the door. 'This place has seen crazier parties than this and no one ever got arrested. Well, one person. Maybe two. And there was that time with Mick Jagger but that was in the seventies, you don't need to worry about that.'

'I am not ending up in a police cell again,' I shouted, gripping his shoulders as I looked right into his glassy eyes. 'Once was funny, twice was bad, but three times in one year is not happening. Sort it out, Kekipi. Sort. It. Out!'

'Relax,' he said as lights flooded the foyer and Domenico held the door open for the fleeing partygoers. 'It's not like we're doing anything illegal; it got a little loud, that's all. We've turned the music off, they'll slap our wrists and leave.'

'I think someone has drugs,' I whispered, rubbing my wrists. I could already feel the handcuffs. 'What if they find drugs?'

'Of course someone has drugs,' he said before turning to me with a serious expression. 'Do you have drugs?'

'No,' I said, beginning to feel very sick as two officers slowly got out of the car in front of the house. 'Of course I don't. I'm me. I daren't even take Nurofen Plus in case I OD.'

'Good,' Kekipi replied. 'I would have been terribly upset if you didn't share.'

'This is not a joke!' I shouted. 'This is America. Don't you watch the news? Prison here is not fun.'

'Maybe not if you're a top,' he sniffed. 'Calm down, let me handle it.'

'I'm not going to ring in the New Year as someone's bitch,' I told him as the police officers knocked on the open door. 'Amy? Where are you?'

'Oh, for Beyoncé's sake!' Kekipi blew out a giant huff of a sigh, grabbed hold of my oversized sweatshirt and yanked it over my head. 'Tits and teeth, Brookes, tits and teeth.'

'Hey,' I yelped, my voice muffled by the soft fabric before he tossed it to one side, fluffed out my hair, and gave me a look so filthy I felt as though I might catch something.

'Good evening, gentlemen, ma'am.'

The two officers approached us with heavy stares, one with his thumbs tucked into his elaborately stocked utility belt, the other holding his radio in one hand, a gun in the other.

An actual gun. In his hand.

'Good evening, officers.' Kekipi, bare-chested but impossibly charming, waved them inside. 'Won't you please come in, you must be freezing out there.'

'Not really,' one of them replied. 'But then *we're* wearing shirts.'

Well, at least they had a sense of humour.

'How can we help you this evening?' Domenico asked, all smiles and civility. It suddenly became glaringly obvious how the two of them had ended up in their jobs: grace under pressure didn't even begin to cover it. 'I do hope our quiet soiree did not upset any of our neighbours.'

'We had some reports of a disturbance,' the second officer, a giant of a man, said as he stepped inside to take a look around. 'Looks like your quiet soiree got a little out of hand.'

'There were a few uninvited guests,' Kekipi confessed. 'But as you can see, everyone has gone now. It's such a shame when a few rowdy people ruin a lovely, quiet night, don't you think?'

The first officer looked him up and down. Kekipi offered up a polite smile, as though it was perfectly normal to run around an Upper East Side townhouse shirtless with a bottle of Cristal in your hand. And as far as I knew, it was.

'Yeah, real shame,' the officer said. 'Mind if we take a look around?'

'I would be delighted, if you would be so kind,' he replied, shoving me into his path. 'My poor friend here was frightened out of her wits when she heard your sirens. She thought something terrible must have happened.'

I felt him pinch my arm, hard.

'I thought something terrible must have happened,' I parroted. 'I was frightened out of my wits.'

The officer shifted his gaze from Kekipi's bare chest to my barely covered one and from the look on his face, he much preferred what he saw.

'We'll just be a moment,' the second officer said, slapping his partner's back as he headed into the reception room. 'Could you turn the lights on back here, please, sir?'

'Just not all of them,' I whispered to Domenico as he swiped at the console. 'Darker is better.'

Even with mood lighting, the devastation was obvious. Broken bottles, smashed glasses, Christmas trees turned over, paintings knocked off walls and a foot-long rip in the middle of the leather sofa, a stiletto shoe sticking out of the gash.

'Quiet soiree, you say?' The second officer pulled the shoe out of the sofa and turned it over in his hand. 'If you guys decide to throw a real party, you let us know ahead of time, all right?'

'Hopefully you'll have the day off and be able to attend,' Kekipi replied. 'We do apologize.'

'I can't find my tossing phone!' Amy came barrelling down the spiral staircase, still trouserless, her black jumper covered in neon paint. 'And Genevieve is in the bath doing—'

She stopped dead in her tracks and blanched at the sight of the policemen.

'Absolutely nothing,' she said calmly, crossing her legs and scrunching up her toes. 'Evening.'

'OK, just keep it down,' the giant policeman said, handing me the shoe and then tapping his hat at Amy. She curtsied on the staircase, wide-eyed and holding her breath. 'And happy holidays.'

The first officer gave my cleavage one last, lingering look before offering a curt nod to Kekipi and Domenico and following his partner out the door. Closing it behind them and turning every single lock, Domenico surveyed the destruction with a wary look on his face.

'It's not a Bertie Bennett party unless someone calls the cops,' Kekipi said with a shrug. 'No harm done.'

'No harm done at all,' I said, holding up the shoe.

'Unless I find out who this belongs to and rip her a new one.'

'That's a very modern take on the Cinderella story,' he replied, opening the pink cardboard box with the doughnuts. 'Ooh, treats!'

'Good grief. Did I miss an earthquake?'

Al stood in the middle of the room, hands on his hips and a great big smile on his ruddy face.

'No, but you missed a hell of a party,' Kekipi replied, biting into half a damaged doughnut. 'Jane would have been proud.'

'She did love a good get-together,' he said, eyes full of happy memories as he looked at the destruction before him. 'She wouldn't have been happy to see it over before midnight, though. Where did everyone go?'

'Home,' I said, not quite sure I was hearing him right. 'Because the police came. You aren't upset?'

'Upset?' Al dropped his arm around my shoulders and gestured to the chaos. 'You should have seen this place after Mick Jagger came to stay. Where did Amy get to? Do I need to go and bail her out? I think we've still a friend at precinct nineteen.'

'I'm here,' she said, waving timidly from the stairs. 'I'm sorry.'

'Not at all, my girl,' he said, shrugging off his coat and adding it to the clothing pile in front of him. 'Between this and the presentation, I've never been so proud. You're a wonder.' He looked up at her as he said it, holding her gaze. I saw her give him a small smile back.

'And she knows how to throw a bash,' Kekipi added. 'Now, Genevieve's doing what in the bathroom, Amy?'

'Nothing,' Amy said. 'Definitely not tripping balls with one of the waiters from the presentation.'

'Good for her,' Al said, flapping a hand at it all and starting up the stairs. 'I don't know about all of you, but I'm exhausted.'

'Amen to that.' Kekipi picked his shirt up from the pile of discarded clothes by the front door and tossed it over his shoulder. 'What a fantastic night.'

'You've all gone completely mad,' I said, taking one last look at the devastation before following them up the stairs, forcing one tired foot in front of the other. If this was Kekipi's idea of a fantastic night, I would hate to see a terrible one.

'Tess,' Amy said, slipping her arm through mine as the others peeled off to their rooms, leaving us en route to the fourth floor. 'What happened? With Nick?'

'Nick happened,' I told her, holding out a hand to cut her off when she opened her mouth. 'And no, I don't need you to go and chop off his balls. At least not tonight, let's give him twenty-four hours.'

'Well, don't be upset when you open your present and you're not surprised,' she said.

'Ho ho ho,' I said, pushing open our bedroom door. 'And a merry Christmas, every one.'

CHAPTER SIXTEEN

'WAKE UP! IT'S CHRISTMAS.'

Amy announced Christmas Eve by jumping up and down on the bed and bashing me in the face with a pillow, still wearing her paint-splattered sweater and stripy pants.

'It's Christmas Eve,' I corrected, grabbing the pillow out of her hands and throwing it across the room. 'And it's early.'

'It's nine,' she said. 'That's not early. Come on, Tess, I have so many things I want to do today.'

'Like what?' I reached up to touch my hair; the night's adventures had turned my silky straight locks back into a curly disaster. I assumed it had happened right as the clock struck twelve.

'Skating in the park, a carriage ride in the snow, Saks, Bloomingdale's, Tiffany,' Amy said, opening the curtains to reveal another bright, sunny, snowy day, 'and as much hot chocolate as my body can handle. We're going to have a perfect day.'

'That sounds amazing,' I said. And it did. 'But I have

to submit my photo for the Spencer prize by two and I still have to pick a bloody photo and get it framed.'

'There's a framing place right down the street,' she said, still bouncing up and down. 'I've had stuff done there and they're nice and they're Jewish so they don't celebrate Christmas and won't be getting pissed in the back. They'll fit you in.'

'You're amazing,' I said, meaning every word. 'Do you think we can we fit our perfect day into a perfect afternoon?'

Amy pouted. 'Yes,' she said. 'But only because I love you very much.'

'Thanks,' I smiled, preoccupied with my newly charged phone. 'I'll make it up to you.'

'I still have some making up to do,' she replied, crawling up the bed and back under the covers. 'I don't know what I was doing last night.'

'I'm sorry I left the presentation,' I said, tossing my phone down and turning my head to look at her properly. Her short hair was sticking up in every direction and she had dark blue circles underneath her eyes. She looked exhausted. 'And I'm sorry if I made you feel like I didn't believe in you.'

She shrugged and flickered an eyebrow. 'There's a slim chance I was the one who didn't believe in myself,' she said. 'Which is ridiculous given how awesome I am.'

'Still, I could have been more supportive,' I admitted. 'I think I might have been a tiny bit jealous.'

'In that case, you're a complete twatknacker,' she said, bashing me in the head with a pillow. 'I've been totally shitting it ever since you left Milan. I didn't have a clue what I was doing last night and if it weren't for the fact you've been here all week, I'd have been sat in

271

the back of the wardrobe with my knickers on my head, sobbing.'

'That's ridiculous,' I told her. 'You're doing brilliantly at all of this. Why didn't you say anything?'

'Do you know what I would do every time I started freaking out?' she asked. 'I'd think, "what would Tess do in this situation?"'

'I'm not sure about that,' I said, slightly weirded out that she was the second person in a week to say the same thing. 'Tess has been making some really sketchy decisions lately.'

'I disagree. Tess is the best,' Amy replied, a look of quiet certainty on her face. 'Tess follows her dreams, Tess is brave – Tess tells boys how she feels even when it's scary which is Beyoncé of her.'

'You've been spending too much time with Kekipi,' I muttered. 'But if you say so.'

'Tess takes advantage of every opportunity that comes her way,' she said. 'You're working your arse off to make this happen when it would be so easy to trot back to your old job and I'll be buggered if I'm going to let Nick Miller bring you down now.'

'Fair enough,' I said, the aching sick feeling that had been buried in my stomach starting to fade away with her words. 'Shall we agree that we both feel terrible but we're both brilliant so we should eat things, drink things and buy things until we feel as awesome as we are?'

'Like I said, Tess is the best,' Amy said. 'Can I see your photos?'

'Yes.' I sat up, suddenly excited, and grabbed my laptop from the bedside table. 'You want to help me choose my entry?'

'Show me, show me, show me,' she said, clapping.

'Well, there's these,' I said, flipping through the shots from Sadie and James' shoot. It didn't have New York in the photo as such but the gorgeous evening gown and elegant tuxedo and general tone of the image really couldn't be set anywhere else. It screamed Manhattan elegance to me. 'And I took these in the park the other night. They're so different, I don't know which to choose.'

'What about this one?' She pulled up the photo I'd taken of Al from the terrace. 'Wow, I've never seen Al look like that. When did you take this?'

'Yesterday morning,' I said, zooming in on the image. 'But he didn't know I was there.'

'Before the presentation?' Amy asked. 'No, he looks so sad. It's a really good picture though, Tess.'

'I know,' I admitted. 'But I'd feel weird submitting it for a competition. It's really personal, I'd have to ask him if it's OK and I don't want to upset him again.'

'I understand,' she said, scrolling back through the others. 'They're all good. I'm not helping, am I?'

'Not really,' I said with a smile. 'But you're trying. Maybe this one?'

I opened one of the photos of Sadie and James. It wasn't one Angela was using in the magazine, but it was one of my favourites. James was holding a party popper in the air and Sadie had her arms high above her head, neon-bright streamers standing out against their black outfits and the white background. The colours were bold and deeply saturated and the lighting was clear and stark. Everything popped.

'It looks like something from an advert or something,' Amy said, giving my worried expression a second look. 'No, it's a compliment. I mean it looks totally professional.'

'I just don't know,' I sighed. She half fell off the huge

bed and staggered over to the bathroom, smoothing down her morning manga hair. 'It looks like something Ess might have taken. That's good though, isn't it? He's really successful?'

'If you say so,' she said, hanging off the bathroom door. 'Shouldn't it look more like something you took?'

'I *did* take it,' I replied, stubbornly. 'I think I'm going to send this one.'

'I'm going to have a shower,' Amy said. 'Whichever one you choose will be perfect. They're all really good, Tess.'

I'd never felt so unsure of myself before but it wasn't because I didn't think my photos were good, it was because I knew they mattered. I didn't really expect to win the Spencer prize but I wanted to make a good showing. I wanted to have something to show Agent Veronica that would convince her to have faith in me, something that she wouldn't write off as a favour from a friend.

The photos from the park, the photos from the shoot, the photos of Paige? They were all nice but nice wasn't good enough. The picture of James and Sadie had something, even if that something was two celebrities. That was the one, I decided, popping it on a memory stick and turning back to my phone while it loaded.

There was nothing from Nick. I knew he was currently on a plane somewhere over the Atlantic Ocean. But they had phone signal from JFK, didn't they? And his apartment. And the cab in between.

But I did have a missed call. Leaning back against the pillows, I picked up my phone before I could think better of it and dialled.

'Hello, Mrs Grinch,' Charlie answered on the first ring. 'You're just in time for the song.'

'Hello,' I replied, smiling. 'I can't believe I'm missing our Grinchmas.'

'Yeah,' he laughed. 'Binning me and Grinchy off to live it up in New York with Amy. How's it going over there?'

'Oh, you know,' I said. 'Missing our routine to be honest.'

'What, listening to me sing Slade songs all the way up the M1 and then eating your mum's shit sprouts?' he asked. 'I still don't know why she insists on doing them every year. No one ever eats them. Ever.'

'Because she's a martyr,' I reminded him, calming down just a fraction. 'But I'd probably even eat a liquid sprout about now. It's beautiful here, though.'

I could hear the soundtrack of the movie for a moment, the happy Christmas song in the background, and imagined myself snuggled up on Charlie's sofa, cup of tea in my hand, Cadbury's selection box between us. He would eat the Crunchie, I would get the Buttons.

'Tess,' he said. 'What's the matter?'

'Nothing,' I said, almost certain. 'Just weird being away. I'm quite worried they won't have pigs in blankets, if I'm honest.'

'You're in America, not Hell,' Charlie said. 'I'm sure you can sort some out.'

'You're probably right,' I said, cheered by the sound of his voice. Having him back in my life made me miss him even more in a strange way. 'What are you doing tomorrow?'

'Seeing some friends,' he replied, no stress in his voice at all. 'I'm in charge of the Christmas pud.'

I smiled.

'Marks and Sparks' finest then?'

'I'm not going to make the bugger myself, am I?' he

said. 'They'll still have some if I go this afternoon, won't they?'

'Definitely,' I lied. 'Go and get your shopping done.'

'All right then,' he said. 'If you're sure you're all right.'

'All the better for speaking to you,' I replied, considerably happier than I had been before I made the call. 'Thank you.'

'I'm always here for you,' Charlie said. 'You know that. Apart from those six months when we didn't talk at all, you know I'm always here for you.'

I let out a choked laugh and squeezed my nose together to stop myself from sniffing. Sniffing led to more crying and there was no crying at Christmas.

'And if you can't find a single pig in a blanket in all of America you can always come home,' he said. 'Planes don't know it's Christmas. I could even boil some sprouts to death for you.'

I looked through the window and saw a crosshatched pattern of vapour trails in the sky. What do you know? He was right.

'I've got Amy to look after me,' I told him, wishing he could hear her singing the dirty version of 'Good King Wenceslas' in the shower. 'I'll see you when I get home.'

'You will,' he promised. 'Merry Christmas, Tess.'

'Merry Christmas, Charlie,' I said before I hung up the phone.

Lying back on the bed, my thoughts inevitably circled back round to Nick and the night before. He was angry with me and I couldn't for the life of me fathom why, I clearly was not the arsehole in this equation. Turning up on his doorstep had done nothing to resolve my confusion. If anything, I was more messed up than ever, but one thing was certain now, I'd done all the running

I was going to do. He knew where I was and he knew how to get hold of me. Although given that I'd told him to call me when he wanted to talk like grown-ups, that was never likely to happen, he wasn't capable.

'I'm not going to ruin today,' I announced to the bedroom. 'I'm not going to let Nick Miller ruin Christmas.'

'Good,' Amy said, popping a wet head out of the bathroom. 'And now get your arse out of bed and into the shower. It's a holly jolly holiday and I want to be drunk by three o'clock at the absolute latest. It's traditional.'

'Well,' I said, pushing back the covers and trudging towards the bathroom, 'who am I to argue with tradition?'

'Babychams all round!' Amy shouted. 'Babychams for all!'

'You're getting married a week today,' I told Kekipi as he scooped spoonfuls of rice onto his plate. After a day full of Amy's Christmas traditions, we were indulging in one of Kekipi's. Chinese takeaway for Christmas Eve dinner. 'That's insane.'

'I know,' he said, handing me the little white box full of sweet and sour chicken. 'I really shouldn't be eating this.'

I held up the takeaway box for Amy to snap a pic on her phone.

'Straight on Facebook,' she said before diving in with her chopsticks. 'You look awesome. It's not like you need to worry about fitting into your dress, is it?'

'No, but I do need to worry about marrying a man who is a foot taller and twenty pounds lighter than me,' he replied, merrily shoving wontons into his mouth. 'It's OK for women. Even if you gain a little weight, you still have boobs to distract a straight guy. Everything I have, he has. He can tell straight away if something's not quite right.'

'Never thought of it like that,' Amy said, snapping at thin air and coming up with nothing. 'Can I have a fork? I'm tired.'

'I'm tired, you're drunk,' I corrected. It had been a good day. I'd tracked down a professional photo lab that had printed my picture with brilliant colours, and taken it to the lovely people at Amy's framing shop, who mercifully accepted my groaning credit card without there being an embarrassing scene, where it had been printed and framed while I waited – well, while Amy waited and I went out in search of snacks – and once I had hand-delivered it to the Spencer Gallery, Amy and I set off on our Christmas extravaganza. I couldn't think of any other occasion when I had consumed so much sugar in such a short space of time. Every time I ate something, Amy drank something. I was amazed that she was still vertical, let alone capable of speech.

'Did you know eggnog is really boozy?' she asked Kekipi, squinting across the table with one eye. 'And if you put peppermint schnapps in hot chocolate, it's delicious *and* it'll get you wasted.'

'More wine?' he asked, topping off her glass and righting the cockeyed Santa hat on her head. He was a terrible enabler. 'I can't believe he's going to make an honest man out of me. I'll finally be respectable after all these years.'

'He's marrying you, not working a miracle,' Amy said. 'Domenico is only human.'

'This is true,' Domenico said as he walked into the kitchen where we were all crowded around the table. 'Did you save me a spring roll?

Kekipi had declared that Chinese takeaway in a formal dining room was 'just wrong' and I was inclined to agree. The kitchen was much cosier. And we were going to be stuck with takeaways for the foreseeable. Genevieve had been given a few days off for the holidays and, after her experiment with mind-altering substances at Amy's party, I wasn't entirely sure how soon she'd be coming back.

'You two need to watch how much you put away,' Kekipi said as Amy rummaged around in the drawers, looking for a fork and settling for an ice-cream scoop. 'If you can't fit into your bridesmaid dresses, you'll be banned from the wedding.'

'I should be your best man anyway,' Amy argued, through a scoopful of rice. 'I look brilliant in a suit.'

'She does have more balls than most men I know,' Domenico replied. 'And she would throw you the best bachelor party.'

'Oh, I'm definitely doing that,' she promised. 'It's all planned out, don't you worry.'

'I wasn't worried,' he said, concern on his face as Kekipi clapped. 'Until now.'

'Should we save some for Al?' I asked, looking at the rapidly disappearing food. 'I think there's some more on the kitchen top.'

'He'll probably eat on his way back from church,' Kekipi said. 'There's a diner on the next block he loves.'

'Church?' I was surprised, Al didn't strike me as the religious type. 'Is that a thing?'

'Not so much for him,' Domenico explained. 'But Janey was Irish Catholic. They always went to Mass on Christmas Eve, so now he goes and lights a candle for her.'

I nodded and smiled but didn't say anything. Al loved his wife so much that he went to a church he didn't believe in and lit a candle, after she had died, while all I could inspire in the man I loved were snarky comments and radio silence.

'That's really lovely,' I said, determined not to wallow in my Miller misery.

'Is that your phone?' Amy turned too quickly to look over her shoulder and promptly fell off her stool. My phone rattled across the kitchen counter where it was charging again. 'Tess?'

'It's my mum,' I said, disconnecting the charger and staring at it for a moment. 'What time is it at home?'

'Umm, midnight?' Kekipi said as Domenico hauled Amy up off the floor.

'Something must be wrong.' I swiped to accept the call and walked straight out of the kitchen, my hand tapping against my chest. 'Mum, is everything OK?'

'Merry Christmas to you too,' she replied curtly. 'I can't call my daughter without there being something wrong?'

'No, you can.' I sat down on the bottom step of the staircase, in the dark. 'But you usually don't.'

'Because I'm such a terrible mother,' she said. 'I apologize.'

Well, this was going well. Things weren't great between my mum and me. I knew we loved each other in that 'you came out of me so I'm stuck with you' kind of way but I often found myself wondering whether or not she actually *liked* me. Having spent a fair part of this year not talking to each other at all, our stalemate had finally been broken in the most middle class of ways: when I had to ask if I could redirect my mail to her house so I didn't miss my monthly subscription to the Hotel Chocolat chocolate club while I was in Milan. Since then we'd had an uneasy truce built on text messages and Moonpig birthday cards and passive-aggressive Facebook posts. It was the new Yorkshire way.

'I'm sorry . . .' I tugged on the end of my ponytail. Bad daughter. 'It's late where you are so I was worried.'

'I'm sorting out the turkey,' she explained, rattling the oven door to verify her story. 'And I've got all the kids coming tomorrow so I thought I'd call now before things get busy. I'm sure you've got very exciting plans over there.'

'Not really,' I admitted. 'Just lunch with Amy and everyone.'

'Hmm,' Mum replied. 'Doesn't sound much like Christmas to me.'

'You should see it, Mum,' I said, looking out the window in the front door. 'It's all snowy and pretty and there are lights everywhere, people ringing bells. It's really nice.'

'Sounds like it would give me a migraine,' she sniffed. 'Lesley from the newsagent's didn't like it when she went. Too loud, she said. Filthy as well.'

'Filthy dirty?' I asked. 'Or filthy *dirty*?'

'You know very well what I mean, Tess Brookes.' I heard the oven door slam shut. 'Well, as long as you're all right. We will miss you.'

'You will?' I asked, surprised. Mum and I didn't always get along terribly well. Or at all. 'Mum, are you dying?'

'Have I got to be dying to say something nice now?'

'Well, yeah, sort of,' I replied. 'I mean, I'll miss you too. It'll be weird doing Christmas without you.'

'No one does Christmas the same as your family,' she said with sage wisdom. 'Won't be the same no matter where you are. How's the photo thing going?'

If there was one person who was really upset about me being made redundant from Donovan & Dunning, it was my mother. We'd barely spoken since I told her I wasn't looking for a new office job, but when we had, it was mostly so she could remind me I wasn't married, didn't have any children and was wasting my time on a hobby instead of looking for a proper job and a husband, the most important factors in a life well-lived, according to her.

'It's OK,' I said slowly. 'It's hard, to be honest, but I entered a competition today.'

The last thing I wanted was to give her a stick to beat me with, but at the same time, she was my mum and I still found it difficult not to tell her when things were tough. It was like parental Tourette's, even when I knew she wouldn't help, I couldn't stop myself.

'A competition?' She immediately perked up. 'Do you think you'll win?'

Mum liked it when I won things. It gave her something to brag about at the supermarket.

'I don't know,' I said, ignoring her sigh. 'But I'm excited to have entered. And I did a shoot for a magazine the other day.'

'In New York?' she asked, an edge of pride in her voice.

'Yes, I'll send you a copy of the magazine when it comes out if you like?'

'I'll have a look,' Mum replied. 'You haven't thought any more about going to work for Charlie, then?'

'It would be *with* Charlie,' I corrected with more confidence than I had felt for a while. 'As partners. And no, I don't do that any more, Mum. I'm a photographer.'

'I just don't understand how you can turn your back on years of hard work,' she muttered. 'All them hours for nothing. You didn't chop and change like that in my day.'

'I wasn't planning on it,' I told her. 'But it's done now.'

'And what happens when you change your mind again in five years and decide you want to be, I don't know, an opera singer?' she said, clucking down the line. 'Or a chicken farmer?'

'I can't sing and I'm scared of chickens,' I replied. All that clucking and pecking put me right on edge. 'So I don't think that's going to be a problem. Mum, why are you so sure I'm going to mess this up?'

'I don't think you'll mess it up!' She sounded shocked. 'I'm just worried about you, that's all.'

Never in my twenty-seven years and eleven months had I ever heard my mother say she was worried about me.

'I've never had to worry about you, Tess,' she went on. 'Your sisters haven't got what you've got; they're not ambitious like you. All they wanted was to get married and have a family and they can do that here, where I can keep an eye on them. But you were always different.'

The words every child wanted to hear.

'You were always good at things, Tess,' she said. 'And you've done well for yourself. I don't want to see you throw all that away. Why can't you just settle down with Charlie? You don't want to end up like Amy, do you?'

'There's a difference between settling and compromising, Mum,' I said as kindly as I could. 'I wouldn't be happy if I went back now. And Amy's making a lot more money than I am right now, you wouldn't believe it.'

'But you'll be happy struggling?' she asked. 'Not knowing where your money's coming from?'

'It's going to come from working.' I rested my head against the wall and stretched out my long, tired legs. 'Same as it did before. It might take a bit longer and it might not be as much, but you don't have to worry about me, I promise.'

'I don't understand why anyone would want to struggle at your age,' Mum said with a sigh. 'Why do you make things so hard on yourself?'

'I don't *want* to make things hard,' I said. 'But I do want to be happy and this makes me happy. I think the struggle will be worth it.'

I heard assorted sighing and tutting across the ocean while my mum attempted to come up with an argument and failed.

'All I want is for you to be happy,' she said, finally.

'I am,' I replied, sitting on the staircase of the New York townhouse while some of my best friends ate Chinese food and got tipsy in the next room. How could I not be?

'And for me not to have to worry about you,' she added.

'I don't know if I can do anything about that one,' I said. 'But it's nice to know that you do.'

'Well, of course I do,' she muttered. 'Right. I need to go to bed. Christmas dinner isn't going to cook itself in the morning and no bugger else is going to help me. Certainly not you, off gallivanting around New York.'

And with that, normal parental service was resumed.

'You could always try and call tomorrow if you find the time,' she clucked. 'I'm sure your sisters would appreciate it.'

'I'll call in the morning,' I promised. 'Merry Christmas, Mum.'

'I'll talk to you in the morning,' she said, hanging up, her goodwill exhausted for the season.

'Everything OK?' Amy asked as I reappeared in the kitchen and plugged in my phone. 'What did she want?'

'Just to say Merry Christmas.' I hopped back onto my stool and gave my best friend a hug.

'Wow, something must be wrong,' she said, handing me a fortune cookie. 'She's definitely not dying?'

'Absence makes the heart grow fonder,' Kekipi said, his mouth full of moo shu pork. 'You'd be amazed.'

'What does your fortune say?' Amy asked, watching while I cracked open the cookie.

'*The greatest risk is not taking one*,' I said, raising my eyebrows at the table. 'So there, you've all been told.'

'Mine said the same,' Domenico said, waving his slip of paper in the air. 'But I think my risk is marrying this one.'

'Mine was eating everything on the table.' Amy popped the top button of her jeans and opened her own cookie. '*It never pays to kick a skunk.* What the bloody hell does that mean?'

'The fates have spoken,' Kekipi said in an ominous voice. 'Now, who wants another drink?'

Huddled around the kitchen table and snapping at each other with chopsticks, I realized I was incredibly happy. Sat there with Amy, Kekipi, Domenico and a Chinese takeaway, I couldn't possibly have asked for more. Slipping my fortune into the back pocket of my jeans, I raised my glass in a toast and wondered what the next year could possibly bring that would top this.

CHAPTER SEVENTEEN

'Ho, ho, ho and a merry Christmas.'

It seemed like a terrible waste for Al not to dress up as Santa Claus on Christmas morning. Kekipi, Domenico, Delia and I were sitting around the Christmas tree in the living room, drinking Amy's peppermint schnapps hot chocolate and waiting on the master of the house to present himself before we opened our gifts.

'There you all are,' Al declared, opening his arms up to a hug from his goddaughter.

His curly white hair was fuzzy from his pillow and his beard seemed fluffier and whiter than ever but it was his red flannel pyjama bottoms and holey *Rolling Stones* T-shirt that made me wonder if he really *was* Father Christmas. None of us had seen him on Christmas Eve, and he certainly had the look of a man who had spent the night delivering presents to children all over the world. Amy presented him with his spiked hot chocolate and he settled himself in on his huge leather settee with a very contented sigh.

'How long have you all been awake?' he asked, looking

around at the huge piles of presents that covered the vintage carpets almost entirely. 'I was worried I'd slept through lunch.'

'Not quite,' Kekipi replied. Apparently we were all ignoring the fact that he was wearing his sunglasses inside. With his pyjamas. 'But we have been awake for a while, haven't we, Amy?'

'It's not my fault you don't sleep with earplugs,' she replied, straightening the collar of her polar bear PJs. 'Or that you don't respect the classics.'

'There's nothing classical about being woken up by "Dominic the Christmas Donkey" at six o'clock in the morning,' he replied, adding more schnapps to his cocoa. 'In Hawaii, we celebrate on the beach at a reasonable hour. Kana Kaloka should take all your presents back and burn them.'

'I don't know what that means,' she declared, taking the schnapps. 'And I don't care to.'

'You're lucky,' I told him, my matching polar bear pyjamas accessorized with a pair of Uggs I'd picked up on sale at Bloomingdale's the day before. 'I've been up since five. That's when the high-pitched puppy whining started.'

'*I love Christmas*,' Amy wailed, her head thrown back with frustration. 'Can we *please* open the presents now?'

'Speaking of presents,' Delia, the only one of us who had managed to get completely dressed, said. 'You should open mine now, I have to be at church in an hour.'

'I can't guess what it could be,' Al said, as she presented him with what was clearly a surfboard, completely wrapped in shiny red wrapping paper.

'It's a surfboard,' she said, as he tore open the wrapping. 'Sorry, there's no really great way of disguising it.

I figured you could keep it here. So you can go surfing in the Rockaways. I know you miss it.'

'That's very sweet of you,' he said, giving her a quick kiss on the cheek. 'I think it might be a bit too chilly to catch any waves today.'

'But it'll be great in summer.' She picked up her exquisite Hermes handbag and gave him one more hug. There was always time for an extra hug for Al. 'OK, I have to go meet Cici but I'll be back tonight. Have a great day, you guys.'

'That's a nice board,' Kekipi said, admiring Delia's gift. 'Wasted on these waves, Al.'

'It'll be much happier back in Hawaii,' he agreed. 'As will I.'

'Are you going back soon?' I asked, while Amy scurried around, distributing gifts to each person in the room. 'It's not that long until fashion week, is it?'

'A little over a month,' he nodded. 'But I won't be here. I came to a decision last night, I'm re-retiring.'

Amy stopped dead in the middle of the living room, a white Stormtrooper helmet on her head and a big stuffed bear wearing a grass skirt and a coconut bra in her arms.

'You're re-retiring?' she repeated. 'What does that mean?'

'It means I've had quite enough,' he replied, his eyes opening wide as he sipped his hot chocolate. 'That packs quite a punch, doesn't it? Very good.'

'But what does it mean for the business?' Amy asked from inside her helmet. 'Is this because of the party? Because I'm really, really sorry about the party.'

'This has nothing to do with that at all,' he said with a smile. 'It's more to do with the presentation, if I'm honest. I'm an old man, Amy. I miss my home, I miss the beach. This is a young man's game and I haven't got the appetite for it any more.'

Amy bowed her head, the saddest Stormtrooper you ever did see.

'Not to interrupt, but is that for me?' Kekipi asked, pointing a lightsaber at her helmet. 'Because it's fantastic.'

'I'm surprised, that's all,' Amy said, removing the helmet and handing it to an ecstatic Kekipi. 'After the reviews were so positive? I can't believe you'd kill the line now.'

'I'm not killing anything,' Al said. 'I'm retiring, not shutting up shop. I thought you'd be glad to have me out from underneath your feet.'

Amy tightened her grip around the bear's throat.

'What do you mean?' she asked.

'I can't think of anyone better to take over, can you?' he replied. 'You've spent the last six months shadowing me, why wouldn't I choose you to take over the business?'

'Me?' Amy looked stunned. Aged twenty-eight, five-foot tall and clad in bright blue polar bear pyjamas, it was fair to say she wouldn't be most people's pick to run a business, let alone a fashion line, but then Al wasn't most people. 'You're kidding me?'

'I'm not, I'm afraid,' he said, stroking his beard and taking another sip of his hot chocolate. 'You'll need business support, of course, but we'll hire someone for that. Edward Warren has been very impressed with you and promised me he will step up his support with the manufacture and design end of things. And I will stay on as creative director for now, but I won't be hands-on with the business every day. Really, this cocoa is very good. Is there any more?'

Amy stood in the centre of the room, completely silent.

'This is if you're interested,' Al said. 'Otherwise I can always ask Kekipi.'

'The keys to the kingdom, at last!' he declared, inside the Stormtrooper helmet, his lightsaber held aloft. 'Only, I'm going to pass. Thanks, though.'

'Thank goodness,' Domenico muttered. 'I was about to retract my proposal.'

'You can't be serious?' Amy said, folding her legs up underneath her and sitting down right where she had stood. 'You can't *really* want me to run your business.'

'I want you to try,' he replied. 'I don't expect you to do it on your own and I know you still have a lot to learn, but I believe in you, Amy. You understand what I'm trying to achieve and I trust your instincts. I don't want to hire some seasoned CEO to take AJB and turn it into something it's not. You created the presentation from scratch and it couldn't have been more perfect if I'd done every last thing myself. It couldn't have been more perfect if my Janey had been running the show. You've proved to me that you can do it, now it's time to prove it to yourself. Merry Christmas.'

'Bloody hell,' she said, staring at the carpet, dazed. 'I got you a hat. It's not even a very good one.'

The doorbell rang as Al roared with laughter.

'I'll get it,' I said, scrambling to my feet while Domenico kissed his Imperial Stormtrooper on the top of his head. Who went round ringing doorbells on Christmas Day? We weren't expecting any guests as far as I knew.

'Two packages for Tess Brookes.' A man in brown overalls waved a black handheld device at me. 'Sign in the box.'

'Oh,' I said, startled, as he dumped one giant cardboard

box and a small paper carrier bag inside the foyer. 'OK. Thank you.'

'Happy holidays,' he grunted. 'And Happy New Year.'

'You too.' I stared at the packages as he climbed back in his truck and drove away. I tried to pick up the box but it was far too heavy. Accepting defeat, I shoved it towards the living room, the brown, taped-up gift bag resting on top.

'What is it?' Amy asked, jumping to her feet and grabbing the gift bag. 'Who is it from?'

'No idea,' I said, hands on my hips. 'Let's open it and see.'

I scratched my nail underneath the edge of the packing tape and tore it off with a loud rip. The flaps of the box flew open to reveal a cornucopia of festive English goodies: Christmas crackers, yule log, Quality Street, bottles of Baileys, boxes of After Eights, mince pies, jam tarts – and a huge netted bag of sprouts.

'Oh my GOD!' Amy grabbed a huge box of Jaffa Cakes and pressed it to her heart, spinning around the room. 'I haven't had a Jaffa Cake in months. I have *missed* you, my love.'

'Who is this from?' Kekipi pulled out a box of Ferrero Rocher and handed it to Domenico, who screwed up his face in disgust. 'Who hates you this much?'

Ripping open a white envelope, I pulled out a glittery Christmas card.

'It's from Charlie,' I said, watching a folded sheet of A4 float down to the floor. 'It's everything we usually have at my mum's house at Christmas.'

Al pulled out a bag of Buttons. 'How thoughtful.'

I picked up the piece of paper, read it, picked up the bottle of Baileys and went to sit on the sofa.

'What does it say?' Amy asked, chasing after me with a Jaffa Cake in each hand.

'It's a job description,' I said, handing her the piece of paper. She rammed both Jaffa Cakes into her mouth and wiped her hands on her pyjama bottoms before taking it. I opened the Baileys and took a swig out of the bottle. 'For a position at The BrookesWilder Agency.'

'It's got a ring to it,' Kekipi said, reading over Amy's shoulder. 'He's offering you *how* much?'

'I know.' I gulped down a mouthful of cream liqueur and shuddered. 'And that's for four days a week. I'd have one day off to work on my photography.'

'That's terribly generous,' Al said. 'Terribly thoughtful and terribly generous. He must value you a great deal, Tess.'

'It's not her values he's interested in.' Amy picked up the brown paper gift bag, tore it open and tossed me what looked like an oddly shaped leather handbag while she scanned the note that came with it. 'Oh, piss off, knobchops!'

'What is it?' Al asked.

'What does the note say?' Kekipi asked.

'I'll go and make more cocoa,' Domenico offered.

'It's a camera case,' I said, slipping the cushioned leather strap around my neck. 'For my camera.'

It was truly beautiful. Soft brown leather with a long, cushioned neck, no obvious brand or label, just true craftsmanship. I reached out to grab my camera from the side table and slipped it inside.

'Perfect fit,' Al said.

'As if it were made for me,' I replied. 'It's gorgeous.'

'My present is better,' Amy said, shoving a piece of paper down the back of her pyjama bottoms. 'Let's open my presents.'

'What does the note say?' Kekipi asked.

'What note?' Amy asked, all innocence.

'The one you're trying to hide in your knickers,' he replied, picking her up off the ground and shaking her. 'Give it up, Miss Smith.'

'This is sexual harassment!' she yelled at Al. 'Or short-person harassment. It's definitely harassment of some kind.'

'You haven't said yes to the job, yet,' he pointed out. 'My hands are tied.'

'What does it say?' I asked, stroking my camera case. My head was swimming and I didn't know if it was from the spiked hot chocolate, the job offer, or the incredibly thoughtful gift.

'Oh,' Kekipi said, his face falling. He looked up and locked his eyes on mine. 'Let's open Amy's presents, shall we?'

'What does it say?' I demanded, still clutching the bottle of Baileys. 'Amy!'

'It says he loves you,' she said, sticking her fingers down her throat. '*Tess, I love you. I want to try. I'll call you soon.* Lame.'

'It doesn't say lame,' Kekipi qualified. 'I believe that's her review of the note.'

'Thanks,' I nodded. 'For clearing that up.'

Charlie loved me? All of a sudden I felt light-headed. What happened to being friends, just friends, again?

'Let's not do anything rash,' Amy said, folding up the note into the tiniest possible square and dropping it inside a huge glass vase. 'Let's sit down, eat this tin of Quality Street and get back to him after dinner. You don't want to ruin his Christmas, do you?'

'Do you think he knows it's been delivered?' I asked,

suddenly sweating. 'They'll email him, won't they? He'll be expecting me to call or something.'

'There's the time difference,' Amy argued. 'And you might not have been home when they delivered it. Tess, don't do anything stupid. Sit down and eat some chocolate, you're not thinking straight.'

'You're right,' I said, standing up, my camera snugly in its case around my neck. 'I need some fresh air.'

Without another word, I grabbed my handbag and someone's coat from the cupboard and walked right out the door.

Christmas Day in England saw the world stand still. The shops were closed, the roads were quiet and hardly a soul left the house unless they were testing out a new bike for the first time on their way to eat more turkey and roast potatoes than could possibly be healthy. But New York did not play by the same rules. Fifth Avenue was as busy at 9 a.m. on 25 December as it was on 24 December and 23 and 22. Delivery men rode their bicycles on and off the pavement, buses mowed down the left-hand lanes of the road, while taxis honked at each other as they swerved around corners, and dozens of people, bundled up in hats, scarves and gloves, buzzed towards the park with their families, cups of coffee, and all creatures, great and small.

I joined the stream, entering the gate right next to the spot where I'd broken in two nights before. Instead of walking the tree I'd shinned up, I made a sharp right, heading for the lake. A big red padded jacket over bright blue flannel pyjamas and tan Uggs, with a camera hung around my neck, and not a single person looked my way.

I loved New York.

Eventually I ran out of steam and sat down on an empty bench right by the edge of the lake, the water still and green and dotted with tiny icebergs.

I couldn't stop wondering what my family were doing. It would be the afternoon in England now. Were they having dinner? Had they finished already? Was *The Sound of Music* on telly? I had promised them I'd call, I thought. I'd just give them a quick bell. They could always ignore it if they were eating.

'Hello?' My sister, Mel, answered the phone.

'Merry Christmas!' I boomed, causing a flurry of ducks to take off across the water.

'We're eating,' she replied. 'What do you want?'

'Nice to hear from you too,' I said, kicking a stone with my toe. 'I just wanted to say Merry Christmas.'

'All right,' she said. 'Anything else?'

'You're in a festive mood then,' I sniffed. My sister was rarely the most exuberant of humans but this was impressive, even for her. 'Cheer up, Mel, anyone would think it was Christmas.'

'It might be Christmas in New York with all your fancy mates,' she replied, sounding more and more like our mum every day, 'but I've already had to drive forty minutes in the pissing rain with two screaming toddlers – and given that my husband is well on his way to getting shitfaced with Brian, it looks like I'll be driving back again tonight. So, I'm not really in the Christmas spirit, no.'

'Fair,' I replied. 'Is Mum there?'

'Mum,' she bellowed. 'It's Tess.'

'Tell her I'm eating,' she shouted back.

'She's eating,' Mel relayed. 'Can I go now?'

'Yeah,' I said, deflating as I spoke. At least Charlie was

right about one thing, Christmas Day at my mum's house would have been about as much fun as elective surgery. 'I suppose.'

'Liz wants to know, when are you coming home?' she asked, speaking for our younger sister. 'You know she's up the duff again?'

'I didn't, actually,' I replied. 'When did she announce that bombshell?'

Liz had always wanted a thousand children. It wasn't a huge surprise that she was on her second before she had turned twenty-four.

'She saved it for today, didn't she?' Mel muttered. 'You know how she likes an audience. I thought she might have texted you.'

'Thankfully not,' I said, slightly annoyed that she hadn't. Oh, the contrariness of sisterhood. 'And I'm not sure when I'll be up. Some time in January, I should think?'

'Well, you've got a load of post here,' she said. 'Nothing that exciting from the looks of it, but there's a whole bloody bagful.'

'There shouldn't be,' I said, frowning. I'd asked Mum to shout if anything important turned up. She had yet to shout. 'Can you see it? What's it say?'

'I'm not your bloody secretary, Tess,' she snorted, although the sound of shuffling plastic bag suggested she wasn't quite so offended. 'I'm not opening fifty bloody letters and reading them all to you.'

'I know,' I said, even as I heard her tearing into an envelope. '*Dear Miss Brookes, blah blah blah, your smear test is overdue.*'

'Thanks.' That would have been nice to know.

'*Dear Miss Brookes, if you move your credit card balance to us—*'

'Next,' I said. 'We don't need to talk about my credit card balance right now. But hang on to that one.'

'Yes, sir,' she replied. 'Ooh, this one's handwritten. *Tess, this is my fourth letter. I know by now you're not going to reply but I'm still going to write—*' She fell silent, but I could hear her breathing as the paper rustled.

Every atom of breath was knocked out of me.

'I don't know who this bloke is,' Mel said. 'But he sounds like a right tart. Got a massive hard-on for you, hasn't he? Who writes letters these days? And I really did not need to know what you were getting up to under a waterfall in Hawaii. Really, Tess, anyone could have seen you.'

'How many more letters are there?' I asked, still struggling to breathe. 'What does the postmark say? Why didn't Mum tell me about them?'

'There's about fifty,' she said. 'At least. And I don't know, I'm not her keeper. You can't see the postmark, can you? They've got the redirect sticker on them. Can I go and finish my dinner now?'

'From Nick?' I asked. The lake seemed to pull away from me and I gripped the splintered wood of the bench with my free hand. 'There are fifty letters from Nick?'

'Oh no, there's maybe ten, twelve with the same handwriting,' she said, her voice breezy. 'Are you in some sort of trouble? Is he a stalker?'

'What's going on?' Mum shouted.

'Tess has got a stalker,' Mel replied.

'She's such a drama queen,' Liz screeched. 'She can't have a stalker, I'm having a baby.'

'Mel, I'm really sorry to be a pain but could you just open a couple, and take a picture, and send them?' I pleaded. 'I know, you want to finish your dinner but this is really important. You don't have to do all of them right now but I really need to see those letters. Please?'

'You're right, I don't have to do anything,' she snipped. 'But my sprouts will be cold by now anyway. The only thing worse than Mum's sprouts are Mum's sprouts when they're cold.'

'I can hear you!' our mother shrieked in the background.

'I'm sending them and then I'm deleting them,' Mel said, the sound of tearing paper ripping down the line. I wanted to tell her to be more careful with the envelopes, but I also wanted her not to burn them before I could read them. 'I do not want this on my phone, I do not want to have to explain it to Darren.'

My phone buzzed against my ear with incoming texts and I looked up at the sky, all soft white and dove grey, promising snow and I was too scared to open the images. I was also scared about my roaming bill.

'There, have you got them?' she asked.

'I have, thank you,' I said.

'Mum!' a thin voice wailed down the line. 'I need a wee!'

'I'm coming!' she shouted. 'I've got to go. She won't let anyone else take her to the toilet at the moment; it's driving me mental and I haven't brought a spare pair of pants. I'll send the rest later.'

My hands were shaking so much I could barely hold my phone. 'Everything's OK, Mel, it's all fine. Don't worry about it. Send them whenever you can. I'll talk to you later. Love you.'

'Well, now I know something's up,' she muttered. 'Go and have a drink, for Christ's sake.'

She hung up and I cradled my phone in my palm and,

one by one, tapped on the four images in my sister's texts.

> *Dear Tess,*
> *This is my fourth letter. I know by now you're not going to reply but I'm still going to write. I was in Tulum this week (that's in Mexico) and you would have loved it.*

'I knew where Tulum is,' I mumbled. 'Sort of.'

> *I trekked out to visit the Mayan ruins and it was so beautiful. I completed my scuba diving training as well and I can officially teach now. I've been thinking of spending some time in Australia next year – I've got a buddy who has a dive school over there – but I'm not sure. Anything that keeps me moving. Anything that keeps me busy.*
> *Call me, I love you.*

The next note must have been sent later. It was a plain piece of paper with something stuck to the page. When I zoomed in, I saw it was an entrance ticket to the *duomo* in Milan. He had kept the ticket from our visit. At the bottom of the page, there were the same five words.

> *Call me, I love you.*

The next was the second or third in our one-sided conversation. My nose prickled and my eyes stung as I read, not able to stop myself from wondering what might have happened if I'd received just a single one of his notes.

Tess,

I don't know if you received my first letter, if
you're ignoring me or just taking your time.
Maybe you're trying to torture me. God knows I
deserve it but I can't take it.

I'm leaving New York for the summer. I had
planned to come to London, I had hoped I'd be
able to see you, but all this waiting to hear
from you is too much for me. I'll let you know
where I land. I'm thinking Mexico, maybe
Central America, nowhere I won't be able to get
back to you. If you want me to. I hope that you
do.

Call me, I love you.

The last note was just that, the last note.

Tess,

It's been almost five months now. Do you
know that? Do you know how long it's been?
Five months since we were in Milano, five
months since I fell in love with you, five
months since I ruined everything. Either you
don't know or you don't care. Either way, I
can't keep writing these letters. I'm not even
sure if you'll receive this – the post in
Venezuela is not famous for its speedy or reliable service. I'm headed back to New York
soon, I've got some work to do and I promised
my family I'd visit England over Christmas. I
need to start my life again. Without you in it,
whether I like it or not.

I love you.

No 'call me'. He'd given up. The letter was dated mid-November but redirected from London to my mum's house on the twentieth of December. The day I'd left for New York. I closed each of the pictures, saving them to the phone's memory and uploading them to the Cloud forever and ever, safe in a bunker full of memories somewhere I would never know. I skipped through to Nick's number as quickly as I could and pressed call. This time it didn't matter that I didn't know what to say to him, all he needed to know was that I'd read the letters. But it didn't even ring; it didn't even connect to his voicemail. There was nothing on the line.

'Maybe he's still flying,' I told myself, my face wet and my skin stinging. 'Or his battery could be dead. Or his phone might not work in England.'

Or maybe he blocked your number, the voice in my head suggested. Maybe he thought you'd been ignoring his beautiful, heartfelt letters and then showed up on his doorstep, didn't even mention them and now he never wants to speak to you again.

At the bottom of my handbag, a little rubber duck eyed me with disappointment.

I remembered chucking him in there before I left for New York. I should have left him in Amy's bathroom with Pete the Pooper.

'Nope,' I said, fingering the supple leather of the camera case and looking at the glitter pressed into the lines on the palms of my hands. It was from Charlie's Christmas card. He had branded me with sparkles, all the way across the ocean.

'Remember when all I wanted was this?' I asked, as he nestled in between my passport and an open packet of tissues. 'The unconditional love of Charlie Wilder and all the After Eights I could eat?'

He shifted and gave me a judgemental quack.

'Thanks for being so supportive,' I told him as I watched two joggers running around the opposite side of the lake. Who went running on Christmas Day? Weirdos.

Said the woman sitting on a park bench talking to a plastic duck.

'He's gone back to England for God knows how long,' I whispered. 'I don't even know how to get hold of him.'

The duck stared at me, his painted-on eyes full of judgement.

'You know, you're not helping,' I shouted, picking him up and hurling him into the lake. He disappeared into the water for a moment before popping up to the surface and bobbing around a few feet from the edge.

I watched, hands pressed to my mouth as he floated away, bobbing along past three cigarette butts and an empty coffee cup.

'Oh God.' I clapped my hand against my forehead, pushed my hair away from my face and shoved my phone back inside my bag. I couldn't leave him in there. Who else would insult me when I was all alone? 'Hold on, I'm coming.'

The water wasn't deep and he wasn't far away. Gritting my teeth, I crouched down on my knees at the edge of the lake, stretching out over the water and trying to reach him, but his neon-yellow tail wobbled away, an inch from my fingertips.

'Nope, that's not going to do it,' he said, sailing further away.

'Fuck fuck fuck fuck fuck!' I pushed myself up off the

floor, picking tiny stones out of the palms of my hands. Tiny stones and glitter. 'Fuck fuck fuckity fuck.'

It was no 'Rudolph, the Red Nosed Reindeer' but it was quite catchy.

I tiptoed into the water, an inch or so lapping around the soles of my boots, and swiped at the surface as he drifted farther away.

'Fine!' I said, marching right out into the lake until I was up to my knees. 'Fine! I'll get wet through and catch a cold and die. Then will you be happy?'

'I wouldn't say happy,' someone said behind me. 'But it's pretty funny.'

Standing by the bench, clad in her blue fake fur, giant sunglasses obscuring her face, two steaming coffees in one hand and filming me on her phone with the other, was Amy.

'No, don't stop,' she said. 'I'm getting some really good stuff here.'

'I want that played at my funeral,' I scooped up the rubber duck, shoved him in my pocket and waded back out of the water. 'How did you know where I was?'

'I always know where you are,' Amy replied, holding out her hand to beckon me back to dry land. 'That and you put the Find Your Friends app on our phones remember?'

It was useful for those times when Amy woke up halfway across the city and had left her credit card behind a bar, which used to happen roughly once a month but now I thought about it, I couldn't remember the last time I'd had to send an Uber on a quest around London to find her.

'Are you going to come out of there or should I join you?' she asked as I pocketed the duck. 'Looks chilly.'

'It's not actually as cold as I thought it might be.' I waded towards the side. 'But I'd give it a miss if I were you.'

'Good.' She sat down on the bench and shoved her sunglasses onto the top of her head. 'Because I wasn't getting in anyway. I'd ask if you're all right but you've clearly gone completely off-your-tits mental.'

Knee deep in a lake, holding a miniature rubber duck with whom I'd just had an in-depth conversation about my philosophy on life, I shrugged, then climbed out with a wet splodge between my toes. My poor new Uggs.

'Is it the pyjamas?' I asked, sheepish as I sat down beside her. 'Or the fact that I just destroyed brand-new two hundred dollar shoes?'

'The shoes,' she said, looking down at her own pyjamas. 'The outfit is very next season – I should know, I run a fashion business.'

'Oh yeah, congrats on that,' I said. Bending down, I pulled off my boots and emptied out the grayish-green water. 'I think I might have overreacted to the present.'

'I don't blame you,' she said. 'When a man sends me presents on Christmas Day I always nick off to the park and try to Virginia Woolf myself.'

'I wasn't topping myself' I replied, presenting her with the duck in my pocket. 'I was just rescuing my rubber duck.'

'Makes perfect sense,' Amy replied.

'So, it turns out Nick sent me dozens of love letters that my mum didn't think to mention,' I added, taking my coffee and staring at the water as it soothed itself, as though I'd never been there. 'So that's nice.'

'She is a terrible PA, remind me never to hire her,' she said. 'Are you serious?'

'Completely,' I nodded. 'I suppose him treating me like a total moose makes a bit more sense now. Christ.'

'A tiny bit,' Amy acknowledged. 'What are you going to do?'

I shrugged and drank my coffee, letting it warm me up, all the way down to my cold, wet toes.

'What do you want to do?' she asked. 'Honestly?'

'I don't know,' I said. 'Charlie's job offer is amazing and the sensible thing to do would be to take it, but I couldn't take the job knowing he feels that way when I don't. I feel guilty because I did but now I don't. I feel like I've led him on.'

'Regardless of whether or not you take the job, you're still going to have to tell him how you feel,' she said. 'And he might not want to be your friend any more. You know that, don't you?'

'Yes, I do,' I said. 'And it's not fair.'

'Nope,' she agreed. 'But it is what it is. You're not going to send all that food back though, are you?'

'How much of it have you opened already?' I asked.

'Loads,' she said, dropping her head onto my shoulder. 'Most of it. And I licked some of it.'

'I don't know what to say to him,' I said, stroking my camera case.

'And what about Nick?'

'I think he's blocked my number,' I said, my shoulders sagging and my feet squelching. 'So that should be fine.'

'You two need your heads knocking together,' she said, producing a handful of contraband Quality Street from her pocket. 'You're in love with him, he's in love with you, I don't see what's so difficult about it.'

'I think that's the point,' I said, selecting the green triangle. 'It shouldn't be. So maybe it isn't love?'

'It's only difficult because you're both being total knob-heads about it,' she reasoned. 'I don't know which of you is more mental.'

The chocolate stuck to my teeth as I chewed thoughtfully. 'I think it's him.'

'I might agree,' Amy replied. 'Had I not just found you knee deep in a lake, fishing for rubber ducks.'

'Do you think I'm making a mistake?' I asked, already knowing her answer. 'Turning down Charlie and the job?'

'No, I don't. And neither do you. You're panicking because things are changing,' she said with complete certainty. 'I know it's scary but it doesn't mean it's bad. Christ, I'm more scared that things are going so well for me.'

'So change is good and everything is better than it was?' I flicked a leaf off my knee and watched it bob away on the water. 'Awesome.'

'I've got something that might cheer you up.' She pulled a tiny blue box wrapped in white ribbon out of her coat pocket and held it out to me. 'You didn't open your Christmas present.'

'Amy, you shouldn't have.' I took the box in my hands, almost too afraid to pull on the perfect bow. Even I knew where this was from.

'Relax, it's not a ring,' she said, grinning underneath her sunglasses. 'You always get me nice things for Christmas and birthdays and I've never been able to get you anything good before. I wanted to get you something to keep forever, to make up for all the shit presents.'

'This is way too much.' I opened the Tiffany & Co box carefully, lifting the lid to reveal a tiny white chain with a sparkling solitaire diamond pendant set against black velvet. 'Amy, I got you boots.'

'You got me a best friend,' she corrected. 'And I know they say diamonds are a girl's best friend, but I reckon you're better than a diamond. It's like, this year has been so mental and I've got a funny feeling next year is only going to be worse. I wanted you to have something to remind you of me if we're not together.'

'And if things get really bad, I can sell it!' I said, pulling it out and fastening it around my neck. It went perfectly with the pyjamas. 'I love you, you daft mare.'

'I should think so too,' she said, taking a sip from her coffee cup. 'I just gave you a diamond necklace.'

We sat for a while, staring out over the water, just like we had when we were little girls. I'd assumed things would make more sense by the time we were looking down the barrel of thirty. How wrong could you be?

'We can't freak out every time things change,' she said, yawning as she spoke. 'No one can turn back time, you know, life only goes forward.'

'This is unusually deep for you,' I said, turning to look at my best friend, my soulmate. 'Are you all right?'

'I watched *Eat Pray Love* the other night,' she explained. 'I'd make the most of it if I were you.'

'Noted,' I replied checking the time on my phone. We needed to get back to the house. 'Come on, Julia, it's time for dinner.'

Amy jumped up, slinging her bag over her head and hopping from foot to foot.

'Good, I'm starving,' she said, dragging me down the path, my Uggs squelching as I walked. 'I hope there's Yorkshire puddings.'

'You might be struggling for that,' I warned her. 'But there is that bottle of Baileys in Charlie's care package.'

'There *was* a bottle of Bailey's,' she said, wincing and patting her belly. 'Sorry.'

'Your own business and a drinking problem,' I said with a sigh. 'You're so New York, Amy Smith.'

'*Right?*' she replied in her best American accent. 'Now let's get you back inside before you catch your death.'

'And Yorkshire through and through,' I added, weaving my arm through hers. 'Thank God.'

CHAPTER EIGHTEEN

'This is so exciting,' Amy whispered in my ear. 'When will they tell everyone else to sod off home because you've won?'

'I'm not sure it works like that,' I said, nursing my untouched glass of red wine. 'I don't think they announce the winners tonight. This is more like opening night, I think.'

'Well, when will you find out?' Kekipi asked, looking disappointed. 'Why did we bother coming if there's no fireworks and giant cheque?'

'Free bar?' I suggested, smoothing down the sleeve of the new black silk Alice and Olivia dress he had fortunately given me for Christmas. I *looked* good enough, even if I didn't feel it. 'And so we can meet the people who decide who wins the apprenticeship and butter them up.'

'Point me in the right direction,' Amy said. 'You know I'll do whatever it takes.'

'And if he's not interested in that, I can take one for the team,' Kekipi promised. 'Dom won't be here for another hour or so, he's picking up his suit for the wedding.'

'You're an inspiration,' I told him. 'Is Al still coming?'

'Should be on his way,' he said. 'He knows it's important to you.'

I nodded, clicking my fingernails against the stem of my glass. It was a classy affair. String quartet, passed hors d'oeuvres, nice red wine in real glasses. Most of the women were wearing high heels and expensive handbags and everyone seemed to know everyone. I didn't know a soul other than the two reprobates I'd brought along with me.

'Where's your photo?' Amy picked the olive out of her martini and munched, looking around the stark white walls. 'I can't see it.'

'There are loads of different categories,' I said, folding my programme awkwardly with one hand. 'I'm entered in the New Image prize which should be in gallery number three.'

'And which gallery is this?' she asked.

'I don't know,' I said. 'I'm not psychic.'

'Ooh.' Amy raised her eyebrows. 'All right, madam, just asking.'

'I'm sorry,' I muttered, looking around at the mass of New York's tastefully dressed art lovers and then back at my best friend. More than three-quarters of the attendees were head to toe in black, myself and Kekipi included. Amy was as subtle as Amy was capable of being in a bright red, skintight AJB shift dress. Everyone looked at us as they passed by, putting me even more on edge. 'I'm nervous, that's all.'

'You need more to drink,' Amy advised. 'Let me get you a cocktail.'

'No, really.' I waved at Angela and Jenny across the room. 'I'm fine.'

'That's a matter of opinion,' Kekipi replied. 'I agree with Miss Amy. You need to relax and enjoy yourself. This is your first exhibition!'

'I'm kind of amazed they accepted my photo,' I admitted. 'Do you think Al asked Delia to have a word?'

'No, I don't,' he said, pinching a crostini from a passing waitress. 'Because I asked him and he said he hadn't.'

'Oh.' I ignored my grumbling stomach. I was too nervous to eat, I had been all day. I had been all week. Between the exhibition, Charlie's declaration of love, Nick's phone, email and every possible social media channel blocking my every attempt at communication, I'd barely managed more than a piece of toast in the last three days. 'OK.'

'That's a good thing,' Kekipi explained. 'You're here because your photo is good. Not because Al called in a favour. You can be happy now.'

'I *am* happy,' I said, rattling my fingers against my glass again and giving him a big, fake smile. 'See?'

'Ecstatic,' he replied. 'Well done.'

'Ladies!' Angela, wearing a black-and-white stripy jumper with a huge sequined red love heart on the front and perfectly fitting leather jeans, zoomed in on me with kisses and hugs and clinking glasses. For a moment I wondered whether or not I could pull off leather jeans and then I returned to reality. 'And gentlemen.'

'Where?' Kekipi replied, throwing air kisses over her shoulders. 'Is he hot?'

'The hottest,' Jenny replied before giving me a quick hug, her black leather mini dress clinging to every curve. I wondered whether or not she and Angela had coordinated on purpose or if there was a cool leather dress code I'd missed. 'So, where's the photo? Are you excited?'

'Ye-e-es,' I said, still not sure. 'I haven't seen my picture yet.'

'Then let's go find it.' Jenny grabbed my wrist and dragged me along behind her, barging through the assembled crowds. 'Excuse me, coming through.'

'She's amazing,' Amy breathed. 'Where did you find her?'

'You don't find her, she finds you,' Angela replied. 'And then you hold on for dear life.'

The five of us stalked through the gallery, until I spotted a tiny plaque by the entrance to an almost empty room.

'That's it,' I pointed. 'New Image prize. It'll be in there.'

'Tess, look!' Amy ran ahead of us and right up to my picture. 'This is amazing. Your name is on the wall next to it and everything!'

She pulled out her phone, ignoring every sign that asked her not to, and snapped a photo of my photo.

'It looks great,' Angela said. 'You must be really pleased with it.'

The framing shop had done a beautiful job. The black wooden frame and stark white mount set off the bold image of James and Sadie. The colours were clear and bright and the lighting was perfect. It popped right off the wall. Very Ess.

'I couldn't have done it without you,' I said to Angela, looking around at my competition. Nothing else was as bright or colourful as mine and I couldn't work out if that was a good thing or not. 'Really, I literally would not have this photo if it weren't for you.'

'The issue is out on the first.' She smiled and squeezed my arm. 'I'll make sure you get one. I really was pleased with the photos.'

'Thanks,' I said, squinting at my photo. The more I looked at it, the less I liked it. I'd already found half a dozen things I wanted to change. It was weird; I was never insecure like this before and I didn't like it one little bit. 'Shall we go and have a look at the other galleries?'

'No,' Amy refused, taking a selfie of herself and Jenny throwing up gang signs next to my picture. 'I want to look at every other photo in your category and tell you why it's crap.'

'You should be proud,' Jenny said, raising a perfect eyebrow. 'This is kickass.'

'I *am* proud,' I said. And I was. I just didn't need to stare at my own photo all night. 'But we should meet some people, shouldn't we? Network?'

'Oh, Angie!' Jenny pressed a hand to her heart and smiled. 'Look at my baby, she wants to network.'

Angela rolled her eyes and looked down at her phone. 'Another successful project,' she told her friend. 'I'll be right back, I need to call Alex.'

'I'm dry,' Amy announced, turning her empty glass upside down. 'Who wants a drink?'

'I do,' I said, quickly hiding my almost full glass on a little shelf behind me. What I really wanted was a minute to myself. 'White wine if they've got any left.'

'I'll get something wet and in a glass,' she called. 'You diva, you.'

As my friends drifted away, I turned back to my picture and stared. Maybe the colours were too bright. Maybe the focus was too sharp. And was it me, or did James look like he was faking that smile? Before I could leave, a crowd of people entered the gallery, swarming me into a corner. Trying my best to look casual, I stared intently at my neighbour's entry, a black-and-white study of a glass-encased carousel, and gave them a polite, tight-lipped smile.

'Tess Brookes?'

I tensed at the sound of my name, looking around to see who was talking to me but there was no one. Instead, I saw two men peering at my photograph, one of them squinting at my name, printed on the wall beside my photo.

'Represented by Veronica Wright,' one said. 'Have I met her?'

'If you had met Veronica Wright, you'd know about it,' the other replied. 'Trust me.'

Both of the men were older than me, one taller and one shorter. I held my breath and raised my empty glass to my lips, pretending to drink. There was no way they could know who I was but I suddenly felt as though I had a giant neon sign flashing above my head, screaming, 'I Am Tess! Judge me!' because that, I realized as soon as I saw their blue name badges, was exactly who they were. They were judging the Spencer prize.

'Am I missing something?' the tall man asked. 'What am I looking at?'

'I think it's an advert for this dress,' his colleague responded, tapping a pen on the photograph and showing flagrant disregard for the no touching rule and my ego. 'Sadie Nixon is hot.'

Lifting his glasses to take a better close-up look, the tall man winced. 'I've seen better pictures on Instagram. Did she take this on her phone?'

'At least that would make it interesting,' the other argued, shovelling crostini in his mouth while he hurled insults at my photograph. 'The composition is nice. And the celebrity-friend angle almost distracted me from how derivative it is, which is impressive in its own way.'

Thank God I hadn't eaten, I would have almost certainly thrown up.

'I don't understand why it's in here.' The tall man screwed up his face, still staring at the photo while I dissolved into nothing behind him. 'It has absolutely no artistic value. What's the message? What's the theme? Why isn't it in the commercial gallery?'

'It's a shame, really,' the short man nodded in agreement. 'She obviously had resources the other entrants didn't. A studio, professional models – but there's nothing here. No honesty in it, no authenticity; there's no value. She's not telling me anything other than pretty people look pretty.'

'Then maybe she's actually cleverer than we thought,' the first one laughed. 'Maybe she's the only photographer in here who's being honest.'

'And now I'm depressed.' The short man shook his head and walked away, leaving the tall critic alone to stare at my work. 'Did you see the landscape gallery? I think Dan Fraser has something new.'

'I'll be there in a moment,' the tall man said. 'I should look at the others. Who do you like?'

'None of them,' his friend replied. 'But we've got to choose one, right?'

The short man gave me a brief smile as he walked out, throwing a dirty napkin in the bin as he went. My feet felt like lead. It was one thing to think all those things about yourself but it was another to hear someone else say it out loud. Someone whose opinion really mattered. Was the photo really that bad?

'Hello, there.'

I looked up to see the tall man smiling at me, as if there was anything to smile about.

'Hello.'

It didn't cost anything to be polite, even if you were dead inside.

'Having a good time?' he asked, nodding towards the crowds outside our gallery. 'Busy night.'

'Yes,' I replied, staring at my apparently shitty photo. 'It's busy.'

'You're British,' he said, seemingly delighted but thankfully failing to put two and two together. 'Do you live in the US or are you just visiting us?'

'Just visiting,' I confirmed, trying to smile but only succeeding in looking something like a constipated otter. 'I'm leaving the day after tomorrow.'

He was almost as tall as Charlie but with none of his charm. His slicked-back blond hair and flat blue eyes didn't exactly scream creative genius but the cut of his suit and expensive tie did suggest endless pots of money. It was the strangest thing, the richer people were, the more alike they looked. Apparently that was true of Americans as well as English people.

'I like this one,' I said, pointing at my own photo, masochist that I am.

'Really?' He looked mildly surprised, turning back to my photo with new eyes, prepared to reconsider his opinion if it would get me to drop my knickers. 'I suppose there is an energy there. A naïve charm.'

'What's wrong with it?' I asked, trying to see what he saw. 'What don't you like about it?'

'It doesn't tell me anything,' he replied, gesturing to James and Sadie with his wine glass. Now that he turned to face me, he was oddly familiar. But then I always struggled to differentiate men who earned over two hundred grand a year. You'd think with that much money, they would invest in some individualism and yet they seemed so determined to look identical.

'I don't know anything about these people. I don't know anything about the artist. There's no truth here, nothing is being revealed,' he said. 'I've forgotten it as soon as I look at the next image. It's candy, no substance.'

With a reluctant nod, I scratched at the corner of my eye. I didn't even disagree with him. I should never have entered the photo. Why hadn't I chosen one of the other pictures? Something with more guts to it?

'It's fine for what it is. I guess the gallery chose it because they thought the subjects might attend,' he laughed and finished off his wine in one quick swallow. 'But it could be so much more. Would you like a drink?'

'Tess, it's been forever!'

Her perfume hit me before her hug and it was hard to say which was more nauseating. A cloud of heavy, woody notes, wrapped around a bright blonde blow-out, choked any reply out of my throat.

'What are you doing in New York?'

'What are *you* doing in New York?' I asked, all the colour draining from my face.

'Silly!' Vanessa Kittler, my former flatmate and winner of my least-favourite-person-in-the-world award for the sixth year running, tightened her grip around my shoulders, her sharp-pointed fingernails digging into my flesh. 'I always come to New York for New Year, you know that.'

I knew she visited New York all the time and I knew she always went *somewhere* for New Year but since Vanessa was a compulsive liar and had generally considered conversation an optional extra during the six years we had lived together, this was news to me.

'Tess, I see you've met David.' Vanessa waved her crystal-studded clutch bag at the tall judge. 'David Sanders, this is my very good friend, Tess Brookes. I'm so glad you've already met. Tess, David owns a gallery in Chelsea and he's bought lots of my pictures.'

'Tess?' David blanched and pulled at his collar as though his tie was trying to strangle him. Now I knew why I recognized him. He was one of Vanessa's conquests. 'Tess Brookes?'

'See? He's a fan already,' Vanessa said. 'My dearest old friend, famous!'

David loosened his tie and looked around for an escape route while I flirted with the idea of smashing Vanessa's head through the wall. Perhaps that would improve the message of my picture.

'I have to get another drink,' he said, holding up his empty glass as evidence. 'I'll leave you two to catch up. Great to meet you, Tess.'

Vanessa took her arm from around my neck and gave me a full, beaming smile.

'That was fun,' she said, tossing her long, long hair over one shoulder. 'Wasn't that fun?'

'Not really,' I replied, looking over her shoulder for someone I recognized. Didn't Kekipi say he was coming back? 'Bye, Vanessa.'

'Constructive feedback is part of the industry, Tess,' she said in a disappointed voice. 'I mean, it is for bad photographers anyway. You're probably going to have to get used to that if you're determined to stick it out.'

'Probably,' I agreed. I'd missed her backhanded compliments. Oh wait, no I hadn't. 'Good point.'

'He's right, of course, it's a terrible photo.' She wrinkled her surgically enhanced nose at my picture and shrugged.

'And I'd heard such great things about you. Of course, you're not to know. You're brand new at this, you can't expect to walk into the industry and compete with professionals like me.'

Like her? Vanessa was a photographer in the sense that she owned a camera, occasionally took pictures for her friends' websites, and didn't have a proper job. Her dad had been paying her share of the mortgage for the entire time we lived together, my share too, sometimes, but only when Vanessa lied and said I couldn't make my rent so she could pocket the extra cash.

'Honestly I'm surprised you're still playing at the photographer thing,' she went on. 'I assumed you'd have given up by now. You might be shit but you're not stupid, so I don't know why you're still wasting your time. I know I make this look easy but it isn't.'

This probably wasn't the time or place to mention I'd caught her passing half a dozen of my early photos off as her own for the first five years of her alleged career. Oh wait, yes it was.

'Maybe you could lend me some of your fantastic photos and I'll tell everyone I took them,' I suggested. She didn't even flinch. 'Actually, now I come to think of it, your photos are all shite, so don't bother.'

'Not according to David Sanders,' she pointed out. 'He's bought more than a dozen from me.'

'And did the blow job come with the photos or was that a separate transaction?' I asked. She blinked and I knew I was right.

'Sorry,' I apologized, brushing my hair out of my face. 'That's not fair. You are totally entitled to blow whoever you want, whenever you want. But you really do need to stop being such a complete arsehole, Vanessa. Who you have sex with has absolutely zero bearing on you being a massive c—'

'Vanessa!' Amy came bounding across the room like a tiny black-haired terrier and I happily noted that Vanessa looked nervous. It was safe to say the two of them were not friends. 'What are you doing here? I thought it was only going to be photographers and their friends tonight.'

She set her jaw and squared off her shoulders, shaking her hair down her back. 'Your point being?'

'You're not a photographer and you've got no friends,' Amy replied.

'I'm not the one who just had her photograph ripped to pieces by two of the biggest art collectors I know,' Vanessa spat. 'At least my work isn't naïve and pointless.'

'You don't *have* any work,' Amy laughed, clapping a hand on my back. 'You're so funny. When did she get funny?'

'Whatever,' she said with a sniff. 'It doesn't matter. I'm sorry everyone hates your photo, Tess. I'd die if someone said those terrible things to me.'

'What did they say?' Amy asked. 'I'm happy to oblige. Or I could just knock you on your arse again.'

'You lay so much as a finger on me and I'll have you arrested,' Vanessa snapped, stepping back. The two of them never had got along. 'You're both pathetic.'

'We learned everything we know from you,' Amy replied, rolling up her silk sleeves. 'Do I need to make a scene or are you going to leave?'

'I was leaving anyway,' Vanessa sniped. 'Is it me or did both of you get really fat?'

'Have a lovely evening,' Amy shouted as she scarpered across the room, several well-groomed heads turning our way as she went. 'Why do girls always call each other fat when they haven't got a real argument? Are you all right?'

I nodded, looking sadly at my photo. Vanessa could insult my work and call me fat all the livelong day and it wouldn't make a blind bit of difference. The fact was, the judges were right. Compared to the other images in the room, my work wasn't the most impressive. Out of the context of the magazine, it didn't make sense. It was bright and shiny and obvious but it wasn't brilliant.

'I think I want to go,' I said softly.

'Al just got here,' she said, holding out a glass of white wine but I shook my head. 'He really wants to see your picture.'

'There were two judges in here before and they hated it,' I whispered. 'They tore me apart.'

'Shit, Tess, I'm sorry,' she said, sucking the air in through her teeth. 'That was only two people though, wasn't it? Someone must like it or they wouldn't have accepted it.'

'I don't know,' I said, wiping a stray, angry tear from the corner of my eye. 'It doesn't matter. When all this gets back to Veronica, she'll definitely fire me. They send everyone who shows a critique. It's supposed to be helpful.'

'Fuck. Don't worry about it, I'll intercept all her mail, every single bit,' Amy said. I looked across the gallery to see Vanessa laying a red-taloned hand on David Sanders' chest and laughing at something that he evidently didn't find very funny. 'I can't believe Vanessa turned up. Actually, I can. She'll show up in our nursing home. She'd follow you onto the *Titanic*.'

'Let's go.' I turned my back on James and Sadie's smiling faces. 'I don't want to completely ruin our night.'

'Well, there's one other thing I want to show you,' Amy said, a nervous smile on her face. 'I'm slightly worried you're going to break my kneecaps now, but still, you're going to find out one way or another so I might as well be the one to show you.'

'What have you done?' I asked as she led me away from Vanessa and into the portrait gallery. I saw Kekipi, Jenny and Angela, all grouped around a photo with their backs to us, and in the middle of their gang was Al.

'Hello,' I sniffed, trying to muster some enthusiasm. It was so good of him to come; I couldn't just slope off without saying hello. Sloping could wait five minutes. Sloping would come. 'Thank you for coming.'

'Tess, when did you take this?' he asked, turning around to reveal another photo I recognized.

Right there on the wall of the portrait gallery was the black-and-white picture I'd taken of Al on the roof of his house. Printed out and blown up, he looked raw and vulnerable and old, his knuckles knotted together in sadness and anger and a million other emotions all at once. The complete opposite of the bright, colourful photo of James and Sadie.

'Oh God,' I whispered, my heart in my throat. 'How did this get here?'

'I entered it,' Amy said. 'I thought it was your best picture and I was right. Everyone loves it, Tess.'

'It's incredible,' Jenny agreed. 'So powerful.'

'Really intense,' Angela said. 'As soon as I saw it, it was like, bam!'

'Why didn't you show me?' Al asked, his eyes still fixed on his own face. He looked shaken and I felt awful.

'I didn't think about it when I took it,' I said slowly. 'I never intended anyone else to see it. I'm sorry; it was such a personal moment, I should never have taken the picture.'

'But Tess, it's so great!' Amy placed her hand on the small of my back. 'Al doesn't mind, do you Al?'

'A little warning might have been nice . . .' He looked around as a small crowd began to gather. 'Oh dear. I wasn't really anticipating this.'

'I know you hate attention,' I said, rubbing my forehead. 'That's why I would never have entered it.'

'Can we all stop coming up with excuses why it shouldn't be here and marvel at the fact that it is?' Amy said. 'Tess, you have two photos in this exhibition. Two. That's bloody amazing.'

'One I wish I hadn't entered and one that shouldn't have been here in the first place,' I told her as Al held a hand up to his face, fending off the mobile phone paparazzi. 'I'm sorry, Al.'

'I think this is my cue to leave,' he said, turning to me with a smile. 'It's a beautiful photo, Tess. I was right, you are very talented.'

He walked quickly out of the gallery, ignoring all the camera flashes and whispers of 'Bertie Bennett' as he went. Kekipi drew his eyebrows together and sighed, handing Amy his drink.

'I'd better go after him,' he said. 'Don't worry, he's not angry, just surprised.'

'Why is everyone overreacting?' Amy asked. 'It's a great photo! And everyone is saying so.'

'It really is good,' Angela said, while I watched Kekipi dash to the door after Al.

'I'm sorry,' Amy said, hanging her head and looking up at me with her ridiculously big blue eyes. 'I was trying to help.'

'I know,' I said, looking back at the photo and trying to see what everyone else saw. But all I could see was heartbreak. Heartbreak I knew Al was reliving right now. 'I know. I just wish you'd warned me. How did you do it?'

'I emailed it to myself while you were in the shower and had the gallery frame it while they were framing yours,' she confessed. 'One of our assistants had it biked down here. I couldn't let you not enter it, Tess. It's just so you.'

Was it? How come Amy knew exactly who I was when I wasn't even sure?

'I say we move on,' Jenny announced. 'The Standard is right around the corner. *Le Bain* anyone?'

'I'm quite tired,' I said, faking a yawn. 'I might raincheck.'

'Me too,' Amy said, quickly adding her own overblown faux yawn to the mix. 'I'm tired.'

'Well, we'd better see you before you leave,' Angela said, cutting Jenny's protestations off with a hug. 'And don't stress about it, really. This is iconic. This photo is going to make you.'

'Thank you.' I hugged her back and thanked my lucky stars that our paths had crossed. 'But we're leaving the day after tomorrow. Kekipi said he invited you to the wedding. Are you coming?'

'Can't,' she said with a smile. 'Work. But I'm sure it'll be fabulous and I'm sure you'll be back in New York soon.'

'I hope so,' I took one more look at the photo of Al, filled with an unsettling mix of guilt and pride. 'I really do.'

CHAPTER NINETEEN

'*Wiki, wiki.*' Kekipi clapped his hands at the top of the palazzo steps as Amy and I emerged blinking from our Milanese taxi. 'You're late. What happened?'

'We were delayed,' I said, yawning. I still got excited whenever I flew and I had yet to master the skill of sleeping on a plane. Amy had knocked back two glasses of red wine and gone out like a light, of course. 'We're here now.'

Kekipi, Al and Domenico had flown out the day before while Amy and I packed, napped and generally indulged in everything New York City. I was still scared I might never get to return and I was still scared that I might never be able to speak to Nick again.

'Thank goodness.' Kekipi linked his arms through ours, me on one side, Amy on the other. 'I was worried you weren't coming.'

'I thought about it,' I admitted. 'Has Al said anything about the photo?'

'Only that it was fantastic,' he replied. 'And I believe he has enquired with the gallery regarding its purchase.'

'Oh my God!' I looked over at Amy who seemed confused. 'He wants to buy it so no one else can see it.'

'Is she always this cynical?' he asked Amy. She nodded. 'He wants to buy it because it's marvellous. Now be quiet and come inside, you have bridesmaiding to do.'

The palazzo was beautiful. It didn't matter how many times I came through those gates, it still took my breath away every time. The house was impossibly beautiful, with its big gleaming windows and perfect symmetry. The fountain sparkled in the centre of the courtyard, decorated with the same strings of tiny lights I'd seen all over New York. I couldn't wait to see it all lit up at night. It really was my favourite place in all the world.

'Are you nervous?' Amy asked, pushing her giant sunglasses up onto the top of her head. Milan was grey and cloudy but thankfully, not nearly as cold as New York. 'Twenty-four hours from now you'll be getting married.'

'Not at all,' Kekipi replied, nodding. 'There's so much to do.'

'Such as?' I asked.

'Most importantly, my bachelor party,' he said, leading us up the marble steps and into the foyer. There were flowers everywhere, vases and vases full of winter white roses in full bloom and, in the middle of it all, one of the biggest Christmas trees I had ever seen. Now I knew where Amy had found her inspiration for the presentation. Al's Milan home was a Christmas dreamland.

'Of course.' I grimaced slightly and steeled my liver. 'Aren't we cutting it a bit fine, going out the night before the ceremony?'

'Shut up, Tess,' Amy ordered. 'It's all done, I've had it planned for weeks. Just be back down here at six o'clock.'

'Yes, ma'am,' I said with a salute, receiving a slap around the back of the head for my trouble.

'And you, Ms Brookes, are expected in Al's office right about now,' Kekipi said, squeezing my arm. 'Then I need you to look at the photographers we've hired and make sure they aren't terrible.'

'I still wish you'd let me take the photos,' I scolded, suddenly nervous. 'You don't need to pay for a photographer.'

'Yes, we do,' he said. 'You're going to be far too busy getting drunk and dancing and kissing boys to worry about taking pictures. Don't argue with me.'

Apart from the vow I'd made to myself to never kiss another boy as long as I lived, it hardly sounded like a bad plan.

'I'll see you both back here at six,' he said with a small bow. 'I have to go and see a fabulous man about a spectacular dog. Who would have thought getting married was such hard work?'

'It'll be Vegas for me,' Amy said, unfastening her coat and dropping her bag on the floor. I picked it up immediately before Domenico appeared to tell us off. The place was spotless. 'None of this fannying around.'

'I lobbied very hard for Hawaii,' Kekipi said. 'But no, my husband-to-be is a traditional Catholic boy. So we're having a non-traditional gay Catholic wedding that won't really be legal and his church won't recognize. You know, the way God would want it.'

'Amen,' she replied.

'Dom has put you in your old room. I'll have your bags sent up and Al is waiting for you,' he said, letting go of my arm and pulling Amy away down the marble-floored corridor. 'Don't get lost!'

'As if I would get lost,' I muttered, climbing the stairs to the second floor. 'What kind of amateur do you think I am?'

'Sorry,' I said, opening the door to Al's office five minutes later. 'I got lost.'

'There you are.' Al stood and held his arms open for a hug. His bare feet and bright pink printed MC Hammer pants didn't quite match his pale blue shirt, but he looked a million times more like himself than he had in his fancy three-piece suits. 'I thought you must be due around now.'

Al's office was one of my favourite rooms in the entire house. Out of all the elegance and grandeur of his Italian home, he had chosen a smart little corner to make his own, with huge windows that filled the space with light and gave him grand, sweeping views of the park opposite the palazzo. You could see right across Milan from his desk and I could have happily lost days there drinking coffee and watching the world go by.

Leaning in, I gave him a small, sideways hug. He smelled like proper gentlemen's aftershave and Brylcreem. The only thing missing was the smell of the beach in his beard.

'How was the flight?' he asked, pouring me a tiny coffee and proving he was definitely a mind reader. 'Uneventful, I hope?'

'Amy kicked a man in the back of the head without leaving her seat,' I said with a shrug. 'But I think he was more impressed at how flexible she was than annoyed.'

'Good, good,' he said. 'And how are you feeling after the exhibition?'

'Confused, if I'm honest,' I told him. 'I still feel terrible about Amy entering that photograph without telling you first. I shouldn't have even taken it, I'm sorry.'

'Tess, that picture was fantastic,' he said, dropping a sugar cube into his own espresso cup. 'It showed a rare talent and I would have been very upset if you had let it languish on a laptop for the rest of your days. You must learn to have more confidence in yourself.'

'I'm trying,' I said, biting my thumbnail. 'I just want you to know I feel really awful. I tried to get them to take it down but they wouldn't.'

'And rightly so,' Al said, bushy white eyebrows raised. 'Tess, it was a brilliant photograph. I was surprised to see it, of course, but that wasn't why I left. The crowds were a little much for me. You know I don't care for a lot of attention these days.'

'I thought you weren't a recluse?' I replied, almost smiling. 'If the picture hadn't been there, no one would have bothered you.'

'Regardless.' He waved away my concern with a tiny silver spoon. 'We shall agree that the photograph was wonderful and my moment of discomfort was worth it. I apologize if my reaction was a little dramatic. You should be very proud of yourself for that photo, Tess. Anyone can point a camera at something; very few people can capture the feeling behind it. Has the gallery been in touch?'

'I'm so glad,' I said, a heavy weight falling from my shoulders. 'And no; I really was hoping I would have heard something from them by now but nothing. My agent is going to sack me and I don't know what I'm going to do.'

I gave him a broad cheesy smile to make up for the anxious tone in my voice.

'So you're sitting around waiting for someone to come and scoop you up out of the cinders?' Al asked, a chiding tone to his voice. 'I thought we'd been over this.'

'I'm out of ideas.' I sipped my coffee and pinched my shoulders together. 'And I haven't got a fairy godmother as far as I know.'

'You know, I never much cared for Cinderella,' he said, tapping the little silver spoon on his saucer. 'Didn't have enough gumption for me.'

'She did marry a prince though,' I protested. 'She must have been doing something right.'

'She never tried to help herself, did she?' All the creases in his brow furrowed together. 'As soon as the magic wore off, she hotfooted it back to the kitchen without a second thought. That part I never understood.'

'I think she was scared,' I said. 'Wasn't that the point?'

'Why?' Al asked.

'I don't really know,' I said, uncertain. 'They were big on beheadings back then?'

'We're talking about Cinderella, not *Game of Thrones*,' he countered. 'He had already got down on one knee and professed his love. What stopped her from explaining her situation? Casually mentioning that she wasn't actually a princess and she could really use a hand. Didn't she trust him?'

'Well, he was a bloke,' I said. 'No offence.'

'None taken,' he replied. 'There aren't that many gentlemen around these days, I know, but my point is: how different things could have been for Cinders if she had simply explained her predicament to the prince in the first place. What would have happened if he'd found another girl who had the same size feet?'

'Well, when you put it like that,' I said. 'One minute

she's the love of his life, the next he doesn't recognize her when she's staring him in the face.'

'Precisely,' Al said. 'She would still be scrubbing floors if everyone else hadn't been born with giant clodhoppers. And all because she waited around for someone to save her.'

'And don't get me started on the glass slipper,' I said, my voice excitable. 'What kind of fairy godmother puts a girl who has spent her entire life barefoot in glass heels? One trip and she slices her foot off.'

'That's an excellent point,' he said, tapping his finger-tips on the desk. 'But we're going a little off topic.'

'She doesn't even try to get the shoe back,' I interrupted. 'Someone leant her that shoe in good faith and she didn't even go back for it. That's shocking.'

'Again, off topic,' Al sighed. 'Since I met you, I've watched you fight for the things you want and made them happen. Surely you're not going to give up now?'

'I have considered eating a lot of biscuits,' I replied. 'That seemed relatively proactive since everyone now thinks I can't take a photo to save my life.'

He gave me a look. 'I don't think that's quite true, is it?'

'No, really,' I said. 'That's what that man said to me at the gallery.'

'And he represents everyone in the world, does he?'

'Not *everyone*,' I replied. 'But a lot of them.'

Al nodded slowly, thinking.

'I really wanted people to like my photo,' I said, looking down at my feet. 'I wanted to prove to everyone that I could do it. I wanted to prove I'm good.'

'And who is it that thinks you have anything to prove in the first place?' he asked.

I didn't answer. But I did take two of the cookies from

his desk and shoved them both into my mouth at the same time.

'All right, then, if this is so important, what can you do to change this man's mind?' he asked. 'How do we get into his good graces?'

'I know what my old flatmate did and I'm definitely not doing that,' I said, pulling a face.

'I can only imagine.' Al gave a gentle shudder. 'But you have to do something, Tess. You've come so far.'

He was right and I knew it. But I wasn't used to it being so hard to show you could do something well. I felt a flicker of regret for my old job and the untold joys of PowerPoint.

'You're someone who holds herself to a very high standard,' he said. 'It might be that you can't change their minds but you won't know if you don't try.'

'I'll think about it,' I promised. 'I'll think of something.'

'Good,' he said, standing up and rifling through a rack of dresses behind him. 'Now tell me, how do we feel about white?'

He held up a long, off-white dress, all fluttering silk skirts and narrow straps.

'We feel strongly,' I said, transfixed, as he wafted it around on the hanger. 'Is this for next season?'

'Perhaps.' Al held the dress out. 'But for now, it's for you.'

'No way!' I gasped. 'Al, it's gorgeous.'

'You were right,' he said, smiling. 'When you told me making dresses was a worthwhile thing to do. The look on your face right now is priceless.'

'Wait until you show Amy,' I told him. 'She's going to die.'

'As long as she doesn't die before the wedding,' he

warned. 'Domenico has spent hours on the seating plan. I fear he would bring her back to life just to kill her again.'

'And there was me thinking Kekipi was going to be the bridezilla,' I said, still wafting the dress around in the breeze from the window.

'Did you imagine for a second that Kekipi wasn't going to have the most beautiful bridesmaids the world has ever seen?' he asked. 'Designed by me as per his very specific instructions. Although the skirt doesn't pull away to leave a bodysuit as originally requested – but since Domenico nixed the choreographed dance number in the reception, I think we'll all get by.'

'Am I allowed to wear white?' I asked, allowing just the very tips of my fingers to trace the delicate fabric. 'When it isn't my wedding?'

'I don't think you'll be upstaging the bride,' he replied. 'Trust me.'

'Brave, brave Domenico,' I laughed, draping the dress over my arm as I waved my way out of his office. Al was right, I couldn't sit around waiting for my fairy-tale ending. It was only midday, I had a whole afternoon until the stag do and unless I wanted to lose Agent Veronica, I had some work to get on with.

'And so I says to him, Brian, I says, no one's interested, put it away.' Amy sloshed white wine all over her hand as she spoke. 'It's not as though there's anything to see anyway.'

With her mouth wide open, she guided her face towards her glass, attempting to hoover up her drink before she spilled the rest of it.

'It's sad when small penises happen to good people,'

Kekipi said, raising his glass with a sombre face. 'To Brian.'

'To Brian,' Amy and I chorused, Amy throwing back her drink, me bringing it to my lips and then setting it back on the table without taking a sip. A bottle of vodka, a bottle of limoncello and three bottles of white wine, all of them open and none of them empty, sat between us.

It was already eleven and the three of us were safely ensconced in the corner of a bar somewhere in the Navigli where Kekipi assured us the bartender was understanding and the drinks were cheap and strong. Al had dined and run, pleading old age and leaving his credit card behind the bar, disappearing with a promise of a car coming to collect us dead on the dot of midnight. I did not like the chances of all three of us getting in that car.

'Where did you even get those?' I asked Amy as Kekipi attempted to slap me in the face with a penis-adorned deely bopper.

'I am a woman of many talents,' she replied. Kekipi had bluntly refused to wear both the headband and the bride-to-be sash at dinner but was now sporting them both with pride. 'Where were you all afternoon anyway?'

'Working,' I said. Amy was wearing a dress that looked like the stripper version of my gown from the AJB presentation and I felt woefully underdressed in my skinny jeans and backless black jumper. 'Tell us more about Brian.'

'Circumcized,' she replied.

'I can't believe I'm resigning myself to one penis for the rest of my days,' Kekipi said, raising his sticky-looking shot high above his head. 'Whatever have I become?'

'I think you talk a good game,' I said, picking up my glass, waiting for the two of them to neck theirs and then throwing it in the plant plot by the side of me. 'But you love it really.'

Kekipi screwed up his face as he swallowed the stiff liquor. 'I'm still in single figures,' he confessed. 'Tell anyone and I'll hunt you down and kill you like a dog.'

'Kill me like a dog or hunt me like a dog?' I asked.

'I don't know,' he shrugged, pouring out another drink. 'I'm drunk.'

'Room for a little one?'

I looked up to see Paige beside our table, a smile on her face and the same penis deely boppers as Amy was wearing on her head.

'Darling!' Kekipi threw himself into her arms and dragged her down to the table while Amy spilled vodka into four shot glasses. 'You made it.'

'The flight was delayed,' she said, quickly knocking back her shot and shivering. 'I'm sorry I missed dinner.'

'You're here now,' Amy slurred. 'I haven't seen you in so long. You look amazing.'

'You really do,' I said, trying to work out what she had done differently. 'Did you get extensions?'

'No.' She pulled her long blonde hair over her shoulder and smoothed it down. 'I haven't done anything.'

'Fake tan?' Kekipi suggested. 'Eyelash extensions? Teeth whitening? Vagina facial?'

'Is that a thing?' I asked.

'It's a thing,' Amy and Paige replied.

'There's a place in New York where you can get it steamed,' Amy said, sipping her vodka. 'Just asking for thrush.'

'I tried to get drunk on the plane so I wouldn't have to catch up but it was easyJet and the drinks were extortionate,' Paige said, filling up her own glass and throwing it back. 'I didn't want to get kicked off – I'm not Kate Moss. How come you're so sober?'

'Me?' I picked up my wine glass and laughed. 'Three sheets to the wind, trust me. Wasted. We've been drinking forever.'

Amy and Kekipi zeroed in on me with slightly wobbly expressions.

'You're not drunk,' Amy said, pointing at me with a shot glass. 'Why aren't you drunk?'

'I've been working on my tolerance,' I replied, sipping my warm white wine. 'I'm just not as drunk as you so you can't tell.'

'I hate people who bully their friends into drinking when they don't want to,' Kekipi said, mixing Lemon Drop shots in a pint glass and then distributing them to each of us. 'I think that's why I've spent so much time in therapy. Drink.'

'I really don't think it's a good idea,' I said, reluctantly accepting the sticky shot glass. 'You both know I'm a bad drunk. I don't want to be hungover for the wedding.'

'It's my bachelor party,' Kekipi insisted, attracting the attention of every other person in the bar. 'Drink the drink, Brookes.'

'Fine, I'll do one,' I said, staring at the shot, my gag reflex kicking in before I'd even sniffed it. 'And that's it.'

'Yeah,' Amy clinked her glass against Paige's. 'Just the one.'

'Cheers,' Paige said. 'To Kekipi's last night of freedom and Tess's hangover.'

'Cheers,' I replied before throwing back the drink. 'Although I'm not going to get drunk so I'm not going to have a hangover. So there.'

*

'I mean, first he doesn't want me then he does, then he doesn't, then he's sending letters. Who sends letters?' I swiped my hand across the table, knocking the empty bottle of vodka with it. 'I don't understand. Pick up the bleeding phone, Miller.'

'He's a shit,' Amy said, rubbing at her eye and smearing her bright blue eyeliner until she looked like a 1970s David Bowie. 'A shitty shit shit, that's what he is.'

'He really isn't worth the energy,' Paige agreed. 'You're better off without him.'

'I don't care.' I had tried and tried and tried to get my head around it. Filling said head with vodka wasn't making it any clearer. 'Not at all. I'm so over him.'

'Of course you are, love,' Kekipi said. 'That's why we're still talking about him. Who brought him up in the first place, anyway?'

Paige and Amy both pointed at me across the table.

'I wish I was a bloke,' I said, sweeping my arm across the table. 'Then I could just forget about the whole thing and move on.

'I think you'd feel better if you did sex on someone,' Amy said, her head popping up and scanning the busy bar. 'Let's find you a sex person.'

'I think I'd feel better if I had a kebab,' I argued. 'Where's the closest place I can get a kebab?'

'Basingstoke.' Paige shook the limoncello bottle but it was completely empty. 'We're dry.'

'On it,' Amy grunted, standing up and yelling to the barman, 'Another bottle for the table and a new shag for Tess.'

'Have you spoken to Charlie?' Kekipi asked. I stuck out my tongue and grabbed Amy's wine glass from across the table. 'You still haven't replied to his note?'

'I texted him to say thank you for the presents,' I sighed, my topknot collapsing around my face. 'I don't think that counts.'

'What note?' Paige asked. 'Charlie sent you a note?'

'And a care package and a shit camera case or something,' Amy nodded, as the lights got lower and the music got louder. 'He decided to declare his undying love. Oh, and offered her a job. It was all very unprofessional. If he had HR, they'd have a field day.'

'Really?' Paige asked, jolting backwards as her eyes shot wide open. 'He told you he still loves you?'

I nodded. 'Amy's got the note.'

'She's not allowed it,' Amy confirmed. '*I* am the keeper of the note.'

Paige pulled her phone out of her pocket and stood up, dark, wet stains all over her short grey sweater dress. We were messy drunks. 'I'll be right back,' she said, waving the phone in our general direction.

'OK, it's nearly midnight,' Kekipi said, watching while Amy struggled to open the bottle of vodka, her tongue poking out the corner of her mouth. 'And we haven't danced at all.'

'I need a wee,' I said, standing on shaky legs. 'I'll be back in a minute.'

'We'll be on the dance floor,' Amy called, taking Kekipi by the hand and dragging him across the room, pushing tables out of the way and moving back and forth on a nonexistent dance floor, completely out of time with the music.

'*Scusi,*' I mumbled, bumping into a mirror on my way across the bar and trying the toilet door. Locked.

'You're drunk,' I told my reflection as I fished my phone out of my bag. 'Shame on you.'

With one more disgusted look in the mirror, I wiped my face with the sleeve of my sweater and looked around for another toilet. I tiptoed through the little tables, smiling and waving at the other patrons until I pushed open a door and found myself outside.

'This isn't the toilet,' I announced.

'It really isn't,' a tall, copper-haired man replied, striding towards me across the piazza.

'Charlie!' I slapped my friend in the chest and laughed. 'What are you doing here? Wait, you *are* here, aren't you?'

'Good God, you're drunk,' he said, smiling his crooked, bright-eyed smile. 'Yes, Tess, I'm here.'

'You're here,' I said, dropping my head onto his chest and breathing in his total Charlie-ness. 'Why?'

'For the wedding,' he replied, grabbing hold of my wrists as I stumbled backwards into a gaggle of Italian smokers. 'Paige invited me—'

'*Scusi*,' I said, very loudly before turning back to Charlie with a look of pride. 'I speak Italian now. Paige invited you? To the wedding?'

'Yes, and technically, I think you did too but you didn't have an official plus one like she did,' he nodded, offering the smokers an apologetic smile. 'Are you OK? Should we call you a taxi?'

'I'm fine,' I promised, swiping my hair out of my face and poking myself in the eye. 'I get it. Paige invited you because she hates Nick but it's not going to work, is it?'

'What isn't going to work?' he asked, looking around for back-up.

'Me and you,' I whispered. 'I know you love me but I don't feel that way any more and I'm really sorry.'

'What are you talking about?' he asked, a puzzled

smile on his face. 'Is this why you didn't reply to my Christmas card? You thought I was making a move?'

'I might be slightly tipsy right now but the note was pretty clear.' I slapped his chest. 'There aren't that many ways to interpret "I love you", are there?'

Charlie pushed my shoulders upright as I began to stagger forwards.

'Tess, I really don't know what you're talking about,' he said. 'Of course I love you, as a friend – but I thought we'd cleared all the other stuff up?'

'I do love you, just not like that,' I went on, reaching out to stroke his face but accidentally slapping it instead. 'Although Amy says the best way to get over Nick is to get under a sexing. Or something.'

'I don't think that's exactly what she said,' Charlie replied. 'Where is Amy? Can you stand up on your own if I go in and find her? Have you seen Paige?'

'We've totally done it before,' I whispered with an elaborate wink. 'We should just do it again. As long as we agree that it doesn't mean anything and that it's just sexing, we should totally do sex.'

'I don't think that's a very good idea,' he said with a laugh as I lurched towards him with my arms outstretched. 'You're very drunk, Tess. You're more drunk than you were at the graduation ball.'

'I wanted to have sex with you then as well,' I said, kissing his ear. 'But you didn't even notice. Look, mistletoe!'

'Where?' Charlie looked up and I launched myself on him.

'There isn't any,' I replied. 'Shhh.'

'Tess, pack it in,' Charlie tried to unravel himself from my arms as I smothered his cheek in kisses. 'I mean it.'

'I'm so glad you're here.' I grabbed hold of his face and looked him in the eye. 'You're my Charlie.'

Leaning in, I touched my lips to his. He resisted but wasn't this what everyone kept telling me? I was Tess Brookes, I didn't give up without a fight. Especially not when I'd had a couple.

'Oh.'

Charlie broke away, pushing me gently backwards, keeping a tight grip on my wrists. I blinked and followed his gaze to see Paige in the doorway of the bar, her phone in her hand and a devastated look on her face.

'Oh no,' I gasped. 'Are they out of *limoncello*?'

'Sorry,' she said. 'Didn't mean to interrupt.'

'Paige!' Charlie let go of my hands as though they were on fire and I immediately crumpled to the ground.

'I'm going back to the house,' Paige said with a decisive sniff. 'I suggest you find a hotel.'

'Shit.' Charlie looked at Paige, then down at me. He grabbed me round the waist and hoisted me to my feet. 'Paige, she's drunk, it's nothing.'

'It's nothing,' I agreed. 'Wait, what's going on?'

'Just stay here.' Charlie deposited me on a cold metal chair and pressed his hands on my knees. 'And don't move.'

Running his hands through his hair and straightening his collar, he ran across the piazza to where Paige had stalked off and was arguing with a taxi driver. I looked up to see an old man in the seat beside me, a rolled-up cigarette frozen in midair in front of his face.

'*Buongiorno*,' I said, nodding.

'*Buonasera*,' he replied, licking the cigarette paper.

'No,' I shook my head and prodded myself in the chest. 'Tess. Not Sarah.'

'What is going on out here?'

Kekipi and Amy barrelled out of the bar, clinging to the doorframe as they spotted me.

'Paige and Charlie are arguing,' I said. 'And I made a new friend,' I added, patting my table neighbour on the shoulder.

'Why are they arguing?' Kekipi asked. 'Do they even know each other?'

'Why is Charlie here?' Amy asked. 'Oi, cockwomble!'

'That doesn't look much like arguing to me,' Kekipi grabbed hold of my shoulder. 'Are they kissing?'

'Noooo,' I said, rising to my feet and struggling to focus on what was happening. Charlie and Paige were face to face and well, it did look a bit like they might be kissing but they couldn't be, could they? 'Amy, why is Charlie kissing Paige?'

'Oi, cockwomble,' she bellowed across the piazza. 'Why are you kissing Paige?'

I watched as the two of them walked back towards us. They were holding hands.

'I wanted to talk to you about this,' Charlie started. 'Before.'

They were holding hands.

'But I didn't really know how.'

'Nothing's really happened,' Paige added, her head ducked low, her face sheepish. 'Not really. We both wanted to talk to you first, that's why he's here. Tess, are you OK?'

They were holding hands. Paige and Charlie were holding hands.

'I think I'm going to be sick,' I replied, flushing hot and cold from head to toe.

'Me too,' Amy said pointing at Paige. 'This is gross, you can do better.'

'No, really.' I spun around and fell to my knees, one

hand in my hair, the other propping me up against the wall of the bar as I threw up half a bottle of vodka into a Milanese gutter.

'Now it's a proper bachelor party,' Kekipi declared joyfully. 'Congratulations me!'

CHAPTER TWENTY

'Rise and shine!' Kekipi knocked on my bedroom door then opened it without waiting for a response. 'I have snacks.'

'Don't bring them in here unless you want me to throw up again,' I warned him from underneath the cold, wet flannel that was draped across my face.

'Charming,' he replied. 'Suck it up, it's my wedding day and I want a bacon sandwich.'

'Why don't you have a hangover?' I asked, as he pottered around my room, picking things up, turning them over and putting them down, like a middle-aged Hawaiian toddler. 'Why do you look so well?'

'Wedding miracle,' he replied, turning up his nose at the tampon holder he had pulled out of my handbag. 'I'm getting married today, can you believe it?'

'Are you excited?' I sat up in my bed, trying to stay as still as possible. Still was good. He sat down in the armchair by the bed and began to eat a bacon sandwich I desperately wanted but didn't dare attempt. 'Is Domenico excited?'

'We're both thrilled,' he said. 'No, really, we are. Only I'm incapable of saying anything and not having it sound sarcastic at the moment. It's all very strange.'

'Try and knock that off before the vows,' I suggested. 'I'm not convinced your husband will be entirely happy about it.'

He shrugged and dove face down.

'Then he should have agreed to eloping to Hawaii like I suggested,' he said into the duvet. 'Remind me to ask him what fabric softener they use here – it smells divine and I want this at home.'

'Where is home going to be?' I pressed the flannel underneath my eyes, hoping it would do something about the bloodshot monsters I had just seen in the mirror. 'Where are you two going to live?'

'Something else we probably should have discussed before now.' He pulled up his head and rested on his forearms. 'Who would have thought two middle-aged men who have spent their entire careers organizing the homes and lives of other people would be so ill-prepared to organize themselves?'

I lowered the flannel.

'Me?'

'Touché,' he replied. 'Have you spoken to Miss Paige? Or, wait, I don't know Charlie's last name.'

'Wilder,' I winced. 'And no.'

'And how do we feel about their little romance?'

'Not good,' I said, not feeling especially good about anything, really. 'I know I don't want to go out with him but that doesn't mean I want my friend to go out with him. Is that bad?'

'Are you sure you don't mean, you don't want *him* to go out with *your* friend?' he asked.'

'Maybe,' I said, moving the flannel up onto my forehead. 'I can't believe I kissed him. I'm going to have to apologize to her.'

'Apologize to Paige for kissing your ex who you didn't know she was in love with?' he asked. I raised my eyebrows at the L word and felt my stomach lurch. 'Fine, in filthy lust with.'

'It makes perfect sense,' I admitted. 'She's totally his type.'

'What, walking and breathing?' Amy asked, letting herself in. 'Ooh, bacon sandwiches.'

She bounced across the bed and my stomach lurched. Surely I'd puked all it was ever possible to puke?

'Happy wedding day!' She kissed Kekipi on the cheek and snatched the bacon sandwich out of his hand. 'You shouldn't eat this, you'll get fat. I'll take it off your hands.'

'We're discussing Chaige,' he told her, wiping his hands on his trousers. 'Or Parlie.'

'Well, neither of those are going to catch on,' I muttered. 'They're doomed.'

'They are,' Amy agreed. 'Wait until I get my hands on them. You don't shag your mate's ex. It's bang out of order, Tess. I mean, I expect it of that wankpaddle Wilder but I thought more of Paige.'

'I knew she was interested in someone but she said it was complicated.' I groaned lightly. 'Now I know why.'

'I don't know why she couldn't be honest about it.' Amy shook her head. 'It's sneaky.'

'I feel like they've been lying to me,' I admitted. 'And it makes me not want to see them right now. That whole people talking behind your back thing.'

Not to mention that whole snogging one of them against his will thing.

'What I don't understand,' Amy said, pulling a slip of paper out from the back pocket of her jeans, 'is why he sent you the note. It's a bit bloody emo for a job offer.'

'Give it here.' I held out my hand and sat up, the flannel flopping into my lap. I smoothed it out, as puzzled as Amy by Charlie's motives.

'Oh, no.'

'What?' Amy asked thickly through a mouthful of sandwich.

'Oh no, no, no,' I couldn't take my eyes off the note. 'It's not from Charlie.'

Opening the drawer in my bedside table, I pulled out my passport and shook out Nick's note. Nick's first note. The paper was exactly the same, the faint blue grid pattern on a heavy cream background, and the hand-writing . . . I would have known it anywhere.

'You're kidding me.' Amy put down her sandwich. This was serious business. 'Don't tell me it's from him?'

'It's from Nick,' I said, comparing the two notes. I looked up at my best friends. 'Even when he thought I'd ignored all those letters. Even after I showed up and was a total arse and stormed off. What do I do?'

The handwritten note. The bespoke camera case. They were so completely and utterly Nick Miller. How could I have not known?

'Call him!' Amy yanked my phone out of the wall socket and threw it at me. 'Call him, Tess. Fuck, he's walking about thinking he told you he loves you and you haven't even replied. What a cow.'

'Call him now,' Kekipi advised in his best soothing manner. 'He'll understand.'

The pair of them stared at me with huge round eyes.

'I can't, can I?' I pulled on my ponytail and made tiny,

frustrated fists. 'I tried to call before when I got the letters and he's blocking my number. So what, I'm supposed to sit around and wait for him to call me? When is soon? What is soon supposed to mean?'

'Use my phone,' Amy said, throwing her mobile at my face. 'He won't know the number.'

Well, there was a bright idea we hadn't bloody well thought of before.

'Is it OK if I don't do it here?' I asked. 'I need a minute.'

'Of course,' Kekipi said, even as Amy opened her mouth and shook her head. 'Whatever you need.'

'I'm just going for a quick walk,' I said, pulling my New York hoodie on over my pyjamas and slipping my phone into the pouch. 'Clear my head first.'

'Don't go far,' Kekipi warned. 'I don't want to be late for my own wedding because I'm Tess hunting. You're booked in for hair and make-up first, all that hair of yours. We'll meet you in the dressing room.'

'I'll be there,' I promised, sliding my feet into my trainers. 'Just make sure Amy gets properly hosed down.'

'Don't worry,' he said. 'She'll be a regular Eliza Doolittle by the time you come back. From about a third of the way through the film.'

She frowned, sniffed her own armpit and shrank away from herself.

'Fair dos,' she said. 'I am a bit ripe.'

'So classy.' I picked up my coat and left them alone on my bed. 'She's going to make the most elegant brides-maid.'

'Are you OK?' Kekipi asked as I struggled to open my own door. 'Do you want us to come?'

'No, really,' I said, not quite able to smile. 'I won't be long. I need a minute.'

A minute, a new brain and a time machine, I thought to myself. And then everything would be just fine.

After a brief pitstop in the kitchen, I pushed open the door to my secret garden behind the palazzo, cup of coffee in one hand and two stolen pastries in my pocket, and immediately felt calmer. I'd discovered this place the first time I'd visited Al in Milan and it had been my sanctuary ever since, even if it had turned out to be less of a secret than I'd first imagined. Sitting down at the little wrought-iron chair and table set, I felt the chill of cold metal on the backs of my legs, even through my flannel pyjama bottoms and heaviest coat.

The garden looked so different to the way I had found it in summer but no less beautiful. The flowers had all died but the trees stretched up towards the sky, most of their leaves long gone, the branches and boughs basking in the winter sun. Domenico and Kekipi had chosen a beautiful day for a wedding. I had rarely seen a New Year's Eve as promising as this one but then, I'd rarely seen a New Year's Eve. I had worked every year before this, only stumbling out of the office after dark when everyone else was already half-cut. The fact that there was daylight in winter at all was something of a revelation to me.

I placed Nick's note neatly on the table.

Tess, I love you. I want to try. I'll call you soon.

'He wants to try,' I whispered, looking up at the clear blue sky. 'He loves me.'

I wrapped my hands around my coffee to keep them warm and took a tiny bite out of one of the delicious flaky pastries to test my stomach at the exact same time my own phone began to ring. Swallowing so quickly I almost choked, I turned on the speakerphone function.

'Hello?' I answered, wiping my greasy hands on my PJ bottoms.

'Tess-bloody-Brookes.' Agent Veronica was using one of her cheerier tones of voice. 'What the fucking fuck have you been up to?'

'Stuff?' I replied, picking up the phone with shaky hands and switching off the speakerphone. It occurred to me that not everyone in Milan wanted to hear my agent bitch me out on a lovely sunny morning like this. Even if they didn't speak English, most of Veronica's language was universal.

'Haven't you just,' she cackled. 'You've got some explaining to do, my little prize pig.'

'I have?'

'First things first, Ess wants you to assist him on a shoot next week while 7 is off in Aspen with Mummy and Daddy but I've told him to go and fuck himself, so don't worry too much about that,' she said. 'Which leaves the tricky stuff. The photo editor at *Gloss* loved the Nixon-Jacobs shoot you did for them and wants to know if you could get your gorgeous little arse back to do another shoot for them. In New York, next week.'

I couldn't say anything for a moment. Well, that was a surprise. Not Veronica telling Ess to go and fuck himself, that seemed fairly standard, but *Gloss* wanted me to shoot for them again? Already? I silently praised Angela Clark and all who sailed in her.

'And then there's your other option.'

I noticed that she wasn't swearing as much as usual. It was disconcerting.

'I had an email from the Spencer Gallery this morning.'

'You did?' My heart began to race.

'I did,' she replied. 'They fucking hated the photo you entered for the New Image prize.'

'Oh,' I said. 'Good of them to let me know.'

'They went into a lot more detail,' she said. 'But that's the general gist.'

'Right.' I tore off another strip of pastry. 'Wait, how is that an option?'

'It isn't,' she replied. 'I'm not done, am I? They hated your entry for the New Image prize but they loved your portrait of Bertie Bennett.'

I closed my eyes and breathed out.

'They've had several offers on it,' she went on. 'And while you're not technically eligible for the apprenticeship, the David Sanders Gallery has a similar programme that they've recommended you for. And David Sanders has personally confirmed the offer. Anything you want to tell me about that?'

'I met him at the exhibition,' I said. I couldn't believe it. 'I emailed him a copy of my portrait of Al yesterday but I didn't know if he'd seen it or not.'

'He has,' she said. 'Seems pretty bleeding keen on it, if you ask me.'

'Sounds like,' I replied, smiling.

'Shit like this doesn't come around very often, Brookes,' she said. 'This is a golden bloody Willy Wonka of an opportunity.'

'I wasn't sure,' I admitted. 'Vanessa said he'd bought some of her photos so, you know, I was a bit suspicious.'

'A lot of men have bought Vanessa's photos,' she replied, her voice arch and dry. 'And by bought her photos, I mean, given her a length.'

'Yes, I got that,' I confirmed. 'But thanks for clearing it up.'

'He might have shit taste in Vanessa but he's got fantastic taste in art,' she went on. 'I imagine her photos are showing at a very exclusive non-existent show in his basement with all the other ropy old tarts he's seduced with his chequebook. But he has been a patron to some really shit-hot photographers, Brookes,' she paused. 'If you do it, it'll be a tough six months, you won't be able to run off to Hawaii or nick off to do a celebrity shoot when the mood takes you.'

'I honestly hadn't thought *Gloss* would want to hire me again,' I admitted. I felt overwhelmed. 'What do I do?'

'Luckily for you, you've got a fucking brilliant agent,' Veronica replied, pausing to take a drag on a cigarette I couldn't see but knew full well was there. 'You get your arse back to New York next week and we'll book the *Gloss* gig, then you can start the apprenticeship the week after. I hope you're ready to make a lot more cups of cocking tea.'

'So ready,' I replied, the excitement making my voice squeak in a most unprofessional manner. 'I'm really good at tea making.'

I could have cried. I could fly back with Amy, shoot for *Gloss*, eat glazed bacon doughnuts and learn my trade at one of the best photographic galleries in New York.

'Of course, that's not your lot,' Agent Veronica said, interrupting my doughnut fantasy. 'Are you sat down?'

'Yes?' I pressed my palms against the chair underneath my arse to make sure. 'What else can there be?'

'I've had a request from *Booker* magazine to use some of your photographs.'

I knew *Booker*; it was, for want of a better description, the men's version of *Gloss*. A glossy men's magazine full of expensive watches, articles on craft brewing, men with immaculately groomed beards and famous actors answering deep and meaningful questions, while still managing to pack in lots and lots of pictures of women who weren't quite naked, all shot from terribly tasteful and artistic angles.

'Which photographs?' I popped a piece of pastry in my mouth and washed it down with coffee. It had to be shots of Sadie; I couldn't think of anything else I had that they would be interested in.

'Your pictures of Bennett in Hawaii,' she said. 'You haven't got a Scooby what I'm on about, have you?'

'You've lost me,' I admitted.

'I'll forward you the article they want them for,' Veronica said with more incoherent swearing under her breath. 'And you can decide whether or not you want the wanker to have your pictures or not but I need to know today. They're going to print this week – it's all very fucking last minute.'

'Everything is,' I replied with a sigh. 'Send it over, I'll look at it now.' I had about half an hour before Kekipi would come looking for me.

'Grand,' she said. 'But wherever you are, I'd stay away from sharp objects, if I were you. I need a decision today, on the photos and the apprenticeship. *Gloss* want you over there next Monday and Sanders is being a stroppy little cock about getting you started as soon as possible, so call me back when you're done. Actually, call me back in two hours. I've got to get to the offy before all the decent shit's sold out and I'll be buggered if I'm ringing the New Year in with a WKD. Trying to get your life in order is screwing my New Years.'

She hung up without further explanation and I immediately opened my inbox, refreshing over and over until her name popped up. And right there beside it in the subject line: 'Love Is . . . by Nick Miller'.

My heart dropped as I opened the attachment, my hands shaking.

Valentine's Day is often written off as a Hallmark holiday, the article began, *but however cynical or jaded or busy on Tinder you may be, there is no way of avoiding the self-reflection brought about by the holiday.*

Love stories are all around us. On TV, in the cinema, in books and songs. We hear them from our parents and we tell them to our friends, following them as they come to life on Instagram, sometimes culminating in a hashtagged wedding, sometimes collapsing in a broken heart icon on a Facebook feed. But one thing is certain, love is unavoidable, pursued by many, shunned by some but ever present in our lives. But, somewhere down the line, this proliferation of love stories has watered down the real thing. How many times have you heard the word today? How many times has someone told you that they love someone or something – a football team or a cup of coffee or their new deodorant?

It is this dilution of the most fundamental human experience that has made it so easy for us to turn away from the concept. We can live without that coffee; if our football team loses, we'll live; and there will always be another, better deodorant, so we toss our human relationships into the same column, because it's easier. Love is a consumable: we believe love can be replaced or retired, it can be upgraded or lived without.

But that's not true.

Albert Bennett met his wife when he was twenty years old. He was working as a Saturday boy in his father's department store in London when Jane walked through the door, on the arm of her fiancé who had come looking for his wedding suit. Less than an hour later, that man left with two suits and a diamond ring in his pocket. Albert and Jane married six months later, leaving their lives behind and moving to America. The only thing they were sure of was each other.

The couple were married for fifty years, until Jane passed away from cancer, Albert by her side, holding her hand and wishing her peace. She told him she was tired, he told her that he loved her and that she should go to sleep, that he would still be there when she woke up. Jane closed her eyes and did not open them again.

But Albert is still there, waiting.

For a long time, I didn't believe in love like this. I considered it anachronistic and told everyone as much – who needed complete devotion from another human being when you could fly to Europe for less than a hundred quid? Who can commit his life and soul to someone else who might not want to spend all weekend binge-watching Breaking Bad? That kind of love was from another age, full of settling and compromises, unhappiness, dressed up as nostalgic romance for the sake of children and grandchildren and great-grandchildren. That kind of love was for people who didn't have a better option.

Today's love is optional, transient. Today's love

supplemented my life; it was elective, it did not define who I was or make my decisions for me. I had been in love once. I gave up my hopes and dreams for those of another, only to have my initial suspicions confirmed: she had another agenda and putting me first was not part of it. And so it became easy to join the Tinder generation, to make easy, casual connections where you created a new version of yourself on every date and wore yourself like an outfit, ready to be tossed aside whenever the fit became uncomfortable. Winter called for a heavy coat, long nights on the sofa, takeaway and lazy sex. Summer demanded something lighter, cooler, less committal.

And then I met her.'

I broke away for a moment and realized I was shaking.

'Like so many love stories, mine started with the perfect meet. We were working together in Hawaii and it was exciting to be seduced by the romantic setting, the pretty girl, the easy sex – and at the end of the trip it was just as easy to walk away. Or at least it was for a while. When an opportunity presented itself to work with her again, I took it, uncertain why. My father's most often-cited romantic advice was 'never go back', a mantra that was easy to live by when every hook-up is only a right swipe away.

But I did go back and soon I realized why. I was in love.

It made no sense. I didn't know this girl, there was nothing obvious as to why she should have such an effect on me but, as I lay awake in my bed at night, she was all I could think about. And so, like any right-minded man with everything to gain and nothing to lose, I ended it. I ended it like a coward. No conversation, no explanation. I left a note, a step above my usual text message kiss-offs.

For almost six long months I have put myself to bed at night, sometimes alone and sometimes not, but every morning I have awoken, hoping to see her by my side. I still look for strands of her copper hair on my sheets, I keep the T-shirt she wore in my bed under my pillow and I wonder how I could go back in time and have another chance at being brave. It wasn't like I didn't try. I wrote her letters, I sent her notes and photographs and reminders of our time together but it was all too late. The bridge was too badly burned for me to rebuild.

Everything else has been a distraction. Love is not optional; love is not a choice. Love cannot be left-swiped or filtered from your inbox or ignored at a party. To deny love is to live half a life. In creating this huge, modern world we live in, we have made love harder to find. What was once our only ambition has been reduced to a novel app, something to pass the time while you wait for a bus. Love has become the eye of the needle in an all-consuming haystack and it is almost impossible to find. But love should be holding your wife's hand and promising to be there when she wakes, knowing that, one day, she won't . . .

I found it and I let it go.

Don't make the same mistake I did.'

Tears streaming down my face, I closed the email.

Picking up Amy's phone, I dialled his number as fast as my shaking hands would allow. Three short beeps and the call cut off immediately. I tried again, looking up at the birds in the trees and heard the beeps again. The number wasn't blocked but his answering service was off.

There wasn't time for this, I told myself, taking a deep breath and choking down my sobs. I was late for my date with the hairdresser and Kekipi would kill me if I walked down the aisle with a dirty topknot.

Wiping my eyes with the sleeve of my sweatshirt, I stood up and headed back to the house. I was so confused. Surely he would know I would read the article? Surely he wanted me to? Somehow, I had to get hold of him, there would be no waiting for his 'soon', whenever that might be. Stopping, I turned and held up Amy's phone, trying to capture my secret garden. I wanted him to know where I was, I wanted him to know I was thinking about him and that I was done with waiting. I framed a shot of the table and chair, the stark trees with their low, bare branches and the steely blue Milanese sky then texted it to him. If he was words, I was pictures. I had to do something to stop him slipping out of my life.

'A vision,' Al said, letting himself into the dressing room just after the make-up artist had left. 'And if I do say so myself, what a fabulous dress.'

'It's just a dress,' I said, smiling and playing with the diamond necklace Amy had given me for Christmas as he sat down beside me. 'Actually, a stunning one, thank you so much.'

'I've been sent to give you a ten-minute warning,' he

said, looking around the empty room. 'Are the other bridesmaids all prepared?'

'I'm in the lav!' Amy screeched from inside the bathroom. 'I'll be out in a minute.'

I glanced at her dress, still hung on the back of the dressing room door and nowhere near her actual person.

'There was a situation,' I said in a light, quiet voice. 'Someone thought today might be a good day to try something interesting with her hair.'

'It's fine!' Amy shouted. Clearly I wasn't quite quiet enough. 'It'll come off!'

Al rumbled with his familiar chuckle. 'I don't doubt it,' he called back. 'And Miss Paige?'

'MIA,' I frowned. 'That's another situation.'

'So I hear,' he nodded. 'What a pickle.'

'In happier news, I've been offered an apprenticeship with a gallery in New York,' I said, finding a smile in spite of myself. 'I think I'm going to take it.'

'Tess, that's marvellous news!' He leapt up, bouncing to his feet like a man half his age and gave me a bristly, beardy hug. 'I'm so pleased.'

'If nothing else,' I shook my head at my own hands, 'I know this is the right thing to do. Not the easiest, I know, but definitely the right thing. I can't really believe it.'

'Much easier to live with the right things than the easy things,' he assured me. 'In the long run, at least. You may have had help from your friends along the way but no one took the pictures but you. No one went out and seized these opportunities on your behalf. You did this, Tess, and you're the only one who can make it work.'

'I suppose,' I said, looking down at the phone in my hand. 'I have to call my agent and let her know as soon as we're done.'

'You can't call her now?' he asked, fussing with his bedazzled tie. 'Call her now!'

'She's not answering,' I smiled, straightening the knot. 'I've tried twice. She said to call her in two hours and when she says something, she means it.'

'I'm very pleased for you,' Al said. It was impossible not to notice how much happier he looked since we had left New York. His eyes were brighter, his hair was bigger and there was a distinct spring in his step. 'I hope you won't be too busy to come and visit me in Hawaii.'

'You're really going back then?' I asked and he nodded, happiness all over his face. 'I'm not sure I'll be able to duck out any time soon but I can't imagine it would be much of a hardship to drag myself over.'

Just as soon as I transferred my credit card balance, I thought, hoping Mel had kept hold of all my post including the useful junk mail offers.

'You're going to make a beautiful bridesmaid,' he said, placing a hand on my shoulder and giving me a proud, parental smile I couldn't say I'd ever seen before. 'I'll go and have a look for Miss Sullivan and send her your way.'

'You do that,' I said weakly, giving him a double thumbs up. 'Thank you, Al.'

He gave me a little bow and closed the dressing room door behind him.

'Tess!' Amy stuck her head out of the bathroom door, wearing nothing but her knickers and a towel. 'Can you still see it?'

She turned her back to me, looking like a neon-blue Pepe le Pew.

'A bit?' I said, pinching my fingers together in the air. If only her hair weren't so short. If only her dress weren't backless. If only she hadn't decided today was the day to experiment with temporary hair dye.

'Shat,' she muttered, slamming the door shut on herself. 'Give me five more minutes.'

'No rush,' I said, looking out the windows as a stream of white cars arrived and dozens of beautifully dressed men and women began to swarm the palazzo steps. 'It's not like anyone's getting married or anything.'

And, right on cue, the door to the dressing room cracked open and Kekipi slipped inside.

'Is it too late to elope?' he asked, smiling.

CHAPTER TWENTY-ONE

'Gentlemen . . .' Al was taking the utter chaos of the dressing room in his stride. He turned to Charlie and Nick first of all, gracious and warm as ever. 'Perhaps you would like to take your seats? I believe there are two spots in the back row.'

Blinking, Charlie managed to right himself and staggered out of the room, still finding the strength to shoulder-barge Nick as he went. With a dark look in my direction, Nick followed, the unlikely wedding dates finding their seats just as Kekipi's instrumental began.

'I do believe the bridesmaids are up next,' Al said as I yanked Amy's dress over her head and Paige pulled at the zip, wiping her face with the back of her wrist. Amy tucked her boobs into the bodice.

'We're ready,' I said, slightly out of breath and more than a little bit confused. 'Shall we do this?'

'I feel like a five-minute sit-down, TBH,' Kekipi said, standing up and knocking back his champagne in one big chug. 'But we're all dressed up and everyone's here and – Amy, what is that on your back? Did you bone a Smurf last night?'

'Just go and get bloody married,' she frowned, taking her bouquet from one of Domenico's friends and fluffing out her hair.

'All right then,' he said, shooing the bridal party out ahead of him. 'Make me proud, ladies.'

'Happy day, old friend.' Al held out his arm and Kekipi gave him a courteous nod. 'Janey would have been awfully pleased to have been here.'

'It's not the same without her,' Kekipi said, clapping him on the back in a hug that made my eyes water again. 'If we can find half the happiness the two of you had, I will go out a very lucky man indeed. Now, the sooner we get this part over with, the sooner we can all get drunk.'

And it's very hard to argue with a man in a bedazzled tie on his wedding day.

As we all walked up the aisle, pausing briefly to accept our leis, it was almost impossible to believe we'd all been part of a six-way dust-up only moments ago. The splashes of blood on Paige's and my dresses were a bit of a giveaway, but I hoped people might accept them as some sort of avant garde fashion statement.

Standing in front of the assembled guests, I held my bouquet of red roses as low as I could, hoping they would distract from the spatter. Or at least coordinate with it. Amy bounced up and down beside me, bristling with excitement for the wedding and the standoff in the dressing room, while Paige stood to her right, a steely determination in her eyes. I watched her watch Charlie, her eyes never leaving him, all while songs were sung, vows said and speeches made. I couldn't quite tell if she wanted to kiss him or kill him, but either way, if I were him, I'd be afraid. I was still a little bit afraid for myself, and I was fairly certain we'd sorted things out. For the most part, Charlie didn't look at anything other than the floor, a hastily put together ice pack on top of his head, while Nick sat beside him, Al's handkerchief stuffed up his nose. Whatever he had to say to me, it had better be good, for his sake.

I just hoped he wouldn't do a runner.

And then there was Nick, sat in the back row and determined not to meet my gaze. If he stood up to leave, I didn't know what I would do. I was worried Domenico might have hired snipers to keep everyone in their seats – the wedding was planned with such precision, even the military might have said he was overdoing it a touch.

'Aloha, everyone,' the celebrant said with a strong Italian accent. 'We come together today to celebrate the union of Domenico and Kekipi and their commitment to one another. They have asked that we incorporate and share in each of their cultures as we join their lives together. I see you are all wearing your leis, a traditional Hawaiian symbol of affection.'

Seeing Charlie and Nick sat beside each other, one concussed and the other bleeding and both with leis around their necks, and not being able to do anything, was excruciating.

'The essence of our ceremony is the acceptance of each other as lover, companion and friend. This is a decision neither has taken lightly and I would ask you all, as you witness this union today, to stand beside the couple through the rest of their days. A wedding ceremony should set the tone for the rest of your lives together and it is with this in mind that I ask you now, if there is anything you wish to share with one another, before we go forward.'

'No,' Domenico said, Kekipi's hands held tightly in his own. 'Nothing.'

'I think you know everything,' Kekipi replied. 'The worst of it anyway.'

'The wedding ceremony joins you together and sets you free.' The celebrant ignored Kekipi and went on with his script. Probably best, I thought. 'At this point I would ask the assembled guests to take a moment and think on the love in their own lives and the love they share for the couple. I also invite anyone who has words of love to share with the congregation to please speak them now.'

Please don't, please don't, please don't, I whispered inside my own head.

'Can we make requests?' Kekipi asked, looking hopeful.

'Not traditionally,' the celebrant replied.

'What's traditional about this?' he asked, pointing at the crucifix, draped in an orchid lei.

'I suppose you're right,' he replied. 'Who would you like to speak?'

'Do not,' I muttered, pressing my high heel down on his toe, 'do this.'

'But it's my wedding,' he whispered. 'It can be your gift to me.'

He had spent far too much time with Amy Smith.

'Breathing is your gift right now,' I said, staring straight ahead. 'Don't do it.'

'Fine, fine, on with the vows,' he said, rolling his eyes and ignoring the exasperated look on Domenico's face.

I looked over at the back row: Nick still sat in the same place with a face like thunder, Charlie still peered out from underneath his cold compress. While Domenico professed his love, I stared at mine.

'Kekipi, it's your turn.' The registrar nodded at my friend, nudging me back into the moment. I turned and tuned back into the wedding, forgetting everything else as best I could. Which wasn't terribly well to be honest.

'I love you,' Kekipi began, holding Domenico's hand in his, all jokes forgotten. 'While everyone here can see I give you this ring, what only you and I know is that I give you my heart. I give you my life. With this ring, I give you all that I am. Whether you like it or not.'

OK, I thought, as the congregation tittered, maybe not *all* jokes.

'I will be a faithful husband to you,' he promised as Domenico wiped away the same tears that were falling on all of our faces. 'I promise you my unconditional love, my unwavering trust and all that I ask in return is that every time you look at this ring, you remember these words and know that I will love you, always.'

I glanced out at the crowd and saw Al in the front row, happily rubbing his wedding ring, lost in memories I wished I could share. Turning back to the happy couple, I heard myself make a tiny sobbing sound. Happy wasn't even the word. Joyous. Ecstatic. Beyond. As much as Kekipi liked to joke about his romance, I could see how much this meant to him and it filled my heart to know someone so deserving had found something he had thought he would never have.

'I now pronounce you husbands,' the registrar declared with an Italian lilt. 'You may kiss.'

'My first kiss!' Kekipi declared. 'I hope I'm doing it right.'

'My husband, the joker,' Domenico replied, leaning in

to press his lips to Kekipi's. 'What have I let myself in for?'

As the music struck up and the crowd stood to clap and cheer, I inhaled a deep, anxious breath as we followed the happy couple down the aisle. It had been a long twenty minutes since Al had sent Nick and Charlie to join the wedding congregation while Paige, Amy and I pulled ourselves together, and the protection offered by the service felt all too short-lived. The whole time I had stood beside Kekipi, I felt like time was ticking backwards. All I wanted was to grab hold of Nick and tell him exactly how I was feeling.

'Tess!' Charlie grabbed hold of my wrist as I walked by, still arm in arm with Domenico's brother on the aisle. 'We need to talk.'

'I can't right now,' I said, looking past him at Nick who was still refusing to make eye contact. 'Give me a minute?'

'Tess, please,' he insisted, following me out and pulling me to one side while everyone ran out onto the steps of the palazzo, throwing rice and confetti and cheering Kekipi and Domenico. 'I'm sorry.'

Looking up at my friend, I felt several strands of hair fall out of my bun and tickle the back of my neck. I handed Charlie my bouquet and attempted to pin it all back together.

'What for?' I asked, looking past him to see Nick still sat stock-still in his seat. Good, he wasn't going anywhere. 'Getting off with my mate or not telling me you'd already got off with my mate?'

'I didn't plan it,' he replied with the same shaky shrug I'd seen him do a million times before. 'Sometimes these things happen, don't they? You know how cool she is, she's your mate.'

'Seriously?' I looked up at him, completely incapable of staying mad at him for more than seventeen minutes. 'You're going with that?'

'We didn't want to do anything until we'd told you.' He rubbed the back of his neck and looked at his shoes. 'But it didn't quite work out like that. I know you know how it is.'

'I know things don't always go to plan,' I agreed, folding my arms in front of me. 'I'm not mad about you being together, I was hurt because neither of you told me.'

I took my bouquet back from Charlie and felt my world begin to shift back to the way things were supposed to be.

'We both felt shit about it. Paige wanted to tell you but I didn't want you to be mad at her like you were mad at me and you know you've had loads going on, neither of us wanted to dump more shit on your plate. It's all my fault, honest.' Charlie pressed his fingertips against his left cheek as it bloomed purple in the low winter sun. 'I really did miss you. Uglies should never have been bumped, I should never have made a move, and we should still be mates.'

I nodded. He was so right. To paraphrase that wise old woman, Taylor Swift, this was exhausting.

'And I really should have known that, years ago.' I said, looking across the room to see Paige watching, her face taught and anxious. 'You really like her, don't you?'

'Really really,' he nodded. 'She knows all the words to *Back to the Future*.'

'Brilliant basis for a relationship,' I said, finding a smile. 'Anyway, it's not like I can tell you you're not allowed to go out with each other, is it? Wait, it isn't, is it?'

'I'd rather you didn't,' he said. 'Tess, I think I might actually love her. It's really unsettling. In a good way.'

I must have heard Charlie proclaim his love for a hundred women in the last ten years, but something about the music in his voice, and the way she hadn't taken her eyes off him the whole time we were talking, made my heart happy.

He looked over at his new girlfriend with a smile I'd never seen before. 'So, you're OK with it?'

'I'm not going to say it's not weird, but yes, I'm totally OK with it. And I'm going to be in New York while you get the honeymoon period out of the way anyway,' I said, waving at the space between them. 'If you could get all the public snogging out the way while I'm gone, that would be brilliant.'

'Wait, you're going back to New York?' Charlie's smile was quickly replaced by a much less giddy expression. 'You're not going to take the job with me?'

Shaking my head, I tucked a few of the stray strands of hair behind my ears and felt my blood fizz with anticipation.

'Better offer?' he asked, glancing over at Nick.

'An amazing offer,' I replied, following his gaze to where Nick still sat, shoulders slumped. 'But not what you think. I've been offered an apprenticeship, I'll tell you all about it later.'

'Tess, that's such good news!' He swallowed me up in a familiar hug and I was almost certain I heard a sigh of relief. 'Gutted to lose you, but I'm so proud of you. But what's the deal with *him*?'

'That's what I'm about to find out,' I said, patting his back and breaking off the hug.

'I know we're probably still on thin ice,' Charlie said.

'But if he messes you around, he'll have me to answer to.'

'You, Amy, Kekipi, Al, a woman called Jennifer Lopez who isn't *that* Jennifer Lopez,' I replied. 'You don't have to worry but it's nice to know you've all got my back. Go and see your girlfriend.'

I watched as he crossed the foyer to Paige, almost running, and I smiled as he swept her up off her feet and spun her around in his arms. I had to admit it: they were a sickeningly good-looking couple. She looked over his shoulder and mouthed something my way. It was either 'thank you' or 'fuck you' and I chose to believe the former as I gave her a thumbs up. I wondered if, when things had settled down, I couldn't charge some sort of Bizarro World matchmaking fee. Possibly they owed me a pony.

Rather than follow everyone out into the gardens, I slipped back into the ceremony room, away from the celebrations, away from the music and laughter.

'Hello,' Nick said.

I sat down in the seat next to him, Charlie's empty seat, and smiled, entirely uncertain of what came next.

'Hello.'

The colour from his lei was beginning to run into his white shirt, leaving a pale pink stain right over his heart.

'Come to give me the consolation prize?' he asked.

I squinted, confused. 'Come again?'

'You might think I'm an arsehole but I'm not an idiot,' he replied. 'You told me he was the love of your life the first time we met. Good for you. Just don't ask me to be happy for you, all right?'

'Charlie?' I asked, trying to add up the numbers to make the same conclusion he had come to. 'You think I'm with *Charlie*?'

'You were the one who said there was someone else who needed you,' he said, not quite so certain of himself this time. 'I knew I shouldn't have come. Too little, too late.'

'We're not back together,' I corrected him and saw a spark of something. 'I meant Amy, you arse. Charlie and me weren't ever together. But showing up to the wedding would be too little, you're right.'

The spark flattened, leaving his skin grey and his eyes bloodshot, the toll of disappointment and an overnight flight showing on his handsome face.

'The article, on the other hand,' I said as lightly as I could, 'and all the letters. They were quite good.'

Nick stiffened but didn't say a word, the corners of his mouth twitching in an almost-smile.

'And the camera case. And the note that I didn't know was from you. You really should sign your name to things, you know. It's terribly arrogant to assume you're the only man sending me beautiful letters and thoughtful gifts.'

'Fair point,' he replied.

'I didn't know about any of it, Nick,' I said softly. 'My mum's been getting my post for months.'

'You didn't get my letters?' he asked, softening towards me.

I shook my head and reached out for his hand. 'And your gift got delivered with some other stuff. I really didn't know.'

'I really didn't think the note was that cryptic,' he said, and the smile that twitched the corners of his mouth grew, covering his entire face and finally finding his eyes. 'But possibly, a signature would have helped.'

I nodded, gnawing on my already bitten-down thumbnail, and squeezed his thumbnail between my thumb and forefinger.

'Why didn't you say anything when I was in your apartment?' I asked, watching the white nail turn red again.

'I was so angry. You turned up at my place out of the blue, all righteous indignation and really, that dress was very off-putting.' His eyes flashed with the memory. 'All those letters, Tess, I poured my heart out and you sat there in my kitchen, demanding to know why I hadn't called you. It felt like I was talking with someone I'd never met before.'

'New Year's resolution,' I suggested. 'We really need to work on our communication skills.'

'You say it like it's easy,' he said, ducking his head, just for a second, as two high spots of colour appeared on his unshaven cheeks. 'I flew to Milan to see you after you ignored a dozen letters, a thoughtful Christmas gift and a declaration of love. Doesn't that tell you anything? Other than that I'm a complete masochist?'

'Getting on a plane is easy, trust me,' I told him, taking my turn to try a wry smile. 'Telling someone how you feel isn't.'

'How weird is that?' Nick asked, pulling my hand away from my mouth and holding it in his as he spoke. 'There are things we do every day that should be terrifying, and we do them without blinking, but telling someone we love that we love them is still the scariest thing in the world.'

'Did you mean it?' I asked. 'What you said in the note. You really want to try?'

'I meant it,' he said. 'I want to.'

He turned towards me, pushing the chairs in front of us out of his way before getting down on his knees, still holding my hand.

Oh, fuckityfuckityfuckballs.

He cleared his throat and ran his thumb over my bottom lip then grinned.

'I'm not going to ask you to marry me.'

'Oh,' I said, breathing out. 'The whole kneeling on the floor thing was a bit misleading then, wasn't it?'

'It was a bit,' he agreed. 'But I wanted to look you in the eye when I say this.'

'All right then,' I said, impatient and excited. 'Let's hear it.'

'I love you,' Nick said, his tired eyes, his grey-blond hair, his strong brown hands, all of him on his knees in front of me. Tears stung my eyes. Wedding make-up be damned, I was going to cry. 'I argued with myself, I made excuses, I told lies – and it was all because I didn't want to be in love with you.'

'Not really feeling this part,' I said, the tears wavering. 'I think the kneeling bit might have given me false expectations.'

'Shut up and let me finish.' He rapped my knuckles hard. 'I didn't want to be in love with you because the last time I felt anywhere close to this, I got hurt. Painfully clichéd, I know.'

'I didn't say that,' I replied. 'You did.'

'I did,' he agreed. 'And those clichés cost me six months with you, but if they cost me the rest of my life, I don't know what I'll do.'

'Go back to New York?' I suggested. 'Get on Tinder? I've heard it's very good.'

'I suppose I could,' he said, his fingers so tight around mine they almost hurt. 'But I don't want to. I want to be with you.'

And there it was.

'I love you, Tess,' Nick Miller, all blue eyes and bended

knee, said with a smile. 'You make me laugh, you make me want to try and you make me better. I visited some of the most beautiful parts of the world in these past few months and the only thing I could think about was you. The only person I wanted to share it with was you. And I know it defies logic and I know it won't be easy but I love you and I want you and if you feel the same, it's got to be worth a go, hasn't it?'

'Probably,' I replied, my ears tickling as my tears began to fall freely. 'That wasn't that hard, was it?'

He shook his head and shuffled closer towards me. 'Easier than I thought,' he said gruffly. 'I want to be with you. Whatever that means and wherever it takes us. I want to see everything and go everywhere and I want to do it together because doing anything on my own doesn't make sense any more.'

'Right then,' I replied, leaning in closer and closer.

'How was that?' he asked. 'I didn't practise but I think it was all right for off the cuff?'

'You had an entire plane ride to think about what you wanted to say and you didn't work on it at all?' I clucked my tongue as he took a strand of hair from in front of my face and tucked it back behind my ear. 'And you have the audacity to call yourself a writer.'

'I am a disgrace,' he said, leaning in until I could feel his breath on my face. 'Whatever do you see in me?'

'It's mostly the sex,' I replied. 'Don't read too much into it.'

'Oh my GOD,' Amy screamed, tearing through the chairs like a miniature silk-clad Incredible Hulk. Nick pulled away, a heartbeat before our lips could meet. 'You're getting married? You're getting married!'

'We're not getting married,' I said, my arms around

Nick's neck, my temple resting against his forehead. 'Calm down.'

'Why is he kneeling on the floor then?' she asked, hands on her hips. 'That's just taking the piss.'

'I know,' I assured her. 'We've covered that.'

'What's this?' Al and Kekipi followed Amy, pops of glitter and confetti decorating Al's beard and sticking to Kekipi's slicked-down hair. 'Who's getting married now?'

'Tess Brookes, if you're stealing my thunder,' Kekipi warned, 'I will not be held accountable for my actions.'

'They're not getting married,' Amy said, disappointment audible in her voice. 'He's just on one knee for shits and gigs.'

'Then what is going on?' Kekipi demanded while Al gave me a simple nod and a wink. 'Are you two actually together or is this a cunning way of getting out of buying me two separate wedding gifts?'

'It's your day,' I said, standing up, Nick close by my side, his hand in mine. 'I'm just here to eat cake and embarrass myself on the dance floor.'

'Me too,' Nick promised, squeezing my hand tightly. 'Boy Scout promise.'

'You were never a Boy Scout,' Kekipi declared, waving a warning finger in his direction. 'You don't fool me, Nick Miller.'

'Shouldn't we be outside with the photographer?' Al asked, a guiding hand on Kekipi's back. 'And your husband?'

'Yes,' he sulked. 'I suppose. As long as those two aren't up to anything.'

'If you mess her around again, I'll destroy you,' Amy said, giving Nick a quick side hug. 'I know I said that before but this time I mean it. I'll literally tear your balls off.'

'I believe you,' he replied. 'And I'll do my best.'

'Don't,' she warned. 'Do better.'

'What do we do now?' Nick asked, slipping off his jacket and draping it around my bare shoulders as they left us alone in front of the altar. 'What's next?'

'Let's start with this,' I replied, throwing my arms around his neck and leaning into a kiss. I closed my eyes and felt him all around me, more certain in that moment than I ever had been before. I knew who I was, I knew what I wanted and I knew where I was going. The rest, we could work out along the way.

'As the rest,' I said, pulling away to see him smiling at me. 'I'm not sure. But I'm excited to find out.'

The sun was beginning to set as everyone assembled for the photographer, laughing and smiling and kissing as the night turned cool and the shadows grew long. I wasn't sure if Nick meant what was next with the wedding or with us, but as far as I could tell, it really didn't matter.

Epilogue

'Amy, I can barely hear you, you're breaking up,' I said, trying to balance two brown paper bags full of groceries in my arms and open the door to my apartment at the same time. 'Where are you?'

'Milan but I'm in the car,' she replied. 'Get out the bloody road, you knobjockey!'

'Tell me you're not driving.' I slammed the door shut behind me, my heart in my mouth as I heard a car horn honk down the line and sirens wailing in the background.

'Of course not,' she said with a sigh. 'As if they'd let me drive. GET OUT OF THE ROAD. I'm meeting Edward Warren to go over spring–summer. Next spring–summer. I'm knackered. Anyway, how's you?'

'Good,' I replied, dropping my shopping on the counter and immediately positioning myself in front of the air conditioner, putting Amy on speakerphone and holding up my arms. 'It's so hot, I think I'm going to die.'

'That's how you know you're not in England anymore,' she said, laughing. 'Milan is hot as balls as well.'

'It's so humid,' I told her, turning in a circle and

waiting for the frigid air to cool me down. Even though my studio apartment was tiny, it was impossible to keep more than ten square feet of it bearable and it was still only June. I didn't know if I was going to survive July and August. 'But I seem to remember Al's palazzo is fairly well air conditioned.'

'When I settle in one spot, I'll get my own place,' she replied, acknowledging the slightly accusatory tone in my voice. 'You could have moved in with Delia, she offered.'

'I know,' I admitted, dropping down onto one of the little wooden chairs by my kitchen table-slash-work-space. 'But it didn't feel right, I don't even know her. And I'm coming and going at all hours.'

'And you're scared of Genevieve,' Amy added.

'And I'm scared of Genevieve,' I agreed. 'This place isn't so bad. Apart from the heat. And how the hot water is really, really hot. And how you can smell the rubbish in the street when they don't pick it up until the evening. And I thought I saw a mouse the other day but I'm sure it was just a cockroach.'

'Oh, that's much better,' Amy said. 'Just a mouse-sized cockroach.'

'I've got to go,' I told her, opening my laptop and rubbing smeared mascara away from underneath my eye. Make-up was utterly pointless in this weather but I didn't want David to think I'd stopped trying already. Things were going well at work: my month-long apprenticeship at the David Sanders Gallery had turned into a three-month trial run, which had become a six-month assistant job with two different photographers. 'I've got some pictures to edit tonight and we're breaking down the exhibition at the gallery tomorrow morning.'

'I bet you're totally diesel now,' she said, over the sound of more honking horns. 'Have you got guns? Are you super buff?'

'Ripped,' I said, flexing my puny arms. 'Remind me, when are you back in New York?'

'Two weeks,' she replied happily. 'Prepare thy liver.'

'I will,' I promised. 'Have fun in Milan. And don't kill anyone.'

'I'll try to try,' she said. 'Love you.'

Hanging up the phone, I turned on the tap until the water ran almost cold and filled up my glass before settling down in front of my computer. When I wasn't slogging my guts out at the gallery or trailing around New York setting up studios and, as Agent Veronica had predicted, making an awful lot of coffee, I was starting to pick up my own jobs. I'd done more work for *Gloss*, a couple of shoots for *Booker* and even a few bits and pieces for *Belle*. I was busier than I'd ever been. I hadn't left the apartment for anything other than work in days but I couldn't remember a time when I'd felt so content.

'Let's get this done and then you can order Chinese,' I bargained with myself, rubbing my eyes as my laptop flickered into life. 'It's just a few shots. It won't take long.'

'What won't take long?'

I span around in my chair to see the front door open and felt all the cool air rush out as Nick walked in.

'What are you doing here?' I asked, jumping to my feet and crossing the tiny apartment in three strides. 'I thought you were in London until the weekend?'

'I wasn't doing anything there that I couldn't do here,' he replied, carry-on suitcase at his heels as he hoisted me up off the floor and planted his lips on mine. 'And I missed you.'

'I missed you too,' I said, peeling myself away from him, sticky skin against sticky skin. He'd been away for eight days and they were eight days too many. 'You should have called, I would have made dinner or something?'

'This isn't dinner?' he asked, rooting through my brown paper bags. 'Pringles, Twizzlers, Diet Coke. You've got all the major food groups covered.'

'You know I like to get my five a day.' I fished around in the bottom to produce a banana. 'Ta-da.'

'You work too hard and you don't look after yourself,' Nick said, wiping a smudge of mascara I'd missed from my cheek. 'Am I going to have to start making you a packed lunch every day?'

'I wouldn't hate that,' I admitted, catching his hand in mine. 'It's been a busy day, I haven't been eating this all the time, honest.'

It was true. I'd been eating Chinese takeaways, pizza, sushi, Thai food and everything else I could get my hands on. It was a good job I was working as hard as I was, otherwise I would have been the size of a house.

'I wish you'd stop being so stubborn and move into my place,' Nick said, frowning as he looked around my dark little studio. 'How do you sleep in this heat?'

'You want to go to sleep?' I ran my hand playfully down the front of his shirt, toying with his buttons. 'Is the jetlag that bad?'

'Jetlag could never be that bad,' he replied, kissing me again. 'Plus, I'm starving.'

'I really do have to finish off this edit.' I pulled away and planted myself in my wooden chair. 'It won't take me more than an hour.'

Nick looked down at me, tired and proud and hungry and a million other emotions written on his face.

'All right but I'm taking these,' he said, snatching up the tube of Pringles and hurling himself onto the Ikea bed that butted up next to the table. It really was a small apartment. 'And if you're not done in an hour, I'll be taking myself out to dinner.'

'I promise,' I said, downing my glass of water and grinning at my laptop. 'Where do you want to go? I could do Italian or we could try that new Mexican place round the corner?'

I tapped and clicked at my computer, checking the time on the clock next to the window. The sun was already beginning to set and thankfully, the air outside was cooling off, even if the apartment was still stuffy and close.

'Nick?' I turned towards the bed, expecting to see his cheeks filled with Pringles and a guilty look in his eyes. Instead, I saw the man I loved, stretched out on top of the covers, still wearing his button-down shirt and travel-rumpled jeans, fast asleep.

Smiling, I stepped away from the computer and picked up my camera, snapping a picture of his peaceful face.

'Stop it,' he said as I sat down on the bed beside him. 'I'm just resting my eyes.'

'Go to sleep,' I said, kissing the top of his head the way he always kissed mine. 'I'm glad you're here.'

'I need your freezing feet to cool me down before I can go to sleep,' he muttered, smiling even though his eyes were closed. 'I missed you, Tess.'

'I missed you too,' I said, brushing the hair back off his face. 'Now let me finish off these photos.'

'My very own Annie Leibovitz,' he whispered into a yawn. 'I can't wait until you're incredibly successful and I can retire a kept man.'

'One day,' I promised, settling back down in front of the computer as Nick rolled over onto his side, reaching out to rest his hand on my leg. 'One day.'

Acknowledgements

I feel like everyone in this list is getting really bored of seeing their names on these pages but that's just tough luck. If you will insist on sticking around, you're going to have to be thanked.

Rowan Lawton, thank you for all that you do. I mean, the agenting obvs but really all the rest of it as well. Lynne Drew and Martha Ashby, I literally couldn't do it without you, which you quite clearly already know, thank you so much.

To everyone else at HC, we'd be here all day and I know you're already sick of me so I'll just send cupcakes later, OK? Special thanks to Sarah Benton, Liz Dawson and Louise Swannell for dealing with me this summer, champions the lot of you. Massive thank yous to Blaise McGowan and Georgie White at James Grant and Liane-Louise Smith and Isha Karki at Furniss Lawton, thank you for being so on top of things when I quite clearly am not.

We're reminded daily that the internet is a wonderful and terrible place and I really want to add a special thank you to the people who genuinely make the inter-webs, and therefore the world, a better place. Talking to you all on Twitter and Facebook and Instagram reminds me I'm not alone, even when I'm feeling a little lost, and I appreciate your comments and photos and messages more than you could ever know.

It's been a funny old year and without these people, God knows where I'd be right now. So thank you Della Bolat, Ryan Child, Kevin Dickson, Philippa Drewer, Ilana Fox, Bren Lee Gomez, Mhairi McFarlane, Rosie Walsh, Terri White, Rachael Wright and Beth Ziemacki. Robert Kelk gets a special thank you for being the best damn brother that ever there was and there's a huge hefty thank you for Jeff Israel. Thank you for looking after me, feeding my kittens when I go away and taking me to San Diego to see Taylor Swift. If that's not the sign of a keeper, I don't know what is.

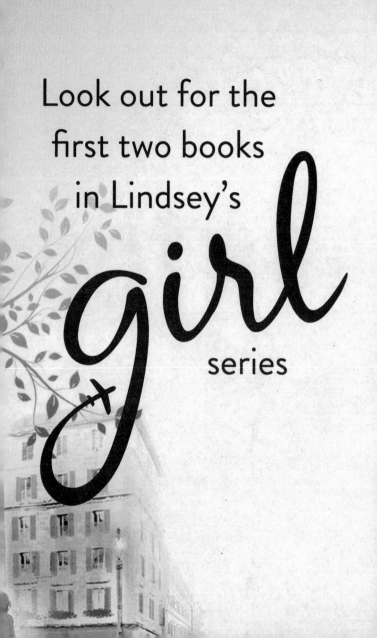

Look out for the
first two books
in Lindsey's

girl

series

what a girl wants

LINDSEY KELK

From the author of the bestselling *I heart* series

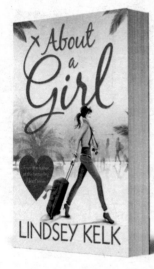

About a Girl

LINDSEY KELK

DISCOVER LINDSEY'S

I heart SERIES

There are lots of ways to keep up-to-date with Lindsey's news and views:

**Check out Lindsey's new website at
lindseykelk.com**

 **Like her on
facebook.com/LindseyKelk**

**Follow her
@LindseyKelk**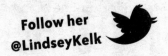